THE RADICAL NOVEL RECONSIDERED

A series of paperback reissues of mid-twentieth-century
U.S. left-wing fiction, with new biographical and critical
introductions by contemporary scholars.

Series Editor

Alan Wald, University of Michigan

Books in the Series

BURNING VALLEY

Burning Valley

PHILLIP BONOSKY

Introduction by Alan Wald

UNIVERSITY OF ILLINOIS PRESS

Urbana and Chicago

© 1953 by Phillip Bonosky
Reprinted by arrangement with the author
Introduction © 1998 by the Board of Trustees of the University of Illinois
Manufactured in the United States of America
P 5 4 3 2 1

This book is printed on acid-free paper.

Library of Congress Cataloging-in-Publication Data
Bonosky, Phillip.
Burning Valley / Phillip Bonosky : introduction by Alan Wald.
p.   cm. — (Radical novel reconsidered)
ISBN 0-252-06684-7 (alk. paper)
I. Title. II. Series.
PS3552.0638B87   1997
813'.54—dc21   97-18470
CIP

INTRODUCTION

The Wager of Benedict Bulmanis

Alan Wald

The existence in the early 1950s of working-class novels advocating social revolution in the United States is often missed because it is unexpected. After all, the height of the McCarthyite witch-hunt and infamous Red Scare seems an unpropitious moment for a young fiction writer such as Phillip Bonosky to launch a literary career as an unabashed partisan of Communist-led industrial unionism. In 1948, when Bonosky's short stories were already appearing in *Colliers, Story,* and *New Masses* magazines, leaders of the Communist Party were arrested under the Smith Act for allegedly teaching the overthrow of the government. In 1949, the CIO expelled all known Communists and Communist-led unions. In 1950, Alger Hiss was convicted of perjury for supposedly lying about espionage activities, and the "Hollywood Ten" began their prison sentences for refusing to divulge information to the government about the Communist affiliations of themselves or their associates. The year that *Burning Valley* appeared (1953) was the same year that Julius and Ethel Rosenberg were executed under the charge of conspiring to give the secret of the atomic bomb to the Soviet Union.[1]

Recent books about cold-war culture suggest that left-wing novelists grew suddenly silent in their craft at this time of national crisis.[2] Without minimizing the chilling effect of the witch-hunt on culture, or denying the heroism of those who squarely opposed it even to the point of serving prison terms (as did Dashiell Hammett and Howard Fast), I find that an examination of the written record tells a less simple and more intriguing story. The political commitment so admirably expressed in writers congresses, manifestos, and political defense committees of the 1930s was not a mere sham propaganda operation engineered by a "clandestine army" of Communist agents, some sort of shallow sentiment that would collapse entirely at the appearance of loyalty oaths and frame-up trials.[3] Social protest was at the heart of a major trend in U.S. literature; while Communist-led organizations of the 1930s may have promoted that trend, its foundation was in an even older legacy of fiction that embodied excoriating social critique, one that existed at least as far back as the turn-of-the century muckrakers and naturalists. Nor was it necessary for the "proletarian novel" to be an object of fascination among critics for writers such as Bonosky to aspire to dramatize the class and race oppression that they had experienced and witnessed firsthand. The desire to produce radical fiction grows out of life experience.

What distinguishes the cold-war era from the World War II years and earlier is not the absence of the radical literary tradition, which had been influenced by—although not created by—writers with Marxist and Communist views. Rather, publishing outlets for such literature were narrowed; political commitments were less explicit and sometimes masked; and attention by critics to race and class was much diminished from the days when radical novels were reviewed in the major publications. Left-wing writers wrote, but usually without the expectation of conventional success.

Nevertheless, their literary output was remarkable given the obstacles put in their way and the temper of the cold war. Along with *Burning Valley,* Walter Rideout's *The Radical Novel in the United States, 1900–1954*[4] cites a dozen other conventional "radical novels" appearing between 1951 and 1954: *Iron City* (1951) by Lloyd Brown, *Spartacus* (1951) by Howard Fast, *Swing Shift* (1951) by "Margaret Graham" (Grace Lois MacDonald), *Barbary Shore* (1951) by Norman Mailer, *We Fished All Night* (1951) by Willard Motley, *A Lantern for Jeremy* (1952) by V. J. Jerome, *Silas Timberman* (1954) by Howard Fast, *Goldsborough* (1954) by Stefan Heym, *Brownstone* (1954) by Arthur Kahn, *The Ecstasy of Owen Muir* (1954) by Ring Lardner Jr., and *Morning, Noon, and Night* (1954) by "Lars Lawrence" (Phillip Stevenson). As important as such publications were for sustaining the left-wing cultural critique,[5] the majority of these were not brought out by the leading publishers that had printed works of pro-Communists in the 1930s and 1940s (Viking Press, Covici-Friede, G. P. Putnam, Alfred Knopf, John Day Company); most appeared only because of the remarkable efforts of left-wing institutions such as International Publishers, Masses & Mainstream, Independence Publishers, Citadel Press, and Blue Heron Press.

Today, when it is safer to identify political associations of five decades ago, one might augment Rideout's list in several ways to indicate an even stronger left-wing cultural presence in the early 1950s than is usually acknowledged. For example, there were novels published in 1951–54 by pro-Communists who were unknown to Rideout or who did not produce narrative structures corresponding to his four main typologies of radical theme and form.[6] Among such neglected efforts are John Sanford's *A Man Without Shoes* (1951), Abraham Polonsky's *The World Above* (1951), Robert Carse's *The Beckoning Waters* (1953), Samuel Ornitz's *Bride of the Sabbath* (1953), and John O. Killens's *Youngblood* (1954). Some Communists turned from writing relatively conventional novels to mass-market pulp fiction, as did Sam Ross in *This, Too, Is Love* (1953), Louis Falstein in *Slaughter Street* (1953), and "Ed Lacey" (Len Zinberg) in *Sin in Their Blood* (1954).

To these one might add numerous other novels by writers once variously drawn to the Communist movement whose radicalism was attenuated but not entirely absent: *Fortress in the Rice* (1951) by Ben Appel, *Foundation* (1951) by Isaac Asimov, *The Loneliest Girl in the World* (1951) by Kenneth Fearing, *Thelma* (1952) by Vera Caspary, *Go Tell It on the Mountain* (1953) by James Baldwin, *The Old Man and the Sea* (1953) by Ernest Hemingway, *East of Eden* (1952) by John Steinbeck, *The Narrows* (1953) by Ann Petry, *Maud Martha* (1953) by Gwendolyn Brooks, *Cast the First Stone* (1952) by Chester Himes, *The Sun Is Silent* (1951) by Saul Levitt, *The Troubled Air* (1951) by Irwin Shaw, *The Killer Inside Me* (1952) by Jim Thompson, and possibly *The Catcher in the Rye* (1951) by J. D. Salinger.[7] The science fiction writer C. M. Kornbluth, who had participated in the Communist movement in his youth, collaborated with a former Party member, Frederik Pohl, in writing a classic, *The Space Merchants* (1953).[8]

Of course, many novels were published in 1951–54 by writers with no evident left-wing affiliation, past or present. These include *Requiem for a Nun* (1952) by William Faulkner, *The Beetle Leg* (1951) by John Hawkes, *From Here to Eternity* (1951) by James Jones, *The Natural* (1952) by Bernard Malamud, *The Long March* (1952) by William Styron, and *The Cane Mutiny* (1952) by Herman Wouk.

Even if this last group should ultimately be judged the largest and most influential, two crucial points must be recognized about the cultural moment of the early 1950s. First, the authentic literary character of the decade, like that of the preceding two, will remain unknown to cultural historians until the substantial presence of the Left is acknowledged, studied, and theorized. Second, the diversity of the achievements of the radical tradition should encourage scholars to go beyond the citation of books merely because the authors wrote against the grain of McCarthyism, although this aspect should be honored. Even the books recognized by Rideout are more often listed as museum pieces than discussed as part of a living radical tradition.

Burning Valley, in particular, is unique and precious not just for moral reasons. It can be distinguished from all predecessor novels by the craft and artistry with which the author, a lifelong Communist, interrogates the parallels between the construction of racial and ethnic oppression. Moreover, it vivifies the double role of religious ideology in the context of working-class life and struggle. In short, this 1953 revolutionary novel of class, race, ethnic and religious strife provides compelling testimony that the radical tradition of the 1930s not only survived but explored new terrain in the subsequent decades. Bonosky stands as a living link in this continuous, if sometimes underground, stream of devoted novelists who artistically recreate working-class ethnic experience from a Marxist sensibility. While he once may have appeared to be a vestige of a literary moment that mostly died out, today he can be more accurately assessed as bridging the decades between the 1930s and the 1960s, when radicalism once again moved from a marginal to a more central location in cultural life.

❀ ❀ ❀

It would be simplistic to blame "the canon" alone for the obscurity into which *Burning Valley* has fallen in the forty-five years since it was published. The Left's own commitment to study more expansively the boundaries of fictionalized social experience has been tardy in the consideration of European ethnic groups, especially the Southern and Eastern European proletarianized ones most disparaged by the dominant culture. The only reference to Bonosky in radical scholarship is in Rideout's study, where his name is misspelled "Bonovsky" and the setting of his novel is said to be "a coal-mining town" instead of a steel-mill town.[9] The one substantial scholarly citation of *Burning Valley* of which I am aware appears in Thomas Gladsky's study of Polish-American literature, *Princes, Peasants, and Other Polish Selves*.[10] Gladsky draws special attention to the secondary character Dobrik, a Communist union organizer, as a kind of teacher-mentor figure, noting that Dobrik means "good" in Polish. Unfortunately, Gladsky never mentions that the fifteen-year-old protagonist, Benedict Bulmanis, and his family are Lithuanians, and he confuses the father, Vincentas, with the son. But Gladsky lauds *Burning Valley* as historically important for the centrality of its ethnic proletarian characters. Moreover, he aptly quotes Bonosky's 1954 public tribute to the proletarian writer Michael Gold, author of *Jews Without Money* (1930), to whom Bonosky gives credit for awakening him to the literary potential of his own experience:

> In short, *I* was missing in American literature—that is, my town, the people I knew . . . the men who died workers, just as they were born . . . Lithuanian Kilbasai and Serbian Tamburitzas and Joe Magarac . . . who wrote about all that? Nobody. It didn't exist. . . .
>
> I felt I stood outside of the permissible literary realm . . . I had pride in myself . . . but the books I read did not.[11]

Born in 1916, the fourth of eight children, Bonosky was the son of Jonas Baranauskas (1887–1951) and Barbara Maciuluite (1886–1962).[12] Both of his parents grew up in Lithuanian peasant families, emigrating to the United States around the turn of the century. They met in Duquesne, Pennsylvania, one of the historic steel towns circling Pittsburgh, and were married in the St. Peter and Paul Lithuanian Catholic Church, the family's lifelong parish church, in Homestead, a nearby famous steel town. Employed in a mill belonging to the U.S. Steel Corporation, Jonas Baranauskas began working twelve hours a day, six days a week, and maintained this grueling occupation for forty years. Eventually, all the Baranauskas children worked in the mill, including the daughters during World War II. One daughter, Toni, followed her brother Phillip into the Communist Party; it is to Toni, another sister, Barbara, and his wife, Faith, that *Burning Valley* is dedicated.

In many respects, the history of the Baranauskas family parallels that of the Bulmanis family in *Burning Valley*. They commenced family life by renting a company-owned shack near the mill. When wages rose due to the increased demand for workers during World War I, Baranauskas set aside money for a four-room duplex. He took out a mortgage in 1922, making weekly payments for the next thirty-five years.

Safety conditions in the U.S. Steel mill were intolerable, but efforts to improve safety were denounced as Communist plots. Until the 1930s, the organization of a union and the holding of strikes were illegal, forcing the creation of secret underground unions such as the one described in *Burning Valley*. Union organizers took their lives in their hands, as do Bonosky's characters Dobrik and King, the former of whom is brutally beaten while the latter is killed. According to Bonosky, in 1909 his father saw mounted deputies, state police, and special police hired by the coal operators shoot down protesting workers in cold blood, tie them to their horses, and drag them through the streets. During the 1919 steel strike, an unknown number of workers were killed by troopers. Moreover, in an episode crucial to the background of *Burning Valley*, African Americans were imported in boxcars from the South and herded into the mills as scabs, breaking the strike and creating long-lasting racial antagonisms.[13] In *Burning Valley*, the Polish and African-American union organizers, Dobrik and King, seek to undo the racial disunity. At the climax of the novel, the 1919 boxcar episode is brilliantly reworked and reversed as the workers rescue themselves from imprisonment in the mill by escaping in boxcars.

Like the Bulmanis family in *Burning Valley*, Bonosky's own family used Lithuanian for intrafamily communication. His father was illiterate and both parents could only speak broken English. For them, the center of Lithuanian-American culture, education, and socializing was the church, St. Peter and Paul. There Bonosky was baptized and made his first communion and confessions; his older brother, like Benedict Bulmanis, served as an altar boy.

Burning Valley concludes as Benedict takes his first steps toward socialist conversion almost exclusively on the basis of pragmatic experience. In Bonosky's own political development, a central part was played by the Carnegie Free Library in Duquesne. The precocious young Phillip passed his spare time in the adults' room among the literary magazines. He was particularly fascinated by the *Bookman*, which in the early 1930s ran articles attacking Marxists, especially Michael Gold. Bonosky was struck by the *Bookman*'s failure to give Marxists a chance to represent themselves. Later, he found a copy of Marx's *Capital* on the shelves.

By the time he graduated from high school in 1934, Bonosky had published poems in the school paper. Yet he found it impossible to envision a role for himself as a writer because the subject matter of almost all the literature he encountered was far removed from his life experience. Moreover, after graduating high school he was forced to do what every young man in Duquesne did: go to the mill employment office to beg for work. Since employment was irregular in the Depression, he soon found himself laid off, and he decided to save his parents the expense of feeding him by running away. Once he got beyond the hills he encountered thousands of other workers wandering about looking for jobs, and he joined their migration on foot and by jumping on freight trains.

In 1935, at age nineteen, Bonosky found himself in Washington, D.C. Unable to locate work, he joined the Workers Alliance, a Communist-led organization of mostly African Americans that fought to secure means of survival for the unemployed.[14] Within a year he also joined the Communist Party and began writing for the *Daily Worker*. The Transient Bureau allowed young men separate quarters if they attended school, so Bonosky also enrolled at Wilson Teacher's College, borrowing textbooks where possible. He financed a second year with savings he had accumulated from odd jobs and the twenty dollars a month he received from the National Youth Act, a New Deal program.

Every spare moment was spent immersed in the new works that were coming out in translation from the Soviet Union by Mikhail Sholokov and others. In particular he was struck by Aleksandr Fadeyev's first novel, *The Nineteen* (1927), concerning a band of Communist guerrillas in Siberia. The band unites individuals from different backgrounds, and the psychologies of many diverse types are cleanly depicted. Another novel exerting a strong influence was Aleksandr Ostrowski's *The Making of a Hero* (1934), about a poor youth who joins the revolutionary underground to eventually become a writer.[15] From these authors Bonosky assimilated the idea of creating a new kind of hero for his own writing—a hero from the working class, his own class, who comes to consciousness of the view of that class as historically the most important of our epoch. In conjunction with the new proletarian novels of the United States, these works made Bonosky feel that, for the first time, he had appropriate examples and models. These books demonstrated that his own life experience—the polluted towns, the filth, the violence, the foods, the cultures, the ethnic mixes—

might be the basis of an authentic literature. Moreover, he could now envision how the main characters in such environments would not just be objects of disgust or, at best, pity and sympathy but actors in their own right who had the potential to transform their environment. It was in this year, 1936, that Michael Gold came to lecture in Washington, D.C., and Bonosky stayed up all night talking to him, an encounter that further bolstered his confidence and sense of mission.[16]

Nevertheless, the political demands of the Depression came first, and in 1938 Bonosky decided to return to Duquesne. He obtained a job in the same plant where his father worked, devoting himself to the difficult task of organizing the workers into what would become United Steel Workers Local 1256. By 1941, the union and the Left were in a strong position; a CIO local was functioning, with Communists openly elected to the leadership. However, the relationship of forces changed during and after World War II; Bonosky was fired and then blacklisted as a Communist by U.S. Steel.

In these years he had been writing for the CIO paper and in his spare time producing some fiction and literary criticism. During the 1940s and the early 1950s Bonosky published about thirty stories in popular magazines as well as in Communist journals. At some point in the decade he read Thomas Bell's remarkable *Out of This Furnace* (1941), which he recognized at once as "a minor classic." Bell had come from the same region and used much of the same material that attracted Bonosky. Nevertheless, while he felt an affinity for the older writer, who was Slovak and also pro-Communist, Bonosky had already formulated his own literary views and the direction of his craft.[17]

In 1948, living in New York City, Bonosky became a leading contributor to the Communist literary journal *Masses & Mainstream* and then an editor. He also taught writing classes for a circle of left-wing African-American writers in the Harlem Workshop of the Committee for the Negro in the Arts, a precursor of the Harlem Writers Guild. One of these writers was John O. Killens, in whose Brooklyn home the group sometimes met.[18] In 1953 Bonosky published *Burning Valley,* set in the 1920s. The year before, he had reason to anticipate that Angus Cameron, the vice president of Little, Brown and Company publishers in Boston, would bring it out under the firm's imprint. But Cameron was forced out because he refused to allow his political activities to be monitored. Consequently, Bonosky was obligated to solicit contributions so that the novel could be issued under the imprint of Masses & Mainstream, Inc. Although it received no reviews outside of the Communist press, nearly five thousand copies were sold.

That same year Bonosky published a labor biography, *Brother Bill McKie: Building the Union at Ford.* In 1960 he published a second novel of western Pennsylvania, *The Magic Fern,* treating the cold-war witch-hunt in the Pittsburgh area. Then came a political analysis of the Chinese Revolution, called *Dragon Pink on Old White* (1962), and a book about the Catholic Church in Lithuania and Vietnam, *Beyond the Borders of Myth* (1967).[19] By 1968 the *Daily Worker* had changed its name to the *Daily World,* and Bonosky served as cultural editor from 1968 to 1974 and then Moscow correspondent from 1978 to 1982. He published *Are Our Moscow Reporters Giving Us the Facts About the USSR?* in 1982 and *Washington's Secret War Against Afghanistan* three years later. In 1987 a collection of his short fiction appeared as *A Bird in Her Hair and Other Stories.* He continues to live and write in New York City, his articles often appearing in the *Weekly World* and *Political Affairs,* publications sponsored by the Communist Party of the United States.

❁   ❁   ❁

Among the features of *Burning Valley* most likely to engage today's readers is its multifaceted dramatization of ethnicity and race. European ethnicity is treated not as a cultural essence or merely a quaint, residual quality; rather, it serves precise functions for the legitimation of class privilege. At the bottom of the ethnic hierarchy, which bears some resemblance to White Supremacy, are the poor immigrants from Eastern Europe, stigmatized by the epithet "Hunky," a term used for Hungarians, Czechs, Poles, Slovaks, Serbs, Croatians, Russians, and Ukrainians. Father Brumbaugh, the well-to-do new priest from Boston, has very pale golden hair, blue eyes, pale eyebrows and lashes.[20] In contrast, Benedict describes himself as having a "brown, flat face, with its flattened nose, its yellow-gray eyes" (73). Brumbaugh came to "Hunky Hollow" under the belief that the community would be predominantly of his own ethnicity, but he now finds himself baffled and repelled by the Eastern European cultures that he encounters:

> "Nationalities I never met before," said the priest with a slightly harassed expression. "How am I supposed to—" He lifted his shoulders, and let them

drop. He turned to Benedict, and studied him. "For instance, what are *you*, Benedict?"

Benedict squirmed. "Lithuanian," he said uncomfortably. . . .

. . . "Whatever that is," [the priest] said. "And there are Bulgarians and Hungarians and Slovaks. . . . They come and talk to me in broken English and wave their hands in my face. . . . Why does everybody eat garlic here, Benedict?" he asked. . . . (110)

With the African Americans obviously on the bottom rung of the ladder, the European ethnics are faced with a clear choice. They can continue to persecute Blacks, splitting the forces of potential resistance in both the workplace and the community; or they can make common cause with the Blacks, thereby increasing their strength and moral authority. Translated into the terms of current discussions of the issue, the European ethnics can either opt for the short-term benefits of "the wages of whiteness," an especially dubious choice in light of the contempt in which the "Hunkies" are already held by their class superiors; or they can repudiate "white skin privilege," becoming in effect "race traitors."[21] The Communist union organizer Dobrik personifies the latter option. The police are shocked by the way in which he identifies with the African-American struggle, declaring in amazement and disgust, "You ever see such a white man?" (45) In contrast, the African-American Mother Burns says approvingly, "Mr. Dobrik is like a colored man" (272). Benedict exemplifies the young person who will have to make a choice of whether to assert caste privilege. His initial inability to comprehend this choice is suggested when the troopers find him in Mother Burns's shack; they ask if he is a "white n——r" (117), which elicits a hasty denial.[22] Dobrik would have answered differently.

Beyond the issue of understanding the need for class solidarity, however, there are many signs that Dobrik looks to the African Americans not simply as allies but as a vanguard, exemplary force. At times, Bonosky even seems to associate Dobrik and his activities with the radical traditions of Black culture. One example is the secret union meeting in the woods that Dobrik organizes; not only does this recall clandestine meetings of slaves to organize rebellions, but Dobrik also uses "call and response" methods to elicit full participation and agreement from the workers. Clifford King, the Black organizer, is martyred, as his last name suggests, in the tradition of "The Black Christ," memorialized in poetry by Countee Cullen and Langston Hughes.[23]

Of course, the treatment meted out by the company and the police to the Blacks in "The Ditch" prefigures the treatment the "Hunkies" will themselves receive; only the blindness of race chauvinism prevents the Europeans from seeing this. One route to the repudiation of "whiteness" may be suggested by the evolution of Benedict's father, Vincentas. While not so politically developed as Dobrik, Vincentas is eventually impelled to challenge the illusion of becoming "American"; he comes to see this as nothing less than a betrayal of one's own heritage through an assimilation process that will never bring the acceptance for which one yearns. Looking at two young policemen recruited from his own community, Vincentas muses: "They had been turned into *Americans*—these children exiled from home, these children who had come from their blood and bone—into *Americans,* he thought, into killers, into barbarians, neither remembering nor wanting to remember their parents, their language nor their past. . . ." (231)

Bonosky is impressive in his ability to dramatize the notion that an authentic alliance between the two groups must be forged in the process of struggle if proletarianized whites and Blacks are to find unity. It is not enough for the Europeans to "wise up" or mechanically imitate the course mapped out by a saintly hero like Dobrik. They must repudiate their own arrogance, which underpins the false messiah of race privilege, and they must sometimes even confront their own ignorance. The changing relation between Benedict and Mother Burns reproduces the dynamic of national self-determination of an oppressed nationality on the level of personal relations. At first, Benedict is incapable of seeing beyond his own paternalistic relation to Mother Burns; despite his youth, he regards himself as her religious teacher, believing that he can uplift her. Later, as the objective events of the class struggle transform their lives, Mother Burns delivers to him what amounts to a verbal slap in the face as she takes action on her own, making her scornful statement, "Help yourself, boy!" (272) This prefaces his final choice of passing over to the side of the Communists.

There are other indications that Bonosky designed aspects of *Burning Valley* to suggest that the African-American struggle, rather than being the object of pity or a cause for a policy of "uplift," is in fact a model for the working-class movement as a whole—especially the more disparaged groups of European ethnics. Bonosky is most likely adapting the Communist orientation for Black culture, "National in form, Proletarian in content," in the episode where he has the Communist Dobrik sign his leaflets "Joe Magarac," after the folk hero.[24] Likewise, the "two languages" spoken by Vincentas Bulmanis, fluent Lithuanian and broken English, and his "greenhorn" act, serve to use the prejudices of the "whiter" Europeans to mock and manipulate them. This resembles the manner in which Black slaves and servants manipulated whites for their own ends by pretending to be simple or servile. It also shows how features of Eastern European ethnicity function as sites of resistance as well as oppression.

Bonosky's treatment of gender is more conventional. His narrative of gender relations with regard to the struggle of the "darker" European ethics remarkably parallels the depiction of gender in literature of the mid-century African-American radical and the proletarian culture movements. Such parallels are less the result of conscious artistic strategy than the shared cultural legacy of patriarchy. The African-American scholar Robin D. G. Kelley has noted the excessive masculinity associated with models of Black proletarian revolt,[25] while socialist-feminist scholars such as Paula Rabinowitz have analyzed the masculinist tropes of much class-struggle fiction.[26] In *Burning Valley,* the Polish-American Dobrik is depicted as a model "tough guy" who can take it. In contrast, the middle-class Brumbaugh is highly "feminized," as in the following description:

> [Brumbaugh] held out his hands and took Benedict's into his own white ones, so soft Benedict barely felt their touch, and Benedict had to raise his taut eyes to meet those eyes now. They were profoundly blue eyes, almost indigo, under pale eyebrows, pale lashes. His face was almost marble white, with faint childish blue veins still visible in it; under thin golden hair almost too light to notice the skin was pink on his cheeks. His voice was musical, with tones Benedict had never heard before, an alien, sweet voice. (15)

Moreover, the older Father Dahr, who radiates the spirit of the working class of Hunky Hollow, is a "man's man" despite his priestly vocation. He challenges Brumbaugh's claim to masculinity in no uncertain terms in front of the protagonist: "'Tell him, Benedict,' [Dahr] cried . . . , 'tell him when he is called to administer the last rites—ask him how will he recognize the human being who is handed to him on a shovel, scooped up from the furnace floor; . . . ask him if he is the man for these men and these parts!'" (168–69)

Like many of the classics in the proletarian literary genre by male authors, *Burning Valley* fails to develop any of its female characters, including Benedict's mother. (Even though the Bulmanis family is modeled on Bonosky's own family, the daughters have been removed.) As a result, emotional affection and physical attraction are most evident in homosocial episodes among males, which are presented in two forms. On the one hand, there is much male bonding, including the interracial bonding of Dobrik and King, that is proletarian, robust, and sometimes joyous. The passage where Vincentas Bulmanis and Father Dahr dance together is a showcase for Bonosky's literary talent and is worth quoting at length:

> Father Dahr clasped his arm around Benedict's father's neck and said something to him. . . . Then they both laughed together, slapping each other's back and bobbing their heads. Somebody brought each a glass of dark liquid and they quaffed it off; and their faces seemed to sweat more and grow brilliantly red, polished like apples. Then the two accordions crashed into another song, and flinging up their arms both his father and the old priest re-entered the square. They danced walled off by spectators. The old priest's collar came loose and hung open over his black coat. They danced *at* each other, their hands gripped behind their backs, walking around at first in a wary circle on their heels. Unexpectedly, his father broke into a few menacing steps, which the old priest mocked. Then his father, provoked, went beyond *that,* and the old priest showed great scorn; and before they knew it they were both whirling and turning in crazy competition, as the incredulous cheers of the crowd mounted, shocking the tissue lanterns. The collar came completely loose now and fell, and nobody noticed it; and it was trampled into the dust. The old priest's hair whirled in a flame of passion. (82–83)

Brumbaugh, watching from the crowd, is horrified by the uninhibited expression of masculine sensuality on the part of Dahr; the casual manner in which the priest's collar falls off, and vanishes, underscores how Dahr's human qualities in the here and now take precedence over his otherworldly offices. In contrast, the garb of the priesthood dehumanizes Brumbaugh, resulting in what Bonosky seems to depict as demasculinization. In the case of Benedict, caught between the two priests, there is sexual confusion. As a consequence, the contemporary reader may find strong homosexual undertones in a number of scenes in which Brumbaugh and Benedict are paired. In Brumbaugh's presence, Benedict frequently giggles and feels giddy, as at their first meeting: "[Benedict's] face burst into flame, and his throat became dry" (15). There are also scenes of affectionate physical contact between them, when the upper-class priest assumes a mother-wife role: "'How unhappy you look!' [Brumbaugh] whispered with a soft moan. He let Benedict's head fall back into his lap; he caressed the bent head absently, and searched the room with distressed eyes. He looked down at the shaking shoulders, and felt Benedict's hot hand as he touched it with his own" (157–58).

While Brumbaugh's behavior occasionally may suggest effeminate and repressed homosexual associations, Benedict is tormented by confusion during sexual episodes, especially those involving nudity. Most dramatic is the early scene when Benedict finds his younger brother Joey swimming naked with two other boys. He has just come from a walk with Father Brumbaugh and is reminiscing warmly of how he "had flushed happily and shivered under the pressure of Father Brumbaugh's ethereal hand on his shoulder" (22). Now he is filled with complex emotions at the sight of Joey and his friends, troubled by their lack of shame and feeling a resentment about Joey's nakedness, that "somehow it reflected on himself" (22). In a scene fraught with hints of sadism and humiliation, Benedict forces the naked Joey to fall down on his knees to pray for forgiveness for stealing a toy wagon, refusing to accede to the boy's plea to be allowed to first put on some clothes. In a subsequent episode, Benedict is discovered by a girl his own age while he is destroying some of his father's bootleg liquor. In shame and anger he throws a rock, aimed specifically at her bare legs (90). Finally, Benedict reveals considerable insight into his own confusion following the episode where he seeks out his older brother Vince in a whorehouse; ostensibly he has gone there to save Vince's mortal soul, but, in fact, he later admits it was because he wanted to get a glimpse of the naked women (159–60).

Bonosky's treatment of race, gender, and ethnicity resonates in powerful and educational ways with themes that preoccupy contemporary discussions in cultural studies. In contrast, a few of the characterizations in this first novel may strike some readers as simplified. Figures such as Vince, Brumbaugh, and Mother Burns seem one-dimensional, while Dobrik and King are highly idealized. Yet, Vincentas and Father Dahr are surely more complex, combining their proletarian solidarity with some degree of arrogance and pride. What the reader must recognize is that all of these characters are depicted from an adolescent's point of view.

Moreover, Bonosky made a rather daring choice by employing Benedict's consciousness as a window on the world in a novel that devotes painstaking detail to recreating experience from a class and materialist perspective. After all, this teenager is depicted as insufferably arrogant, prideful, and holier-than-thou, an almost unlovable kid who orders his mother about, bosses his younger siblings, and nags his father and older brother incessantly with regard to their moral failings. Nevertheless, these repulsive traits are balanced by Benedict's strong emotions and evident powers of imagination, such as when he transforms the long stairs that lead out of the valley to the hills into "praying stairs" and uses that vantage point to fix the valley in his gaze (10). Such a capacity for fantasy and a will to reorder the universe anticipate, perhaps, a literary talent that might, if properly nurtured and channeled, one day transform experience into art through an imaginative vision.

The literary strategy of *Burning Valley* is reminiscent of a classic bildungsroman such as *The Portrait of the Artist as a Young Man* (1915), of which this has some features of a proletarian version.[27] Indeed, there are few works of literature in our history where the authenticity of proletarian life and experience resonate so richly—sometimes too painfully—on every page. While the voice behind the experiences and emotions depicted is primarily that of Bonosky, it is likely that readers from families who worked in steel mills and coal mines will feel a shock of recognition, as if this novel embodies some aspects of a collective childhood of a broad stratum of the working class. The psychology of Benedict, in great detail, and that of the other characters, more sketchily, is inflected by class origins. The subtleties of adolescent proletarian consciousness are at the heart of the narrative as Benedict evolves through a sequence of epiphanies.

Characteristic of such revelations are several episodes in which his efforts to "do good" in the capitalist world result in his being taken as a thief. For example, there is the opening scene where he attempts to come to the aid of a drunken old man and is rebuffed (10–11). Likewise, his effort to return the wagon that his brother Joey stole from a Protestant family in the city results in accusations against him, largely based on his ethnic appearance and association with Hunky Hollow. Later, after realizing that the police can easily be mistaken—they had actually believed that an altar boy might be a criminal—Benedict wonders if the police might also be wrong about Dobrik in their characterization of the Communist as an evil man.

Bonosky does not try to enter the consciousness or inner life of any characters outside the young protagonist, and he tries to closely follow the level of perception and consciousness as Benedict evolves through a sequence of conversions and reconversions. At each stage, Benedict has a need for a mentor-guide and for a moral system that can account for contradictions of his environment. Thus he journeys from a worldview structured by Catholic doctrine to a class-conscious outlook. Yet, what may be *Burning Valley*'s signal contribution to socialist culture is its demonstration that religious discipline, ideals, and utopian dreams need not be repudiated by revolutionaries, only re-established on firmer Marxist principles to re-enchant the secular world with the glow of revolutionary passion.

❖　❖　❖

While most readers of this reissue of *Burning Valley* will be familiar with Karl Marx's famous statement that "religion is the opiate of the masses," few will be aware that the 19 September 1954 issue of the Communist *Daily Worker* featured a cartoon "wanted poster" for Jesus Christ, charged with "Sedition, Criminal Anarchy, Vagrancy, and Conspiring to Overthrow the Established Government." Beneath a drawing by the cartoonist Art Young (1866–1943) of a long-haired, bearded, disheveled-looking Christ ran the following text: "Dresses poorly, *said* to be a carpenter by trade, ill-nourished, has visionary ideas, associates with common working people, the unemployed and bums. Alien—Believed to be a Jew. . . . Professional agitator. Red Beard. Marks on hands and feet the result of injuries inflicted by an angry mob led by respectable citizens and legal authorities." Accompanying the drawing was the review of a new book issued by the Communist Party publishing house, Archibald Robertson's *The Origins of Christianity* (1954). The reviewer, Ben Levine, emphasized not only the centuries-long association of Christianity with struggles against oppression but also that "the Psalms and prophetic writings of the Old Testament, collected and edited in 500 B.C. contemporary with the Periclean Age in Athens, are part of that militant tradition."[28]

Among the most challenging issues probed by *Burning Valley* is the relationship it suggests between Marxism and Christianity in general, and Marxism and Catholicism more specifically. The novel continues earlier Marxist treatments of religion in terms of the theories of alienation and of ideology.[29] But Bonosky's double vision of religion in the context of the working-class experiences vivified in *Burning Valley* also pushes us into new territory that requires some fresh thinking. This is partly due to the manner in which Bonosky moves the issue of religion from the realm of the abstract to that of the concrete. For example, the novel depicts religion of a specific type—Lithuanian Catholicism of the so-called Hunky Hollow, as distinguished from Irish Catholicism of the nearby city (presumably Pittsburgh), the German Catholicism of Father Brumbaugh, and the Protestantism of the city and the mill owners. In addition, Bonosky dramatizes the functions of Lithuanian Catholicism in the context of a fairly precise mode of production of capitalism in the 1920s with the expansion of the steel industry that requires as much control as possible over the lives of its wage-labor force. Moreover, during the decade after the crushing of the Great Steel Strike of 1919, religious leaders were forced to carry out their offices in the face of the institution of paramilitary units commanded by the industrialists in the communities around Pittsburgh.[30]

Burning Valley, however, renders religion concrete in a third way. The novel deals with a panorama of characters in relation to the religious themes, including Benedict Bulmanis, a teenager who wants to be a Catholic priest; Vincentas Bulmanis, his father, who is a mill worker (who also sells bootleg liquor) and who will not attend church services but happily volunteers his work skills to repair the church roof; Father Dahr and Father Brumbaugh, two priests who interpret church doctrine from opposing class perspectives; Dobie and Clifford, a pair of union organizers, the former Polish and the latter African American, who act in very Christian ways; and so on.

Whether or not *Burning Valley* is in some sense a religious novel cannot be resolved simply. The author, of course, is unambiguously pro-Communist, and Benedict, the center of consciousness in *Burning Valley,* progressively becomes disaffected from both priests as he is drawn to the Communist organizer.[31] Yet there is never a point where Benedict intellectually rejects Catholic doctrine to embrace Marxist doctrine; to the end, Benedict retains most of the categories and values that he always held as a believing Catholic. However, through his epiphany-like experiences and revelations, Benedict begins to impart to such values and categories a class content, seeking guidance from the Communist organizer instead of either priest. At times, the book comes close to arguing that Communism is the authentic realization of Catholic ideals, which the church institutions have perverted.

That the craft of *Burning Valley* aims to transform our thinking about religion, rather than simply bash religion, is evident from the outset. The title, *Burning Valley*, refers factually to the valley where the events take place;[32] both the mill and the dump are said to be "burning" and to light up the valley, so the burning literally refers to fire from the industrial process (250). At the same time, both "burning" and "valley" are words resonating with religious associations. There is the Burning Bush witnessed by Moses, and from which he heard God speak; and frequently, in the Bible, God's judgments are accompanied by fire—such as the destruction of Sodom and Gomorrah.[33] Moreover, the Bible is filled with acres of valleys; not just the obvious "Valley of the Shadow of Death," but the valley where Moses was buried, the valley of salt, the great valley that will be formed when Christ returns to the earth to rule, and so on.[34] Benedict is named after St. Benedict, who created the foundation for the Benedictine order, which emphasizes collective living and collective manual labor.[35] *Burning Valley* is a novel about an adolescent who declares on the very first page his desire to become a saint, generally meaning a pious layman or a priest who belongs to God and who lives his life accordingly. Never in the course of events does he abjure that goal; he only discovers more appropriate forms to realize his ideals.

To what extent is Bonosky's thinking about Marxism and Christianity a departure from traditional approaches? As Michael Löwy points out in his study of liberation theology, *The War of the Gods,* the most popular view associated with Marxism—regarding religion as a narcotic preventing oppressed people from taking action—is not distinctively Marxist. This was a widespread view among a range of radical social critics in the mid-nineteenth century, and Löwy explains how Marx's own well-known statement along these lines, in his critique of Hegel's "Philosophy of Right" (1844), discloses a far more nuanced response to religion. The famous passage reads: "Religious distress is at the same time the expression of real distress and the protest against real distress. Religion is the sigh of the oppressed creature, the heart of a heartless world, just as it is the spirit of an unspiritual situation. It is the opiate of the people."[36] Löwy observes that this analysis departs from the pure and simple Enlightenment critique depicting religion as a fraud perpetrated by the religious establishment to maintain its power. Moreover, the early statement is a pre-Marxist formulation in that it lacks the class analysis evident in *The German Ideology* (1846), co-authored with Engels. There, religion is treated as ideology, and in subsequent writings Engels employs historical materialism to demonstrate that Christianity played different roles in diverse historical periods. In particular, Engels demonstrated that factions of clergy sided with feudal lords while others allied with the peasants. Engels thus recognized that the clergy was not necessarily a socially homogeneous body and could divide according to class composition and allegiances.[37]

Moreover, Engels's research on the Peasant Wars in Germany called into question the conventional "Marxist" view that Christians transpose a better world to the hereafter, while socialism demands it now. Löwy points out that Engels's favorite figure, Thomas Munzer, an Anabaptist theologian who was a peasant leader, "clearly wanted the immediate establishment on earth of the Kingdom of God," and that Munzer described this earthly utopia as "a society without class differences, private property, or state authority independent of, or foreign to, the members of that society."[38]

Thereafter, twentieth-century Marxists have tended to follow in the footsteps of the German Karl Kautsky, who regarded early religious currents as precursors of socialism in their thrust toward social equality, even though he dismissed their beliefs as masking their progressive content. Lenin's views were similar, although he opened the Bolshevik Party to those with religious beliefs so long as there was unity around the political program. The Polish revolutionary Rosa Luxemburg denounced retrograde policies of the church in the name of its own religious traditions.[39] Antonio Gramsci wrote of the utopian dimensions of religious ideas, claiming that differentiations can be made in Catholic culture among liberal, modernist, Jesuitical, and fundamentalist trends.[40]

Only with the work of Ernst Bloch, Löwy maintains, does the theoretical framework of Marxism's relation to religion undergo a qualitative change. In a statement surprisingly similar to Ben Levine's view in the *Daily Worker*, Bloch argues that, in its protest and rebellious forms, "religion is one of the most significant forms of utopian consciousness, one of the richest expressions of . . . the Principle of Hope."[41] In Löwy's summary, Bloch holds that religious thought has a capacity for creative anticipation contributing to the imaginative space of what he calls the "not yet being."[42] Löwy judges this to be more than advocacy of a "dialogue" between Marxism and Christianity; it is an actual fusion of the two, reminiscent of the unification of Christianity and revolution during the sixteenth-century Peasant Wars in Germany.

Pursuing this alternative Marxist tradition outside Europe, Löwy also cites the famous Peruvian Marxist José Carlos Mariátegui, who gave special emphasis to spiritual and ethical dimensions of revolutionary struggle. There is a noticeable parallel with Bonosky's portrait of Dobrik and King in *Burning Valley*. Like Mariátegui's revolutionaries who resemble devout Catholics, the two Communists are invigorated with a "faith" in the potential of ordinary working people and poor peasants; they feel solidarity for working people in all nations and of all colors; they burn with moral indignation; and they give total commitment to the revolutionary struggle at the risk of their lives.[43]

Burning Valley, then, is closest to those writings in the Marxist tradition that reject the one-dimensional Enlightenment view of religion as a mask of mystification. Moreover, Bonosky recognizes the potential for a subversive trend in religion when embraced from below, by a rebellious population, and, like Engels, can visualize sections of the clergy identifying with that rebellious interpretation of doctrine. Where *Burning Valley* departs from the view of Marx and Engels is in their belief that such a subversive role was primarily a phenomenon of the past. Bonosky's treatment features a split in church personnel as well as in doctrinal interpretation set in the twentieth century; this is especially impressive because, in the era in which Bonosky wrote, such developments largely went unnoticed in radical literature.[44] Of course, there had always been some groups of left-wing Christian socialists, worker-priests, Catholic workers, radical or revolutionary Christian pacifists, and so forth, in the United States, and the Black Church had occasionally produced leaders active on the Left. But in 1953 such developments would have appeared to many to be exceptions to the main trend of twentieth-century religion.

Yet it was only a little more than a decade after *Burning Valley* was first published that developments in the Christian Church in Latin America refuted the view that the subversive tradition in Christianity was tied to the past and was dying out. More surprising, it was specifically the Catholic Church that evidenced not only the kind of class split in its clergy that Bonosky dramatizes in *Burning Valley* but a new revolutionary interpretation of doctrine that seems compatible with the Marxism of Dobrik and, incipi-

xxvi

ently, of Benedict.[45] What seems to have come to the fore is the very tradition of an aggressive identification of Christ and the poor that was emphasized in the *Daily Worker* cartoon.[46] Thus, as documented by Löwy's *The War of the Gods*, starting in the early 1960s, Latin American Catholic organizations began passing resolutions declaring capitalism "intrinsically evil" on grounds that seem identical to Marxism—because it prevents the full development of human beings, because it turns people against each other, and even because it promotes private property rather than social property.

These are all reasons why *Burning Valley* should be reclaimed for its prescient anticipation of a recrudescence of the kind of "church of the poor" that existed in earlier times. Yet this assertion hardly does justice to the richness and boldness of the philosophical implications of Benedict's final evolution. After all, evidence is slight that Benedict is enroute to becoming a worker-priest, not only because of the moribund depiction of the prototype of such a figure (Dahr) and the comparative vitality of Dobrik. Rather, the autobiographical nature of the novel suggests that its narrative is more likely the making of a proletarian (or, in Gramsci's terminology, organic) intellectual. Finally, there is the disturbing violent climax of *Burning Valley,* when the forces of nature, in the form of a storm and flood, conjoin with the class warfare of the corporations and their hired police to crush and further immiserate the workers of Hunky Hollow. This episode, recalling aspects of Richard Wright's story "Down by the Riverside,"[47] in which the oppressed are assaulted by nature, seems to invert the biblical floods and plagues that came to punish the unrighteous. Hence, anyone sitting passively by in hopes of a divine intervention to save the persecuted ought to think twice about the wisdom of that stance. Humanity, it seems, can really only count on its own resources.

What, therefore, are the terms by which we might interpret Benedict's final choice? Here we might consider Löwy's comments on Lucien Goldmann, a student of Georg Lukács who, in his book *The Hidden God* (1955), argues that religion and Marxism share a refusal of pure individualism and a belief in "trans-individual values."[48] Löwy attributes to Goldmann the view that both religion and Marxism involve a kind of "faith" based on a "wager." Christians live their lives based on a wager that God exists; Marxists live their lives based on a wager that the emancipation of humanity on earth is a real process in which they are participating and to which they are contributing.

Of course, Goldmann favors the Marxist wager because it is not supernatural or transhistorical but based on something we must accomplish by our own activity. This seems an appropriate description of the fusion of Marxism and Catholicism achieved by Benedict at the end of *Burning Valley*. The power, beauty, and purity of Catholic ideals—of service to humanity consecrated to the achievement of some higher goal—remain the objects of Benedict's desire. But Benedict Bulmanis has changed the terms of his wager: the goal will now be achieved by class solidarity and struggle. For him, unlike the religious apostate, "faith" has not collapsed into disillusionment; rather, it has moved to the higher ground of finding its foundation in human self-emancipatory practice.

Thus, *Burning Valley* places its greater emphasis on one's need to reformulate appropriate ideas before effective action is possible. This produces further evidence that one would be mistaken to classify Bonosky's work as a mere throwback to the "proletarian novel" of the early 1930s, even though the earnestness of the novel seems antiquated today, and, in fact, such earnestness diminishes in Bonosky's later work.[49] But *Burning Valley* does not end with Benedict reading the *Communist Manifesto* and leading a new strike; instead, he buries one brother, unsuccessfully tries to induce another brother to return to the family, and takes oranges to the imprisoned Communist Dobrik. In other words, the thrust of *Burning Valley* is toward the development of ideas preparatory to action. In that sense Bonosky's work realizes the argument of his colleague Charles Humboldt, in whose 1947 essay "The Novel of Action" the proletarian literature tradition is critically associated with Lukács's critique of "naturalism." Humboldt suggested that this earlier body of literature, like the naturalistic novel, "performed such great service in describing the effects of society upon men, but ignored man's capacity to return blow for blow." He advocated that Marxist novelists aspire to create a "novel of action" that "presupposes an equal interchange between the individual and society, a constant welling-up of ideas and emotions created in the midst of contradiction and conflict."[50] It would be difficult to formulate a more compelling characterization of the method of *Burning Valley*.

Yet there is also significance in the novel's setting during the dark days of the 1920s, to show how the ground was prepared for the radical upsurge of the 1930s. After all, Bonosky composed *Burning Valley* in another dark period, that of the cold war. His motives for publishing it could not possibly have been fame, wealth, or "success" in conventional terms. In addition to satisfying his own artistic drives and standards, and honoring the people and culture from which he came, there is no doubt that Bonosky hoped that *Burning Valley* would assist in creating a climate of ideological clarification preparatory to a new radical upsurge of the working class like that of the 1930s and its great leap forward in creating the CIO.

Unfortunately, no such event took place, although the witch-hunt faded and inspiring rebellions of people of color, students, and women exploded in the 1960s, leaving a liberatory mark that continues to the present. In the 1990s, however, as we face century's end, the working class of the United States—of all colors and nationalities—remains imprisoned in chains of economic exploitation and cultural mystification. As *Burning Valley* is reissued, unionization is at an all-time low since the 1950s, the social safety net inherited from the New Deal is being dismantled, and race hatred is in many respects on the rise. All else having failed, is now not the time for a reconsideration of the wager of Benedict Bulmanis?

NOTES

I am grateful to Phillip Bonosky, David Demarest Jr., Annette T. Rubinstein, and Douglas Wixson for their comments on a draft of this introduction.

1. A useful review of the experiences of the Left in this era can be found in Griffin Fariello, *Red Scare: Memories of the American Inquisition* (New York: W. W. Norton, 1995).

2. Such studies are informative, however, for documenting the right-wing cultural assault on the Left and the complex role of the "New Liberalism" of the era, as well as some of the activities of leftist writers when called upon to "name names." See Arne Axelsson, *Restrained Response: American Novels of the Cold War and Korea, 1946–62* (New York: Greenwood, 1990); Thomas Hill Schaub, *American Fiction in the Cold War* (Madison: University of Wisconsin Press, 1991); and Stephen J. Whitfield, *The Culture of the Cold War* (Baltimore: Johns Hopkins University Press, 1991).

3. This outrageous caricature of the leftist cultural movement was revived in Stephen Koch's *Double Lives: Spies and Writers in the Secret Soviet War of Ideas Against the West* (New York: Free Press, 1994).

4. Walter B. Rideout, *The Radical Novel in the United States, 1900–1954: Some Interrelations of Literature and Society* (1956; rpt., New York: Columbia University Press, 1992).

5. Of course, the heterodox radicalism of Motley and Mailer should be treated differently from the pro-Communism of the other novelists, although both writers had been close to the Party in the 1940s.

6. Rideout describes the typologies as follows: "1) those centered about a strike; 2) those concerned with the development of an individual's class-consciousness and his conversion to Communism; 3) those dealing with 'bottom dogs,' the lowest layers of society; and 4) those describing the decay of the middle class" (*Radical Novel*, 171).

7. Biographical information about Salinger remains scarce, due to the reclusive writer's lack of cooperation in research efforts; however, some left-wing sympathy may have encouraged him to submit work to *Anvil* under the editorship of the pro-Communists Jack Conroy and Nelson Algren, as Douglas Wixson reports in *Worker-Writer in America: Jack Conroy and the Tradition of Midwestern Literary Radicalism, 1898–1990* (Urbana: University of Illinois Press, 1994), 441.

8. Two other groups of writers once connected with radicalism made noteworthy contributions. There were novels published by one-time Communist sympathizers or former members with a special anti-Party animus, such as *Invisible Man* (1952) by Ralph Ellison, *The Golden Nightmare* (1952) by Walter Snow, *The Outsider* (1953) by Richard Wright, and *Most Likely to Succeed* (1954) by John Dos Passos. Each of these features a Communist villain worthy of a Hollywood matinee melodrama. The early 1950s also saw the publication of novels on radical themes by left-wing veterans of the Trotskyist milieu, such as *The Adventures of Augie March* (1953) by Saul Bellow, *The Groves of Academe* (1952) by Mary McCarthy, and *Limbo* (1952) by Bernard Wolfe. Judith Merril, the former Trotskyist turned science fiction writer, collaborated with the prolific Kornbluth on *Gunner Cade* (1952) and other works.

9. Rideout, *Radical Novel*, 260.

10. Thomas S. Gladsky's *Princes, Peasants, and Other Polish Selves: Ethnicity in American Literature* (Amherst: University of Massachusetts Press, 1992) is commendable for its inclusion of often neglected works of pro-Communists, such as Joseph Vogel's *Man's Courage* (1938), Jean Karsavina's *Reunion in Poland* (1945) and *Tree by the Waters* (1948), Millard Lampell's *The Hero* (1949), Howard Fast's *The Proud and the Free* (1950), and V. J. Jerome's *A Lantern for Jeremy* (1951). In contrast, Bonosky is absent from the most important recent book on ethnicity, Werner Sollors's *Beyond Ethnicity: Consent and Descent in American Culture* (New York: Oxford University Press, 1986). He is also neglected in discussions of Catholicism in mid-century U.S. literature, as in "Catholic Lives," edited by Thomas J. Ferraro, a special issue of *South Atlantic Quarterly* 93.3 (Summer 1994). Ferraro's *Ethnic Passages: Literary Immigrants in Twentieth-Century America*

(Chicago: University of Chicago Press, 1993) omits entirely Poles, Czechs, Lithuanians, and other groups depicted in *Burning Valley.*

11. Quoted in Gladsky, *Princes, Peasants, and Other Polish Selves,* 328.

12. Information about Bonosky comes primarily from a personal interview with him on 7 December 1989 in New York City; an interview with his brother, Frank "Butch" Bonosky, in Duquesne, Pa., on 21 February 1997; and numerous letters exchanged between Bonosky and me from 1988 to 1997. In addition, I have consulted correspondence between Bonosky and Charles Humboldt [Clarence Weinstock] in the Beinecke Library at Yale University and discussed Bonosky's career with *Masses & Mainstream* associates such as Lloyd Brown and Annette Rubinstein, as well as with other left-wing writers such as José Yglesias and Paul Sporn. I am especially grateful to the Catholic scholar Toby Terrar for sharing with me his draft manuscript "Catholic Communists and Their Contribution to Liberation Theology: The Case of Philip Bonosky." Terrar summarizes, quotes, and cites in his bibliography a number of uncollected essays and reviews by Bonosky that contain much biographical information. Bonosky also published a memoir of his father, "The Life and Death of a Steel Worker," *Masses & Mainstream* 5 (Apr. 1952): 14–21, and a memoir of returning to the scene of *Burning Valley,* "Margin for Maneuver," *Masses & Mainstream* 9 (Nov. 1956): 35–46.

13. See the chapter on "The Great Strike" in David Brody, *Steelworkers in America: The Non-Union Era* (New York: Harper and Row, 1969), 231–62. For a discussion of the legacy of racism in the region, see John Hinshaw and Judith Modell, "Perceiving Racism: Homestead from Depression to Deindustrialization," *Pennsylvania History* 63.1 (Winter 1996): 17–52.

14. See Franklin Folsom, *Impatient Armies of the Poor* (Niwit: University Press of Colorado, 1994), where there are numerous references to the Workers Alliance, including Bonosky's activities as president of the Washington, D.C., local. Some details of Bonosky's activities are contained in "A Letter to Mrs. Roosevelt," *Mainstream* 16.1 (Jan. 1963): 3–22.

15. I am grateful to Rachel Rubin, a specialist in U.S.-Soviet literary relations, for alerting me to the importance of these novels. In light of recent rethinking of the socialist realist tradition, a comparison of U.S. radical novels to Soviet novels would be valuable. For examples of this new scholarship, see Régine Robin, *Socialist Realism: An Impossible Aesthetic* (Stanford: Stanford University Press, 1986), and "Socialist Realism Without Shores," edited by Thomas Lahusen and Eugeny Dobreko, a special issue of *South Atlantic Quarterly* 94.3 (Summer 1995).

16. See Bonosky's important tribute, "Salute to Mike Gold," *Masses & Mainstream* 7 (Apr. 1954): 43–49.

17. Bonosky to Wald, 7 Feb. 1997. The authoritative discussion of Bell's nov-

el is David P. Demarest Jr.'s "Afterword" to the 1976 University of Pittsburgh Press edition. An important discussion of Bell appears in the doctoral dissertation by Betty Ann Burch, "The Assimilation Experience of Five American White Ethnic Novelists of the Twentieth Century" (University of Minnesota, 1973). Bonosky offers a final tribute to Bell in his review of Bell's posthumously published *In the Midst of Life;* see *Mainstream* 14.12 (Dec. 1961): 56–58.

18. Bonosky to Wald, 7 Feb. 1997.

19. Bonosky's English-language books have been translated and published in the former USSR, China, Poland, the former German Democratic Republic, Bulgaria, Lithuania, and Vietnam. In the Soviet Union the press run was 100,000 and in Lithuania, 15,000. However, most of the royalties received from those editions have been available to him only in the currencies of the various countries.

20. *Burning Valley* (this edition), 15. All subsequent citations will appear parenthetically in the text.

21. See Noel Ignatiev and John Garvey, eds., *Race Traitor* (New York: Routledge, 1996). See also David Roediger, *The Wages of Whiteness: Race and the Making of the American Working Class* (London: Verso, 1991) and Theodore Allen, *The Invention of the White Race: Racial Oppression and Social Control* (London: Verso, 1994).

22. Throughout the novel Bonosky does not spell out the hate epithet "nigger," presumably because he and the publishers felt that it would be offensive.

23. See Countee Cullen, "The Black Christ," in *The Black Christ and Other Poems* (New York: Harper and Bros., 1929) and Langston Hughes, "Christ in Alabama," in *The Panther and the Lash* (New York: Random House, 1967).

24. There are several references to the Magarac story in Archie Green, *Wobblies, Pile Butts, and Other Heroes: Laborlore Explorations* (Urbana: University of Illinois Press, 1993), 9, 52, 355.

25. See Robin D. G. Kelley, *Race Rebels: Culture, Politics, and the Black Working Class* (New York: Free Press, 1994), 103–21.

26. See Paula Rabinowitz, *Labor and Desire: Women's Revolutionary Fiction in Depression America* (Chapel Hill: University of North Carolina Press, 1991).

27. In fact, *Burning Valley* has many elements of "The Proletarian Bildungsroman" as theorized by Barbara Foley in her excellent chapter in *Radical Representations: Politics and Form in U.S. Proletarian Fiction, 1929–1941* (Durham, N.C.: Duke University Press, 1993), 321–61.

28. Ben Levine, "Christianity Born in Fight on Oppression," *Daily Worker,* 9 Sept. 1954, 4.

29. Alienation, because the Marxist theory of the origins of religion involves the notion that the religious act is one of alienation; that is, one in which we give up some powers of control by projecting an idealized image of ourselves into the heav-

ens, comparing ourselves unfavorably to that image, and living with the promise of a joyous afterlife to compensate for our miseries here and now on earth. Ideology, because religion is seen by Marxism as functioning in the superstructure as a form of ideology—as an imaginary way of living our lives that tries to mask and resolve the real material contradictions of our situation.

30. These are the so-called coal and iron police who simply did what the owners wanted, including beating and even killing anyone who tried to organize a union, evicting people from their homes when the land was needed for expansion of the mill (as is the situation in this novel), forcing workers to go to work, forcing them to stay inside the plants, and so on.

31. While Benedict should not be read as a literal portrait of Bonosky in every respect, it is worth noting his recollection that "I discarded almost casually my religious beliefs, inherited in my early teens, finding them inapplicable from both a practical and spiritual point of view." Bonosky to Wald, 7 Feb. 1997.

32. According to the Pittsburgh regional specialist David Demarest Jr., the literal place of Burning Valley in Duquesne is now called Thompson's Run. Demarest to Wald, 8 June 1997.

33. The Burning Bush is referred to in Exod. 3:2, 3; Deut. 33:16; Mark 12:26. Sodom and Gomorrah is referred to in Gen. 19:24–28. There are also important references to burning in connection with judgment in Lev. 10:1–6 and Num. 16:2, 35.

34. See Deut. 34:6; II Sam. 8:13; and Zech. 14:4–5.

35. St. Benedict was an Italian monk, called Benedict of Nursia, who died around 547 A.D.

36. Quoted in Michael Löwy, *The War of the Gods: Religion and Politics in Latin America* (London: Verso, 1996), 5–6.

37. Moreover, Löwy observes that Engels's writings develop Marx's earlier ideas about religion serving to legitimate the established order as well as protesting that order in which Löwy notes three parallels to modern socialist movements: that they start as mass movements; that they are movements of the oppressed, often hunted down by rulers; and that they preach liberation from slavery and misery (*War of the Gods*, 8–9). An additional important study of Marxism and religion is Paul N. Siegel, *The Meek and the Militant: Religion and Power Across the World* (London: Zed, 1986).

38. Löwy, *War of the Gods*, 9.

39. Löwy cites Luxemburg's 1905 essay "Church and Socialism" in which she argues that modern socialists are more faithful to the original principles of Christianity than the official clergy (*War of the Gods*, 12).

40. Gramsci also wrote: "Every religion is really a multitude of different and often contradictory religions: There is a Catholicism for the peasants, a Catholicism

for the petty bourgeoisie and urban workers, a Catholicism for women, and a Catholicism for intellectuals." Quoted in Löwy, *War of the Gods*, 13.

41. Ibid., 15.

42. Ibid.

43. The Peruvian Mariátegui's ideas about socialism being inseparable from the attempt to re-enchant the world through revolutionary action bore fruit decades later when his influence became evident in the writings of the founder of modern liberation theology, another Peruvian named Gustavo Gutiérrez.

44. Even Ignazio Silone's *Bread and Wine* (1937) does not go that far; the novel features a committed Communist disguised as a priest who increasingly blends the two roles.

45. Catholicism, after all, was strongest under feudalism. Still, it can be argued that precisely because it was Protestantism that evolved with the rise of capitalism, there are elements inherent in Catholic theology resistant to capitalism.

46. Indeed, there is a kind of popular tradition in Catholicism of seeing poor people as the earthy image of Christ's sufferings, and there are popular parables about helping out a poor stranger who may indeed be Jesus Christ himself.

47. Richard Wright, "Down by the Riverside," in *Uncle Tom's Children* (New York: Harper's, 1938).

48. Löwy, *War of the Gods,* 17.

49. See the later stories in Bonosky's *A Bird in Her Hair* (New York: International, 1987). His views on the tradition of the U.S. literary Left can be found in several essays: "The Background of American Progressive Literature," *Zeitschrift für Anglistik und Amerikanistik* 9.3 (Autumn 1961): 253–60; "Reclaiming the Thirties in American Culture," *Political Affairs* 72.10 (Oct. 1992): 19–25; and "The 'Thirties' in American Culture," *Political Affairs* 38.5 (May 1959): 27–40.

50. Charles Humboldt, "The Novel of Action," *Mainstream* 1.4 (Fall 1947): 395.

BIBLIOGRAPHY

Reviews of *Burning Valley*

Aronson, James. "A Fine First Novel." *National Guardian,* 22 Feb. 1954, 7.

Brown, Lloyd L. "Men of Steel." *Political Affairs* 33.4 (Apr. 1954): 61–65.

Gold, Michael. "A Memorable Novel by the Son of a Steelworker." *Daily Worker,* 20 Dec. 1953, 8.

Humboldt, Charles. "Steel Worker's Son." *Masses & Mainstream* 6 (Dec. 1953): 53–57.

Sources on Phillip Bonosky

Published

Bonosky, Phillip. "The Life and Death of a Steel Worker." *Masses & Mainstream* 5 (Apr. 1952): 14–21.
———. "Margin for Maneuver." *Masses & Mainstream* 9 (Nov. 1956): 35–46.
Gladsky, Thomas S. *Princes, Peasants, and Other Polish Selves: Ethnicity in American Literature.* Amherst: University of Massachusetts Press, 1992.

Unpublished

Terrar, Toby. "Catholic Communists and Their Contribution to Liberation Theology: The Case of Phillip Bonosky." Undated ms.
Wald, Alan. Interview with Phillip Bonosky, New York City, 7 Oct. 1989.
———. Interview with Frank Bonosky, Duquesne, Pa., 21 Feb. 1997.

Additional Sources

Demarest, David P., Jr., ed., *From These Hills, From These Valleys: Selected Fiction About Western Pennsylvania.* Pittsburgh: University of Pittsburgh Press, 1976.
Humboldt, Charles. "The Novel of Action." *Mainstream* 1.4 (Fall 1947): 389–407.
Löwy, Michael. *The War of Gods: Religion and Politics in Latin America.* London: Verso, 1996.

BURNING VALLEY

For my sisters, Barbara and Toni
. . . and for Faith

PART ONE

1.

"I will be a saint," Benedict said. "I will live humbly all my life. I will be poor."

In his pocket he carried a rosary; around his neck, tapping lightly like a leaf against his heart, always hung his scapular, the image of St. Benedict on it old and faded.

This was not the first time Benedict had made this vow. He felt as though he had always believed it; that somehow it had been in him since he was born, for he had never had to struggle to his belief: it was there waiting for him when he found the words to say it.

For two years it had seemed very simple to him to be a saint. It was harder now that he was almost fifteen, but his determination was only more stubborn. "I *will* be a saint!" he said.

On top of Honey Bee Hill, as it had originally been named, Hunky Hill as the people in the City called it, Hungry Hill as they in the Hollow called it, he stood and gazed over Hunky Hollow. He often looked down at the Hollow from that point—coming home from school or from a quick dangerous visit to the City: because it seemed like a little town spread out before him, small enough, snug and safe enough for his eyes to encompass, and his saintly authority to cover. It was the diocese of his inner dream. Unlike the City which spread out in all directions and wandered finally away into remote little patches of miners' houses and steelworkers' shacks, the Hollow was cupped in by Honey Bee Hill on this side, and some three miles across the valley by the slag flats and the Northern Railroad: then to the west by the incinerator, with its big brick chimney, its steaming dump; and finally to the east by the railroad bridge and the Mill.

There were four main streets, curving like lines of wonder around the base of the Hill: Highland Avenue, Washington Avenue, Vanderbilt Street, and Kuckuck Alley. Running at right angles to them, more or less, and down to the Ditch, were Shady Avenue, Carnegie Avenue and Mellon Avenue; and then a couple of alleys which were called Toe Alley and Rosy Lane.

From this high point he could see *their* house, Grammar School —that is, *public* school—then St. Joseph's, with parochial school beside it, then the parish house, then the convent: all at the foot of Honey Bee Hill where Highland Avenue ran into it.

It looked like a world: there was the Ditch, full of mine water coming out of the hills back of the Flue Dust; there was the slag hill, and the Northern Railroad running on it, bringing cone-shaped hot-metal cars from the Mill to dump here. There was the Flue Dust Mill, with the Flue Dust pond behind it; and behind the pond the woods going Benedict didn't know how far back, the burnt-out and worked-out mines, filled now with eerie dripping water and bottomless pits.

Benedict smiled seriously and began to descend the hill down its long wooden stairs. He knew exactly how many steps were in those stairs. He'd counted them hundreds of times. There were three hundred and forty-eight. He counted them now, slowly, with his tongue clicking them off, as he descended: sometimes confusing the counting with the beads he fingered. When he had decided to make it a praying stairs, it had taken him 10 seconds to say a Hail Mary; it had taken him exactly an hour to reach the top. Then he had gone down again saying Our Fathers. "In the Name of the Father, and of the Son. . . ."

As penance for lying he had made Joey climb the steps saying Hail Marys.

No one should be poor, but it was a sin to wish riches. *He* was poor, but this did not count: he *wanted* to be poor. A priest had no need for wealth.

He felt as though sunshine had come inside him and illumined his body.

On the midway landing he found Mr. Donkas who was lying on his back with his red mouth open, drunk. There was a ragged gash on his forehead, and Benedict leaned over him and murmured a prayer. As he crossed himself, Mr. Donkas' eyes suddenly flew open, his hand jerked out, and Benedict was caught by the wrist.

"You try rob?" Mr. Donkas cried.

He twisted Benedict's hand until he gasped and tears came burning into his eyes. When it seemed impossible to endure it any longer without crying, Mr. Donkas' hand suddenly fell away.

"I'll pray for you," Benedict mumbled and staggered down the steps. Mr. Donkas roared after him and then rolled off the platform and went back to sleep among the dandelions.

All the sunshine was gone.

He wept, struggling with himself against humiliation, against pain.

"Oh, God," he beseeched between clenched teeth, "test me! Make me suffer more, God; test me. Test me even more, God!"

For even now he felt stronger than the humiliation of the encounter. By the time he reached the bottom of the steps he would feel serene again.

A great sewer pipe jutted out of the hill and over the steps and a thick stream of gray water arched over the alley and into the ditch that ran down the hill. Benedict held his breath, without knowing that he did, and then walked quickly down the back alley to St. Joseph's. It was Saturday. He was on his way to confession. Reluctantly on his way, however, and so he dawdled a little as he went down through the dirt alley behind the board-fenced yards. Women in shawls were digging up the black earth, and the steamy smell of manure filled the air. He passed cow sheds, in which cows heavy with calf mooed dreamily. The pleasant green smell of fresh cow dung hung over his passage like an arbor.

The steeple of St. Joseph's was like a compass point to him. From it and the incinerator stack he estimated distances, for they could be seen from almost any point for miles around, deep in the woods behind the Flue Dust, from on top of Honey Bee Hill, from the slag dump, even from as far away as the burnt-out tipple of the old Robbins mine, if one climbed the charred boards up to the rusty wheel.

From it he really estimated his life.

11

He entered the mossy gate of the parish house yard, and passed through the yard where Mrs. Rumyer, like the women along the way, was digging in Father Dahr's garden.

"Hello, Mrs. Rumyer," Benedict said politely.

She was startled and jumped painfully when he spoke.

"Is he coming tomorrow?" Benedict asked.

Mrs. Rumyer turned back to her work, stuck a pitch-fork into the ground, and didn't answer.

Benedict passed through the red-stone walk, through the closed-in garden, with its wooden wall and pergola of scuppernong that hung over it. The walk led past the back porch of the parish house to the sacristy of the church. Once inside the door, he stood with his back against it as though listening. No matter what he had been thinking of on his way to church, whether he was happy or sad, or dreaming only, the moment he entered through the door it seemed as though he stepped into an air that was entirely separate from the air on the outside. Here was a different realm. He stood still always for a moment, composing himself, returning his thoughts to piety. The odor of incense and wax candles, the ancient odor of dust and of human grease which clung to the backs of the pews, rubbed over and over by new generations until the wood shone—this, mixed with the aroma of dead lilies from the altar—never failed to make his heart beat faster, his skin to tingle. He shuddered and suppressed his joy. A silence that seemed almost tangible surrounded him; as though it was the same cocooned silence that had come down to him through the Catholic ages, existed in every church in the world, the almost-material flesh of religion, separated and united in time and space. He felt as though from this he could step into Rome's St. Peter's as though he had not moved an inch.

Tomorrow he would be here again, directing the altar boys, preparing for both Low and High Mass—here he would be at five a.m., again at seven, then at noon, serving at all masses.

He passed through the sacristy into the church. From the top step he looked over the shadowed interior. He surveyed it critically, as though he were the priest in charge, testing the atmosphere and silence, the smell and look. Paint peeling from the ceiling hung in long faded streamers, scarring a depiction of Christ's miracle of

12

the loaves: and the sight of this hurt him like an immoral thought.

But the walls were beautiful—everything in place, the Stations of the Cross, the windows through which the sun was shining, casting a rosy bar of light as though from heaven itself. A few women and children sat in the back pews; others were kneeling. Still others were preparing to enter the confessional.

He took his place humbly at the end of the line, conscious of his humility, bowing his head. "Holy Mary, Mother of God, pray for us, sinners, now and at the hour of our death. Amen."

"It has been one week since I last confessed, Father," he said.

The little gate separating him from Father Dahr clattered open. A rank smell of bad teeth, mixed with a faint sting of whisky, filled the cubicle, and he bowed his head. Anguish gripped his heart.

"I have no sins to confess, Father," he said.

Father Dahr turned his profile like a coin and asked hoarsely: "Who are you?"

"Benedict," he answered, flushing.

"Ah, yes." Father Dahr peered at him through the gloom. "How was that, son?" he said.

"I have no sins to confess," Benedict repeated, with stubborn pride.

There was a silence. He waited, suddenly feeling as though the old man's thoughts prickled him, so that he could sense their skepticism. He bowed his head lower.

"Why did you come, then?" finally the old man asked.

Again Benedict flushed. He felt the weariness in the priest's voice.

"I come every week," he murmured. "I—was born in sin. . . ."

Again there was silence.

As though dreaming, the priest repeated: "Nothing? No sin all week? Not even a thought—you have been pure both in thought and deed all week?" he asked.

"Yes, Father," Benedict replied.

"Perhaps," the old priest said, leaning toward him, "you are guilty of the sin of pride?"

"I don't understand what you mean," Benedict said.

The priest wiped his eye, as though a secret beam had suddenly troubled it. "None of us," he said through a thick voice, "is without sin. You—I—" He waited for a moment, which stretched into a long silence, until Benedict could hear the silence rise and shudder. In sudden fear he began to pray. It was only as the words separated from his prayers that he heard the priest's voice again: ". . . and he'll be my assistant, you understand. *Assistant* pastor: my curate. A very young man, I'm told. Here with you, tomorrow, of course. Low Mass, and I want you to be sure. . . ."

"The new pastor, Father?"

Father Dahr's head jerked up.

"*Assistant!*" he cried. Benedict lowered his head. "Yes," the old man added, finally, in a softer tone, "I want you to be sure to——"

"Yes, Father?"

"Sure to——"

Benedict waited. Moments passed. He had not raised his head. He could hear, as though the church were a huge ear, the sound of day, of the eternity beyond life in which he believed; as though in this cubicle he had placed his ear against a shell and were listening to a distant religious sea.

"Father!" he whispered urgently. He poked his finger through the mesh separating them and touched his shoulder. "Father!"

Soft snores came through. He poked harder. The old man started and cried: "Yes?"

"I'm still here, Father," Benedict said, in a low tormented voice. He added: "You fell asleep."

The priest coughed.

"How many more are waiting?"

"I'm the last," Benedict said.

"Go now, son," the old man said. "Try not to think impurely and practice impure deeds on thyself. Ten Our Fathers and 20 Hail Marys."

"But, Father——" Benedict cried, flushing.

The old man made a tired sign of the cross blindly at him and clattered the door shut between them. Burning like a torch from head to foot, Benedict felt the darkness whistle around him.

He stumbled out of the confessional, his eyes almost clenched together, and sank to his knees. His prayer now was so secret

14

almost he was not aware of it. His heart seemed to hold its beat. He prayed without words: that God would hear him, even him, and help the Church, and somehow restore Father Dahr, or take him mercifully back, now that he was so old, for he no longer knew what he did, nor how his disgrace had made Benedict suffer, how deeply. . . .

He ignored Father Dahr's instructions, and rose to his feet. For a moment he felt impelled to go into the confessional and wake Father Dahr, who would now be asleep, and take him. . . . But Father Dahr would no longer know him: he would sleep till late this night, or morning. . . .

Instead, he left the church, again by the rear door, and crossed through the little yard to the back porch of the priest's house. He knocked. Mrs. Rumyer, the housekeeper, opened the door.

"Father Dahr——" Benedict began and abruptly stopped. Beyond Mrs. Rumyer, his back to the door, bending over a suitcase, stood a young priest. He had not even taken his topcoat off. He turned when he heard Benedict's voice; and when his eyes fell on Benedict, Benedict couldn't go on. His face burst into flame, and his throat became dry.

"Yes?" Mrs. Rumyer, her gray-streaked hair fallen over her face like a poodle's, confronted him. She turned to the new priest. "This is him," she said.

The priest's face lit up and he took a step forward.

"Oh, so you're Benedict!" he cried.

He held out his hands and took Benedict's into his own white ones, so soft Benedict barely felt their touch, and Benedict had to raise his taut eyes to meet those eyes now. They were profoundly blue eyes, almost indigo, under pale eyebrows, pale lashes. His face was almost marble white, with faint childish blue veins still visible in it; under thin golden hair almost too light to notice the skin was pink on his cheeks. His voice was musical, with tones Benedict had never heard before, an alien, sweet voice.

"I've already heard about you," he continued, slightly smiling at him. "From Mrs. Rumyer, from Father Dahr. I am Father Brumbaugh."

Benedict nodded.

15

"Where is Father Dahr?"

"I've just come——" Benedict began, his voice croaking. He pointed wordlessly back to the church.

"Confession, Father," Mrs. Rumyer explained, grabbing hold of her hair with both hands and parting it, her scalded-red face suddenly emerging.

"How long——?"

Benedict felt tears helplessly rise to his eyes. His head whirled and there was a buzzing in his ears. He stumbled.

The young priest's eyes rounded and he stretched out a hand, but Benedict recovered himself and giggled. Something knocked in his forehead like the knuckle of a hand.

"Are you feeling ill?" Father Brumbaugh asked with alarm.

Benedict shook his head stubbornly.

"I've fasted all day," he murmured.

Father Brumbaugh stared at him.

"But why?"

Benedict looked away. A tiny shadow of pride crept into his face. "Before Communion," he said softly, "I fast—from Friday midnight."

Mrs. Rumyer snorted.

"Don't believe it," she said. "More's likely there's no food at home. Work's been slow, Father. Work's been slow. Everybody's fasting, to tell the truth."

The young priest turned surprised eyes from one to the other.

He would never harm him, he thought deep in himself. It seemed as though God had heard even his most intimate thoughts, and this was his answer, his perfect answer. He thought of Father Dahr snoring in the confessional, sunk in a heap; and he wanted never, never to have to admit to *him*, standing there so pure, spiritual, with a hand so light its touch was almost unfelt, that this was so. He acknowledged that a duty to protect the young priest from such reality, somehow to cherish him, had fallen on his shoulders—as though only he understood the perfect gift of his coming.

Mrs. Rumyer extended a slice of bread with butter on it and, ashamed, he shook his head.

"Take it, take it!" she insisted. She put a bit of butter on her finger and suddenly buttered his lip. "There!" she said.

His eyes blazed at her. She stuck the bread in his hand and he let it hang at his side.

"Father Dahr will be busy for hours," he said.

"Are there so many——?"

He nodded dumbly.

"What shall I do, then?" the young priest asked, helplessly.

"I'll lay away your things," Mrs. Rumyer said, taking hold of the suitcase. "Why don't Benedict show you our parish," she added. "Show him!" She jerked her head at Benedict and her hair fell over her eyes.

Benedict turned to Father Brumbaugh. The priest hesitated, then shrugged.

"He won't be back for——?"

"An hour," Benedict said.

"Then I'll go."

He turned to Mrs. Rumyer, and his hand reached out toward her as if to part her hair. "Be sure to——" He didn't finish. Mrs. Rumyer was already out of the kitchen. His face reddened.

"Does she——" he began.

"Father Dahr likes her," Benedict said.

The young priest looked at him.

"She works hard, though," Benedict granted. "She knows how to take care of him."

They passed through the yard. Underneath the porch, there was a sudden squeal and from between the gaps in the lattice-work covering the bottom of the porch three tiny kittens darted out.

"Oh," Benedict cried. "I forgot about them!"

"What?" the other asked, surprised.

"Father Dahr told me to drown them," Benedict replied.

They passed through the gate, which was weighted by three old horseshoes hanging from a chain, out into the back alley.

It was unpaved, and a gutter ran through the middle of it; and a little boy was playing in the gutter. Benedict didn't notice this, but Father Brumbaugh said: "Tell him to get out of the gutter."

"Rudy!" Benedict commanded. The little boy, whose bare shanks and dirty dimpled knees were visible from beneath his dress, lifted his round moonface to them. Benedict handed him the buttered bread. "Run home!" he said.

The little boy dropped the stick he was holding, and with the bread in his mouth pattered down the alley.

"Come with me up Honey Bee Hill," Benedict said.

They walked through the alley and up the path to the wooden steps.

"Is it true?" Father Brumbaugh asked.

"What, Father?"

"What the housekeeper said?"

Benedict flushed. "I don't remember what she said, Father."

"About your fasting?"

"No. We have enough to eat at home," Benedict answered sullenly. "I *always* fast Friday night for Sunday communion. I never eat on Saturday."

"Why?"

"Because I'm a saint," Benedict wanted to answer. Instead he replied: "I wish my repentance to be a sincere and true one."

The priest stared at him with a hesitating disbelief. "This is unusual," he finally said.

They came to the steps and began to mount. Benedict's tongue ached with unconscious counting. Half-way up, he stopped. He looked over the railing for Mr. Donkas, but he was gone. He touched Father Brumbaugh's elbow slightly and turned him around. "You can see everything from here," he said.

The young priest put his hand on his heart and panted slightly, with a painful little smile. Then he raised his eyes and surveyed the valley.

"It's small," he murmured.

"Oh, people from the City come here, too," Benedict answered proudly.

"Why is it——" the priest began. "Why, a *German*——"

"We were settled first by Germans," Benedict explained. "This is the oldest part of the city. Oh," he added with sudden satisfaction. "General Braddock marched through here on his way to Fort Duquesne in 1755."

"Oh," the priest said.

"There," Benedict directed, pointing his arm like a rifle. "That's the Flue Dust."

"What's that?"

"It's where the iron ore used to be processed," Benedict answered. "They don't work it anymore. They didn't work since the War. But you see all the red dust—reaching up the valley to the pond? That's iron ore dust; it's all red up to the pond. Then there's the woods." He turned his arm to the west. "That's the garbage furnace. You see how big the smokestack is."

The priest lifted his head and a pained expression crossed his face.

"What smells so?" he asked.

"Smells?" Benedict repeated, sniffing.

"The smell!"

Benedict snuffed loudly. "I don't——" he said innocently.

"There's a *smell*," the priest cried. "Like—eggs, rotten eggs, and —oh, indescribable—dead rats?"

"I don't smell anything," Benedict replied anxiously.

"What do they burn up there?" the priest asked.

"Dead horses," Benedict replied promptly, "and cats and rats, of course. Maybe you smell the *Furnace*," he cried, light breaking on his face. "Oh, that *smells!*" he said fervently. "During the summer when the wind comes down from there—whew!" He laughed boastfully; then suddenly cut his laughter short as his eyes fell on the young priest. He had his hand on his heart, and in his violet eyes tears shone.

Slowly Benedict turned to look at his valley again.

"Over there," he resumed, in a low, faltering voice, "is where they dump the hot-metal cars. The hot-metal cars come up here from the Mill and dump the slag over the hill on the other side of——" He could never utter the word. "—the other side of the— Ditch," he finished.

The young priest's lips were moving. An expression of anguish had settled on his pale suffering face.

19

"Where have they sent me, Lord, where have they sent me?" he prayed through strained lips.

Silently they began to descend the steps.

2.

Benedict walked far out past the church, past the incinerator, with its vast mass of festering garbage that had been burning slowly for years, along a dusty, slag-covered road, which even now in June raised a dust behind him. The smell of the furnace followed him: and now he was uneasily conscious of it, identifying it out of the air; and he realized, somehow with a feeling of guilt, that it didn't smell unpleasant to him. It was a—familiar odor, that was all; it colored his cells and ran through his blood.

But at a certain point in the road, it faded, and now the smell of the desert of slag took over. To the right of the road stretched a long, empty land: it was a dark gray, as though once a volcano had erupted, perhaps somewhere up in the hills, and had covered this area with lava, with slag. Nothing grew here: it stretched as far as the eye could see—a vast table of gray rock—only crisscrossed far down the other end by tracks on which the hot-metal trains stood with their bell-shaped ladles filled with the yellow-hot slag. The table came to an abrupt end: here was a cliff over which the slag was dumped; then there was the Ditch, and on the other side of the Ditch were rows of houses, or rather shacks, built originally of packing-case lumber covered with tar-paper. The Company had built these shacks to house the Southern Negroes who were brought up in sealed freight cars after the World War as scabs to break the steel strike, and they had lingered after; and so the other people began to call it N----r Ditch, because the Company kept them living on its southern side.

He crossed the Ditch and began to climb the slag hill, along the narrow path practically cut out of the molten stone. Alkaline dust filled his mouth and nostrils, with a taste of sulpher, never separated from the slag. Nothing grew here. It took years to accumulate a dust fine enough to make a soil, even a sandy one. Farther up, daisies sometimes found a foothold and ached all summer in the hot stone. A tough grass also took a whiskery hold, and lured sometimes a tattered butterfly, like a white petal, from hill or woods, to its uncertain green. But there was no tree, no bush, nothing but the gray unbroken rock, like a vast plateau of desolation. Between this plateau and Honey Bee Hill, which rose like a tarnished emerald, the valley stretched three miles wide. Honey Bee Hill rose only as high as this plateau, so that one could have thrown a bridge directly over the valley connecting the Hill.

Farther along, to the west, away from the valley, the molten rock suddenly gave way to a red dust. Now, as if by magic, slag disappeared and red flue dust, a mixture of fine iron ore and coke dust, like a vast bloody earth, appeared. It rolled in mounds and valleys, mountains and crevices, like the sand dunes in a desert. Again nothing grew here, except perhaps the hardy daisy, or the surprisingly delicate "horse tails", where a dark crust had formed over the ore. When a wind blew, the dust rose up in a storm and reddened the countryside for a mile around; reddened the faces of the people who walked into it; reddened the roofs of the houses, when it reached so far. A tiny creek cut through the dunes, showing amazingly clear water running over rusty stones. It smelled as sour as pickles, but it was laced with green all along its way to the Ditch.

In the middle of this vast desert of red earth was the "Flue Dust." "The Flue Dust" was a great iron barn, covered with red dust. Here some part of a blast furnace had once existed, but had been dismantled: and now there was only the barn, with lonely and forgotten machinery, tangled with cobwebs and crusted with rust. Two old men, who seemed more like men left behind by some inexplicable catastrophe, guarded the works, mostly from boys, who were afraid of its ghostly look anyhow.

Beyond the "Flue Dust"—again acres of red earth, into which shoes sank deep, and whose light dust covered face and clothes and hands coppery as an Indian. Then, between two vast heaps that rose to flint-like peaks, as though time had cast its own pig-iron, was the Flue Dust pond. It was fed from the hilly woods, which lay beyond, by mine-water streams: and it was as red as blood.

Three naked boys were swimming and wading in it when Benedict arrived. He had come to get his brother, Joey, but wanted also to take the long walk in order to think and meditate. The humiliation he had felt as he caught a glimpse of the Hollow through Father Brumbaugh's stricken eyes had disappeared. On their way back to the parish house, he had confided to Father Brumbaugh that he, too, was destined for the Church; and then he had added, with his particular pride, that he already performed the duties of an acolyte although the Bishop had not yet confirmed him in this. Father Brumbaugh had been impressed. He had said: "We'll be good friends, Benedict"—and Benedict had flushed happily and shivered under the pressure of Father Brumbaugh's ethereal hand on his shoulder.

On his way out to the pond, he had tried to humble his delight by adding to himself that, in return for Father Brumbaugh's arrival, he, Benedict, would strive to carry out his duties more earnestly, more humbly, with even greater self-sacrifice. By this, he included not only the formal duties and obligations demanded by the Church, but his own additional saintly ones as well.

Fortunately, Father Dahr was home when they arrived. Mrs. Rumyer had gone to the church and roused him. But Benedict had not lingered to hear what they had to say to each other.

To see the three naked boys made him feel a little uneasy, but he didn't quite know why. There was nothing sinful in nakedness itself, he acknowledged; but still—nakedness. They seemed too unashamed. He felt most uncomfortable because Joey was just as naked as the other two boys, and he resented it, as though somehow it reflected on himself.

He stood at the edge of the pond, which was set like an almond-shaped eye in the middle of the red-ore dunes, watching them. There was a raft in the middle of the pond, and the three were playing a game. There was Joey standing on it, painted red from head to foot, his hair plastered down like a helmet, his eyelashes red, the ridges under his nose red, the spit from his mouth diluting the color of his chin to pink. He was laughing and war-whooping around the slippery raft, batting the heads and fingers of the two other boys with a stick as they tried to knock him off and take possession. His washboard ribs folded in and out like an accordion as he yelled. Nobody saw Benedict.

He laughed, too. For Joey was so triumphant, and he danced about so comically, and rapped the knuckles of the other two boys with such delight that Benedict couldn't help sharing his feeling. He watched until the two other boys ducked under the raft, tilted it, and spilled Joey, startled, with arms outflung, into the rusty water.

"Joey!"

Everybody turned to him. Their red-streaked faces stared.

Joey waited for awhile before he answered: "Wha—at?"

"Come on home!"

"No, I don't wanna go," Joey replied.

"Come on home," Benedict repeated, ominously. The two boys snickered. "Come on home, you know why."

"No!"

Silence. "Put your clothes on," Benedict ordered. But Joey didn't move. "You hear?" Joey was standing belly-deep in the water. His face was splashed with red-and-white bars, his navel was a red button. "You didn't go," Benedict accused.

"I did!" Joey cried back hotly.

"Don't lie!"

"I di!" He crossed his heart with a great staggering cross, and Benedict screamed:

"Don't do that! Do you want to go straight to hell—*now?* You lied! You didn't go to confession—you lied!"

Joey's face turned pale underneath the paint. The other two boys also looked frightened at this. They began to come out of the water. They wiped themselves dry with their underwear, which they then stuffed into their pockets. Their soaked scapulars clung to their bony chests. They began to shiver, for it was still chilly.

Joey stood rebelliously in the water, staring down at it, while his hair slowly caked together.

The other two boys, who knew Benedict's reputation for holiness, now dressed without a word, and left them—with Joey still in the water.

When they disappeared beyond the dunes, Benedict said: "Didn't I tell you *never* to steal? Didn't I?"

Joey's naked shoulders flinched as though he'd been hit.

"I didn't swipe nothin'," he whined, casting a frightened look at Benedict. His face seemed to shrink; his shoulders began to quiver slightly. His voice now was weakly defiant.

"I found the wagon today!" Benedict measured his words out. Joey's red-fringed eyes flickered. "Tell me whose it is!"

"I didn't swipe it!"

"Tell me!"

There was a silence.

"Why didn't Pap buy me one?" Joey cried suddenly, tears of self-pity gathering in his eyes.

Benedict ignored this maneuver. "That's why you didn't go to confession, isn't it? You were *afraid* to go! It would have been a mortal sin to go and then *lie,* too! You didn't want to take the wagon back, so you couldn't go to confession because you'd have to tell Father Dahr you stole it. Do you want to go to Morganza?"

Joey shuddered. His lip began to tremble. His chin wobbled. In a moment fresh tears were drawing pale white lines down his red face.

"Don't let them take me, Benny!" he wept, his face crumpling. "I'll bring the wagon back—only come with me. Come with me, Benny!"

Benedict looked into his uplifted tearful face. A gust of tears rose to his own eyes, and he said abruptly: "Get out of the water."

Joey, shivering violently now, waddled out of the pond. He stood trembling before Benedict, who looked sternly at him, his lips set.

"Get down," he ordered. "Kneel!"

"Let me put on my clothes," Joey begged.

"Kneel!"

He sank to the dust, shaking. Benedict knelt beside him.

"Pray," he said in a muffled voice. "Pray after me."

His teeth chattering, Joey had to repeat five Hail Marys, ten

24

Our Fathers and an Act of Contrition. Then Benedict closed his damp eyes and prayed for Joey alone. Then, only, did he allow Joey to dress, which he did with shaking hands that couldn't get the buttons through the holes.

"Mother'll know you swam in the Flue Dust," Benedict said, "and she'll whip you. Lucky if Father don't find out!"

"You won't tell?" Joey cried, terrified.

"You know I never blowed on you," Benedict said proudly.

They began to walk back over the red dunes, silently for a long time, and then finally Joey, whose peaked white face had emerged from the mask of paint, asked: "Will they pinch me, Benny, if they find out?"

"I'll take the wagon back myself," Benedict replied. "They won't arrest you. I'll say *I* took it."

"They'll pinch——"

"Me?" Benedict smiled. "No," he went on with serene pride, "they'll see I'm not a thief."

Again they walked slowly. Joey didn't even think of thanking Benedict; it was impossible to.

They lived on Washington Avenue in a four-room house, of which the two lower rooms were really a cellar; or rather, because the Hollow slanted down to the Ditch, the house was built on an incline, and the porch, which was on the level of Shady Avenue, led into their father's bedroom. The kitchen and "front" room were of red brick, and the kitchen, since it was underground and got air and sun only from under the porch and a side window, was almost always dark. You went into the "front" room through the kitchen. It had no windows at all. The kitchen opened out into the back yard, which right now was printed with a kind of Japanese script of lettuce, and smelled of horse manure, a rich and moist odor. Beside it was the toilet: a modest little shed with a crescent moon cut in the door, and a little star held between its horns. Beyond the toilet was the gray ditch, which ran freely down to the big Ditch, and through which the neighbors drove their cows on the way up the valley for grass.

Benedict went around to the back of the house with Joey. He inspected the garden, most of which he himself had planted, to see if anyone had rooted through it: then, satisfied, he went on behind the toilet. Joey suddenly disappeared. Benedict dragged the red-and-yellow wagon, "Lightning," from behind the toilet and parked it outside the door.

"Mama," he said, when he entered the kitchen, "make Joey go to church tomorrow!"

She turned from the stove. The kerosene lamp in the kitchen was lit. She was spooning through a big pot on the coal-stove, and sipping a little from her spoon. She was small and plump, with brown oily face and gray, sometimes, yellow eyes. Her black, straight hair was always worn pulled back into a ball behind her head. "*Cigona!*" he had called her because she was dark. "Gypsy!" At the wings of her nose were two wens: dark and fascinating.

She was afraid and proud of Benedict. Now she turned, her face reconciled to catastrophe, and asked: "What did he do?"

"Nothing!" Benedict said sullenly.

His mother stared at him for a moment, and then cried energetically: "I'll whip him!"

Benedict shrugged his shoulders impatiently.

"Does he care?" he cried.

She sipped the soup loudly, and Benedict sank on a chair and laced his fingers over his head. She watched him secretly, playing with the soup. Finally, with skepticism, he asked: "Where's Papa?"

She didn't reply. A little boy, in a dress, tottered into the kitchen. Benedict trapped him between his knees.

"Why were you playing in the gutter?" he cried fondly, pressing the little boy's nose. He turned to his mother: "Rudy was playing in the ditch when I found him with Father Brumbaugh. He was dirty, Mama! He made me feel so ashamed. Why do you let him?"

Rudy broke away from Benedict and ran to his mother. He hid behind her skirts and peered at Benedict with one dark blue eye.

She spanked him. "I *told* you to stay in the yard," she said feebly. She cast a quick glance at Benedict, and added more fiercely: "The next time, you'll see!"

A dry ache arose in Benedict's stomach. The smell from the soup pot came tantalizingly. He shouted: "Did he?"

Startled, his mother dropped the spoon into the pot, and Rudy hid completely behind the skirt.

"Don't talk like that," she said, coming forward, sucking her finger. "He went to the chipping mill and the rolling mill——"

"Oh, Mama!" Benedict cried, getting up and going to his mother. She turned her head away with a guilty laugh, but he pulled it back into the light. Under one of her eyes there was a purple wedge. He looked bitterly at her. "Why, now?" he cried; and before she could answer he accused: "You let him! You let him!" He ran to the kitchen cupboard and tore it open. He pulled out a half-filled bottle and took it to the sink.

She caught his hand before he could tilt it. "Are you crazy?" she cried, staring down into his hot eyes. "You don't understand!" she said, wrenching it angrily out of his grip. "Do you want him to come home and not have something to make him forget? Go, go!" she cried. "Work all day *yourself* in the Open Hearth—come home, you, so tired your bones are dragging in your skin! And then to have this worry like a boil in your head! Go away!" She pushed him, and carefully corked the bottle and returned it to the cupboard. She turned around again, looked at him, and then dropped her eyes. "If *I* don't say anything," she said softly, "why should you?"

"Doesn't he hate the church?" he demanded.

She tilted her head. "It's not for you to judge," she said.

"He mocks God!" Benedict cried, and her hands flew up to her breast and she crossed herself passionately twice. Her eyes were so frightened, he turned from her and dropped his head.

Joey entered the kitchen. He sidled away from Benedict and asked in a whisper: "Mama, supper?"

"In a minute," she answered.

His blond, straw hair was still streaked with red, and a wavering red line followed his cheek around his ears and disappeared down his neck.

She put bowls on the table.

"Where's Vince?" she whispered. Joey shrugged, his shoulders coming up to his ears. She glanced at Benedict with his face lowered in his hands. She set three places and filled the bowls with soup. The three sat at the table and waited. Without lifting his head, without moving from his chair, Benedict prayed: then they ate.

After soup, she dished out small pieces of soup meat. This they ate with brown bread. When it was over, Joey said: "Mama, I'm still hungry."

She looked at him angrily. Rudolph banged his spoon on the table. "More," he said, laughing.

Benedict raised his head. "Give them more, Mama," he said.

"There is no more," she replied.

"There's more," he said quietly.

"Papa's," she returned. "I have to save some for——"

Benedict rose from his chair and picked up Joey's bowl and went to the stove. He filled it and replaced it in front of Joey. Joey sat still, with the tips of his fingers touching the table.

"Eat!" Benedict commanded.

The yellow head shook.

"Eat!" Benedict said between clenched teeth. The nervous fingers moved toward the bowl and then shot back as though they had touched fire. Rudolph, who now received a bowl, dived into his. Benedict set a bowl for his mother.

"Eat, Mama," he said.

"I couldn't," she cried, with a laugh. "Look how full I am!" Like a child, she threw out her stomach and patted it. "See?"

Joey lifted his head with a smile watching her and Rudolph began to bang his spoon in glee.

Painfully Benedict whispered: "Eat, Mama."

"Go, go," she said.

He returned to Joey. Slowly, Joey lifted a spoon and dipped. Benedict's smoldering eyes followed him. A hollow throbbing was in his head. His eyes burned. The pain through his chest and stomach nevertheless comforted him: it was not a new pain. The dry, exalted emotion in his head seemed as though he had been weeping for days until his eyes had exhausted themselves and his brain was a dry empty cell.

Nobody asked him to eat.

When they were done, he went upstairs to their bedroom. There, in a corner near the window, he knelt before a small chapel, decorated with nothing but a gilt crucifix and two small, now dead, candles standing in shallow red cups. Through smarting eyes, he prayed. "Do not forsake me, God," he begged. "Help me to make our life as You would wish it, Lord. Show me the way, oh, my God!"

His mother was holding up a long white envelope to the light when he came downstairs. "A letter came," she said, her voice lowered, whispering it.

"I'll read it when I come home," Benedict said, glancing at it. "It's from the Company," he added, staring at the printed return address.

"Maybe it's about a job for Papa?" she coaxed, coming near.

He tore it open and read it rapidly.

"No," he said. "They want us to sell the house."

She looked blankly at him. Suddenly she cried with horror: "Sell the house? What does it mean? Why should we sell the house?"

"I don't know, Mama," he answered impatiently. He handed the letter back. "I have to go. Show it to Papa when he comes home."

He went to the toilet and dragged the wagon out. Joey was waiting. "Let's go," Benedict said, pulling the wagon behind him.

They started up Shady Avenue and cut over to the wooden steps that led up the Hill. Then, with Joey lifting the back, they carried the wagon up the long flight of stairs, stopping every ten steps to rest a little. It was growing dark. A gray, cat-like dusk had suddenly settled on the Hollow. It seemed to have arrived more quickly than the street-lights could be put on—in one of those moments when they weren't watching. The dark houses were shrouded, and the gentle darkness softened the ragged lines and blended the Hollow in a soft gray twilight. Far to the west, a spear of yellow flame shot up from the tall dark stack of the incinerator. It pricked the sky, and then disappeared.

Midway up the long stairs, they paused and looked over the Hollow to the slag dump. A train of some ten hot-metal cars, their bell-shaped ladles looking like upright thimbles at this distance, shuddered into position. The tracks came to the very edge of the abyss over which the molten slag would be dumped. Benedict remembered how Father Brumbaugh and he had stopped at this point earlier that day and gazed over the Hollow.

"Joey," he said. "Can you smell anything?"

Joey sniffed.

"No," he replied.

The sky suddenly lit up. The Hollow was mercilessly exposed, as though suddenly caught in some shameful act; the houses appeared startled and nakedly ugly. One of the cars had dumped its slag. The slag tumbled out in a huge red-hot boulder. It teetered for a moment against the blurred horizon, and then began its fiery descent down the side of the hill, fragments breaking off and shooting like stars from a whirling wheel. Midway down the hill the boulder burst; its yellow-hot heart was revealed for an intense instant, knifing their eyes, and then it disintegrated like a huge bomb into the air and rolled in a thousand pieces down the hill, bounding and shattering as it went, until it came to a glowing rest at the bottom, a hundred yards away from the Ditch. Another boulder followed: it dissolved quickly and lay like a burning tongue along the whole length of the hill. A third followed, like a tiny river of flame and gas. The sky flared. A sudden roof of flame covered the valley, and the dazed windows of the homes reflected its bitter light. The shacks of the Negroes across the Ditch were lurid and sharp. The tar-paper tacked to the front walls had begun to curl and soften, tortured by the heat.

The two watched this common sight in silence. But even at this distance, some three miles away, they thought that they felt the terrible heat. Their faces were garish, like faces in a disaster.

"One man just fell in!" Joey observed in a hollow voice.

"Stop lying!" Benedict ordered, and started up the stairs.

When they came to the City, somehow they both immediately felt different. They came as strangers, outlanders. Benedict felt alien even though he knew there were Catholics in the City, too, who would certainly have a high opinion of him because of his religious devotion. He had gone to St. Mary's here—once even served Mass; but it was an Irish Catholic Church, and he had not liked it.

"Where is it?" he asked at each corner. "Here?"

"No," Joey said. His face had become pale; when he was afraid, it seemed to shrink.

Protestantism was evident everywhere in the City. There were Protestant churches, a public library, and public schools. They skirted the business section of the City and came into its tiny residential area. The streets were bordered with sycamores, and in front of each of the brick houses was a strip of lawn.

"Here?" Benedict asked.

Joey nodded dumbly.

"Which one?"

Joey pointed. Benedict stared at it and hesitated. "That one?" he asked. Again Joey nodded. "You sure?"

"Yes," Joey whispered hoarsely. "Benny, just leave the wagon, and let's run!"

Benedict turned on him.

"And be thieves? No. We have to show them we're not thieves. We have to *tell* them!"

Joey cast a despairing look at him.

"Well, wait for me," Benedict said at last.

He pulled the wagon down the walk through the lawn. Lights were on in the house, an orange blurred light in the sitting room. He turned to cast a wan look back at Joey who was hiding behind a large lilac bush, whose tiny leaves were sticking out like ears. He arrived at the door. There again he paused. As though in a stern dream, he had come this far without questioning: now his hand trembled as he lifted it.

Suppose it was a Protestant family? Here, in the City, he had always felt a threat to his beliefs, not only because he was Catholic, but somehow also because he was . . . poor; because he lived in Hunky Hollow, and somehow they seemed to know this at a glance. Here, in the City, they couldn't know of him as they did in the Hollow; he couldn't tell them that poverty was no disgrace, it was . . . humility. The face of disdain was the face of the City. Against his resolve, he flinched. Suppose, he thought . . . and the eyes of Father Brumbaugh staring through a silver tear at the valley came back to him.

He heard a voice inside the house, and turned to run. Then, his hands shaking, he closed his eyes and pushed the button. The bell tones looped melodiously through the rooms. The door opened almost before they had died.

"What do you want?"

The face that looked down on him was *that* face. It had the unmistakable characteristics of Protestantism: the voice was oh, so certainly the City's, his father's middle-class, Anglo-Saxon, Company enemy: it was the voice of those people who, in his imaginings, Benedict could not visualize touching money.

"I——" he stammered. He grasped wildly for the thought of himself, his image; that Benedict who mounted Calvary, on whose tongue the taste of God's bread lay like his breath. The man was tall, and he had brought his pipe to the door: his hair was very gray, his nose was long and narrow; his lips were almost invisible.

"I brought your wagon back!" he cried.

The man tightened and looked over his head. "Ada!" he called, "here's Roger's wagon!" And then, before Benedict knew that he would, he had him by the shoulder and was dragging him into the house.

He couldn't speak. He dragged his legs, and the man lifted him off the ground and swung him into the hallway. Over him he could hear the panting voice of the man now say: "Here's the thief that stole your wagon, Roger!"

They crowded around him. He was huddled on the floor, with his back against the wall. He lifted his face to them. There it was, from the three of them: the face of disdain: that look of tolerant contempt at the dirt on him, the rags he wore, the "foreign" face, the broken language—half-English, half-foreign. Ever since he was three—two—one. A woman, her son, and the man.

"Let me go," he said. He felt blind.

"So you stole it, did you?" the man said.

Benedict found it hard to answer. "No," he said finally. "I didn't steal it. I was bringing it back. . . ."

Somehow he felt that his words were wrong. They sounded strange and stilted in his ears; the others couldn't understand him, and always asked him to repeat.

"So you *did* steal it," the man cried.

"No, no," Benedict replied. "I said I was bringing it back. . . ."

"So you stole it, then?"

"No!"

Finally: "Who stole it, then?"

But Benedict didn't answer.

"Where are you from?"

Benedict stiffened.

"You're from Hunky Hollow, aren't you? Aren't you? You don't have to tell me—I can smell!"

Benedict lowered his eyes and selected a prayer. His lips moved slightly.

"We'll see what you've got to say!" the man said.

Benedict closed his eyes, and immediately against the dark curtain of his mind he saw the chaste crystal steeple of a church rise up sheerly from the darkness. At its peak shone a cross, dazzlingly white. Then, suddenly, he was inside: he was before an enormous ivory altar covered with lilies; the suffering visage of Christ looked down on him as he lay prone upon the altar steps. The dust of the carpet was in his mouth. A chalice rose with blinding power above his head. "Holy, Holy, Holy, Lord God of Hosts! Heaven and earth are full of Thy glory!" He heard the deep ragged voice of Father Dahr, and then suddenly it became the clear, silver voice of the other, soaring: *"Kyrie eleison! Christe eleison! Kyrie eleison! . . ."*

The boy and the woman watched him. His eyes flickered briefly open, and he saw their curious, half-frightened expressions; the way they stepped back a half-step. *They're afraid of me,* he thought. The man was in the hall telephoning. *They think I'm a freak.* He could run to the door, those two couldn't hold him. He'd scream and jump up an down and bare his teeth at them, and the woman would faint, the boy run. . . .

The man was back. "I've called the wagon," he said. "Now, you've got just ten minutes to make up your mind." He stretched his arm out to clear his sleeve from his wrist-watch.

It was strange how all those faces looked alike, he thought. They had only one expression.

"Is he the one, Roger?"

Now the twelve-year-old boy stared at him, examined him, measured him; Benedict could feel his body estimated, judged. The little boy was safe over there, on the side of the Company. A flush of humiliation spread over Benedict.

"I'm not sure, Dad," he said in precise and legal English, which they understood. "He looks like the hunky who stole it, all right!"

Out in the street he'd make him eat those words. He'd knock him down and push his nose in the dirt. He'd make him say, "I eat shit!" Then he'd chase him all the way home, yelling: "Lacey pants, lacey pants. . . ."

"Three minutes," the calm voice said crisply.

Benedict couldn't look at him directly; he didn't know why. He felt his eyes quivering. A curse word sounded in his brain with some one else's voice, and his mind paled and he bowed his head.

"He's going to cry!" the woman said with alarm.

Benedict's head flashed up.

"Five minutes gone," pronounced the man, glancing at his watch.

He felt at bay.

Sometimes the kids of the Mill officials would stand on the Hill at the top of the steps and yell down at them:

> *Hunkies, niggers, Jews and Wops,*
> *We eat cake, they eat slops!*

And the boys would start up the steps after them, and chase them into the protection of barberry bushes and golden-toned bells. . . .

He closed his eyes. *"Credo in unum Deum,"* he said. *"Patrem omnipotentem Factorem coeli et terrae, visibilium omnium et invisibilium. . . ."*

"What is he saying?" the woman cried.

"Mother, that's the *way* they talk—that's hunky talk," the boy said with authority.

"Three minutes left," the voice declared.

"Ad Deum," Benedict intoned. The altar was before him. Father Dahr's voice sounded in his head: *"In nomine Patris et Filii et Spiritus Sancti. Amen."*

It was already tomorrow—Sunday. The white light of the Mass spread over him. The altar, covered with nothing now but burning candles and white cloth, embroidered in gold thread, rose before him, the long candle sticks gleaming from their own reflected light, the closed and curtained doors of the Tabernacle behind which rested God's body and blood. . . . A pain went through his stomach and then seemed to kick, like a foot, in his head. He thought he was kneeling: if he bent forward, he would fall flat on the floor. The smell of his mother's soup somehow filled the room, and the surprise of this made him open his eyes again.

"Please let him go," the woman said. "Besides, they're not coming. We have the wagon back! Don't you want to let him go, Pups?"

"No," the boy said decidedly.

"It's not just the question of the wagon," the man replied.

"Maybe he *didn't* steal it!" she said.

"Somebody did, didn't they?" he answered her with irritation. "What do I care if he just doesn't happen to be the exact one in this particular instance? *Somebody* from Hunky Hollow did! And if he didn't happen to steal this particular wagon, I'll bet he's stolen something else he wasn't caught for! They're all guilty of something! The point is to protect our property from Hunky Hollow," he said, "from *Hunky Hollow*, you understand, not from this or that man or boy!"

There was no smell of soup here. It had been in his mind.

He would prove to Father Brumbaugh how loyal he was, how devoted to the Church: by every kind of proof he would show his selflessness, his consecration to the duties of priesthood, he would amaze them all by the depth of his sacrifice. . . .

"*Dominus vobiscum.*"

"*Et cum spiritu tuo.*"

"*Oremus . . . per omnia saecula saeculorum.*"

"*Amen.*"

"But still," the woman said, "if he didn't steal it, it seems . . ."

"Why doesn't he say *who* did, then?" the husband snapped.

Benedict wondered if Joey was still outside; if he had seen what had happened, or had guessed, and had run back to the Hollow. It was time to speak.

He opened his eyes and said calmly: "You must let me go. I didn't steal the wagon, but I can't tell you who did."

He spoke as though reading from a primer.

He stood up. "Don't call us 'hunkies' ", he said with grave dignity, "even if we do come from the Hollow. *I* serve Mass."

The doorbell rang. As though only now the thing leaped out

of fantasy—the silhouette of the uniform through the window—and he screamed. He twisted out of the hands of the man with the watch, still held out as though ending a race, stumbled through the hall into the kitchen. A dog outside began to bark. He grabbed hold of the doorknob and pulled . . . and pulled . . . and screamed and kicked at it with his feet, and twisted and pulled. . . .

3.

They had taken him out of the police-wagon and led him into the lockup. Two drunks had lain in blood and mess on the floor, and he had sat pinned in a corner of the van with his eyes closed, praying. A long-legged policeman sat at the rear with his legs barring the exit.

His face was so pale, a policeman asked him if he was sick. He didn't answer; he hadn't heard. It seemed as though he had taken a submarine ride, under some big ocean whose weight had pressed against his lungs, on his eyes, over his brain, and he floated sluggishly on a current that was thick and sticky as blood. Although his eyes were closed, instead of darkness, there was a brilliant sun shining that cut into his eyeballs. He drew into himself, scooped into a little corner.

His feet stopped. A forefinger nudged his shoulder. He opened his eyes. Before him, leaning like God out of the clouds, sat the police lieutenant elevated on a dais behind a high bench.

"What's your name?" he said, and it was for the second time.

"Benedict Blumanis," he answered through a dry mouth. A big dry stone filled it and his tongue was glued to the stone. "B-u-l-m-a-n-i-s," he spelled automatically for the lieutenant.

"Address?"

Benedict hesitated. "Sir," he said.

"Your address?"

The lieutenant was pink from his fingers up through his neck to his hair.

"Sir," he repeated. "Please call Father Dahr at St. Joseph's. That's on Highland Avenue. Please call him."

"Address?"

He trembled. "I don't want to give you my address," he said.

The lieutenant looked at him. It seemed to Benedict for the first time; his eyes were a sharp blue.

"Let's have your address," he said.

Benedict tightened his lips.

"If you don't give me your address," the lieutenant said, "we'll have to keep you in jail until Monday."

"822 Washington Avenue," Benedict said.

"Charged with——?"

"Petty larceny," came a voice. It was the policeman whose leg had barred the way out.

"By——?"

Then, out of the back, Mr. Brill materialized, and in a clear, legal voice gave his name, address, what was stolen, when, who. . . . Benedict couldn't look at him. He suddenly shivered: he was in the presence of a Lie. He was mortified for Mr. Brill. A nausea took hold of him, and his shoulders shook violently for a few seconds, and a sweat broke out on his forehead. It seemed to him that Mr. Brill had compromised himself forever; that he was damned forever, wherever he went, whatever he did. He was a chemical engineer in the Mill, he was telling the lieutenant. Benedict was overwhelmed by the profound crime that Mr. Brill was committing: at the same time he was terribly astonished. He closed his eyes and said a prayer while the voice of the damned man went on over his head.

"Okay, take him!"

A hand gripped Benedict. "Call Father Dahr!" he cried. He braced his feet against the floor, and shouted: "Call Father Dahr!" From his soul he was crying: Call for my Church to speak for me!

Mr. Brill was gone; the lieutenant was leaving. The room was empty, and there was no sound except for the distant clang of steel, and the loud sobs of someone crying. The sobs were so tremendous they seemed to be coming out of a wounded animal, some elephant weeping in the jungle. They were his sobs, but someone else seemed to be weeping them. Two men lifted him up between them. His legs flailed the air and his arms stuck out rigidly like dragging oars. They carried him screaming down a corridor, opened a door, and dumped him down on a cot.

He rolled off it and fell on the stone floor with his face against the cold concrete, his arms flung over it. His forehead ground into the sandy stone and bled, but he was unaware of its bleeding. A hand touched his shoulder, and he shook it off, kicking out with his feet. He heard a voice, but screamed against the stone.

Then, in a while, he could feel nothing, only a deep tide of some sea dragging him out into itself. Green water whirled around his head, and drowsy icicles dripped water, touching his forehead, penetrating his eyes. It was salty and warm, drifting in between his teeth and slowly sinking under his tongue. A cool forefinger made a salty cross upon his forehead, a wet forgiving touch. Silence arrived. A warm lip was pressed against his ear. Breathing filled him.

When he awoke, there was a man sitting on a bunk in the corner, and yet appearing to hunch up to the naked electric light, as though he couldn't get enough of it. He was busily scribbling with a stump of pencil on a piece of brown butcher paper. He had on a khaki shirt, a black tie, a pair of gray pants that were slightly split at the seam. His frowning brown face was screwed on his writing. His eyebrows were thick and brown, and his brown light hair had slight touches of gray in it. His face was broad and his nose was big and fleshy; his broad cheekbones caught the light, and the light brightened the gray, fascinated, calm eyes. There were little laughing wrinkles around his eyes.

He caught Benedict's eyes on him, and lifted his heavy hand, but kept on writing with the other. He wet the stub of the pencil with his tongue, leaving a black wet blot on it, and wrote. His tongue came out once in a while and thought with him.

"They'll be shutting off the juice in half an hour," he explained, jerking an ear at the light without taking his eyes off the paper. His pencil whispered.

Benedict looked around. There was nothing here but the bunks on opposite sides of the cell; a toilet bowl without a cover, a tiny sink.

"Did Father Dahr come?" he asked.

The man lifted his head to sign that he had heard and would answer in due time and kept on writing.

Only they two were in the cell. He was on a bunk—and only at that moment he realized that he was no longer lying on the floor but on a bunk, on a bare mattress through which he could feel the iron springs. He lay still. There was a monotonous humming in his head; his eyes ached without pain, as though the pain had finally been washed out of them. He turned over and stared at the floor. His hand hung over the bunk. His chin was pressed into the hard mattress. He wanted to die.

Jail was not separate from life. The wagon came down into the Hollow almost every day to drag someone off to jail—Mr. Petraitis for beating his wife one day, Mrs. Godalis, who made bootleg whisky and was turned in by a stoolpigeon, another day; one of the Negro men from the Ditch for reasons nobody knew. Then they had come for Anthony next door—not with a wagon, and he wasn't home, but two policemen and a plainclothesman: and later they brought him to his father's door, having caught him hiding in a chicken-coop, and had asked his father: "What do you want to do with him?" "Take him to Morganza," his father had replied, standing in his underwear at the door, looking down on Tony whose wrist was handcuffed to the cop's. "I can't keep him home." Everybody had seen, everybody knew.

He could see his father coming into the room, taking him by the arm and shouting: "You, too?" Laughing a dry bitter laugh, saying, "You, Meester Holy One, you be in jail just like crook! Like t'ief!"

A sick wave of fury against Joey came over him. Where was he now? Home, happy that *he* had escaped! And tomorrow was— Sunday.

His head sank over the side and he felt the blood rush to his forehead. *Father Brumbaugh!* That pale face came and wavered before him and disappeared in a mist. He closed his eyes and his head hung as though his neck was broken.

The light went out.

"Damn, damn it!" the man cursed. He laughed immediately after; then the pencil fell out of his fingers to the floor and he dropped down on his hands and knees to search for it. This brought him to Benedict's cot. A sudden light flared up and Benedict opened his eyes and flinched.

"It rolled somewhere here," the man said, gasping as he reached a long arm under the cot. "Very precious bit of pencil to me." He wet his fingers and transferred his hold to the burnt tip of the match. "Ah!" he cried with intense satisfaction. His fingers had touched it. "Now!" He got up off his knees and squatted in front of Benedict. Only the watered light from the corridor came into the cell. Sounds, so unfamiliar and so iron, came from the jail's depths. Steel on steel, concrete, a tin pan, the whisky voice of a policeman husky with fog.

"*Now,* what did you say? Before the light went out, I mean?"

Benedict turned his head to the wall.

"Oh," the other grunted with surprise. "I see, I see. A boy like you in this place." There was a silence in which he seemed to be chewing. "I know you didn't steal it, sonny. No, no. They're all wrong out there! They'll find out soon enough, don't you worry, and they'll all come here to apologize to you. Now, you see if I'm not right!"

Benedict said to the wall: "Did Father Dahr come?"

"What Father Dahr do you mean, sonny?"

A long, heavy shudder shook the walls of the jail, and then a muffled roar followed it. Benedict didn't notice this familiar sound from the Mill; but the man said: "That's the Bessemer! Am I right?"

Benedict turned.

"Would you ask them to call Father Dahr?"

He got up from the floor and knocked on the bars with the ring on his finger. A turnkey came running.

"Lay off them bars or I'll——"

Benedict's cell-mate interrupted him lightly, but with a kind of playful authority: "Keep your shirt on, Buster. All we want in here is a little hunk of constitutional justice for my partner here.

Wants you to call up a certain Father Dahr—right now. Where's he live, son?"

"Highland Avenue," Benedict said in a choked voice, sitting up.

"Highland Avenue. Got that? Now, run back to your lieutenant and tell him if he don't follow out these important instructions, I'm going to bang on these bars till the whole town comes down with an ear-ache!"

He turned his back on the turnkey as though he had not the slightest doubt that he would be obeyed, and said: "We're going to get your Father Dahr if we have to send the whole police force after him." Then he laughed at a joke Benedict did not understand.

He reached into his shirt and brought out a little brown bag, tightly wrapped. He handed a sandwich to Benedict. "You look like you might have skipped a meal," he said. Benedict accepted the thick brown-bread sandwich and bit into the raw bacon. Then he spat it out.

"What's the matter?" the other cried, startled. He smelled his own sandwich.

Benedict handed it over. "I have communion tomorrow," he explained sadly.

The man took back the sandwich, turned it over and looked at Benedict. Benedict repeated: "I have communion tomorrow." And then, without warning, he was crying bitterly, and the big man came and sat down beside him, clucking in an embarrassed way, and put a big sweat-smelling arm around his shoulders. "Now, now," he coaxed, "now, now. What's the big matter?"

"I *didn't* steal the wagon!" Benedict sobbed. "I only brought it back. I'd never steal anything! I'm going to be a priest, and I'd never never steal. My father's going to despise me now, and everybody's going to despise me! Father Brumbaugh's going to despise me!"

"No they're not!" he heard the big man declare. "Why nobody's going to despise you! They're all going to know you're innocent! It's a dirty shame that they dragged you down here. It's class justice," he said with a wink, "that's what it is! I'm telling you they're all going to be apologizing just as soon as they find out who really did steal that wagon!"

41

"They'll *never* find out!" Benedict cried tragically.

"Why not?"

Benedict shook his head.

"Why don't you tell me about it?" the man asked. "Maybe we can help you somehow?" He looked down at Benedict's fallen head. "No? All right! Let's say we understand why."

He released his arm and lifted Benedict's face with his hand. "Don't worry, now. Be a brave boy, and don't worry as long as you're in the right. You got to fight back! Understand? Even a jackass kicks back. Do you understand?"

Benedict nodded without conviction.

"Only," he said. "As long as they don't know who really did it, and I won't tell—they'll keep——"

"It was a good friend of yours, wasn't it?" the man guessed shrewdly.

Benedict nodded.

"And you won't tell on him!"

"But we brought the wagon back!" Benedict cried.

"And *then* they——?"

Benedict nodded. The other laughed, and Benedict looked resentfully at him. "That adds up!" the other said, slapping his thigh. "*You* took it back, didn't you?"

"We're not thieves!" Benedict said.

"But why did *you* take it back? Why didn't you make *him?*"

Benedict lowered his eyes. The other one watched him keenly.

"Why, you're a martyr," he declared. Benedict didn't notice the slight touch of amusement in the man's voice. He lowered his head.

"But now you'll have to tell, won't you?" he demanded.

Benedict said, muffled: "I never can!"

"But the other one won't come up and say *he's* guilty; he'll let you——"

"I never can!" Benedict repeated in a despairing voice.

"Even if they send you to reform school for——" He put his arm over Benedict's shoulders and added, in a warm low voice: "Maybe we can find some way out without stooling on anyone," he said.

Benedict's eyes held great blinding tears as he raised his face.

"Only Father Dahr can help me," he said sadly.

The other stared down into the passionately mournful eyes and brought his big thumb up to his nose and rubbed it thoughtfully. Then he picked up his sandwich again and took a bite out of it. "Oh," he said suddenly, pointing to his mouth as he chewed, "I don't go to communion." Benedict nodded understandingly. He chewed massively, looked at Benedict and asked: "Have you got a drink?"

Benedict shook his head gravely.

"Dry," he explained. "I thought you might have a drink on you."

Benedict smiled slightly. His "partner" leaned over and peered at him.

"Now, that's a lot better," he said. He listened to the sounds in the hall and then asked: "Does your father work in the Mill?"

Benedict nodded.

"Is he working now?"

Benedict hesitated. He hated to admit that his father was unemployed.

"Not exactly," he said.

The big head nodded. "But the Mill's working full blast. Full time. Why did they lay your father off?"

Benedict shrugged uneasily. "I don't know," he said.

"Does your father own his house?"

Benedict said "Yes" hesitantly, studying the other's face.

"How do you make out at home?" he now wanted to know.

Benedict was uncomfortable. "What do you want to know for?" he asked sullenly.

The other one gave him a quick smile, touched his knee reassuringly and said: "That's why I'm in here," he said, and winked, "for asking questions. But there's no harm doing it *here*—I'm already in, they can't put me *in*-er." He waited for Benedict to smile, but the smile didn't come. *"Furstay?"*

Benedict made a neutral motion.

"Good! No more questions."

He squinted at the barred window, through which a gray light filtered. "Would you do me a big favor?" he asked, pulling out a small box of matches. "Would you hold this match?" He lit it, and gave it to Benedict. Benedict held it in his fingers, while the man hastily pulled out his brown paper, lifted up his knee and leaning into the match-light began furiously writing with his stub pencil. "Closer! Closer!" he commanded. The match went out. "Light another one!" Benedict did. More and more he wrote. Benedict watched fascinated. He forgot his sorrows. The match burnt his finger and he dropped it with a cry. The other waited impatiently in the darkness while Benedict fumbled for another match. The moment the light appeared he was back with the pencil.

Steps came down the hallway, and suddenly the man cupped the match out. Steps stopped at the cell, and they could hear the key groping into its hole.

Benedict's cell-mate stood up to face the door. His expression had become wry; he licked his lips a couple of times, rubbed the palms of his sweating hands against his pants legs, and just as the door opened the smile cracked his broad face again.

Three men stood in the entrance, all dressed in plainclothes, looking somehow all the more like police because of that. One of them was unusually tall—over six feet, stringy and thin, with a tiny head and hollow cheeks. But the other two were men who could have been fat, except that the fat was hard muscle; these two were smiling as though they were coming for a social visit. The bean-pole bent his head to enter the cell.

"Well, well, if it isn't our old friend, Dobrik!" one of the fat men said. "I though Attorney-General Palmer deported all you Bullsheviks five years ago!" He turned to his tall partner and added: "You know he just must love this town of ours—he keeps coming back!"

The tall man, his little ostrich head swinging loosely, laughed. Dobrik's smile was like a guard over his face.

"Hello, boys," he said.

"You know, Dobrik," the first man said, shaking his head, "I'm disappointed in you! Why the hell do you keep coming around where you're not wanted? Why don't you go to Rooshia where you come from? Ain't you a Bullshevik?"

They had been coming into the cell all the time. Their tone and manner was so cordial that Benedict watched them with a smile. At the same time an ambiguous undertug in their voices puzzled him.

Dobrik, also smiling, had stepped back; and then suddenly the smile blotted out of his cheeks, and he cried: "Not before the boy!"

And the same man answered with that same congenial voice: "We wouldn't think of it!"

Before Benedict could register it, the same man suddenly swung his fist up from his hip and Dobrik staggered back against the whitewashed wall. A rattle of whitewash flakes fell on the concrete floor.

The man who had hit him clucked his tongue disapprovingly. "You Bullsheviks just *will* never learn! You know these hunkies and greenhorns and n - - - s in this town are satisfied the way they are! Why do you keep on coming in to stir up trouble? Didn't we teach you and Foster a lesson in the Steel strike? Now, do you call that right?"

And again his fist broke out from his stubby body and caught Dobrik flush on the mouth. Blood jumped out of his mouth like a red ball.

"Look at that!" the policeman said with disgust. "There you go getting yourself all busted up—and for what? To help a lot of goddamned n - - - s! You ever see such a white man?" He turned to the others incredulously. "Now I always took you for a guy with a lot of sense, Dobrik, but I just guess you have to learn the hard way."

He stepped back and the tall man stepped in, and for a moment Dobrik looked up at his tiny waving head, and the tall man looked down; and then he brought his hands locked together up into that steep height and very carefully brought them down on Dobrik's head. Dobrik's knees buckled and he staggered. The blood was coming out of the ruins of his smile and running down his shirt. When he stood up again his eyes were glazed.

The three men stood and shook their heads.

"Now, ain't that a sight!" the first man said, disapprovingly. "If I was as careless as you are with your health, Dobrik, I'd be a dead man right now!"

45

Now it was the third man's turn. He walked leisurely up to Dobrik, whose hands were lifted over his face.

"Don't you know the Company just don't *allow* no union in this town?" he said, as though instructing someone very dull-witted. "We thought we taught you that after the war!"

Then he lifted Dobrik's head by the hair and smacked his face back and forth until the teeth rattled.

Benedict stared in horror. The first man, at that moment, caught sight of his face and calmly winked.

When he let Dobrik's loose body slump to the floor, the first man kept looking sadly at him, shaking his head.

He walked over to Benedict's cot, and Benedict shrank back against the wall. The man observed this and said plaintively: "You 'fraid of me, son?"

Benedict's eyes were stiff with fear.

The big hand that came through the air to pat him on the head was stained with blood! He shrank deep into himself and closed his eyes. The hand came to rest on his head, and the top of his head seemed to explode into fire.

"Just don't you pay any attention to none of this," he heard the man say in a fatherly tone. "Do you go to church, son?" He patted Benedict again, and Benedict nodded violently. "Why, son, you just keep on going to church and grow up to be a God-fearing Christian, and you'll never get to be one of them Communists, son! Why, look at him!" the man said indignantly. "Now, ain't he a disgrace?"

Suddenly Benedict began to shudder: he felt it in his ankles first; then it climbed spiral-like in twists of cold up his legs and watery knees; his thighs began to quake, and then a cold knife seemed to twist in his bowels and in his groin; his mouth opened helplessly for breath and he gasped as though drawing air in through a thick cloth.

He felt the shadow of the man pass off his face; and then he heard the three talking soberly in the middle of the cell; and then there were footsteps going, and suddenly, like a bell of gold, the doors clanged iron shut.

He opened his eyes.

Dobrik was still lying on the floor where he had been knocked, and his face was level against the concrete, with a pool of blood curling like a tail out of his mouth.

Benedict stared down at him; a heavy rock of horror was loaded in his stomach. He could not lift it. His face was cold white. The sweat that had broken out on it had turned icy, and when it dashed against his wrists he shivered.

Then he got slowly down, as though instructing his body, and crawled over the scratchy floor, crawling around the blood, and stopping at the head. He peered into the half-open eyes, his heart going and coming; and without knowing what he was doing, he lowered his mouth and began to breathe his hot breath on the parted eyes, as though on dying coals. He could see the eyelashes quiver.

Suddenly the body jerked, and there was a vital groan that came from Dobrik, and his face lengthened, opening his mouth, which was a mush of red, and a great sigh escaped him. His eyes opened wide. He looked up into Benedict's face, and to Benedict's horror, the same deliberate smile that had been on it until the last moment, struggled painfully back. Then, to Benedict's added horror, he said: "How do I look?"—and grinned.

Benedict got up on his knees, and by taking hold of the white-washed wall, pulled himself to his feet where he swayed dizzily, looking down on Dobrik's back as he struggled to rise.

On his feet, Dobrik lifted his head, then suddenly wobbled and fell against Benedict, pinning him to the wall. Underneath his thick body, smelling of tobacco and rain, he felt a strange comfortable smothering. Dobrik was trying to apologize, as though this were some unforgivably clumsy thing; and pulled himself by force off the boy and took a grip on his arm, leading him back to the cot.

They both sank down on it simultaneously; and again he was in danger of being pinned. He sat beside Dobrik, whose head was lowered and whose hands held it up by the brow. They said nothing. Benedict finally took out a handkerchief and whispered: "Do you want this?"

Dobrik lifted his head and stared a long while at it as though trying to identify it; and then, again with a casual courtesy as though nothing out of the ordinary had happened, said: "No, no —I'll use my own," and began to search methodically through all his pockets. He found nothing, and Benedict put his handkerchief into his hand, and with it Dobrik began to wipe his face, then the stains off his shirt. He poked a finger into his mouth, tapped his teeth, and then said ruefully: "If I don't get no sense, I'm going to lose them all."

He tried to get up for water; but there was none. He picked up a tin cup and wobbled over to the toilet, and sank down on his knees. He flushed the toilet and inserted the cup; then he doused himself over the head with it. He shook himself like a dog, and when he turned to look at Benedict, his face was streaked with pink bars. He was grinning. "Did you notice that skinny guy?" he said with a lop-sided grin. "Didn't his head look like an ostrich?" He walked more firmly across the room this time, and sank down with a sigh. "They'd never caught me," he said, "if I'd waited till dark. I must be a lousy organizer!" Then he sighed again, turned to Benedict and said: "You know what?" He gave him a dry smile. "I kept looking at that tall fella. Last thing I wanted to say to him: 'Juke your head when you go out, or you'll bang it on the top bar!'" He smiled and shook his head, as though he couldn't understand the oddness of himself, and fell silent.

Benedict drew his knees tight and clasped his hands over them. All the horror began to fade, he didn't know why; things loosened in him and subtly flowed away: and a spinning glow, like a white light, slowly took shape in his chest throwing off warmth as though from a wheel. It was warm in the cell. His heart, as though waiting at the door for the moment, now began to beat like a loud barking. He felt his face flush hot, and the tears began to come slowly out of his eyes, and lingeringly flow down his cheeks. He tasted the salt of his tears, pensively sinking his tongue into a pool of warm spit. Idly, he crossed himself.

"I know about you," he said at last, without turning to where Dobrik sat sunk in deep thought, his narrow eyes almost closed, his big cheekbones flaked with the drying blood. "You're the union man."

Dobrik seemed not to hear.

"Aren't you?" he asked. "That's what they say."

"What?" Dobrik asked, lifting his committed eyes.

"They talk about you."

"Who?" Dobrik asked. "You mean, the men?"

Benedict nodded. "My father," he said. He lifted his troubled eyes to Dobrik and said: "But why do you desert the church?"

Dobrik stared at him now.

"The church?" he said.

"Why don't you ask for God's help?" He stared at Dobrik's face and said earnestly: "Was it true?"

Dobrik leaned over to him and said: "What?"

"What they said." Then he shrugged swiftly, and added: "Why did you let them beat you?"

Dobrik smiled and waited till Benedict looked at him.

"I wouldn't tell them what they wanted either," he said.

"The names of——"

"Yes," he said. "The names of people. . . ."

Benedict nodded. "You mean . . . in the union? I know," he said quickly. He added in a tormented voice: "Why, if you don't love God, do you——"

But he couldn't finish. The silence deepened. Dobrik had only watched him and not tried to answer. They sat and said nothing for an hour. Once, Benedict lifted his head, startled, and said: "Communist! That's what they said you were!" But Dobrik had fallen asleep and didn't hear.

4.

Benedict could not sleep. He stood up and walked about the cell; stopped beside Dobrik's sleeping body, and once, secretly, as though he could be seen, lifted his hand in a benediction. He found the other uneaten sandwich, and the memory of Dobrik eating made him burn with a vague remorse. He knelt once on the cold floor and dropped his closed eyes into the cups of his hands and prayed, reaching into the profoundest depths of his belief: shuddering, suddenly, as he remembered the three men entering the cell, and twisting his head in muffled agony as though to drown the jagged vision.

There, pinned to the stone floor by an anguish and a fear that held him mercilessly in a cold pain, he listened to himself and to the gigantic whispered echo of the jail, and beyond it the hoarse crying of the Mill in its torment of fire and iron.

He knelt, frozen, his knee-caps aching, staring out of the window over which orange-tinted clouds, touched by the Bossemer glow, sometimes floated. His head nodded, and he drowsed there on his knees . . . coming suddenly stiff awake as the door clanged open behind him.

He jumped to his feet and faced the door with terror. Dobrik, too, had awakened, and now rolled out of the cot and stood leaning as though into his own pain. But there was only one man in the doorway; he held a ring of keys.

"Come out, Dobrik," he said. "We got a delegation ready to escort you out of town."

Dobrik gave Benedict a wry grin. "Well," he said dryly, holding his hand out. "I'm afraid I have to go. Now, don't worry." He turned to the jailer. "Did you do like I said—call up Father Dahr?"

"Yeah, yeah," the other answered. "Come on, the delegation's waiting."

"On whose orders?" Dobrik asked.

"The mayor himself took a personal interest in your case," the turnkey answered with a heavy underlining of his words.

"You know this violates the Constitution of the United States?" Dobrik said ironically.

"Constitution?" said the other with a blank face. "Never heard of it. Come on!" He took a step toward Dobrik but Dobrik lifted up a hand.

"Just a minute," he said. He turned to Benedict. "Don't worry so much. Don't lose your courage. That's the main thing." He poked Benedict gently in the chest. "Remember you're a workingman's son." Benedict nodded dumbly. Dobrik continued to look at him thoughtfully. He lifted Benedict's head by the chin and Benedict looked into his eyes. "I have to leave you, but don't be afraid to be alone. If you're right, you won't be alone." He laughed and poked Benedict on the shoulder. "Will you?"

Benedict shook his head.

Still Dobrik seemed unsatisfied. He looked anxiously at him, at the turnkey, sipped his lip, then turned almost violently, so that the turnkey stepped hastily back, and cried: "Tell the mayor I'll be back! Tell him there'll be a union in this town yet!"

"Tell him yourself!" the turnkey answered.

Dobrik laughed and shrugged his shoulders. "I'll send him a letter."

He turned once more and gave a last pat to Benedict's arm. "We'll be back—take my word." He winked.

"Wash up before you go out," he heard the turnkey say. "People'll think you've been mistreated."

He heard Dobrik's mocking laughter.

And then silence: and the loneliness Dobrik had told him would not come, came like ice. He lay petrified with anguish on his cot. The grace of prayer lay like a frozen goldfish in the crystal paralysis of his mind; and the touch on his face was as cold as the chilled bowl that morning he awoke and his breath exhaled before him like a ghost, and he flattened his face against the glass in the center of which his fish hung suspended with ever-open glassy eyes. . . .

Night had been looking through the barred window into the cell.

There was a Power in the City that was like a machine in the Mill that ground and shook, moved by giganic laws of its own. And yet, as long as the worker remained clear of it, it could do no harm. But let him, in passing by, carelessly let loose a thread—that is all that it needs—or a shoelace dangling from a shoe, a thoughtless swing of a hand, then it will pull the whole man like a shot into its gears and grind him to death.

Everyone knew of the machines in the Mill, and of the Power in the City, and learned how to live with each.

So he had been stunned but not surprised. Some thread had come loose and he had been picked swiftly up and carried along, according to the laws of the Power, which considered nothing, whether his thoughts were good and pure, or whether they were evil. It acted impersonally: just as though he had never dreamed of martyrdom and had never kissed the communion bread. He had looked into the eyes of Mr. Brill and seen that impersonal cruelty.

The church never asked who: only let him be poor! The machine would bow to the church, the sole refuge of the poor and weak. . . .

To live more righteously, to be more holy, to obey the laws of God in every way, in every moment of his life: only in this way could salvation be ensured, fear be destroyed, human beings taught to love one another. There was a way of living that was pious and just, and would not provoke the Machine and the Power, and would in the end wipe away the hidden stain of fear from everyone's eyes. For this he had traveled ten miles every day so that he could go to a Catholic High School in Delroi. There both Sisters and Fathers held him, naturally, in the highest esteem, and knew, of course, that he was destined for the priesthood (and for sainthood, which they could not know.) Father Scanlon had asked him when he had first felt the call, and he had answered with a ringing conviction that had awed the whole schoolroom: "The moment I was born, Father!" Even the Bishop knew of him! He was an acolyte at the age of fourteen, and the Bishop had written a letter to his father, who had looked at it and shrugged. . . .

Benedict tore out the memory like a page. His father's face, with the rough orange bristles on it, the deep-set expression of weariness, the yellow eyebrows, the gray eyes, the voice that mocked . . . God. . . .

He groaned, putting his hand to his forehead. There he felt the dried blood and then the fresh blood that rose.

"Don't let father find out," he begged God.

He tossed on the mattress. His head felt feverish, and he dozed for a moment, only to jump up sharply and cry: "Oh, don't do that!" —and he flung out his hands into the pointed air. His eyes stared wide-open into the horrible vision in his mind. Then, suddenly, he began to shake his finger, and said out loud: "It burnt me!" He laughed. "What are you writing?" he asked the semi-darkness. He smiled. "*Confiteor Deo omnipotenti, beatae Mariae semper Virgini,*

Beato Machaeli Archangelo. . . ." He tried to think of his sins, and his heart sank and he closed his eyes, watching them fall shut in his mind, with despair.

"No, son," he said. "The trinity: in God there are three Divine Persons, the Father, the Son, and the Holy Ghost."

He patted the child on its springy hair and walked solemnly down the red-brick walk, through the sacristy into the church. The organ rolled. *"In nomine Patris et Filii et Spiritus Sancti. Amen. Introibo ad altare Dei."* And it was his own voice answering, too: *"Ad Deum, qui laetificat juventutem mean. . . ."*

The sea of faces murmured back; he blessed their heads, and from the high windows a broad shaft of light descended. Angels like motes floated in the light. There was music now, music that floated through the windows and rose like smoke to heaven.

He twisted on his cot, his knees tangling together. It seemed cold in the cell; he huddled down into the mattress, seeking for warmth, slipping his hands between his thighs, palm to palm. Now, he was tight, rounded in a seamless ball. A drowsiness rose like a hum and he heard the droning of the silence, like a furry bee going in an endless circle. A spinning began in his head, and suddenly a moving darkness that held within it shapes of vague contour. A long spool unraveled: an infinite sweetness spread in a prolonged unwinding of yellow ribbon along which he floated. Suddenly, he began to twist and moan, to writhe on the bed, and a hot sweat broke out on his forehead. He cried in his sleep, and opened his eyes wide. He pulled his hands from between his thighs, rolled over on his side and began to sob with his lips pressing the stiff cloth.

5.

"Here is your Father Dahr!"

The voice shook him more than the hand. He had not heard the door open. He was groggy when he rose to his feet, and the turn-key had to steady him. His eyes were red and his lips were sleep-swollen. His face was yellow. His eyelashes had stuck together and he had to pull them apart with his fingers.

He stumbled down the corridor behind the turnkey and blinked when he entered the booking room. Father Dahr, his soiled white hair showing like a haystack over the bench, dressed in street clothes, the collar turned, his hanging jaws and mottled complexion, the moist gray eyes from which he peered near-sightedly, opened his arms, and Benedict rushed into them. He dug his head into that chest and his shoulders shook.

"Oh, Father, I thought you'd never come!" he cried.

"There, there," the old man replied, patting his shoulder and wiping his eyes. "I came as soon as I could."

Benedict could still smell the faint odor of whisky in the old man's clothes but it seemed to him suddenly a friendly smell.

Father Dahr held him at arm's length to look at him, and a horrified expression came over his face. "What, boy, did they do to you?" He turned to the lieutenant who was lifting papers on his desk. "If you touched a sacred hair of this boy's head," he cried sonorously, pronouncing anathema, "I'll seek out the Pope himself to have your soul fed to the hogs of Hell!" He added sternly: "Are you a Catholic?"

"We didn't touch a hair of his head," the lieutenant, lifting his pink head over the bench and shifting his eyes from one to the other, said calmly, "and I'm a Catholic."

"I hurt myself," Benedict mumbled.

"Now," Father Dahr said, shaping his coat with a pull and a tug, "let's go from here." He looked around and gave a hearty shudder. "This is a horrible place to put a child!"

"We only got one jail for man and boy," the officer replied. "We could send him to Morganza. And not so fast. A few questions." He picked up a page and studied it. "Weren't you here before?" he asked Benedict suspiciously. "Is your name Vincent?"

"No," Benedict said flushing.

Father Dahr made an impatient gesture. "I want to take the boy to his home," he said sharply. "It's been a terrible ordeal for the lad. Why are you sitting there asking foolish questions? Let us go."

"How can I let you?" he asked. "He's booked here for stealing a wagon."

"I *didn't* steal it!" Benedict said between clenched teeth.

"Who," the officer said deliberately, "did?"

"I can't tell!"

"See?" The officer shrugged.

Father Dahr looked from him to Benedict, plucking at his vast hair, and snorted: "What? What? What wagon, who stole what?"

"A wagon," said the lieutenant.

"He said *I* stole it," Benedict added under his breath.

"No," the lieutenant observed. "*I* don't—a Mister Brill does. A Mister Brill of 4287 Arbor Avenue. What were you doing up there? What did you leave the Hollow for?"

"Bringing back the wagon back to its owner," Benedict said, flushing. He turned to Father Dahr. "Father, I was bringing it back. I didn't steal it. I can't tell you who stole it, I just can't, even if I have to stay in jail." He saw Dobrik's concerned narrow eyes squinting at him. "Didn't I bring it back?" he cried. "What else do they want?"

Father Dahr turned to the bench. "Yes," he growled, "what else do you want?"

The lieutenant sighed. "Bail?"

"Bail?" Father Dahr blinked. "Bail?"

"For the boy."

Father Dahr spread his hands, then dug down into his pocket and brought out sixty-three cents in change. "This is all I have."

The officer shook his head.

"Not enough."

Father Dahr dropped his hands, then his head. He brooded. Finally, with a slow process of hands and fingers, he brought a rosary out of his pocket and placed it beside the coins. "Is that enough?" he asked.

The officer stared at him. A flush started at his neck and mounted up his face.

"All right, Father, I'll remand him in your charge." He stamped a paper in front of him. "Stay in the Hollow where you belong!" he said, eyeing Benedict.

He shuddered when the door closed behind them and they were out in the still-dark street. They walked in silence along the maple-bordered road. The shadow of the jail seemed huge: it seemed to cover the town, and Benedict could not shake its weight off his mind. He walked fast, almost ran.

"Slower," the old man gasped.

The morning of that night seemed an eternity away—a different country away. He couldn't believe it had only been last morning that he had gone so reluctantly to confession, met for the first time, with such an elevation of spirits, Father Brumbaugh; that he was hurrying now as though he believed they would change their minds and come running after him.

The old man coughed and wheezed.

"Slower, slower," he pleaded. And as Benedict slowed down, "The transparent hyprocrite," he said with self-satisfied malice. "I knew he was no Catholic. But like the devil he was afraid of the cross anyhow. Did you see how red he got?" He put his arm on Benedict's shoulder. "Slower." He panted hoarsely and then asked: "Who was the man you sent to me?"

Benedict stopped abruptly. "Man?"

Gratefully, Father Dahr stopped, too, and wiped his face. "Yes, the man who came knocking on my door, called to me out of the darkness, frightened me so I'm still shaking—sneaking in the shadows of the yard. I'll never be able to go into the yard at night again," he said.

Benedict stared at him.

"Said to me it was you—in jail. Said you sent him to me. 'Go away, the devil!' I cried. 'Benedict in jail!'"

Benedict flinched and turned his eyes away.

"Then he disappeared like a ghost. I thought 'twas an evil dream. And only later did I think to myself: 'Bad news comes by the devil.'"

"Was he——?" Benedict said wonderingly. His heart had begun to pound; his flesh seemed lifted by wings. He started to walk again.

"I clutched my sixty-three cents in my pocket," Father Dahr went on dramatically, "and a prayer was bubbling to my lips when I saw him suddenly rise out of the lilac bushes and come to me."

"Someone I met in jail," Benedict said curtly.

"In jail?" Father Dahr stopped and held Benedict back by the shoulder. "A thief?"

"No!" Benedict replied firmly, "nor the devil either!" And for a moment the conviction took hold of him that somehow the world had got twisted and the good were in jail and the bad were out. "No!" he said again sharply, as though Father Dahr had doubted it.

But Father Dahr had slipped away from him. "Keep watch!" he urged in a ragged whisper, and disappeared down an alley. Benedict, who had been overcome with shame and guilt at his morning thoughts about the old man, now stood beside the telephone pole and fumed. He felt disgraced. Nevertheless, he waited at the pole and fidgeted and watched up and down the graying street.

"Ah," said Father Dahr in a refreshed voice when he returned, "what did you say his name was?"

"I didn't say what his name was!" Benedict snapped and turned his face frowning away. He walked ahead. His body ached as though horses had driven over him, as though an immense toothache had set up inside him. He felt impelled to get the City behind him, the shadow of it off his back and out of his mind, and yet he dreaded coming home. He heard Father Dahr gasping behind him and reluctantly slowed down.

"I was told that you already met our new—our new Father Brumbaugh?" Father Dahr said carelessly when he had caught up.

"Yes," Benedict said, a shadow crossing his face. "This morning —I mean, yesterday morning." He saw the young priest again, standing so slender and pale on the worn wooden steps, looking over the valley with a lost and suffering expression. His heart went out to that image. He seemed in this moment to understand that anguish, as though he had looked down, from this peak, not only from the Hollow but from the day's troubles as well. "Yes, I met him," he said. "I showed him the Hollow."

"What did he say?" the old man asked eagerly.

Benedict scuffed at the sidewalk.

"He said he liked it," he answered, and turned quickly from Father Dahr's searching eyes.

The old man hurried to keep up with him.

"Yes, yes," he said practically, nodding his flowery head. "He'll be of great help to me. I'm *old*, Benedict," he said with a plaintive and reproving laugh as though Benedict had always insisted he was young. "I need someone young, that's plain. And so the Bishop has sent me this David—as a staff, yes, a staff to lean on. Make my life easier. And this young man is everything one could look for. Young, and, like the young, you know——" He squinted at Benedict. "Didn't he say it was too little?"

"What was too little?" Benedict said unsympathetically.

"Oh," Father Dahr said deprecatingly, "the Hollow, the City, the church. He comes from Boston, you know."

"No, he didn't."

"Yes, he'll be a big help to me," the old man resumed, affirming his words with a bobbing head. "It was time—my duties have been——" he looked sidewise at Benedict.... "heavy," he said.

Benedict's face remained unchanged. The old man put his arm on his shoulder.

"Why do you think he really came?" he asked wildly in a whisper.

Benedict stared at him.

"What, Father?" he cried.

The old man lifted his hand in a nervous flutter of fingers. "Nothing, nothing," he said hastily. His eyes shot around the landscape. "You said he was no thief?"

"Who?" Benedict asked tartly.

"The man you sent to me!" Father Dahr said reproachfully. "The one who lifted me from slumber to give me your message."

Benedict flushed. He walked foward silently.

"I'll serve Mass for you this morning," he said earnestly, looking up honestly at the old priest. They exchanged glances and the old man's eyes fluttered; he took a step forward and left Benedict behind.

"Father Brumbaugh has asked me to let *him* celebrate Mass today," he said.

Benedict stared at Father Dahr's back. Finally he asked in a low voice: "Does Father Brumbaugh know——?"

"About you?" The old man shook his head. "No," he said, turning his head and smiling wryly at Benedict. "You'll serve Mass this morning with him," he said.

When they arrived at the top of the wooden steps leading down Honey Bee Hill, they both stopped to gaze over the Hollow. The hot-metal cars were still being dumped, and as they watched, the sky lit up with the nervous glow and a huge yellow ball slid out of the inverted car and began to roll down the hill. It leaped high into the air at one point and shattered into a million fragments, and then it rolled like fiery raindrops down to the bottom. The slag field was in shadow, and beyond, where the red ore fields began, only darkness gleamed, its shining black fur lit like a brooding cat's by the fire. The Mill, sleepless, shuddered in the distance, and the iron bars, like gigantic trees, fell and shook the air. Workers were coming home, emerging darkly out of the City and clattering in their heavy work shoes down the steps.

They came to the bottom and Benedict said good-bye.

"Sleep well," the old man said, turning down the alley, and yet turning once, half-way, to wave back at the darkness where Benedict had been.

There was a light on in the house when he arrived. The clock in the public school rang hollowly. He could smell the upturned earth, the manure which so richly nourished it, the sour odor of the toilet, with the smell of lime, the flat odor of the ditch outside the yard. He could smell the worms, and the cows that mooed darkly shut inside the sheds that lined the ditch.

He held the knob a long time, listening to the world that lay outside——the yard slumbering under the moonlight and the flaring light of the burning slag dump; the City that lay like a waiting trap over the hill. He leaned his hot ear against the door, and then slowly turned the knob.

They were sitting in the yellow kerosene light. His mother's quick dark eyes lifted to him. His father, whose heavy round shoulders were hunched over the table, had one broad hand choking the neck of a bottle of his homemade brew. He was wearing a vest of sheepskin, with the yellowish fur turned inside, and underneath it a blue working shirt. Benedict stood at the door. Slowly, his father's head rose from his hunched shoulders and ponderously turned to the door. When their eyes met, Benedict flushed, stared for a moment into the heavy gray eyes of his father, and then dropped his.

"Holy bum come home now," his father mocked in a voice that was low and heavy. His father's eyes seemed to sink even deeper into his head. There was a heavy motionless sweat on his red forehead. He lifted a weighted hand and then dropped it with a splash on a wet spot on the table. "Uh!" he cried, staring at Benedict, and speaking in English which he reserved for scorn, "what Father Priest say you in jail?" His jaw jerked up. "Tell dis to me. What you say?"

On the table in front of him lay the morning's enevelope and a folded paper. Something had spilled on the paper. His father stared moodily at him, his head nodding; then his eyes turned slowly back to the table, lingered on the paper in front of him, and then returned to Benedict. In that process Benedict felt a mysterious condemnation, as though in some way he and the paper were linked.

The room felt as though there had been a long silence in it before his father spoke. His furry eyebrows, thick as caterpillars and as round, twitched.

"Come here," he ordered through his thick voice.

Benedict hesitated.

"Come here!" He lifted his hand and swept it heavily downward. "You hear I say, 'Come here'?" he cried, ominously.

His mother urged him forward. He took a step.

On the wall above the table, a finely-wrought china figurine of Christ, hanging from the cross, His feet transfixed by a nail, His breast pierced, His bloody hands outspread, with His bitter crown of thorns aslant on His head, stared down with suffering eyes. Below Him was a blue calendar, advertising the First National Bank, with Mill pay-days printed in red. A pale yellow clock ticked nervously.

His father stared at him, his sparrow eyes lost somewhere deeply in his brooding thoughts.

"Where you be all day?" he asked, studiedly.

60

There was no answer to this. Benedict set his lips.

"Like Vince—you, too!" his father cried. Benedict flushed again, knowing what a model of vagrancy his father considered Vince, his brother, to be.

"Where you be all day?" his father roared, crashing his rock fist on the table. A glass jumped and fell over and rolled slowly along the table. His mother watched it nervously until it reached her and then quickly snatched it up and hid it in her lap.

He bent his head and began to move his lips.

His father's face purpled, and then he laughed flatly. "Police come here!" he cried, his head sharply lifting again. His gray eyes watered. "Knock on mine door. I open door. Say, 'Vy you come here? I'm workingmans, not gambler, not t'ief: you got wrong address!' But, no, no, they say, 'No, Meester, no got wrong address, got right address!' 'My Wince?' I say, 'What Wince do now?' But no, they shake head, not Wince this time—this time, *you!*" He leaned his head far over toward him. Now the sweat had begun to move on his forehead. His eyebrows rose and his eyes gleamed. "You!" he repeated, thunderously. His hand, with its gripped fist, rose slowly in the air. "You tell me what you do or I knock head off!" He swung the fist in a heavy slash through the air, and his mother ran to the sink and poured herself a glass of water. She drank it, peering at them over the rim, which magnified her yellow eyes. The water glistened on her lip.

"I did nothing," Benedict said. He stared at his father's heavy working shoes. He spoke in precise English, as perfect as his father's was broken. "It was a mistake. They let me go when they found out."

"Meestake?" his father repeated with heavy thoughtfulness, nodding his head. "What kind of meestake be in jail?"

His voice sounded obscure, and Benedict looked at him more closely. He was staring now at the table; his heavy hand was set squarely in the center of the typewritten paper, with the fingers spread over it. The hand was so big—the paper was so small! He could crumple it. But the paper was vast; it had a great power—it was the messenger from out there, from the City. You could tear it up, grind it into the dirt—but next day another one would come; and the day after a policeman would follow. . . .

A sigh spread inward, relaxing his body.

His father mumbled something, turned and again studied him. But now there was no trace of his accusation. His face was heavy with worry.

"You read good?" he asked ponderously.

Benedict nodded.

"Here, read!" he said, closed his thick fingers over the paper and lifted it stiffly with his arm unbent and handed it over to Benedict. His heavy head did not follow the motion.

Benedict took the crumpled paper and smoothed it out. It was the same letter his mother had showed him that morning.

"Dear Sir:" the letter began, "Pursuant to the agreement of Sept. 19, 1913, which you entered into with the First National Bank——" Benedict looked up at the calendar—— "for the purchase of property located at 822 Washington Avenue, we wish to inform you that the holders of the mortgage for said property now wish to call in all deeds and. . . ."

"What say?" his father asked.

He read on silently. The window at the top of the wall turned faintly orange, and he knew that another train had begun to dump its slag over the hill. A rooster crowed, hailing this false and fiery dawn. A cow mooed. A dog barked hoarsely, echoing it. The day stirred its dozens of images in his mind, and a sea of weariness rocked him as he read. The language was tedious and obscure, the letters blurred, and he could not understand them. He felt his father's heavy drooping eyes turned on him, knowing all, his mother's anxious face, as though it were raw flesh exposed to him. His brain stumbled, the air was pointed with the sharp odor of alcohol.

He dropped the letter to his side and said, without looking at his father: "The Bank wants to buy back the house," he said at last. "I think that's what it says."

He handed the letter back to his father.

"I'll write them tomorrow and tell them we can't sell it," he assured his mother.

His father took the letter.

"It say what else?"

"Also that the next payment is due on July 15. The next interest is due on August 1."

His father nodded. "Denk you," he said formally.

For a moment they stood motionless in the silence that locked them together in the room. Benedict shuddered.

"I'm going to bed," he said. "Mama, wake me at four. I have to serve Mass."

She nodded, without looking at him. One hand was lying on the table, as though it had begun to reach for his father's hand, and something had stopped it. She stared at it as though trying to understand it.

He left the kitchen and climbed the dark stairs to their bedroom. Weariness dragged him to the floor. He groped his way between the two beds in the room, sank down before the homemade chapel, and prayed. Sleep swung in and out. Crossing himself, he climbed into the bed where Joey lay curled in the middle of his warm nest. Joey stirred and said sleepily: "Benny?"

"Go back to sleep," Benedict answered, slipping down between the covers and surrendering to the rush of odor that rose from the quilt drenched in so many years of their slumber.

"I waited for you," Joey said thickly.

"Go to sleep," Benedict said.

There was a breathing silence, and then again Joey's voice arrived: "Benny wake me up with you. I'll go to church!"

Benedict tried to answer, but he was smelling the musk of sleep, and his voice was covered with feathers.

"Benny?" Joey's sleep-footed voice came again, doggedly. "Thanks for taking back the wagon," he said. His voice was low and purged; he added from an immense parabolic distance: "I knew they wouldn't pinch *you*, Benny!"

But there was no answer.

6.

Dawn had not yet broken when Benedict stumbled out of the house. He had awakened himself. Passing through the kitchen, he had found his father slumped over the table; the letter was plastered on his left cheek and his right cheek lay flat against the wood. He had stopped to stare at him in the half-darkness. The kerosene light was turned down low. His father's breath came softly, as though spent. His face was relaxed, and his mouth was slightly open. He stared at him for a long disturbed moment, thinking uneasily of Noah and his sons, and then thoughtfully left the house.

The northern sky was burning. They had been dumping all night. He hurried along Shady Avenue toward the Ditch, carrying his surplice, which his mother had washed and ironed, over his arm. His stomach rumbled: and for a moment his mind hesitated before the vision of the day ahead: this Mass, and the Mass to come, and the duties that he would have to perform.

He shook off the feeling in the kitchen after walking a few blocks. No matter how else he felt, he always felt a subdued pride as he walked swiftly through the silent, dawn-chilled streets on his mission of piety—awake and serving God while all others slept. Duty was profoundly sweet. He walked down Shady Avenue to Highland. Instead of turning off on Highland, however, he continued on to the strip of houses lining the Ditch. No one was stirring here either, but he walked more cautiously, in spite of himself. He kept in the middle of the street and cast quick glances into the shadows of the alleys. No one but himself and Mother Burns knew of this pre-dawn mission which he conscientiously fulfilled every Sunday of the year regardless of the weather.

The Negro woman watched for his coming from the window, sitting there looking out on what little world she could see, a little lace cap on her head, a black shawl over her shoulders. She was always awake when he arrived: she'd tap with her ring on the window when she caught sight of him and he'd wave politely back to her. The door as always was open. All he had to do was turn the knob and push back the cat, Tom, and he was in one of her two rooms.

Father Dahr had brought him to her. Because she wanted to become a Catholic, Benedict had accepted the duty of preparing her for acceptance into the Church with particular devotion. He had never known a Negro who was a Catholic, and he felt that her call to the Church was proof even in this small community of the shoreless power of Catholicism. Her son had worked as a janitor in the church, and had been converted by Father Dahr, who had been impressed by his success: it was the only person he had ever converted, and he considered it almost a miracle. Benedict had taught Mother Burns' son the catechism, something of the Bible, church history and other religious matters that prepared him properly: and Benedict had attended the baptismal ceremony which Father Dahr had nervously performed. And then one day Sam Burns had left for Detroit, and had never come back.

Mother Burns lived on what he sent. She had listened to Benedict struggling over the catechism with Sam, and when he left, she had suggested that Benedict continue with her. Benedict wasn't sure that she could read, but he had never had the audacity to ask her or try to trap her.

He came in with a very efficient, business-like and slightly frowning air. "Now, Mother," he said immediately, putting his surplice down on the table, which was covered with a great delicately crocheted lace table cloth, yellow with age, "I hope you did study all week what I told you."

"I did, I did, Master Benedict," she replied, getting up from the chair at the window and leaning on her cane. Her hair was almost snow-white. She fished for her glasses in a pocket and came painfully to the table. "It's in my bones this morning," she explained. "It's a frisky morning," she continued looking at the morning through the half-open door, without, however, disapproval.

"I have to be at church to serve," Benedict said sternly, and relentlessly opened the catechism. He had flinched at the word 'Master'; it had sounded too important for him. "But you're not a Mister," she had explained to him.

She took her place at the table with a sigh. "I been settin' waiting for you almost an hour, staring out across the crick to that tumbling fire," she said. "I fear someday it's going to leap over the crick and burn down the houses."

"No, Mother Burns," Benedict assured her authoritatively, and he thought she listened to him with faith in his words. "That won't happen."

From a sideboard in the little room, which was furnished with a dull-red couch, two wicker chairs, one a rocker, and the round table he was sitting at, she brought a dish of cookies. She disappeared into the kitchen, and he cried after her: "No tea for me, Mother Burns! You know I can't take tea. I told you that before!"

There was no response, and in a moment she was back carrying two cups of tea, from which little figures of steam floated, like ascending souls. He had given up trying to make her understand that he couldn't eat or drink before communion. She put the tea and the molasses cookies down before him. Benedict closed his eyes, crossed himself, and lifted the tea to his lips. In that moment of prayer he had explained the circumstances to Christ. The warm tea flooded his empty stomach and sped through his body, warming his finger tips and toes.

Then he opened a gray-covered catechism, on which a figure of Christ with uplifted hands was engraved, and looked expectantly at Mother Burns.

But she wasn't ready to begin yet. He had to answer several formal questions first.

"And how is your poor Ma?"

"She's doing all right," Benedict answered as though there was only one condition his mother, or anybody's mother could be in: ailing.

"And your Pa?"

"Fine, Mother, fine."

Her head nodded delicately in a kind of approving rhythm to all the answers. Her eyes had a reddish-brown shade in them. Before she could go on with the other questions, Benedict himself ran down the list.

"Joey's all right, too, though he had a little cold."

66

"Had a little cold?" she said with interest.

"And Rudolph's all right, except he hurt his big toe."

"Hurt his big toe?" she approved noddingly.

"And Vince is all right," he said.

"That's the bad one," she identified, nodding again.

Then he opened the book and looked at her speculatively: "Lesson eighteen," he warned. He was very tolerant of her, and sometimes her eyes flashed. But she nodded her head and looked admiringly at him with her bright eyes, as though it was he who was the star pupil. The dawn was sitting in the doorway like a cautious cat. The night had been long. The devils had been walking. "Lesson eighteen," he repeated. "I explained all about the saints, relics and images," he began with slight pomposity, "last Sunday." She nodded vigorously to assure him that lesson had taken. "Now, we're going to think about the third commandment of God." He stopped to make sure she was ready. "What is the *second* commandment of God?" he asked.

"Are you comfortable?" she wanted to know.

"The second commandment of God is: Thou shalt not take the name of the Lord thy God in vain," he said severely.

"We had that last week," she reminded him.

"*I* know," he said ominously. "What is the third commandment of God?" he asked, and answered: "The third commandment of God is: Remember to keep holy the Lord's day." He looked at her. "What does that mean?"

She knew. "Take a rest," she said, "on the Sabbath."

"That's right," he answered.

"What is forbidden by the third commandment of God?"

"Work," she answered.

"Yes," he replied. The tea-cup rattled on the table. Suddenly the Mill whistled roared hoarsely, and they listened abstractedly. "By the third commandment of God all unnecessary servile work on Sunday is forbidden," he said. "What is servile work?" he asked himself. "Servile work is that which requires the labor of body rather than of mind."

Footsteps went by the shack, and sometimes someone called:

"Morning, Mother Burns!" and she cried back, without needing to see who it was: "Morning, Mister Drew."

"Servile work," Benedict explained, "is the kind of work you do with your hands."

She nodded her head. "Seems like I been doing that all my life," she commented, nodding.

Benedict looked at her.

"Well——" he began hesitatly.

"And on the Sabbath," she said, still nodding, "a man takes his rest."

"That's right," he said.

"Weren't no Sabbath at Mr. Charley's," she said, staring down at the floor.

"Where?" Benedict asked, leaning toward her.

But she wouldn't answer.

The clunk of the bucket against something metal in someone's pocket came to them.

"White and black *both*," she said vigorously.

"That's right," he answered, and again he stared at her. Her lips were pursed tightly and she tapped the floor twice with her cane.

"What's next?" she asked, folding her hands expectantly.

He frowned at the catechism. He looked uncertainly at his other books. "Let's turn to the Bible," he said. He opened the big book which lay on the table before him. It was bound in rusty leather, buckled with a brass lock, and bore inside the date 1845. The fly leaf had, in painful purple characters, the cryptic story of Mother Burns' life: only births and deaths were registered, as if nothing else happened or mattered, except that one relative had before it the dates, 1845-1864, and someone had added the legend: 'he never sen freedom.'

"Now the serpent was more subtile than any beast of the field which the Lord God had made: and he said unto the woman, Yea, hath God said, Ye shall not eat of every tree of the garden?" He stopped here and coughed. "I'll close the door," he said, getting up. Outside the fog was thick and smelled strongly of sulphur smoke and steel.

"Yes, close it," Mother Burns said, looking anxiously at her lace curtains.

When he returned she leaned over the book and asked: "Is this the serpent?" placing her finger on the page. Benedict looked. "No," he said. "This is." She gazed curiously at the word. "I'll never forget the looks of that word," she said finally.

The acrid smell of the burning slag seemed suddenly to invade the room. Benedict started to read again but was stopped by an attack of coughing. A siren began out in the dawn: they listened to it swell; and without saying anything to each other, both went to the door to watch the police car swing into the alley, go past the window, and haul up in front of one of the houses down the line. The police jumped out of the car, and they could hear the loud pounding on the door. They parted the curtain only slightly, and stood back in the shadows.

"Maybe I'd better go now," Benedict said in a low voice.

She seemed not to hear him. She had narrowed her eyes to penetrate the fog.

"But I'll come back next Sunday," he said.

He picked up his surplice and started for the doorway. There was a slight tap on the window, and he stopped and looked back at where Mother Burns was drawing the curtains together again and coming past him to the door. She was hurrying, and her eyes were lit. She opened the door slightly, and the fog came in; and with it a tall Negro man had also slipped in. He glided across the room to the window and parted the curtains slightly and peered out. The faint glow of dawn reflected from the ivory curtains on his face. There was a tense alertness in the poised grace of his body; his eyes were alight with a kind of private amusement, which rode above the taut muscles of his face.

He dropped the curtains finally and laughed softly.

"They'll be jumping mad out there——" he began, and catching sight of Benedict, he stopped and said sharply: "Who's he?"

Benedict's lips grew dry. He licked them.

Mother Burns' wrists jerked nervously. "Now, he's just a friend of mine——" she began.

The man glided across the floor and grabbed Benedict suddenly by the shoulders. His strong fingers caught the bone and pressed tightly. Benedict paled.

"Do you know me?" he demanded turning Benedict's face up to his.

Benedict shook his head.

"Cliff!" Mother Burns cried.

"Never seen me before?"

Benedict stared up at reddish-brown eyes from which all amusement had gone, and shook his head violently. The pain of the fingers dug into his shoulders paralyzed his neck.

"No!" he said, choking.

"You never been here today!"

"Clifford," Mother Burns cried, an angry gleam coming into her eyes. "Let that boy go this instant!"

He turned to her and laughed shortly, then his fingers loosened. "What you doing with this boy?" he asked.

She gave him an angry glance and only said tartly: "Mind your own business!"

The sirens were going again, and the man slipped back to the window and flattened himself against the wall to peer out without touching the curtains. Mother Burns gave him another sharp glance and then turned to Benedict.

"I have to hurry," Benedict cried, his face desperately white.

"I'll be waiting for you next Sunday, same as always," she answered calmly, casting a look at her visitor whose tense face was once again lit with that taut smile. Benedict turned to go, and in that moment, Mother Burns lifted her hand to her face and said: "I clean forgot to ask you one thing!"

He looked at her. She reached down into the folds of her skirt and brought forth a long white envelope with the familiar return address printed in the corner, and at the sight of it his heart stumbled.

"Mother, I can't stay!" he cried wildly.

"I know that!" she said quickly, and stuffed the letter back into her pocket. She looked over her shoulder to the window and then lowered her voice: "Don't pay no mind to that," she advised.

"Them police is looking for him, but he's no criminal. He's just a union man, that's all."

Benedict's lips parted, and he turned to stare back at the other one leaning against the wall, his muscles poised, his long thin-veined hand slightly touching the dimpling curtains.

Then his breath came out as though he had been holding it in forever, and he said: "I have to go!"

Outside he stared at the dawn, which gleamed green-gray through the fog. The police car started to whine again, and he flattened himself against the wall and watched it go by, its red light winking like an angry eye. An enormous boulder of flaming slag rolled down the hill, bounded far into the air and exploded. The pieces flew for yards about, and some fell hissing into the Ditch. This was the first time the slag had touched the Ditch: the very first time. He cast a last glance at the frail tar-paper cabins, and then, hearing a bell that rang soundlessly in his mind, walked back to Highland Avenue and the church, bending his head as though before an evil snow of long white envelopes.

7.

No one was in the sacristy when he arrived. This was the moment he loved most of all: he alone in this ante-chamber to the sanctuary, surrounded by the spare furnishings—the two rows of drawers set in the wall, filled with altar cloths; the steel cabinets in which the articles for the Mass were stored: the censer, the incense boat, the aspersorium, incense, candles, the chalice which had risen so often above his bowed head, gleaming in polished gold, the church books, and other utensils. He put on his surplice and cassock (which had been hanging in the closet: his, waiting for him), feeling, as he did, a sense of calmness, of deliverance (from everything that was: the City, home, that moment of cold terror, the Ditch, his hunger), a feeling as though his uniform covered him away from the world, in its black and white, drawing him to the vast past as though to an immemorial strength.

He worked swiftly, confidently: picked up the cruets of wine and water and entered the church. Already a few bowed heads were there: women in black shawls bent over their knuckles, blue and bony with work, their wispy lips forming words of prayer. Men who came in their working clothes, to go straight to work once Mass was finished: beside them sat the zinc buckets whose warm coffee-filled bottoms reminded them still of bed and wives, touching them warmly on the thighs.

The rounded church ceiling bent over them like a huge listening ear: their prayers rose faintly like their breaths on this cold morning. Benedict genuflected and carried the cruets to the credence table on the Epistle side of the altar and then returned to the sacristy for the finger bowl and the towel. He lit two candles, one on each side of the Tabernacle.

The door to the sacristy was just opening when he returned.

"Oh," said Father Brumbaugh, surprised. He stood long and slender in the open door, the pale rose light of the dawn behind him. He looked at Benedict for a moment and smiled seriously. "Come and help me," he said in a still voice.

Benedict thrilled and bit his lips gently, then brought the chalice to him and watched him prepare it. The priest's eyes closed for a moment and his long narrow lips moved. Then he began to put on his vestments: Benedict handing him the cincture, making sure that the tassels were on the right; pulling the alb to make it hang evenly all around. Father Brumbaugh donned the maniple and stole, his eyes lowered, and his eyelashes throwing tiny shadows on his upper cheek. When he put on the chasuble, he looked at Benedict. "Everything is right, Father," Benedict whispered. Father Brumbaugh nodded; his eyes turned inward again.

He knelt and closed his eyes, and began the prayers preliminary to Mass. Benedict watched him with a painful pride, as though somehow he were responsible for him; as though, through him, the church had attained its natural grace. Almost angrily he shut out the memory of the morning: peace and beauty and reverence alone, all these in this quiet room smelling of faint incense and scented soap, were his, and to be his: his eyes followed the graceful arch of that bent neck. But he could not keep out of his memory, even as he watched the young priest kneeling submissively on the prie-dieu, his sensitive head bowed, his gently-molded, blue-veined lids closed over his eyes, the hundreds of times he had watched Father Dahr kneel, and sometimes sway, on that same bench, redolent from a week's neglect, scratching absently where the winter underwear itched, the fumes of tobacco and beer swirling around his furry head.

His eyes were wet; he wanted to touch the young priest on the elbow and whisper: "Thank you for coming to us, Father." He shivered slightly in anticipation of the moment they two stood alone before the altar—he, Father Brumbaugh's faithful right hand; and his heart filled with humility, his eyes closed like a wing over his pride. So he imagined St. Augustine had looked, or his patron saint, St. Benedict, as Father Brumbaugh looked, his pale hair slightly waved, molded gently to the graceful lines of his head. No longer would he have to apologize to the world for Father Dahr. Now, *he* had come—from whose handsome eyes purity shone, whose pale complexion and soft voice implied long sessions devoted to contemplation and meditation. A swift picture of himself, in sudden contrast, passed through his brain: the brown, flat face, with its flattened nose, its yellow-gray eyes, looking like his mother's, the dirty straw-colored hair, the inflamed nostrils. . . .

He felt all the more pleased with Father Brumbaugh instead.

Always the church seemed to wait like a great listening shell, as though a holy sea washed its shores, expanding horizons into the religious past. A certain kind of murmur came through the closed doors, as though prayers long said there still reverberated among the dust and shadows, mixing with the new, settling in a soundless ocean. There was some kind of depth, some kind of repose which ignored beyond its walls the tar-paper shacks along the Ditch, the flue dust, the slag heaps, the incinerator, Mr. Brill: as if these were the infested ornaments of a life that would soon pass, leaving the church standing, stone on stone, for eons to come.

It was here that he came, humble and powerful at the same time, mortal and immortal. This was his realm. The profound yearning of his heart for harmony and faith, for permanence and eternity, for the irreducible justice of the holy laws, made by God, sanctified in heaven forever, was answered here. Here, in this church, whose echoes flew like birds from wall to wall, was the only art he knew, the only music, the single love: his whole soul responded to it.

He watched Father Brumbaugh cross himself, and prepared to leave. At that moment the door to the sacristy burst open and filling the open space behind which the sky shone now like milk, stood Father Dahr. Benedict's heart felt a blow. Father Brumbaugh's head was still lowered, his sheltered eyes still bent.

Father Dahr put an arm behind him against the jamb and swayed slowly in an unsteady arc. He caught sight of Benedict and cried, in a hoarse, responsible whisper: "You're late!" He aimed an arm uneasily at Benedict and added: "I've been waiting *hours* for you, boy!"

Father Brumbaugh turned, his hands still clasped.

Still pointing, Father Dahr continued heavily: "All right, I'll forgive you this time! Now, on with the vestments." He took a step forward into the room, and staggered.

Benedict came to him and took him by the arm.

"Go back," he whispered with lowered, shame-stricken eyes. "Go back, Father!"

Father Dahr lunged to the cabinet and opened it.

"Boy," he cried authoritatively, "come here!"

Father Brumbaugh's face had grown pale; at the same time a tight, painful smile slightly altered his lips. He watched Benedict struggle with the old man in silence; his chin was slightly raised, his eyes were blue-black.

"Sit down, Father!" Benedict cried hoarsely, leading the old man to a stool and trying to push him on it.

"We've got to serve Mass!" Father Dahr cried angrily.

"No, Father," Benedict said. "Father Brumbaugh is serving. It's all right."

The old man turned his heavy moon eyes on Benedict; his coxcomb hair rose like an arched back.

"Father Brumbaugh," he muttered. "Father Brumbaugh."

He sank into a heavy brooding spell, from which he roused himself to whisper ponderously to Benedict: "They've moved me, boy. They've moved me. You won't find me in the old bed anymore."

"Yes, Father," Benedict said. "Father Brumbaugh will serve."

The old man looked at Benedict. "Don't you want to help me?" he asked.

"Yes, Father, I do," Benedict answered seriously. "But you're sick. Father Brumbaugh is going on. . . ."

He turned a pleading glance at Father Brumbaugh, but the young priest, who was now standing, watched him with a faint, bitter smile.

"He'll be better soon," Benedict cried, "if we can only get him to the house."

The old man's heavy hand fell on Benedict's shoulder. "It's late," he said sternly. "Must be ready. Come, my—my——"

"Please, Father," Benedict cried. "Let me take you to the house. Father Brumbaugh will——"

The old man's hand tightened on Benedict's shoulders so that he winced and his knees wobbled. He had gripped the same spots that Mother Burns' visitor had. For a moment his eyes dimmed.

"Your hand is hurting me, Father," he said, with a laugh.

Father Dahr stared down into his wide eyes, and gradually the hand loosened on his shoulder, and his head fell forward as though the heavy hair bore it down. There was a terrible, hidden groaning in his chest, and Benedict took him by the arm and led him toward the door. Mrs. Rumyer appeared and efficiently took the old man under the arm and pulled him down the steps.

"I got him," she said. "Go on with the Mass. Old man," she scolded him, "you're a terrible sight!"

They were silent for a long moment after the door closed behind the two. Benedict kept his eyes on the floor. He felt as though he were slowly burning alive. The smell of an acrid fog seemed packed around his head. Muted sounds came from inside. He raised his head slowly, and his hands shaking, raised them to the man standing rigidly in the middle of the floor, his white face showing two red lines like an angry bite on each cheek.

He lowered his head and went through the door. The little bell tinkled and the Roman words slowly formed in his mind:

"*Ad Deum qui laetificat juventutem meam. . . .*" as he crossed the threshold.

A rustling wave of soft sighs greeted them, an uneasy shuffling of feet. Benedict didn't look out at the congregation. He performed mechanically, moving from side to side of the altar, responding in a tight low voice. There was a sting in his face, as though he had been slapped.

Father Brumbaugh's voice came clear and sweet. Kneeling, he was conscious of the young priest's movements, and as the Mass progressed, the memory of Father Dahr, the insistent memory of Mother Burns faded, and he felt himself absorbed again by the color and light, the murmurous silences, the silver movements of his body, the grace of the Father's. An inward repose, a deep contentment arrived, and he felt an elevation in his forehead, in the muscles of his cheeks, in the sweet straining of his upthrust throat. The people behind him lived and breathed: he felt a mature gentleness toward them, as though he were older than any of them; and he loved them, too, for being there this morning, kneeling on the hard benches, bowing their heads, repeating prayers that came to him no longer as words but as feeling alone.

"*Misreatur vestri omnipotens Deus . . .*" Father Brumbaugh intoned.

The candle-light flickered and the gold responded.

"*Amen,*" he said.

He made the sign of the cross, synchronizing his motions with those of Father Brumbaugh. He listened to the priest's clear eloquent voice, and responded again: "*Amen.*"

He saw Father Dahr stagger once drunkenly through his mind, and a flash of pain cut through him. The Mill whistle, muted as though it, too, understood that it had entered a church, lowered its voice calling for delinquent workers who had fallen asleep in church with Christ's name on their lips. The wail of a siren also came, slender and low: he lifted his head abruptly, but it was gone as he lifted it. He heard snores. He stole a glance at Father Brumbaugh, his eyes filled with pain for him, wondering if he heard them, too. He lifted his eyes to look longer at the priest, and in lifting became aware that Father Brumbaugh's voice was faltering, and then, as he stared, it suddenly stopped. Benedict followed his horrified eyes. There, between the lace curtains covering the Tabernacle, a mouse had poked its tiny blunt head. It looked out upon the church for an instant, and then whisked its head back in again.

Benedict stared at the rigid back, at the contour of the face, the one white cheek. Sweat, big horrible drops formed on the priest's forehead and rolled down his cheek. His shoulders suddenly shook, as though from internal sobs, and the muscles of his face, like tight wires, began to throb. Tight, tiny sounds came out of his throat.

Behind them the church prayed; the voices went on by themselves. Benedict waited. In the long moments that followed it seemed to him that some great catastrophe could happen: some vast tumbling of columns, of foundations, of roofs and cities. . . .

"*Domine, exaude orationem meam,*" the voice came high and uneven.

"*Et clarmor meus ad te veniat,*" Benedict responded.

"*Dominus vobiscum.*"

The candle flame leaped suddenly as though a hand had reached to snuff it out.

"*Et cum spiritu tuo.*"

8.

Although his father never went to church (except for funerals), still he never refused to help it. His father was always on call to repair the roof, to plaster the ceiling, even to paint the altar: and now he had left early to help build the picnic tables in the black walnut grove which, covered with red dust and soot, nevertheless still was green. This was how they would welcome Father Brumbaugh to the parish. There would be a bazaar and a picnic. His mother had hunted in the woods and on the hills for days before, bringing in huge baskets of dandelions and sassafras roots, and two rabbits which she had trapped herself.

They worked together, he and his father. While his father sawed or nailed, he held the board for him. His father ordered him about —get me a plank, hand me a hammer, get me some nails—with a rough kind of equality and left-handed respect that made him flush. The other men came naturally to his father, who without anyone saying so, was recognized somehow as the organizing force. They asked him where the booths should be erected, how to string up the lanterns, and where to pound out a square for dancing. His father always knew where.

They even built an oven in the side of the hill. They strung wires from tree to tree and hung paper lanterns on them. Miraculously the grove took on strange new shapes and brilliant new colors. How amazed Father Brumbaugh would be! Nothing like the ladies' Sodality! How his eyes would light up as he came on the scene—the green-and-yellow lanterns bobbing on the line, the casks of root-beer foaming yellow-brown, the white cakes spread out on the table, the table heaped with food: all for him! Benedict passionately anticipated the moment, and a tiny smile curved his lips as he watched.

The women started coming with the food they had cooked at home—cakes, *kugelis, blynai,* pies, *kilbasai,* pickle and in jars from the cellar, sauerkraut with caraway seeds, *kopustai,* pikalilli jellied fruit; they started coke fires over which to roast goat. He saw his mother carrying two large pots, and ran over to help her.

"Mama?" he inquired.

She threw him a triumphant look.

"I caught two rabbits," she whispered.

He smiled at her and took one of the pots away.

"Look," he said to his father, lifting up the lid.

His father, who was smoking a strong-smelling cigarette, rolled by himself, nodded; he seemed not to have heard. He was looking beyond the people. Benedict glanced at him. There was a dull flush on his cheeks.

"Go away," his father said sharply, and Benedict, humiliated, brought the pot over to the table.

The grove was a bouquet of delicious smells. The little fires were burning on the hill-side, squirrel-tails of smoke arching over them. Children were beginning to run; they would run now all afternoon and evening until they got sullen with exhaustion and sank to sleep with pale roses on their cheeks. But they wove in and out with their shrill laughter. He saw his little brother squatting underneath a table.

He said: "Joey, what are you doing there?"

Joey cast him a glance. "Sittin'," he said.

Benedict left him there.

Suddenly there was music. Two accordions began to roll out their long, hoarse, teasing notes, and there was Mr. Grazulis dancing! He was down on his old haunches kicking out his feet stiffly; and the men and women began to clap and tap on the hard ground with their toes. Benedict smiled foolishly at the old man, whose white hair flew about his head as though it were spooned; his face got dangerously red, but his feet never missed a step. Then the accordions suddenly shifted into a quiet sobbing song, which might have been Russian or Slovak, and the women around Benedict put their aprons to their eyes. But the players departed from the sadness with a crash of chords and leaped into a furious polka. Benedict watched the old people snap into unexpected life, as though they had been bit; it shocked him for a moment; and then he was roaring at the funny picture of his aunt and her husband as they pranced up and down the hard earth, finally stopping out of breath.

Everybody was eating something, but he had no money to buy. The money would go to the church: it would be presented to Father Brumbaugh.

He felt a nudge on his shoulder. He looked up into his father's reddish-grizzled face. "Here," he said, handing him some coins. "Get something for Joey."

"And for Mama?"

His father stared at him, but said nothing. Benedict hung his head taking the money. He went to look for Joey but now he was gone. He went to his mother.

"Mama?" he said, holding out his open hand to her.

She looked into his eyes, then ladled out a dish of rabbit stew and put the money she took from him into a cigar box. She kept twisting her lips. He went away from her and dipped his bread in the stew and ate it. The taste was suddenly like his mother—it filled his mouth, and his eyes swam. He found his father and said: "Papa, have some."

His father pushed him angrily: "You eat—eat——" he cried.

Benedict walked away, looking for his brother. He saw Joey in the distance playing with a baby goat that was tied to a crab-apple tree, and did not go to him. Soon that goat would have its throat slit. He felt tears swell behind his eyes. He could see Joey's puckered face as he talked to the goat.

But music was still playing—"hunky" music Mr. Brill would call it. For a moment he was terrified that Father Brumbaugh would come! He couldn't bear to be there anymore. He left the grove: it was already darkening: and took a path down through the elder bushes to the spring. Women and his boy friends were coming back from the spring with pails of slopping water.

The spring smelled of cows. They had trampled the soft ground into swamp around the wooden hogshead that had been sunken to the brim. He could smell worms and moss. The acrid odor of burning mines back in the woods came here too.

He saw Tony, the Italian boy who served Sunday Mass with him, and walked into the woods because he didn't want to talk. In the shadow and half-hidden by a tree he saw his father.

"Papa?" he called.

His father turned quickly, showing for a moment the man his body had hidden from view, and waved him away. The man with whom he had been talking stepped farther back into the shadow. Benedict stood still. Then he took a step forward, and once again called: "Papa?" He was about to come even nearer when his father stepped abruptly out of the shadows; the man shook his hand—their two hands clung together in the moonlight—and then instead of coming with his father up the path to the picnic disappeared in the opposite direction. Benedict stared at his vanishing back, shivers breaking over him.

"Come—come——" his father said harshly, taking him by the shoulder and turning him around.

He looked questioningly into his father's face; and his father returned the glance with a frown; then said as though remembering anger: "Why aren't you at the picnic?"

Benedict shrugged but couldn't explain. He wanted suddenly to take his father's hand but instead walked silently by his side back up the path. They had never been out of hearing of the gayety; but now it engulfed them like a light turned on. The lanterns were lit and the lights danced off flushed faces and bright eyes, and again Benedict's heart lifted. Now when he met Tony he ran up to him and put his arm around his shoulder.

"Remember we're playing the Jay Birds Saturday," reminded Tony, his brown, earnest eyes turned on him.

Benedict laughed. "I didn't forget," he cried.

"We'll beat them n-----s!" said Tony, his moth-lidded eyes fluttering gently. Don't say *that*, Benedict said to himself, flushing. The smile on his face that had included Tony and himself seemed suddenly betrayed; his eyes withdrew.

"You know, Tony——" he began, but bit his lips. The other boy's dark eyes were turned with supreme innocence and trust upon him.

"We'll beat 'em if you play, Benny!" Tony said proudly.

He teetered for a moment on the edge of those admiring eyes; then, suddenly, without a word, turned and walked away. He felt his face a mask of pride and guilt.

There was dancing still: and as he pushed through the crowd, which was laughing and clapping, he drew back, shocked: it was his father and mother there in the middle of that rocking crowd doing the polka. His mother's face was white and beaded with sweat, and she was laughing breathlessly and with embarrassment; but on his father's face was a look of lusty abandonment . . . and Benedict turned quickly away and hid his head in the smothering crowd. The laughter unfolded like a rose behind him. He turned back, tempted into happiness.

Benedict caught Joey's bemused face, with its uncertain smile that seemed to have been forgotten on his tiny face as he stared at the strange sight of his father and mother dancing! He must be drunk, Benedict thought, unable to look at his father. He felt

that his mother must be suffering, although he was uneasy at
the strange glimpse of merriment, uncontrolled and penetrating,
which he caught once or twice on her face. Suddenly he thought
that once his father and mother must have been like that, young.
His lips parted with surprise.

The polka drove on: and suddenly his father, flushed and
aroused, tore one of the accordions away from the players and
started pumping it himself. How the people cheered! There was
nobody in the cleared square now but his father who was playing
as he danced. Then, shooting out from the crowd, erupted his
little brother, helplessly drawn by the rhythm and the gayety; he
sank down on his thin haunches and followed his father soberly
around, mimicking his motions, kicking out his legs and crossing
his thin little arms fiercely together. Benedict smiled at him, whom
he loved at that moment. When Joey fell to the ground with a
look of pain and dismay, everybody laughed: and he got up and
walked slowly back to Benedict who put his arm around his
shoulder.

But his father kept on dancing—whirling around on his heels,
jumping up, kicking, whirling again; and all the time the accordion,
accompanied by the other one in the background, kept time with
his feet.

A roar of laughter and applause rose up when he stopped:
and suddenly out of the crowd stepped Father Dahr, clapping his
hands, his thick hair rising like a portentous bush. Benedict was
afraid that he, too, would try to dance; and his heart sank as the old
priest squatted down and began creakingly to dance, while his
father played. Father Dahr's face was a flaming red: the neck
cords stood out white and rigid against his scarlet skin. Faster
and faster his father played, a malicious look on his face: faster
and faster the old priest danced: and faster and faster the people
clapped.

The music ended with a great crash, like a falling tree, and
Father Dahr threw up his arms triumphantly as the applause and
laughter shook the swinging lanterns above their heads. Father
Dahr clasped his arm around Benedict's father's neck and said
something to him, and his father laughed and lifted up the ac-

cordion. Then they both laughed together, slapping each other's back and bobbing their heads. Somebody brought each a glass of dark liquid and they quaffed it off; and their faces seemed to sweat more and grow brilliantly red, polished like apples. Then the two accordions crashed into another song, and flinging up their arms both his father and the old priest re-entered the square. They danced walled off by spectators. The old priest's collar came loose and hung open over his black coat. They danced *at* each other, their hands gripped behind their backs, walking around at first in a wary circle on their heels. Unexpectedly, his father broke into a few menacing steps, which the old priest mocked. Then his father, provoked, went beyond *that,* and the old priest showed great scorn; and before they knew it they were both whirling and turning in crazy competition, as the incredulous cheers of the crowd mounted, shocking the tissue lanterns. The collar came completely loose now and fell, and nobody noticed it; and it was trampled into the dust. The old priest's hair whirled in a flame of passion.

Suddenly Benedict saw *his* face: it came into bright focus out of the bewildering wheel of lights, sounds, and smells. It was as white as a scar. It was staring at his father and the old priest, and then looked around at the people, and an expression like terror fled through his eyes and he seemed to shrink and dissolve into the crowd.

The agony of alienation in that face was so intense that Benedict felt it, and his own face pulled with sympathy. It was the same face the young priest had turned to Benedict as Benedict proudly showed him the valley that was to be his parish, his priestly vineyard. Benedict wanted to hush the accordionists; he wanted to go to Father Brumbaugh and reassure him somehow. . . .

He stood chained to the other's agony until the music stopped.

Then Father Dahr, climbing on a bench his father had made, shouted: "Everybody be quiet!" He had to shout it several times, roaring out: *"Tchekai!"* and following it with a mild Slovak curse, which brought shocked laughter from the women and then the silence he wanted. He held up his arms. "Is everybody spending money?" he cried; and the little boys answered: "No!" "It all goes to the church—so spend, spend what you have! God will provide! There's food, there's drink——" He stood with an innocent expression on his flaming face as they roared a knowing laughter at him. "Only soft drinks," he said when he could speak again. "I want to thank the men who built the tables and booths," he said. "I want to thank the mothers who cooked the food. I want to thank the children——" he paused and looked sternly down, "for behaving themselves, for listening to their mothers——" There were hoots from the rough boys but Father Dahr ignored them. He lifted his voice again and roared: "I am glad to see that we can still have pleasure and enjoyment even in the face of . . . events; even though our thoughts may be dark. But daylight will come! Take heart; don't lose faith. Daylight will come! God is more powerful than Mammon: God is with you, my friends." He stopped to wipe his flaming brow. Then he resumed in a quieter voice. "This picnic—this picnic—is for a big reason. We have a new assistant pastor! You saw him last Sunday. Today you will meet him; he will talk to you: open up your hearts to him! He is your shepherd: teach him, protect him, cherish him. Remember that he is young; remember that he will need your help!" He pounded his fist into the open palm of his hand. "Help him!" he roared so that his voice bounded back from the hillside. "Teach him that God can be found here—yes, here in this foresaken valley—here among you God will be found, if one will search. God is in your work-hardened hands; God is in your faces; God goes with you as you go among those fiery furnaces—your souls are in God's hands."

He stopped suddenly, and his head fell down and his hair closed over his brow. Then he turned blindly to the crowd and called: "Father! Where are you, Father? Will you come here and speak a few words to your people?"

He looked over the crowd, straining above them.

"Father!" he cried.

Everybody turned to search with him. Benedict climbed on a table and looked over the heads of the people. He strained into the darkness that had come like a closing hand over them; and it seemed as though in a gash of light he saw someone hurrying already half way up the side of the hill—hurrying with the black skirts of his gown flinging dust behind him.

84

He didn't hear Father Dahr anymore. He jumped off the table and stooped to the ground. He picked the collar out of the trampled dust and shoved it into his pocket. Then he pushed himself through the crowd, walking toward the woods. At a distance he spied Joey standing desolately at the crab-apple tree and then walking round and round it for the absent goat. He went past Joey down along paths that circled old abandoned mines whose deep pits yawned perilously at his feet. There were scurries in the underbrush. Overhead a thin moon, curved like a watermelon rind, stood propped up on one end in the sky. The music dimmed behind him, and as he walked the pain in him thinned out like the music. Father Brumbaugh's pale face died behind him like the last flicker of an altar candle. An owl flew clumsily over his face crashing through the branches of the tree. He took the collar out of his pocket and blew the dust from it and smoothed it out. . . .

There was a light on in the kitchen; and when he tried the door he found it locked. His father, first separating the curtains to see him, unlocked it.

"Go upstairs to bed—quickly!" he ordered.

Benedict hurried through the kitchen, throwing a glance at the four men sitting at the table. They had turned the oil lamp down and sat in half-shadow. He stopped suddenly and stared; and then broke free of himself and ran upstairs.

Joey was already asleep and wandering in the wild land of his dreams. His bony body turned, and his husky voice spoke to someone unnamed and unremembered. Benedict slipped into the warmth beside him.

Torn deep from sleep, suddenly he shot upright in his bed. Joey gasped and came wildly awake like a frightened swimmer out of deep water. His father came into the room.

"Why did you shout?" he asked.

Benedict stared at him.

"Papa," he said. "I know that man!"

"What man?" his father cried impatiently.

"The man from jail!"

His father stared at him.

"Go to sleep," he said to Joey, punching him gently down into bed. He stood silently in the room, breathing thoughtfully. Then, when his voice came again, although it was soft and even gentle, it was full of something Benedict could feel almost as though it was his rock-like hand.

"Benedict," he said, "listen to me. Go to sleep and forget who you saw in the kitchen. Go to sleep. Do you understand?"

Benedict crouched back into bed.

"Benedict?" his father demanded.

"Yes, Papa," he promised, his head lowered. "I'll remember what you said."

His eye were wide open. His father lingered a moment longer, as though he wanted to say something more; then with a last, "Go to sleep," he left the room. When he was gone, Benedict whispered to the room: "I saw you, Dobrik!" and the darkness seemed to close in on his voice and hush it.

9.

Daylight made the night unbelievable.

As he came into the kitchen, his mother was crooning, her large face holding back a teasing smile. Rudolph was on her lap, his up-turned pudgy hand laid in hers. She was stirring porridge with her forefinger in his palm, while he grinned deliciously and hunched his shoulders with painful anticipation. Joey watched them dreamily.

"*Vire, vire koshe . . .*
Visi vaikai atsiloshe. . . ."

Rudolph began to giggle. Gravely she continued to stir her finger into his hand.

"*Tam dave, tam dave——*
Mazuilytei nebeliko,
Chiur, chiur pabego i mishka. . . ."

she suddenly cried, her finger scuttling up his arm into his arm-pit while he screamed with helpless laughter, and Joey smiled, too, holding his squirming brother until she was through tickling him.

Benedict stared down at his little brother's tear-splashed face, his helpless agony of laughter, and looked at his mother who was laughing too. He hesitated, reluctant to break through this moment.

His father was bending over a copper kettle; a fire was burning underneath, and from the long copper coils the purest alcohol dripped. The kitchen smelled of corn sugar crystals and mash.

"Papa," he said, blurting out the words. "I need some money."

"Shut door," his father commanded in English.

He shut the door behind him. For a moment he stared at his father, remembering him parting the curtains of the window; then he shrugged it away.

"The church asked me again for the tuition," he went on doggedly. "We didn't pay yet for last year. I mean for Joey," he said.

"Tell Joey go next time public school."

He let silence follow. He wished his father would speak in their own tongue.

"I *have* to pay, Papa," he said, holding back a swift flare of anger. "He's behind now. I need to buy books for him."

He had tossed all night, it had seemed to him, the collar clutched in his hands.

"Public school give books free," his father answered. He was busy among the coils, bending down to examine them. "I pay school tax! Go, get from public school!"

"I *can't* let Joey go to public school!" Benedict cried hotly. "Father Dahr said that——"

His father stood up from the coils to look at him.

"Who tell Father Dahr?" he asked sarcastically, imitating Father Dahr. He had mocked him the night before with his dancing feet. Benedict could not reconcile the moments. He felt himself going. He gripped his hands into fists and dug his finger-nails into his palms.

"Don't, Papa!" he cried, turning his face away and speaking into his shoulder. He lifted himself to his toes and leaned forward. "You want to send us all to Hell!" he shouted, his face flaming. "*You'll* go instead—you, you!"

His father laughed, shrugged his shoulders impatiently. He squatted down again to the fire, but turned his head back.

"I go Hell?" he said quietly. He nodded his head several times and picked a bottle up and squinted at it. Then he put another empty one under the coils. "Mill boss lay all mans off—lay *me* off. I'm work 15 years in Mill. Now lay off. What for lay off? You no t'ink about dat? *What for Mill lay off, huh?*" He looked at Benedict and raised a finger at him. "You tell me what for? You don't know! You no t'ink about dat! I tell you what for! Now, they say: 'Mr. Bulmanis, you come me sell house!' *What for?*" he roared suddenly, so that the cat jumped off the window sill and ran under the stove.

Benedict kept his lips shut bitterly.

"Go!" his father cried passionately, "go ask Father Dahr what I'm do now? Go tell him ask God what I'm do now?" He pointed at his forehead. "There—you no got there!" He shook his head and shrugged again hopelessly. "You take money to priest, he build house, he eat foods—but you, now you go with raggy behind." And he jutted out his behind. He lifted his eyes to Benedict, and even in the half-gloom of the kitchen, with the alarm clock beating like a cricket, Benedict could see his gray bitter eyes, the expression of heavy disillusionment in his glance at him, almost of contempt. "You say, 'Papa, give me moneys for Joey school.' Now, I say: 'Where you going to find money eat?' " He spread out both heavy hands and snorted. "What for?" he asked in Lithuanian, then repeated quietly, his eyes drifting off Benedict, "What for?"

The room settled into silence. They could hear the drone of the cat who had fallen asleep under the stove. He stiffened himself, and with his head lowered, he said, "We're not going to lose the house!"

His father glanced at him. "You say!" Then he turned to the table and picked up the bottle which he had removed from under the coils and wrapped it in a newspaper.

"Take this Mr. Dragraubaus," he said. "Buy books."

The wrapped bottle hung in the air between them. With his eyes away, Benedict finally lifted his hand to accept it. He left the house.

He would take the bottle out into the field and break it against a rock!

He wandered up Shady Avenue, past Kuckuck Alley. A smoke, like a blue-gray shadow, hung over the valley: the air was still, and the echoes came from down by the Ditch where boys were playing baseball. He wanted to join them, and lingered listening to their voices on the still air. A dry, naked stench, of endlessly burnt paper and leather and soaked rags, of bones and dead animals, of hair and tin came with a sly wind from the incinerator, when all else was still. He turned back to Kuckuck Alley, past the rows of cow-sheds, into which angry little boys were moving the huge moony animals, prodding them and slapping their manure-stained hides. Lilac bushes toppled huge bosoms over the back fences. A pale unstained evening moon was already hanging in the sky.

He stopped before a house, set like the others a little off the dirt road, a broken picket fence guarding it, a gate with a rounded wooden arch opening into the front yard. Irises, darker than the shadows, lined the walk and the fence.

"Hi, Benny," an impertinent, searching voice cried, and Benedict turned to a long-legged skinny girl coming up the lane behind him, her yellow hair hanging in long pigtails. "Watcha doin' here?"

He hid the package behind him.

"Nothing," he said. "Taking a short-cut."

"Oh, why?"

"Because!" he said flatly.

"Are you bringing my old man some moonshine?" she demanded clairvoyantly.

"No," he said.

"What're you hiding behind you?"

"None of your damned business!" he snarled at her.

"Oh, you swore!" she said smugly.

He shut his eyes and grit his teeth.

"My father said anyhow he's not going to buy any more moonshine. They laid him off the Mill."

Benedict stared at her.

"What?" he croaked.

"So take it back—or drink it yourself," she said. "Or the cops will come and pinch your old man for making it. *I* know!"

"Sap," he said.

She went inside the gate and closed it.

"*I* know," she chanted, rounding her lips. "*I* know something you don't know!"

She was like an evil spell; he couldn't break himself loose from her. He stood facing her with his hands behind his back. The bubbles in her mouth sparkled, and she hung on the gate with a malicious glee, as though she had all the world in which to swing.

At last she delivered her pronouncement.

"You're a hunky," she said, "and they don't let hunkies be priests."

He shouted furiously. "But I'm going to *be* one! I'm already studying!"

"You'll see," she said calmly, "you'll die first—of poison!"

He stared horrified at her.

"They'll put poison in the wine."

He picked up a rock from the alley and threw it at her bare yellow legs running into the house. Then he turned and ran back.

There was nowhere to go, once he reached Honey Bee Hill, except to follow the road to the City; so, instead, he walked in the opposite direction, along the foot of the Hill, moodily watching his toes as he walked.

The ground was silver, silver from the moon. In the north, the perpetual dawn, the perpetual sunrise, rose over the Ditch, over the shacks, and sprayed long streamers of slag that fell hissing into the sour water. Negro men and women, with their children under their arms, staring out of their tar-paper shacks, the yellow bite of the molten slag in the center of their eyes, watched from their windows. Would the molten river come to them? It moved, inch by burning inch, across the green grass, turning all living things to ashes, and burying them in the same instant; preserving in a hollow mold forever the frightened sketches of field mice, whose bones and flesh and skin were gone in a tiny gray smoke, leaving just this sketch of air behind.

Benedict saw it over the roofs of the houses, and, for the first time, his heart caught, as though it had almost fallen over some unexpected cliff: where would the slag dump stop? He had seen, he thought, someone else in the half-lit kitchen, darker than the shadow. . . .

St. Joseph's tolled: and he stopped to hang his head and think a prayer. He set the bottle down on the ground and took off his baseball cap, and then knelt in the cow-trodden path to cross himself. He prayed passionately for strength, as though he felt trials that lay ahead; as though, even, he needed strength to combat those of the past, which would never cease, as though the past also remained treacherously alive. He tried, with his mind's eye, to cast a dissolving glow of piety over the bristling face of his father, the thick heavy shoulders which could carry a house, the sarcastic English coming broken from his lips: but he could only see his half-contemptuous, half-sad expression, and hear his bitter voice.

"Lord, help me!" he cried, biting the tips of his fingers, clutched together in a passionate grip.

He got up from his knees, and swung aimlessly, looking up and down the alley, pushed by troubled winds. He saw the bottle lying in the dust, picked it up and crashed it against a rock. The freed alcohol swiftly mounted the darkness and escaped above the sheds. He watched the spot where it disappeared bitterly, unsatisfied by his deed. A sudden regret caught him as he remembered Joey and the unpaid tuition and the books that should have been bought.

He decided to talk to Father Brumbaugh, to open his heart to him and ask for guidance. Perhaps, he thought, now—now that his heart was filled, now that his mind overflowed. . . .

The wooden gate squeaked loudly, and he listened fondly to it, and walked down the red-brick path through the upturned yard. Without his being aware of it, a pleased smile had slightly parted his lips, his pulses had quieted themselves, his heart returned to its silence.

The lights were on in the kitchen, and voices came faintly to him. He opened the screen door, and raised his hand. The knock remained suspended in the moonlight.

"I will *not!*" he heard Father Dahr's heavy storming voice, edged with a cry he had never heard before. "This is *my* church, this is *my* parish, I've served here for 30 years, as poor as them all, and I'll not, I'll not——"

"Don't shout," he heard Father Brumbaugh reply coldly.

"I'll shout, I'll raise the roof, I'll do what I need to do!" Father Dahr roared, his agonized breath coming through the walls. "You don't order me in my own church. I *built* this church before you were born yet, and I've served in it, and these people are my people, and I'll keep serving them till it's time for me to go. But it's not for you——"

"You'll not repeat your performance of yesterday," the young priest said in a hard bitter voice. "I was ashamed to show myself! No, you'll not repeat it, if I have to report you to the Bishop myself!"

"Ashamed!" Father Dahr cried hoarsely. "Of *me!* You're ashamed of the people—they're not good enough for you! Run, run now, report me! That's your job anyhow—to spy on me! Tell him you saw me running down the alley naked as the——"

"That's enough!" Father Brumbaugh cried acidly, and Father Dahr's voice ended suddenly, and somehow Benedict knew that Father Brumbaugh had left the room. He could still hear the heavy breathing of the old man on the other side of the closed door. His hand was still in the air; he needed now to lean against the wall and shut his eyes. His head beat as though it held his heart.

Moments later he staggered out of the yard into the alley, forgetting to close the gate behind him.

10.

He didn't go home. He straggled up and down the alleys and the vacant lots, trying to shake off the feeling he had carried with him out of the parish yard. But it clung closer than feeling; he felt stained by it. The cows stank, the alley was stuffed with garbage and the ditch water flowed gutter-deep; old paper fled down hill chased by a vindictive wind that had risen from nowhere. The moon shone high and white. Only the sky, because it was so far that this air did not reach it, seemed untouched: a vast moon-swept ceiling stretched over these houses, the hills that surrounded them, to a finer world, he was certain, beyond the rivers, beyond the railroad tracks, to that place that Father Brumbaugh came from.

He couldn't go home. He remembered the broken bottle of whisky and again felt a pang of regret. He *had* to have some money! He didn't trust his father. He remembered the day Joey was ready to start school, and his father had announced that starting with Joey all his children henceforth would go to public school. This had begun one of the bitterest battles he had ever waged with his father. He was determined to die rather than let Joey loose for the paganism of the public school! On schoolday, he and his mother had taken Joey secretly to parochial school and had him enrolled: and then they had kept paying his tuition from what money they could save. Benedict had a separate fund which he kept for his brother alone: money he raised selling junk and even stealing out of the pockets of Vince, his brother, when he came home a gambling winner. Then his father had found out, and, instead of stopping Joey from going to parochial school, he had shrugged his shoulders and made a circular motion around his ear; then, later, he had agreed to pay some of the tuition. But now that he was out of work?

Desperate insincere visions of himself going to the City and stealing floated through Benedict's mind. But he shrugged them off.

The smell of the incinerator had been in his nostrils all evening; and he knew where he was walking, though he wasn't consciously directing himself there. He was on the white road, covered with lime stone, which set up a thick biting dust as he walked. It suited him; he wanted to feel pain, to make his bitter thoughts more real.

Nobody ever came this far at night. The moon, over his right shoulder, cast the left bank in shadow, and he walked there. He had not made a decision, but already he was making sure that Blind-eye Coulter, the watchman at the incinerator, wouldn't see him. The sign confronted him like a cross: "No Trespassing," it read, "$50 Fine."

Riches lay in the dump. All day long trucks came churning up the lime stone road, or old horses, themselves later to be dragged there, plodded through the dust, loaded down with the City's exports, and dumped, and went back to get other loads. At first, anybody could go scouring through the dump on the lookout for riches. It was surprising how the City underestimated value: for sometimes it was possible to furnish entire rooms with the castoff furniture that needed just a little repair. Some days the dump was covered with boys and men like raisins on a bun. And then Blind-Eye Coulter, whose one eye was all white, as though the eye everlastingly pondered his inward life, had the sign tacked up and himself went scavenging through the dump collecting stuff that he loaded in a little yard beside the incinerator and sold.

He drank and kept a rifle, and at night sat in the yard in the dark shadow of his furnace and shot at the rats which prowled over the rich heap. Boys came for copper and brass and lead, silk and silver: except that everybody knew that if Blind-Eye Coulter caught them, he kept them locked up in the Furnace, and. . . .

Benedict shuddered. The immense heap lay jagged and dark and moved uneasily. A tense wind came from over it. He heard Father Dahr's ragged voice and his throat ached.

The bright moon had followed him curiously all the way. It had watched him come. The dump was flooded with its light, except for the northern side, over which a rich deep shadow lay, lit only by glints of glass like secret eyes. He looked down at the incinerator, which stood, a long tall column, reaching high with its wavering black finger of smoke, against the creek. Nobody was stirring there. Nothing stirred either on the dump, except where a prowling wind rustled paper and snuffled among the growing potato plants whose long tendrils shone white and naked in the silver light. Small, perpetual fires burned: the dump suffered an endless purgatory under which its huge bulk sometimes softly shifted and spilled unsettled garbage down its side before it sank into a profounder and deeper sleep. A stench, like a sticky steam, rose from its rotting body. Benedict shuddered again, his teeth cracking against other teeth. He held his breath as he picked his way across the rim, crouching to keep from making a silhouette against the horizon. He found a sack, then a broom-stick which he carried with him and poked into the hill as he walked. He held his breath like a swimmer, letting it out with a gasp and breathing in a short gulp of the infected air.

He found a copper kettle and put it into his sack. Now, a glee suddenly seized him. He stood up and gazed greedily over the dump. The dump was *rich!* All he had to do was poke around it and make his choice of its riches. Rats left reluctantly at his approach, and he shook his stick at them. They slunk, mean gray shadows across the moonlight looking back at him. He spied a broken candelabra that looked, to his engrossed eyes, like real silver and he ran to pick it up. A terrific roar burst across the valley and Benedict fell flat on his face in an oily puddle. Above his head cans began to tumble down. He dug his fingers into the matted earth in terror, and lay quivering against it, as though against a rotting breast. He couldn't open his lips to pray; his thoughts froze in his stiffened brain.

The nosey wind had not been frightened. It nuzzled around him and licked his cheeks. He moved silently. He could barely see the incinerator from where he lay: the peaceful moonlight spread over the yard and not a shadow moved. Then he saw it. A ray of the moon had fallen on the barrel of the rifle outlining it like a livid stool-finger pointing to him.

He lay with his cheek pressed against the dump, and his eyes stared fixedly across the hill. He waited. He couldn't move—not even a thought. He felt as though he were plastered against the side of the hill; it held him, held him to its rotted City riches, while on top of him his body, enormously burdened, lay on him like a stone. The unreal night shone like a clear crystal above him. Terror watched the moon with a single eye.

Above him something moved, and again the gun spoke. A shadow shot high in the moonlight and then fell clawing back with a shriek. It began to crawl clattering through the cans down the hill. He could see its long shadow dragging through the cans while it kept up a frightened gibbering. Again the gun barked. The rat squealed, and moved faster.

Benedict watched it coming with horror. He thought that it would reach him and touch him, staining him with its blood; he heard a distant shriek sound in his mind, his brain swell with the roar of it; he felt his throat tighten and his taut lips strain against the skin. His eyes spread as though parted by fingers. And then the roar in his mind filled the night, and the rat leaped again in the air and fell rolling down the side of the hill, followed by a peal of cans that rattled noisily to the bottom. And then silence that echoed and re-echoed filled the night like a drum, and died away, and was still.

Long afterwards it seemed to Benedict that he had blundered somehow into a malicious dream, wrapped with sickening innocence in a silken coil that wound about him a deceptive spell. A silence waited patiently like a cat with its furry paws before it and its calm eyes watching from the dark. Here he had lost his precious identity. They couldn't tell who he was, and thought he was *the others;* he was in terrible peril, and in the spell, he could not find the voice to cry: *God knows me! Ask Him!* For he heard behind the closed doors the voices of those who should speak for him, whose recognizing glance would restore him to the world, abolish the eyes waiting in the darkness, hold back the leap, make the world with its rational laws go again. These voices were immersed in a controversy that sounded louder than his cries, and even if he banged on the door till his knuckles bled they wouldn't hear him. For he could never move from where he lay. A vast lassitude, a sickness unbled him, and he lay like water. . . . Ugliness fell like a smothering hand. . . .

First in his mind, and then slowly with his hand that reached only partway up, he begged: "In the name of the Father, and of the Son, and of the Holy Ghost, in the name of the Father. . . ." And he heard his voice and saw his hand lift before his eyes and touch his forehead. And came to life.

Then the moon, quietly, slipped away. Clouds pushed awkwardly across the sky. The ragged shadows moved over him and covered the entire dump and moved to the incinerator and darkened it.

Only then did he realize that he was still clutching the candelabra.

He got up on his hands and knees, and then lifted himself upright by pushing against the dump. He staggered, but lifted the sack on his shoulder with the candelabra in it, and started to climb along the side of the dump. A fatigue, as if he had suddenly grown very old, streamed through his body, and the shadow before him looked bent like an old man. Mechanically he continued to poke among the debris, picking up copper wire and brass pans; and when his bag was full, he rounded the hill and started down the lime stone road walking behind his shadow and coughing unprotestingly into his shoulder.

Men were going to work. They came out from among the shadows of their homes and walked quickly, as though they weren't sure they'd find their job when they arrived. Benedict thought he saw Dobrik, but had no interest in this illusion: the shadow that might have been Dobrik was walking swiftly with an anonymous worker, who had clutched under his arm the gleaming aluminum bucket, which the moon, as though summoned for this, brightened with a ray.

He hid his sack behind the toilet, and stood for a moment in the back yard. Then, as though only now he recognized the spot, he limped in through the back door and climbed slowly upstairs.

"Benediktas?" his mother whispered, half-hidden in the darkness.

"Mama!" he cried with anguish.

"Everyone's asleep," she said.

In the darkness he reached for her, and felt her frightened bosom against his cheek, and kneaded his forehead into it. She caressed his head. "Mama," he said over and over pressing his wet lips into her bosom. "He's asleep. Make no noise," she answered.

The breath of the two children in the room rose and fell in sweet pain, and wearily he took off his clothes, and stood and looked into the crumpled face of his brother, Rudolph, and then of Joey, purified in dreams.

Then he climbed into bed and held the vision of beauty tight against his breast.

11.

Early Monday morning they came and began to lay a huge concrete sewer alongside the Ditch. In the afternoon, after he had sold his candelabra and junk, Benedict went down to watch them. Most of the Hollow seemed to be there. A long skinny crane lifted concrete slices into the air from the creaking trucks and laid them, slice by slice, in a wavering cobra-line along the Ditch. The sections were slipped into place by other workers and cemented together.

One always thought, because one's eyes grew from infancy on, looking at the unchanging scenery, transferring it simply into one's soul and slowly building it there memory by memory, until the inner image coincided entirely with the outer, only one's own skin separating the reality from the image—one believed that the self grew out of the native ground like the grass, and nothing could change outside without inside bleeding.

And then one day strangers came from nowhere, summoned by nobody knew what power, and along with them came trucks and cranes and wagons of cement, and without asking if they might, and not caring about that inside of you, or those roots anchored in the ground, they set about changing everything; and all you could do was stand there and watch, and begin to feel odd and strange inside, as though the inside image were being hacked with a knife. You felt something then tearing, and your underwear got sticky, from blood, you thought, except that without knowing you had broken out in a stormy sweat. And standing there in the crowd, clutching your rosary, feeling your scapular rising and falling on your chest, and in your chest the image of God pressed like a leaf against your heart, you suddenly felt as though you had come carrying a bouquet of flowers, and looking down, saw they were only a bunch of wilted weeds.

Benedict was out of breath as he watched. He felt a stitch in his side, as though he had been running, although he had walked down to the Ditch. He looked from face to face in the crowd, searching for tears in anyone's eyes. He wanted to demand. . . .

A tall, cheek-boned man, spitting a long streamer of yellow juice, remarked out of the side of his mouth: "Well, guess we'll be getting rid of them shines anyhow. . . ." And his uneasy eyes turned to look at the shacks, and then back at the men working. His lips got thin, and he clutched his side as though he hurt as Benedict did.

There were at least a hundred people gathered along the road. A few Negroes stood outside their shacks watching with fixed expressionless faces. Across the Ditch, so close now they felt the heat, and could see the cooling slag crusting, and even the air blisters that formed on the crust, the long slanting incline lay strewn with half-broken boulders, which had cooled, and a long burnt-out tongue that lay yellow and sullen along the hill. And now it was obvious to everyone what would happen: the sewer would be laid down and the slag would come steadily on, covering it, erasing the Ditch, going on to the tar-paper cabins, going on over them, obliterating them from the earth, and going on beyond them, climbing the valley, climbing on up the Hill. . . .

So they watched as though in a trance the crane hoist the big, swinging concrete rings, letting them hang suspended for a moment against the slag hill, and then bringing them to rest gently in place along the line. The crane was a clean new yellow, as though imagined for this particular day, and the trucks were new, too, and even among the workers there were new railroad caps and new pairs of overalls. The June sun was clear as glass. Children suspected how pleasant it was, and yelled and admired, and Benedict felt instantly elevated, and then felt sick with treason.

He stood rigidly facing the Ditch, as though his right side toward the shacks was stiff and he couldn't turn in that direction.

Mrs. Tubelis, a Lithuanian who came to see his mother and once put a baked onion on his inflamed toe, spoke to him in

Lithuanian. "*Kaip einasi?*" She looked darkly at the Ditch and spat. "*Rapuzhe!*" she swore.

Benedict smiled. (Swearing, somehow, was ugly only in English.)

"How is Mama?" she asked Benedict with formal gravity but smiling fondly at him at the same time.

"Fine," he said nodding eloquently, although he knew that she had probably seen his mother only an hour before.

"*Ir Tevas?*"

He shrugged. "*Bedarbis.*"

"Ah!" she cried, her voice rising tragically, nodding her head as though once again the sad lot of the workingman was here confirmed; her bosom rose to its full strength and then suddenly collapsed in a profound sigh. "Mill shut down, maybe?" she asked fearfully, putting this unpleasant thought in English, narrowing her eyes for his important opinion and poking her tongue out a little.

He shrugged again. "*Nezhinau,*" he said.

"*Kaip Tevas pasake?*" she asked.

They always finally asked him what his father thought; he shrugged his shoulders, frowning. "He didn't say anything," he said brusquely in English.

"*Ah, mano vyras . . .*" she began, without finishing, and sighed. "My Mister no vork since Tuesday."

Benedict said soberly, with his lips almost closed: "Did a letter come?"

"From Bank?"

He nodded.

She nodded too without speaking. A profound gloom, mixed with superstitious fatalism, came into her face; her eyes fixed and she stared with fallen cheeks into her thoughts. Then she shook, and put her hand on Benedict's fleecy hair and smoothed it with her heavy hard hand, smiling with a tender inward look, and purring: "*Grazhus, grazhus . . .* nice, nice. . . ." And, as though he understood her necessity, he suffered her caresses and stood patiently until she dropped her hands with a long regretful sigh.

It was frightening how fast the sewer was laid. Before the

workers quit at six o'clock, they had already laid several hundred yards of pipe. The Ditch went down for half a mile to a cut in the ridge; it ran then under a railroad bridge, then down into the river. The ridge blocked off the eastern end of the Hollow, except at the south where it parted wide enough to let a road through.

The sun deserted first, and then the watchers broke reluctantly. And then, as though afraid to be caught last there, the others suddenly left, and only Benedict and a few stragglers remained.

He would be late for church soon, he knew. And yet he lingered. His eyes were fastened on the yellow crane, whose snuffling steam had ended, and it had settled into the lonely look of machinery that has been abandoned by workers.

He turned, at last, around his left, and began slowly walking up the street, seeing dimly for a moment, only to be washed out of his thoughts, the knitted cap and cane, and smiling to himself.

Father Brumbaugh was in the sacristy. Already he seemed to be in full possession of it; he moved certainly from object to object. There was a new boy there with him—a redheaded boy, with tarnished freckles, and Father Brumbaugh was instructing him in a low, insistent voice in the elementary principles of the Mass. The boy's face was set and he licked his lips nervously to reply when the priest paused.

Father Brumbaugh nodded to Benedict as he passed through, but asked: "And *then* what?"

The boy stammered. "And then I cross—cross to the Epistle side of——"

"You just *cross?*"

The boy stared blankly at Father Brumbaugh.

"You just cross? That's what I said."

Benedict raised himself behind Father Brumbaugh and smiled painfully at the boy.

"I—I cross to the Epistle side——" faltered the boy.

"That's three times you've done that," Father Brumbaugh observed dryly.

"I c-cross," the boy stammered.

"You have borne that cross," Father Brumbaugh said, "already three times."

The boy's face flushed. Benedict knelt for him, drawing his attention by the power of his sympathy; he kept kneeling and getting up and bobbing, while the boy stared at him with wide frustrated eyes. Father Brumbaugh turned.

Benedict scrambled to his feet. "I'm sorry, Father," he said, bowing his head.

"I understand," Father Brumbaugh replied, his young face somehow in-closed and pale, with a dense shadow lurking somewhere in it, but his eyes weary. "But he'll have to learn himself."

"Yes, Father."

"I want to talk to you shortly," he added. "Will you wait?"

"Yes, Father."

He turned to the redheaded boy, over whose brow a crown of sweat-beads had formed.

"Did you understand *that?*"

"Kneel?"

"Genuflect, yes, when you cross from the Gospel to the Epistle side of the altar and vice versa. Always, unless——"

The boy nodded vigorously.

"Unless what?" Father Brumbaugh asked sharply. The boy's startled eyes flew up. "You shouldn't agree so quickly," the young priest observed.

Benedict left, going through the yard and knocking on the back door of the priests' home.

Mrs. Rumyer let him in, examining him with a sour penetrating look as he entered, pulling loose a hanging button from his coat sleeve. Her hair was pulled back out of her eyes and neatly caught on the nape of her neck; her dress was carefully covered with a fresh rose-print apron. So she wasn't so old after all! Benedict thought with surprise. A workingman and his wife were sitting at the table, waiting to see Father Dahr. The man's wife had a black eye, and he sat glumly beside her, his great horned hands in his lap holding each other as though to keep them out of trouble. They had come for advice from the old man.

"Where's Father?" he asked.

"Which one?" she asked darkly.

"Father . . . Dahr?"

"In," she jerked her shoulder behind her. "Don't go in all of a sudden," she added. "Someone's with him. Give me that coat," she said, slipping it off him as he passed through the kitchen, the dark little hall, dominated by a dark Christ crucified in the shadows, with only his thorns, which had been gilded with luminous paint, glowing.

He was seated in a rocker, facing the shrouded window, and beside him was a bottle of medicine and a teaspoon. A man was with him. Benedict recognized him as the Greek worker, George Pappis. He was standing some distance away from the old man.

Father Dahr said angrily: "What, are you a child?"

Pappis shrugged his dense shoulders, and the flesh of his face seemed to darken with the color of his thoughts. His hands were gripped behind his back: and there was the electric smell of newly-drunk whisky mixed with the sweet of licorice in the room. Benedict could feel that Pappis was drunk, not a simple drunkenness, but one in which his brooding face seemed filled with an agony of will, of struggle; and Benedict couldn't open his mouth to announce himself. Nor could he leave.

"It's one or the other!" the man said harshly.

"But this is an infant's thinking!" Father Dahr replied, roughly, coughing a little with a sound as though of tearing.

Pappis turned on him and cried, his deep voice rumbling: "I'll die before I let them!" He extended both hands in trembling fists and the arches of his arm-muscles were throbbing mounds of strength. "With these hands I'll tear them apart!"

"Ah—you're a fool!" Father Dahr said impatiently, his voice suddenly cracking. He coughed again helplessly for a moment, and then said: "To beat your wife—yes, those arms are good enough! But when it comes to this—all you can do is talk of killing! Whom will you kill? The sheriff? Do you think the idea began with him?"

"But what am I to do?" Pappis roared, staring with bloodshot eyes. "Stand meekly by till they take my life away?"

Pappis struck his head, punched it with his fist three times (as though he were punching his breast, Benedict thought, crying *mea culpa! mea culpa!*) and the blows knocked his head back.

"What can we do?" he cried, his shoulders suddenly sagging.

"Why do you ask me?" Father Dahr said bitterly.

"But you are one of us!" Pappis accused him.

Father Dahr shrugged, and lapsed into a silence which seemed to be waiting in him, like darkness. He said something in a very low voice to himself, which Benedict could not hear. Pappis' eyes meanwhile had begun to dull: a somber melancholy, like a strong odor, exhaled from him: and they stood and sat waiting for something in that room. Finally, Father Dahr rose out of the shadow of his chair, and his voice was tired.

"Do you think I have any power at all—me, half-dead in this old chair? What do you want me to do—go to them and threaten them—with what? They would laugh at me. The time of thunderbolts has passed. . . ." He fell silent staring at the curtains. Pappis too was silent. Father Dahr roused himself after awhile and said again: "What do you want me to do?"

"God knows," Pappis said.

Father Dahr's head tilted gently as though a kind of weight had moved it. A heavy sigh, with a strange high tremble running through it, came from him.

"How many times have I warned you?" he said, staring at Pappis' fallen head.

The other cried suddenly turning to him. "Words!" he said in a muffled voice. "Do you give words to the stomach?"

"To the soul," Father Dahr said calmly.

Pappis stared at him, the presence of violence in his body dominant in the room; then he laughed a hoarse insulting laugh. He fell to his knees shaking and crossed his arms and bent his heavy head. "Bless me, bless me!"

Father Dahr stared at him for a long moment, a paleness in his face, a slight bitterness in his eyes, and slowly he brought up his fingers and traced the ancient cross in the dark air. Then he whispered: "Go, get out now. . . ."

Benedict didn't move for minutes after Pappis, without another word, had stumbled past him. The odor of whisky remained sharp in the room.

He cleared his throat.

"Father?" he whispered. Then again: "Father!"

The pompadour moved slightly; then the cracked, hoarse voice, as though half-locked in rust, coughed and said: "Come in, I know it's you."

"It's me, Father," Benedict assured him, wondering if he had known. He stopped beside the chair and said anxiously: "Are you sick?"

"Sick?" the old man protested. "No, no, not at all! This?" Picking up the bottle. "Clears my throat. Old age stuck in it." He laughed and turned his sallow eyes on Benedict. "How do *you* feel?"

"Me, Father?"

"Oh," the priest said slyly, "a man of your experience. . . ."

Benedict colored. "Thank you, Father, for coming for me," he said.

"Not at all, Benedict; but I'm afraid of jails."

"So am I," Benedict agreed with a slight tremor.

The old priest fell silent, as though this had tired him, and stared at the gently throbbing curtains, which parted from time to time to expose a small part of Highland Avenue.

"Polank and his wife are waiting in the kitchen for you," Benedict said.

Father Dahr waved a hand loosely.

"In time, in time," he said. "I've two confessionals." He laughed a little to himself. "Here they come for—what shall we say?—secular advice?" He nodded his head. "I've told him for thirteen years that he was on his way to eternal hell-fire," he said. "He says to me: 'What's a wife for if you can't beat her?' 'But God frowns——' I tell him. And he looks at me reproachfully, even a little—what shall we say?—for it's not God's word he is looking for here but man's." He stared at Benedict as he spoke, and when Benedict said nothing, he added: "And for which have you come today?"

The slight irony in his eyes was suddenly attacked by a cough, and when he sank into his chair exhausted a silence followed. The room was heavy and dark, like the furniture, like the few gilt-framed pictures, portraits painted in dark thick colors, except for the halo in one, and in the other a gold ring. In the corner near the window was an enormous bowl in which tiny blue fish swam among the thick submarine vegetation that grew round and round inextricably tangled, but glowing mysteriously when a light touched it. Over the mantel, as well as religious objects, there was also a place for mementos from Africa—a spear, a headdress, a bracelet of lion's teeth: memories of an early digression into missionary life.

"Father," Benedict said, "I was down to the Ditch this afternoon."

Father Dahr coughed, and Benedict waited until the tearing of rags ceased.

"I watched them working," he added.

"Working?"

"Laying a sewer."

Father Dahr nodded, but his eyes showed that he had not heard; they closed for a moment, and from behind them, he asked: "Are you and Father getting along well?"

"Yes, Father," Benedict admitted gently.

"He's a fine young man." He mused for a moment, and then added curiously: "Would you like to be like him, Benedict?"

Benedict shivered from head to foot.

"I couldn't be, Father!" he protested, blushing.

"Because——" Father Dahr said, "because he is to you what——" He smiled suddenly and stopped. He stared thoughtfully at Benedict and said: "So you're still determined to take holy orders?"

"Yes, Father," Benedict replied uneasily.

"Why?"

The answer he had given himself always lay ready on his lips, but under the sudden oppression of Father Dahr's heavy sick eyes, he could not find it.

"I wish to serve the Church, Father," he replied, twisting.

Father Dahr muttered and nodded his head. His mottled, green-and-blue cheeks moved silently. He coughed, doubling up in the chair, and brought a large handkerchief to his mouth into which he spat. "A bit of death," he remarked pensively staring down at it. Benedict turned his queasy eyes away.

"Yes," Father Dahr resumed. "I've served the Church too in my time—fifty years of it." He lifted his head and asked him quietly: "Take a good look at me."

Benedict stared at him. "What do you mean?" he asked uncomfortably.

"What do you see?" the priest asked.

"I don't understand," Benedict faltered. "You're old, of course——"

"Old?" he panted. He swung his hand impatiently through the air. "Of course, I'm old! But what do you *see*, Benedict? Look—look deep!"

"I can't see anything, Father!" Benedict cried painfully. "I don't know what you mean." He strained nervously against the chair. "I——" he struggled; then he cried, tormented: "Father, why do you ask me such a question!"

The old man's eyes held his in a long falling moment, his fingers pressed painfully into Benedict's arm. Then he relaxed, and let go. "Give me that spoon, Benedict," he begged.

Benedict, relieved, handed him the spoon, and then opened the bottle, and watched the old man's shaking hands pour out an oily potion, and then dreamily sip it. And instead of taking the spoon out he licked it gluttonously, closing his old eyes over the taste in a kind of exhausted ecstasy.

"Father," Benedict began with a touch of irritation.

The old priest removed the spoon and placed it against his cheek and rubbed it.

"My father——" Benedict began.

"Yes, Benedict?" Father Dahr said. "Your father——?"

"My father got a letter from the Bank," he said, reddening with shame. "It asked him to sell the house back to them. Can they do that?"

Father Dahr tapped his ear with the sticky spoon. "You, too," he said musingly, turning his ironic glance on Benedict. "You too are looking for the secular——" His face grew serious. "I got one also," he said dryly.

Benedict's mouth opened. "*You?*"

"Yes," Father Dahr said calmly. "I."

"Oh, but Father——"

Father Dahr put the spoon down. A bit of oil glistened on his cheek.

"They want to buy the property. The ground, you understand. The church they'll build again anywhere we choose," he said. "They will not disturb the spiritual. They don't offer a price, at all. 'Render unto Caesar——' It's the ground they want, Benedict; they are interested in the material, not the spirit. They do not want the church. They don't mention, of course, the mortgage they already have bought up."

Benedict stared.

"The mortgage," the old man said with a kind of wry humor, "was in the hands of several of our richest Catholic folk in the City; to be protected, one thought, with one's life. But now it seems the Bank has them all: and the Bank is the Company."

He looked at Benedict with his wry expression, and added: "The Company wants to fill up the Hollow. Fill it up from hill to hill, *this* Hollow, Benedict. They want to build a mill on it, another mill. What do you think of that?"

"I don't know, Father."

"From hill to hill," he repeated. "From the slag hill to Hungry Hill. Over the church. Buried."

Benedict said slowly: "And will they——?"

Father Dahr began to cough, and the sweat broke out on his face. When he was through he stared vacantly and dully at Benedict, and Benedict touched him by the arm and asked earnestly: "And will they sell, Father?"

The old man shook his head with irritation, and cried: "Where would they go? Live in the fields like cows? Is money a house?"

Benedict shook his head. His lips trembled, and he struggled several times to form the question like a bubble in hs mouth. "Father——" he blurted. "Father——" His lips blanched and his mouth grew dry. "And the church?" he whispered finally.

Father Dahr stared at him angrily.

"What?" he asked.

Benedict blinked. "The church?" he said hoarsely.

The priest continued to frown, then his face suddenly cleared, and he cried: "Well, would *you?*"

"No!" Benedict recoiled with horror.

Father Dahr shrugged and spread out his hands.

"Yes, Father," Benedict said, with a relieved sigh. "I see now." He looked gratefully about the room, and touched the chair, smoothing the arm of it gently. "But down by the Ditch," he began, "they——"

The old man's head had fallen to his chest. He lifted it and his eyes seemed clouded and he sought for Benedict.

"What?" he asked.

"Nothing, Father," Benedict replied. He got up to go. "I'll come in and see you again," he promised.

"Going?" The old man stirred a little in his chair. "Come and see me again, Benedict."

"I will, Father," Benedict replied.

"Tomorrow?"

He hesitated before answering, surprised that the old man wanted a specific answer.

"I'll come tomorrow," he said.

"Be sure to come tomorrow," the old man said.

"I will, Father."

"Close the window before you go," he said, and he watched Benedict go to the window, and close it, and the wild curtains die down.

On his way through the kitchen, Benedict laid a small bundle on the kitchen table. In it was a collar, very starched and very clean.

12.

They were walking along Highland Avenue west. His hand rested softly on Benedict's shoulder.

"He caught a cold," Father Brumbaugh was saying, "and so

I've asked him to stay in for a few days. I'll need your help more than ever," he added with a slight smile. His face was tired.

"I'll try to help you all I can," Benedict replied with profound sincerity.

Father Brumbaugh paused to look at him and say earnestly: "You *can*, Benedict!"

And Benedict glanced up at his small face, almost wan above the white collar.

"I feel so alone since I've come here," the priest said moodily. "They told me I was coming into a predominantly German Catholic community, but they must have lost track of it, for the Germans have all since left."

"Most of them moved into the City," Benedict explained authentically.

"Nationalities I never met before," said the priest with a slightly harassed expression. "How am I supposed to——" He lifted his shoulders, and let them drop. He turned to Benedict, and studied him. "For instance, what are *you*, Benedict?"

Benedict squirmed. "Lithuanian," he said uncomfortably.

The priest's face registered nothing.

"Lithuanian," Benedict repeated with more emphasis.

"Lithuanian. . . ?" The priest echoed, his helpless look in his eyes. They walked silently for a few steps. "Whatever that is," he said. "And there are Bulgarians and Hungarians and Slovaks. . . . They come and talk to me in broken English and wave their hands in my face. . . . Why does everybody eat garlic here, Benedict?" he asked with shadowed pain on his face. He shrugged however, his brows furrowing, and he went on to Benedict, his tone suddenly changing. "Yes, you can help me a great deal, Benedict. I think you realize this is a hard assignment for me. I'm not used to living . . . in this way," he said with a bewildered wave of his hand. "I don't understand the people. These bare smoky hills depress me. When I wake in the morning, I look out of the window—over there," and he pointed to the slag dump, "and the air's foul. And the poverty, the miserable poverty! Oh, I always thought I could confront it——" He laughed to himself. "But I'd never *seen* it—smelled it. The workers come into the church in

110

their work clothes and leave smears on the benches and dirt on the floors. . . . I've never known of things like this, Benedict! All my life I've lived another way."

The note of lost, bewildered anguish cut through Benedict, and his heart ached for him.

"Where are the better-class people?" the priest cried. "Why don't *they* come to see me? Do they all go to St. Mary's? Nobody has asked me to visit them, to enter their homes, to have tea. And the smells! It was wrong of them to send me here! I'm not equal to it, and I don't dare beg to be sent——"

He dropped his hand from Benedict's shoulder, and Benedict felt as though a weight of words had fallen from him.

"Maybe——" he began, his face aching to be of comfort.

"Oh," the priest protested sadly. "Don't feel so badly for me, Benedict. *You're* at least different. You're more sensitive than . . . all this." He waved his hand in a circle that included the menacing stack of the incinerator as well as the distant gloomy iron shed of the Flue Dust. Its arc also enveloped the church, whose spire rose behind them, and Benedict smiled at the mistake. "I've never even dreamed that a place like this existed," he went on with candid dismay. "Or that the people could have so little, so few comforts, so few luxuries, so little culture. Things I took for granted," he said with widened eyes, "all my life . . . aren't here. Nobody reads, there's not even a piano in the whole Hollow; no music, except drunken music, nothing at all but the red dust and the horrible smoke, and the men swearing and getting drunk on Saturday and roaring under our window." He stared at Benedict with the echo of the shocked memory still in his eyes. "Did you know I had to call the police last Saturday?"

"No," Benedict whispered.

"How can I be the pastor of people against whom I have to call the police?" he asked almost with horror.

Benedict, absorbed in the young priest's vision, shuddered. Father Brumbaugh's face was strained in self-pity, and Benedict suffered for him, and suddenly cried: "Someday *I'll* be a priest!"

Father Brumbaugh looked at him, startled.

"And come here?" he said finally, understanding.

Benedict nodded, his lips set tightly.

"To these workers, these men?" Father Brumbaugh rubbed the back of Benedict's neck. "You *come* from them, Benedict. You're right, then. *You* should be here, more so than I." He turned moodily away, a shadowed bitterness in his eyes, and continued: "These men need a different kind of spiritual guidance," he said. "Priests from among themselves, if there are any. Priests with muscles," he said squeamishly. "Or like you. If the day should come when they should rise against the government," he went on, "if the day should ever come!" He looked down on Benedict with frightened eyes. "Oh, don't be too sure it won't!" he cried, as though Benedict had protested. "What events in Boston, for instance! The policemen's strike! *Policemen,* Benedict," he said lowering his voice. "Thank God," he added, "for Governor Coolidge, even though he is a Protestant!"

They walked on, until the June grass, dark with the oncoming twilight, was underfoot.

"There's only been one strike *here,*" Benedict assured him. "Back in 1919. They don't let them have strikes here," he said. "The Cossacks would kill them."

"The who?" Father Brumbaugh said, startled.

"The Cossacks. The Mill cops. The Coal-and-Iron Police," Benedict explained. "They'd kill them. They'd shoot them."

"Oh, no!" Father Brumbaugh protested.

"Sure they would!" Benedict insisted confidently.

"But why should they strike?" Father Brumbaugh asked helplessly, looking around the landscape as though it had suddenly become more hostile than ever, pregnant with unspecified dangers.

"Because we're all poor," Benedict said carelessly.

Father Brumbaugh stopped and looked reproachfully at him. "Oh, Benedict," he said, "I'm surprised to hear that from you! Poverty does not turn men from God into Communism," he said smiling.

Benedict suddenly turned flame hot.

"But that's what *they* said!" he cried. He turned to Father Brumbaugh and said painfully: "I know somebody, and they say

". . . but, Father, they beat him for not telling who was in the union!"

Father Brumbaugh stared at him.

"But he wants to build the *union!*" Benedict insisted as though Father Brumbaugh had contradicted him.

"A Communist!" Father Brumbaugh finally whispered, half skeptically, half in fear. "You know a Communist?"

Benedict hesitated. He had never told Father Brumbaugh of that episode! He flushed; lowered his head and mumbled, twisting his fingers. "No, Father." Father Brumbaugh gave him a consoling look and patted him gently on the shoulder. They walked silently along the road, and a bitterness welled in him, and he said, without raising his head: "My father got laid off the Mill, and they want to buy the house now."

Father Brumbaugh's eyes flickered; he had been sunk in his own thoughts.

"What?" he said.

"My father got laid off in the Mill!" Benedict said loudly, bitterly.

"Oh," Father Brumbaugh said sympathetically, "but he'll get work again soon——"

"Sure, when the Mill hires him back," Benedict said tersely. He added uneasily: "It has to be soon. Because they want my father to pay on the house on July. They want Father Dahr to, too."

Father Brumbaugh stopped suddenly.

"Father Dahr too?" he repeated.

"Pay on the church—or sell," Benedict answered.

"I don't understand," the young priest said, frowning.

"The mortgage—they want to buy the whole church," Benedict explained with a scoffing smile. "They want to tear it down so they can cover up the Hollow with slag!" He looked at Father Brumbaugh with confident derisive eyes.

"How do you know this?"

"Everybody's getting letters," Benedict replied. "Father Dahr told me about the church."

"*Told* you?"

"When I saw him today."

"Oh," Father Brumbaugh said.

"But," Benedict added triumphantly, "he's not going to sell the church! Imagine selling the church! The *holy* church! I'd let them kill me first," he said proudly.

"Of course," Father Brumbaugh said, but Benedict wasn't sure his expression of pride had registered. They walked farther on into the deeper shadows, until they reached that part of the Ditch that ran by the incinerator. Father Brumbaugh stopped here abruptly and elevated his head. His thin nostrils quivered and he turned Benedict around.

"We better get back," he said.

Their return was faster, and in silence. At the gate, Father Brumbaugh touched Benedict's shoulder and said: "We'll have other walks. You make me feel as though the task isn't as . . . difficult as it seemed to me at first."

"You'll like it after awhile," Benedict declared fervently. "Father Dahr says he's not going to drink anymore, and so——"

"Father Dahr," the young priest said sharply, "does not drink!"

13.

They started running down hill as though a bell had rung. Men, women and children, dogs and even cows streaming down Shady Avenue and along the creek to the Ditch. Benedict ran, too. "There's a fight!" He saw Mr. Dragraubaus, his suspenders over his woolen underwear, clogging along, and Lena, his long-legged daughter, and Mrs. Tubelis who gasped as she ran, clutching her bosom—and from all the side alleys and streets Negro men, women and children joined the stream and outran them all.

The Ditch was gone now. Over it a long mound of rounded yellow dirt, like a long fresh grave, stretched waveringly down to the ridge. The workers had passed beyond the ridge days ago with their yellow crane and new trucks. There was no ditch: the

114

Ditch was gone! But there in the road, white with lime stone dust and the yellow dust from the slag hill, piles and piles of furniture, each pile before each cabin, and going in like blue ants, the Sheriff and his men, and the Cossacks, the Coal-and-Iron police of the Mill (since these shacks were Mill property), taking out a chair and a table and stacking them, with great care, on the road.

Toward the end of the row a group of police were battering down a locked door with some long two-by-fours. The wood splintered: there were shrieks, and the police came carrying a struggling woman and dragging a man with bloody head out into the road: followed then by their furniture which they tossed out into the yellow sunlight.

A Negro man burst through the crowd that had gathered and grabbed the Sheriff's arm. The club, with easy, almost oiled power, lifted and fell, and the crunch made them flinch and duck their heads, and the man pitched on his face in the white road and rolled over on his back with his eyes too surprised to close. A scream rose from the cabin, and a woman tumbled out and before she could go far tripped in her skirts and fell with her arms spread-eagled across the road. A policeman helped her up, and blinded by terror, she thanked him and then, as though she had forgotten turned back into her cabin, aimlessly brushing the dust from her skirt.

Down at the end of the row a man had barricaded himself in. The barrel of a hunting rifle poked out of the broken window. The onlookers had been roped off by the police and stood leaning against the taut hawser, compelled and restrained. As they watched, a policeman shot a heavy bomb through the window of the barricaded cabin. They could hear the glass shattering. Then the smoke began to billow out. "Tear-gas," said someone knowingly.

Almost immediately after the door burst open and a tall Negro man, his fingers clawing at his eyes, stumbled out. A policeman stuck out his foot and he pitched face forward into the dust.

Abruptly, Benedict sat down in the road. He sank his head into his knees and spilled out his stomach. The world reeled: earth, sky, blinding sun.

Someone yelled: "You gonna do that to me, too, Anderson? You gonna put me and the Missus out in the road, too? Come on and try it!"

Anderson, the Sheriff, waved at the crowd and laughed. People laughed back.

"I'll blow you and your boys to hell if you come—and I won't use a hunting rifle!"

Sheriff Anderson pretended to be terrified; he waved his hands fearfully in the sky, shook his head. No, he certainly wouldn't come calling! The crowd, enjoying his performance, booed.

"Count them pieces of furniture, Jake!" somebody yelled. "Make 'em turn out their pockets before they leave!"

"Where you moving 'em to, Sheriff? In *your* house?"

He shook his head with mock horror.

"Bet they ain't going to vote for *you*, Sheriff!"

Sheriff Anderson assumed a tragic pose, shrugged as though what could he do? Duty was duty. Besides, it was well known that the ballot boxes from the Hollow were usually "lost."

"Tella Company go Hell!" somebody shouted.

"N-----s first, hunkies next!" somebody else cried.

"Black clouds passing!" came a cry, and laughter followed.

A stone sailed through the air and nipped the white dust near the Sheriff's foot, and hardly had the dust begun to rise when he had whipped out his gun and fired into the air. The people broke and ran, gathering again farther away. Now, the Sheriff was no longer smiling.

Benedict got up slowly, first on his hands and knees, and then on one foot at a time. He steadied himself in the road, and then noticed that the crowd had fallen back. Methodically, the blue-uniformed police were entering the shacks and bringing out the furniture, and stacking it on the road. A couple of wagons had appeared and the families were loading these and driving off. He crossed behind the cabins and followed the long row down almost to its end, catching a whiff of sickly-sweet gas, and at a certain cabin stopped and shook as though a chill had caught him. He had to will himself to move on. He pushed open the door and called: "Mother Burns? Mother Burns, it's me, Benedict!"

'There was no answer from the webby interior, and, pushing the door open wider, he raised his voice: "It's only me, Mother Burns, don't you hear me? Benedict! I've come to tell you that——"

He stepped inside. The sweet cool smell of vanilla and alum, somehow mixed together, along with the penetrating, never-to-die odor of tar, welcomed him. The crocheted doilies and antimacassars, and the lace frames on pictures made the dark rooms glow with a cool, ancient look, as though this parlor with the haunting motion of the air she had breathed, had lived somewhere else for more years than the cabin had stood on that ground.

Not even the cat was there. He walked from living room to kitchen, and looked outside to see if the toilet door was closed. "Mother Burns," he called defensively. The kitchen, with its cracked dishware and its dwindled look, and the still-burning coal-stove, was empty. A faint panic seized him. He ran to the door, just as it opened, and one of the troopers sang out: "Hey, looka here what I found!"

Benedict backed up.

The trooper entered the room, which shook under his feet.

"Who lives here, kid?" he asked. "Don't tell me they stuck in some white people——"

"Mother Burns. She's out somewhere——"

"She your mammy, boy?" he whined in a high tone. "You a *white* n----r?"

"No," Benedict breathed.

"What you doing here? What's your name?"

Benedict recited his passport: "Benedict Bulmanis. I'm an acolyte for St. Joseph's Church."

"Sure enough?" said the trooper, laying a hand on the table. "Well, that's pretty good, boy, but beat it out of here before we get going."

Benedict stared at him. "Don't——" he cried.

"Now, get going, boy," the trooper said impatiently. His jaw was wadded with tobacco. "You oughtn't be hanging around with n-----s anyhow. Don't you know any better?" He squinted cynically at Benedict and shot a stream of juice out of the door. "Where was you hiding, boy, when they was passing out brains?"

117

Benedict pulled himself together, and said, with great reasonableness: "Mother Burns isn't here. She's out picking dandelions for a salad for supper, I think. Wait till she comes back. Don't put her furniture out on the road. She'll be awfully shocked when she comes back and finds it out on the road. She's an old lady."

"She's going to be shocked anyhow, son," the Sheriff said, entering the room. "We don't make the orders, son. We just carry them out. Besides," he added with a touch of grimness, "it's better this way. No bawling, scratching and clawing!"

"But can't you wait until——"

"Why, we're on schedule, son."

"But, can't you——"

"Now, get out of the *way*, boy."

He felt the need to establish his legality.

"Ask Father Dahr of St. Joseph's who I am!"

"Boy, if you don't move, I'm going to carry you out with the furniture!"

"I tend Mass every Sunday there. They know me. Ask *them!* Father Dahr knows Mother Burns, too. She's studying to be a Catholic. She's an old lady. I'm teaching her the catechism. She hasn't got nowhere to go, she's an old lady!"

The Sheriff put his hand on Benedict's shoulder.

"Son," he said, "you ought to be a woman, you talk so much! Now, be a good boy and take your feet out of here. This ain't got nothing to do with religion. Everybody got a letter asking them to be out of the premises on such-and-such a time and on such-a-such a day, which happens to be *to*day. The law's the law —you got to get to learn that early, son. The Company owns this property, it can do anything it damned well wants with it. And if you don't get the hell out of it in two seconds flat I'm going to arrest you for trespassing. You *furstay* English? Now, lift your behind!" And he gave Benedict a shove that shot him, like a bullet, to the door. He fell against the jamb.

"Ask Father Dahr!" he cried. "*He* knows who I am. I tend Mass there!"

"I don't care if you're the Pope hisself!" The Sheriff picked Benedict up by the back of his coat and helped him, more gently now, out of the open door. Benedict fell flat into the ashes and pulled himself slowly up, shocked at how soiled his clothes were. He rubbed the wet ashes off. He heard St. Joseph's bell tolling, and the sound came to him weakly, as though from another world. He stood in the alley, listening with a frown; and then for no reason a verse which he had composed in seventh grade and which had been printed in a Catholic paper came to him:

Atheists may break God's laws,
Their minds and souls and hearts destroy;
But I am strong in faith because
I am a Roman Catholic boy!

He shook all over. His mouth tasted bitter, and his tongue hurt: he remembered how he had collapsed in the road, and the same bottomless feeling returned. He reached out his hand and caught the trooper's hand and began to jabber to him: "You should believe me, for I never lie: you mustn't be cruel——" And he went sprawling into the dust, knocked so that he twirled like a top on his face and his teeth bit into the sour ashes. He lay paralyzed with the cold taste of the ashes in his mouth. He had locked his hands behind his head; his knees were drawn up. Suddenly he jumped to his feet and began to run insanely down the alley, his face smeared, his eyes burning from the ashes and wide with terror, crashing blindly into poles and trees and walls. He heard his own voice whimpering in his ears. His head hung, too heavy to raise, and his eyes seemed to ball out like grapes and hang loosely from their sockets. His mouth was open and spit dripped helplessly over his chin and his tongue lay flat.

Then he saw her coming. She was pushing a big hand-cart in front of her, and her dark frenzied face was concentrated in an agony of effort. She went puffing by him and he couldn't open his mouth to call her. He watched her go, safe in the doorway, her old skirt kicked into froth by her skinny running legs. His arms began to shake and then his mouth ached with his chattering teeth. Then he sat down and dropped his head into the pool of his arms.

St. Joseph's bell clamored its last note, and the iron silence closed over the entire valley.

After a while, he walked on up the hill and found a hidden place there from which he could look down. Hand-carts, wagons and Model-T Ford trucks carried the last of the furniture away— carried some of it up along the road into the woods where the evicted had set up a tent colony. Darkness came. Then the hot-metal cars appeared from around the ridge in the distance, moved unsteadily into place, and shuddered still. A dark little worker-sprite, almost invisible at this distance and this time of evening, moved in and out among the cars. Suddenly one of the bowls shifted and slowly began to tilt. For a moment it offered itself like a gigantic caked eye to view; then the eye split and a yellow cut appeared. Then the hot boulder lazily eased itself out of the car and slowly began to roll. It rolled half way down the hill before a big yellow chunk broke off and leaped high into the air. The ball gathered speed and turned round and round like a fiery wheel, sending off enormous sparks to light the evening up. Then it suddenly bounded into the sky, lifting its fiery wheel far off the slide, and leaped across the long yellow grave of the Ditch and crashed into the first dark shack. A flame leaped up into the sky, enveloping the tiny shack, which appeared miraculously for a brief moment complete and untouched within the flames; then the fire consumed it, and a sudden smoke rose quickly out of the immolation and twisted, huge and golden, into the night.

But before the shack was gone, another rushing ball came tearing down the side from the second car; it disintegrated before it reached the row, and long fingers of running fire reached across the buried Ditch and groped at the foundations of the huts. And then another swept down the hill, and at the crucial moment of contact disintegrated into flame and lava and burst like a shuddering bomb over the row of shacks. They began to burn furiously. Smoke rose hastily. And then another and another roaring ball crashed down the slope. The huts collapsed in raging fire and were quickly inundated by the liquid slag.

The valley lit up with flame. People watched quietly in a huge amphitheatre along the hills. Darkness settled gingerly on the flames. The huts melted into the fire one by one until the whole area was raging. The train up on the hill left, only to be replaced immediately by another. And again the fiery balls rolled and bounded down the slide and swept over the ashes of the huts. Then, fantastically, there were no huts left at all: not even scars or ashes, for they had all been consumed, and where the row of huts had been was now only the smoking lava. Already the boulders had passed on.

And then, as suddenly as it began, the trains departed, and night quickly settled on the valley. And the people remained on the hillside. Then, one by one, as though shaken out of a heavy dream, they walked sleep-footed down the hill, meeting each other ghostly in the darkness. Doors slammed shut, and up and down the streets came the last haunted cries of mothers for children who had not come home: "Al—bert! Be—la! Jo-o-ey!"

14.

All week Benedict felt a weight on his heart. He couldn't shake it off. The memory of the struggle held no memory of physical pain —but a deeper pain. For he knew that in the depths of his heart he had prayed for—felt that God, perhaps, had been obliged to send—heavenly intercession. "The time of thunderbolts has passed," Father Dahr had said.

But worse than the pain or grief of martyrdom was a kind of . . . humiliation. He had not expected that.

The dispossessed had set up tents and wooden shacks far back in the woods, and among them he was sure Mother Burns also was. He helped his mother care for the twins of Mrs. Carroll who stayed two days with them until their mother could find a place for them.

There his father was, the night he came home, sitting in the kitchen holding on each knee one of the little two-year-old girls and explaining to Benedict's mother that before he came to America he had been in Africa for a year, hunting for work, and had there for the first time seen a black man. He had stared, fascinated by the dark color: but found that work was no more plentiful, though worse paid, than anywhere else: and he had set forth for America. He explained authoritatively that the intense heat darkened the skin, while the little girls ate Mother's Oats from a wooden bowl, soaking his vest and trousers.

"The sun was so hot there," he told her.

The twins' mother, a widow whose husband had died in the Mill, worked in the City taking care of little white children. Because she had a light skin and a faintly aristocratic appearance, a rich family had hired her as a nurse to their children. The prevalence of nurses among the rich had convinced Benedict that the children of the rich were all sickly. She, meanwhile, had hired an old woman to look after *her* children while she worked looking after theirs. But now the old woman was evicted, too. The children had naturally come to Benedict's mother till their own mother found a room in the City.

Benedict wasn't surprised. His mother loved children, and would have planted them like flowers all over the house if she could. He went upstairs into their bedroom where he found Joey sitting cross-legged in a corner staring at a snake—a little green garter snake that had blundered into the yard. He wanted to see it whip its tongue out—learn whether it was forked or not.

"Go downstairs, Joey," Benedict said.

"I gotta go to sleep," Joey protested without looking up.

"Go downstairs!" Benedict ordered.

Grumbling, Joey lifted himself from the floor, put the snake into a big match-box, gave Benedict a resentful look out of still-squinting eyes, and started downstairs.

"Joey!" Benedict called.

"Wha-at?" Joey asked suspiciously.

"You and that Boney made a lot of noise in church Sunday, Father told me!"

"We did not!" Joey denied fiercely. Benedict looked him steadily, with terrifying certainty, in the eye. His brother's eyelids flickered and he dropped his gaze to a bloody wart on his knuckle, which he touched gingerly.

"You think God doesn't know when you do that?" Benedict asked.

Joey shuddered slightly, and started once again to deny, but let his mouth hang open without speaking.

"I'm going to pray for you," Benedict warned, and turned away. Joey hung at the door for a long moment and then let his breath out. The door closed softly.

But no prayers came to Benedict as he kneeled before his own altar. The room smelled of chicken feathers and ammonia. His depression soaked his thoughts. His face was still scratched where he had fallen into the ashes, and the taste of the ashes somehow stayed in his mouth. He had striven humbly to attain the Beatitudes, and had been moved to destroy the barrier between dreams and reality. Christ had forever blessed those attaining and achieving that highest grace, his profoundest dream: the poor, those who mourn, the meek, the just, the merciful, the clean of heart— he was all these—the peace-makers, those who were persecuted. How many times had he received willingly the lash on his shoulders in his waking dreams, suffering for humanity's sake, the sweet Eye of Jesus on his wounds?

He had never been so confused by Evil before. Evil had been plain, though it often came in tempting form: but Evil that came with the sanction of the State was bewildering. He saw his passionate face, suffused with the knowledge and presence of Christ, uplifted to Sheriff Anderson—his sanctity visible to the naked eye —he saw that face and flinched inwardly, and the raw taste of ashes filled his mouth and his stomach began aching to turn. "Get out of here boy!" He heard the big man's voice.

He had not even had the consolation of sweet suffering. They had dismissed him as though they knew him as Mr. Brill had known him, always that way, always with the same expression half of annoyance, half of disgust!

For a moment the tiny altar, adorned today with little bunches of violets, which stood with their broken heads and dried petals in jelly glasses, took on the quality of *here*—he looked around—of home, of the room with the sharp odor of kerosene for killing bugs. He could hear his father talking downstairs, and outside the heavy boom of the Mill came like a straining heart, and somewhere in the darkness dozens of families were lying under tents waiting for morning to come. He hadn't gone after Mother Burns because, he suddenly realized, he could do nothing for her; nothing at all. She would have asked him to pray for her, he thought; and for some reason he had not wanted to be asked that.

He had never felt so helpless before, so robbed of certainty, not even in jail, though that was part of the same thing. Nor could be understand why they didn't *recognize* him—that image of him set like a stone saint in a niche of the church, directly in communion with God, clothed in shining sanctity. They, too—didn't they?—believed in God and the Church? Couldn't they see, then, that piety written on his forehead? Didn't the touch of his fingertips, dipped in how many hundreds of founts of holy water, show at all? His sacred thoughts? His prayers? Did they see him, did they *have* to see him inevitably, as only the poor hunky boy from Hunky Hollow whose shoes were torn and whose coat was old and whose face betrayed the fact that his father worked in the Mill but was laid off now and his mother couldn't speak English or read?

But he shook this picture away proudly.

"As if God cares for *them!*" he said scornfully to himself. "They'll go to Hell, those mean bas——" And this time horror drove through him like a stick. He dropped his head on his rigid hands and pressed his eyes shut and dug his words deep into his brain. "Oh, God, show me the way!" he cried. "Help me, now! Lend me Thy strength. Help me, help me——" And he felt as though the dark night of the senses was closing over him. He threw his hands up into the dark air where other hands were waiting, or were not.

Familiar steps coming up the stairs brought him abruptly to himself. Hastily he crossed himself, got up and was ready to pretend that he was just about to go to bed. Then, suddenly ashamed of his cowardice, he returned to his knees and bent his closed eyes over his clasped hands; but he was saying nothing: he was waiting for the door to open and the raucous, outrageous voice of his brother to say:

"Don't you ever wear them prayers out, Benny?"

He suppressed a shiver, crossed himself firmly, and turned. Seventeen-year-old Vince, whom he had not seen except sleeping for days, long-legged in faded dungarees, a sweat shirt, a brown neck with a big strawberry birthmark on it, a lean big-boned face with yellow eyes and hair streaked with yellow, sat down on the edge of the other bed and took out a cigarette.

"No, I don't," Benedict said sullenly.

Vince laughed. He blew a thick dangling, somehow sensual, smoke-ring into the room, stretched himself, dragging his hands luxuriously along his thighs and across the bulge, mockingly, yawned and sighed. Benedict flushed. Vince looked at him with his alligator eyes and extended a cigarette. Benedict turned contemptuously: Vince laughed again.

"Ah, horse-shit, Benny," he said tolerantly, "why don't you level off a little. Jesus, I never seen a kid so nuts about religion!"

He took a pair of dice from his tight hip pockets and blew on them. He caressed the dice with a look of love on his face. "Watch!" he said mysteriously. He rattled the cubes against his ear, and moaned elaborately: "Come to Papa, baby!"—threw, and a seven turned up. "Want to play?" he asked innocently.

Benedict didn't answer.

Vince rattled the dice again, kissed them with a loud smack, and threw. Again up turned a seven. The red shining dice looked like sin incarnate to Benedict. Still, as he watched, he felt a terrifying temptation to giggle.

"They'll come up seven every time," Vince went on significantly, "even if *you* throw them. Want to try? No? Them's educated dice. Been to college. Look." Again he tossed them, this time carelessly with a flip of the wrist, giving them full freedom to dare to come up any other way, and again the seven came up. "Almost got killed last night," he said, examining the dice, and fitting them together. "Some sucker didn't trust my dice and wanted to look at 'em."

"Are you going to go to confession this Saturday?" Benedict asked grimly.

"Okay," Vince said offhand.

"You promised Mama. At least don't double-cross her!"

"All right, all right!" Vince had a superstitious love for his mother. "Didn't I say I would? Don't stick them little pitchforks in me yet. You ain't got me in Hell yet!"

"And that's where you'll go!" Benedict cried.

"Aa," the other replied uncomfortably, "when I'm dead I'll stay dead."

"How do you *know?*" Benedict asked intensely.

Vince lifted his gleaming narrow eyes. "You'd be *glad* to know I was roasting in Hell right now, wouldn't you, Benny?"

"No," Benedict answered.

"Then why do you keep——"

"Because you were born a Catholic!" Benedict cried passionately. "You took your first communion and confession, and you went to a Catholic school! That's why! Because you're becoming a bum and you'll land in jail, or even worse!"

"Jail?" Vince said slyly. "Heard *you* were in jail, Benny? But I know that's a lie!"

Benedict turned a dull red, and closed his lips.

"Christ Almighty!" Vince swore, while Benedict flinched. "When I heard that, I like to drop dead in my tracks! Benny, you almost got your wish—I almost landed in Hell right then and there! Benny in jail—*our* Benny? *Im*possible! By Jesus, it scared me so much I almost got religion myself. I said to Pogy: 'When they start putting people like Benny in jail and let no-good bastards like you and me walk around free, then that's the beginning of the end!' Pogy turned green thinking about it." His expression of broad humor relaxed. "What'd they put you in for, Benny?"

Flushing deeper, Benedict reluctantly explained: "Somebody thought I swiped a wagon. They let me go when they found out I didn't."

"I'll be damned," Vince said, frankly shocked. "Didn't they *know* about you! *You* swipe a wagon? You wouldn't swipe a breeze in a windstorm! Them jerks don't know their ass from a hole in the ground, Benny, putting you in the jug! You don't belong in places like that, Benny, any more than I belong in church—the hoosegow's my rightful home, people like me belong in it, not you."

"Don't kid, Vince," Benny said with a little reluctant smile.

"I'm *serious!*"

Benedict watched Vince's smoking cigarette moodily. He felt, somehow, as though the energy had gone out of his long struggle with Vince. "I don't care," he said to himself; but the very next moment, said aloud: "You're *dumb*, Vince, you're real dumb! You think you found out the answers to everything, because you're not afraid to smoke, to gamble, or to—well, but there *is* a God, and there *is* punishment for sin, and there *is* life after death. Suppose there wasn't? Wouldn't the thieves and the robbers and the murderers, and everybody with evil power rule the world? If they weren't afraid of something?"

Vince looked at him cynically. "What makes you think they don't now?"

"They don't," Benedict said confidently. He thought of Sheriff Anderson, and cried more fiercely: "They *don't!*"

Vince rubbed his face. "Aa, I don't know," he said, with sudden sincerity. "I don't know nothing about nothing! I just don't know a thing!" He turned to Benedict and cried: "And neither do you!" He fondled the dice, threw them and said: "That's what I count on. I *know* they're going to turn up seven every time, and as long as there's suckers in the world who don't know about loaded dice, I'm going to hunt them out, and they're going to hunt me out, and we're going to play a game together. And me, I'm always going to know that them dice will turn up seven every time; and them, they're going to know nothing—just that they're losing their hard-earned workingman's dough. I'm going to take it, and get me everything you can buy with money."

"Then some day somebody's going to find out that you're cheating and kill you!"

Vince shrugged and looked philosophical. "Well," he said, "in that case, I hope it's fast and sudden."

"But you'll be *dead.*"

And again Vince shrugged. "You can pray for me," he said.

He stared bitterly, however, into his thoughts; laughed, then, shrugged, turned to Benedict and the same teasing sly smile returned to his eyes. "You ought to seen the pair of tits I seen walking down street this afternoon," he said rolling his eyes ecstatically, but waching Benedict at the same time. He did loops in the air. "Like that! Milk-cans like that, I'm telling you!" He pretended that Benny was hard to convince. "Swear to God, Benny!" he cried, turning his eyes to heaven. "I followed her a mile just to watch how she swung 'at thing!"

"Shut up, Vince," he begged in a hoarse voice.

Vince went on. "Je-*sus!*" he cried. "Ba-*by,* I could hardly walk, I was so *in*terested; I mean *in*terested! Then she turned around and give me the high sign! I'd a followed her to hell and back, but I had to catch a floating crap game down by the river with my trusty dice."

He pulled out a small wad of bills, and started counting them ostentatiously.

"Yep," he said. "Suckers born every second!" He yawned. "My hands get tired out just raking it in." He picked a dollar up, looked at it with disapproval and tossed it on the floor. "How'd that get in?" he demanded. "That's hoor-money, you can smell it!" He looked at Benedict professionally. "Throw it out when you get time, Benny."

Benedict snickered. "Show-off," he said.

"Aa, horse-shit, Reverend," Vince said, and stretched out his lean hard legs and then bent over to undo his shoes. "I ain't worrying about gettin' past the Pearly Gates," he said. "All I got to say is I'm Benny's brother and they'll open up them gates wide!"

There was a kind of strange affection in that, and Benedict frowned.

With his head bent, Vince now asked: "Pap working yet?"

"No," Benedict said. Then he added slowly: "You know about the house, don't you?"

"Yeah, Mama told me."

"Well?"

"Well, what? What do you want me to do about it?" he asked belligerently.

128

"Why don't you find a job and help Pap out?"

"Why don't you stick your nose up my ——!" he cried.

"You're no good for anybody!" Benedict shouted. "You don't *care* for anybody, not even your own family! Maybe they'll kick us out of the house, but what do you care? Why don't you go down to the Mill and get a job?"

"I'm too damned young, *furstay*, nut-head?" Vince replied hotly. "They don't want to take me. I got to be eighteen!"

"Tell them you're eighteen!"

"That's all you know about getting a job!" Vince said with contempt. "Don't worry, don't worry," he added bitterly. "If the old man don't want me around anymore, I'll go! I'll go on the bum! Lots of guys do it—I'm tired of sticking around this two-bit burg where everybody knows who you are and you got to kiss the ass of the Chief of Police to walk down the street! We even got to give him a rake-off on our crap games! This ain't the whole world! I'll go to New York or Chicago, change my name—you'll see! After a year or two I'll come back with a roll of bills big enough to choke a horse!"

"Nobody's telling you to leave home."

"No? Then what the hell were you suggesting?"

"Not that. I just want you to help with the house——"

"What can I do? I can get a job right now in Clairville if I want to! At eight bucks a day!"

"What?" Benedict cried.

"Sure, if I want to scab! The mine's down on strike, and a guy come around when we were playing up on the hill and said we could make eight bucks a day. Would you want me to do that?"

"Papa would kill you."

"So all right, then!" He looked bitterly down at his lean brown hands. "So I'll keep on giving Mama what dough I make. She don't have to know where I get it. Yeah, *this* dough! All right, you can spit on it, but it's still money. You want to be holy with your ass sticking out of your pants? Even the priests don't turn down this money."

Benedict began to take his clothes off. The silence boiled between them. He felt he wanted to say something to that hard-set face, those tight lips, those yellow eyes that were almost blank with bitterness, that would make everything dissolve. Even if it was only to make him jeer again.

"I'll go to confession with you, Saturday," he promised. "You'll feel better."

Vince looked across to him and his eyes snapped.

"Yeah," he said. "And if I don't? Do I get my money back?"

"You're going to go, aren't you?"

"If I feel like it."

"Don't give up your religion, Vince," Benedict said earnestly. "Some day you'll need it, and it'll help you."

"Go to bed."

Vince crushed the cigarette out on the iron bedstead and stretched out. Joey slipped into the room. When Vince saw him he jumped out of bed and caught him by the shoulder. "You little bastard!" he yelled. "If I ever catch you smoking butts again, I'll tan your ass till you can't sit on it for a week!"

Joey shook. Vince turned to Benedict and cried with profound indignation. "I caught him smoking the other day! That little seven-year-old bastard! Smoking already! Go to bed!" he cried, letting Joey loose and smacking him across his lean knobby buttocks. "And say your goddamned prayers! Make him say them *all*, Benny! And you say them," he yelled threateningly at Joey, who was already down on hs knees, "or I'll beat the living piss out of you!"

"Say your prayers," Benedict ordered.

"*All* of them?" Joey asked timidly, with his clasped hands over his face.

After supper, Saturday, Benedict said tensely to Vince. "It's time to go to church. You said you'd go today," he added quickly. "He said he'd go today," he repeated to his mother.

She looked appealingly at Vince.

"All right, all right," he mumbled with a persecuted look.

His mother chewed a hard piece of meat and then poked the chewed hunk into Rudolph's mouth.

"Go with him," she urged Benedict.

130

"I can go alone. I don't need a bodyguard," Vince protested sulkily.

His father came in with a basket of dandelions. He looked at the two older boys and they fell silent. He stared at Vince, whom he hadn't seen all week. "Bum," he said finally, like a bark. Vince cast him a yellow-eyed side-glance of defiance. "Bum know where come eat," his father said in English. "To eat he know how come home!"

Vince gripped his fists.

"But for work—don't know where home is."

"Don't start on me, Papa," Vince said in a low, warning voice, his eyes narrowed, long straight lines tensing his face.

His father looked at him. "What?" he said heavily. "What you say, Mr. American's Bum? You speak to me like that," he added in Lithuanian. "Look at me like that with your eyes of an assassin?" He lifted his hand and struck him. "Gambler, bum, no-good! Come home and eat when I'm out of work, when I don't eat myself so you'll eat—you, you——" And he lifted his arm again. His mother let out a short cry as Vince raised his fist. She held the little boy up and turned his face into her shoulder.

"Don't raise your hand to your father!" she cried hoarsely.

The old man struck and Vince staggered against the wall. He stood tensely for a moment, his arms and fists cocked; and then, with a crooked white smile to his mother, he lowered his hands and bent his head, while his father rained blows on him crying: "Go, go—hit your father! Hit old mans! He give you food, clothes, you grow up, American boy, smart now!" And he struck harder, and Vince crouched against the wall with his face lowered. He had put his hands into his pockets. He took blow after blow without flinching, waiting until the blows ceased; and finally when his father fell back exhausted and sat down panting at the table, with his head weaving back and forth as though it had lost its socket, he lifted his head, took one anguished look at his mother, and left the house. Benedict followed him.

He trailed Vince through the back yard, and up through the ditch. He called: "Vince!"

His brother turned a white, bruised face back and cried bitterly: "Go on back home! Get away from me! Get out of my sight!"

"Your confession!" Benedict faltered.

"Go home!" Vince yelled, "I don't want to have to hurt you!" Then he turned and began to run. Benedict ran after him, over a back fence, through a barking yard, down through another alley, just keeping the lanky shape in sight ahead of him. His brother threw back looks of fury, shaking his fist. But still Benedict hung on grimly, driven by some fear he only sensed, but crying doggedly: "You promised to go!"

And as he clambered over still another fence he fell into the waiting arms of his brother hiding there, who then took him by the throat and backed him against the fence, banging his head, crying: "Stop—following—me! You—son—of a—bitch! Go—home!"

His eyes stretched wildly apart, gasping, Benedict croaked: "Let me go, Vince."

Vince took him by the hair and knocked him to the ground and rubbed his face in the dirt. "I don't want you following me," he said hoarsely. "I hate you, your priests and this whole stinking town!"

Benedict choked and tears burnt his eyes. He caught hold of Vince's ankles and gripped them with both arms.

"Stay home, Vince," he begged. "Don't run away!"

Vince kicked viciously.

Benedict turned his smeared face up, and cried: "Please don't run away, Vince! I know you're going to! Stay with us! I'll help you!"

"You!" Vince sneered. "You gonna preach to me! Go home! I don't want none of your help. Just let me be—let me live my own life like I want to! I don't want to see any of you anymore! You make me sick!" he cried, jerking his foot away. Benedict held on to the other one, as Vince dragged him along.

"Let go!" Vince cried, staring down at him, and lifting his foot. Benedict closed his eyes, feeling the foot come down on his head; he gritted his teeth and Vince pushed with his foot.

"Come with me, Vince," Benedict said, between his teeth. "Come to confession. Father Dahr will help. Father Brumbaugh will help. Please, Vince—don't leave us! Stay with us, Vince, Papa didn't mean it! He's out of work and he's worried, that's all. Stay home, Vince!"

He sobbed suddenly and Vince broke away, and he lay flat on the ground trying to get up finally on his hands and knees, and crawling along the ditch as though his legs were broken, and looking up at last for the sight of him, and seeing only a gray cow plodding along down the alley with a long silver rope falling from its great open nose.

PART TWO

1.

Ho, Joe Magarac!

Joe Magarac was eight feet tall, sometimes ten feet, and sometime even twelve. He came to America during the late eighties or in the years before the first World War from a country in Middle or South Europe—from Slovakia, or Bohemia or Serbia. The American entrepreneur had come to his village, just as he had come to all the others, and described in the most glowing terms how well people lived in America, how great the opportunities for jobs were, how easy life was with the golden streets and the great-hearted industrialists who loved no one more tenderly than greenhorns and paid no one more handsomely for their services.

Joe laughed thunderously so that the wheat in the fields a mile away bent as though a wind had charged through it. He felt cramped in the little village of his birth: he needed room for his expanding muscles, he wanted mountains, big rivers, giant trees. So he signed the bargain with the agent, made his X so huge they had to use a whole side of the page to contain it, and parted with his mother's and half his own life-time's savings. Then he walked 500 miles in five days to Antwerp, and found, like the others there, that the agent had rooked him and absconded with his money, and the ticket was no good.

Ai, Joe Magarac!

Joe was wonderfully good-natured and long-suffering as everyone knew, and seldom grew angry. But this was one of those times. He didn't understand English, nor Dutch. All he knew was that he had paid for his passage to golden America, that he was almost penniless; and so when they tried to bar him from going aboard

134

the steamer, he shoved the little men aside, and picking up two or three likewise stranded fellow countrymen under his big arms, stomped aboard.

And this was how Joe Magarac came to America.

He came to Pittsburgh where a relative of his, a puny little man, four feet, nine inches tall, his uncle, in fact, lived. His uncle took him down to the Mill Employment Office next morning, and when the employment officer laid eyes on Joe Magarac he drooled with pleasure for the Company's sake, and signed Joe, without any bother, to the labor gang in the Mill.

That was how easy it was to get a job in America!

The first thing they did was build a special wheelbarrow for Joe. The ordinary ones were too small. This one was ten feet long and five wide, and Joe picked it up as though it were a kiddie-car, and rolled it down through the Mill, filled with clay, or iron ore, or lime stone. When they were ready to tap a furnace, the foreman would yell: "Where's Joe Magarac?" and Joe would come wobbling over to the furnace, and with a poke of his finger unseal the tap and let the molten steel go free. When they had a train of cars filled with the bubbling soup, the foreman yelled: "Where's Joe Magarac?"——and Joe would come running to push the train out of the yard to the rolling mill.

The Company appreciated Joe Magarac—Joe Jack-Ass. He worked like the devil and never complained. Every shift he came to work, the Company would lop off a couple dozen men from the payroll, and give their work to Joe to do. The Mill had two 12-hour shifts, and sometimes when work was heavy, they'd let Joe forget to go home and he would work the clock around; and because Joe couldn't read any English they paid him for only 12 hours. What could Joe do with the money anyhow except drink it up? And when Joe got drunk, he roared up and down the valley like a tornado, knocking down telephone poles and pushing horses into the ditch.

He boarded with the other greenhorns in the boarding-house down by the Mill, and they had to cut out the side of the house to let Joe's legs stretch out. He had the dinner table all to himself when he came down to eat, and this is what Widow Dodracik gave him to eat every morning: ten loaves of sour-dough bread, a whole roasted pig, fourteen dozens of eggs, eighteen gallons of coffee, six pounds of butter, and three barrels of beer. Even so in the beginning he lost a little weight.

Now, as Joe got used to working in the Mill, the Company began to appreciate him even more. They had him lay 30 miles of track single-handed. They brought him red-hot tracks out of the rolling mill and loaded them smoking on Joe's shoulders. He ran off with them to the job, threw down the ties, laid the burning tracks over them, and spit a handful of spikes to nail them down. Then he lifted a locomotive and set it on the tracks and pushed it 25 miles up the valley.

Ho, Joe Magarac!

Then they had him move a mill across the river. He put it on his shoulders and waded through the water to the other side, and came back to carry a dinkey over the same way. Ho, Joe Magarac! the people cried.

After Joe had worked for the Company ten years they gave him a medal.

Ai, Joe Magarac!

The Company sent a hundred agents back to Joe's home country to scour the land for others like Joe. They were proud of Joe. Ho, Joe Magarac! rang up and down the Mill; and rang loudest and fondest in the offices of the Company. For he never complained. He had a great big Slovak grin on his big face, and his yellow-clay hair hung down over it. He picked up a freight car, grunted, and yelled: "Ho, Joe Magarac!"—and up and down the Mill like an echo rang the cry, Ho, Joe Magarac! He never complained, he worked all day and all night, too, if they wanted him, took what wages they gave him, never got sick, never got hurt. He never learned English, except for just the English he should know: "I'm do, Boss!" "Yes, boss, right away!" "Dank you, Boss!" "All right, Boss!" "Mr. Boss, okay, I do!"

Ho, Joe Magarac. . . .

And then one day, Joe Magarac got tired. He woke that morning and didn't get out of bed. Widow Dodracik shook him and teased him and threw water on him, but he wouldn't get up. He just lay there, with his eyes closed. When the Company heard that Joe Magarac was still in bed, and half the day gone, they sent a foreman to wake Joe up. The foreman yelled at Joe: "Joe, get up! Got work to do!"—and for the first time, Joe didn't grin and respond: "I'm do, Boss!" He just lay there.

So they sent the superintendent, and the superintendent promised Joe another medal, and even dropped a tear in memory of Joe's mother, but still Joe wouldn't budge. So they sent for a doctor to examine his mind. Then they sent for the police. The cops came from the town, and from the next town as well. They came with a big wagon, and they brought along clubs and chains and guns. They knocked the bed from under Joe and forced him out, still half-asleep, into the street, and chaining him to the wagon, they dragged him down to the Mill.

And when Joe got into the Mill, he opened his eyes, and saw that he wasn't in his own bed. He got mad. *Ho!* he cried. He broke the chains off his arms, kicked the foreman so that he flew across the river and landed in a mud-hole, and sat down on top of the blast furnace and crossed his legs.

And then he went back to sleep.

Joe Magarac slept on the top of the blast furnace for one month. There wasn't any work in the whole valley for the whole month that Joe Magarac had his Big Sleep. Everybody in the valley walked around on tiptoe so as not to wake up Joe Magarac. His snores were like thunder and shook the houses for miles up and down. He put one foot in the river and dammed it up. The workers stayed home and drank beer, and every morning they woke up they looked out of the window to see if Joe Magarac was still sitting on the top of the blast furnace, snoring away, sleeping like a mountain.

And that month nobody got hurt in the Mill, and no widows were made.

The Company men went crazy out of their minds. They racked their brains for some way to wake Joe Magarac up. But at the same time they were afraid to wake him because waking him might kindle his wrath.

Never had there been such peace in the valley. Never had

the workers rested so much. They came to know their wives and learned the names of their children. They even had picnics on the hills they used to see while working in the Mill. And every morning they woke up wondering if Joe was still resting there, and while he rested, they rested; and the valley was quiet. Ho, Joe!

And then Joe Magarac, on the thirtieth day of his Big Sleep, yawned, stretched out his arms, and a big wind rushed down the valley knocking over trees; and then he stretched his legs and pushed his hands through the clouds and made it rain. So the rain woke him up. And he yelled: "Ho, Joe Magarac!"—and the windows in the valley rattled, and the workers turned to their wives, and the children yelled: "Joe Magarac has woke up!"

He went back to work. And the Company officials sighed and shook their heads and worried about the profits lost and yelled at the workers and pushed Joe as though he were in Hell.

And all the time they had nightmares in their sleep, turning in their beds with the Great Fear that Joe Magarac, the willing Jack-Ass, would one day again grow tired and take his Big Sleep. And so *they* did not sleep well in their fine beds.

Ho, Joe Magarac!

2.

When the workers received a mimeographed letter in the mail, typed in English, Hungarian, Slovak, Russian, Lithuanian and Polish and signed, "Joe Magarac," laughter swept up and down the houses.

The letter was a brief factual description of the situation. It confirmed the news that the Company had indeed decided to fill up the Hollow with slag in order to get several acres of good level land near the river and to the railroad cheaply. It confirmed the fact that the Bank had been quietly buying up the mortgages it didn't already hold; that it had been doing so for years now, and had dated the maturation periods uniformly so that most of them fell in July while the others fell in December. It confirmed the fact that the Bank offered to buy back any property at face value. Then it made the point that in buying up the property the Bank was receiving for practically nothing the streets, alleys and fields. Nobody in the City Council, which happened to be filled with company officials, thought to raise this matter in agreeing to the Company's proposal. The letter pointed out, further, that the property which the Mill would receive from the Bank was already paid for by the Government through an amortization scheme which the Company had demanded as its price for producing steel for the army. That, in fact, when you came down to it, all this land would be an outright gift by the Government to the Company. The letter added that workers who were hard to deal with were being laid off, and so persuaded to sell their property while they could—or have it sold for taxes. Joe Magarac declared that a union existed in the Mill, and that it would fight back. And this letter was signed, "Joe Magarac."

Already thirteen families had sold to the Company and moved out of the Hollow. Not until the moving trucks drove up to the Bogich's place did anyone feel uneasy. And when the truck drove away, piled high with furniture, panic swept up and down the streets. Bogich's house had been almost completely paid up, and he had jumped at the Company's offer to buy at face. He immediately bought another house (from the Bank) in the City. The twelve others followed quickly after. And those left behind, with heavy mortgages, interest that compounded itself, or small down payments, knew that the few empty houses in the City were being snatched up. There was nowhere to go.

"Well," Benedict's father said, taking off his glasses and looking blindly about the room. "Where can we go, then? For us there's nowhere."

He looked out of the window into the garden, where the spring onions were already high enough to put into a salad. Benedict was coaching Joey in his catechism. Joey was sucking on his wart and racking his brain.

"What is the Fourth Commandment?" Benedict read sonorously.

"Honor thy father and mother," Joey answered.

"What does the Fourth Commandment tell us to do?"

Joey bit a piece of his wart and spit it out.

"The Fourth Commandment tells us——?" Benedict prompted.

"——tells us——" repeated Joey, squinting his eyes conscientiously and searching the ceiling.

"——tells us——" Benedict urged.

"——to believe?" asked Joey.

"No," Benedict replied, "——to obey our father and mother."

"That's right," Joey said, relieved.

"Must we be kind to our parents?" asked Benedict. Joey searched Benedict's stern eyes for a hint. "To our father and mother —that's what 'parents' means," supplemented Benedict. "Should we always be nice to them—you know, not bother them?"

Joey nodded cautiously, ready to retreat if Benedict frowned.

"Is it wrong to talk back to our parents?" Benedict asked grimly.

"No," Joey said abruptly, and as Benedict's acid eyes turned on him he said meekly, "You do."

Benedict turned the page.

"What is the Seventh Commandment?" he asked significantly.

"The Seventh? Seventh?" Joey toyed.

"The Seventh."

"Thou shalt not——"

"*Steal!*" Benedict's voice crashed down.

"Oh," Joey said, his head creeping down into his shoulders.

"What does the Seventh Commandment tell us?" Benedict demanded.

Joey looked at his father who was whittling a rung to fit into a chair. Rudolph was lying on the floor and the cat was licking his hair slick on his head.

"The Seventh Commandment tells us never to take what belongs to somebody else. Remember that! Now, what must people do that steal?"

"People that steal," Joey swallowed, his eyes circling the room.

"Must——?" prodded Benedict.

His father looked over to them, turning his grizzled orange face from the light of the window. "Mr. Teacher," he said.

140

Benedict flushed. "I'm busy, Papa," he said.

"Let Joey take rest. Now, I'm ask leetle question, Mr. Teacher." The faintly taunting humble tone made Benedict bite his lip.

"You say, 'Joey, you no steal. No good, you steal, Joey.' Good, good!" He wagged a thick finger at Joey. "Joey," he said sternly, while Joey ducked his head, "you no steal! Go jail, you steal! *Supranti?*" Joey nodded dumbly. "Now," his father continued respectfully. "Now, you tell me, Mr. Fine Teacher, you tell me dis: when *Company* steal, what now dis? Who put Company in jail? When Company steal people house, what now do? You," he cried, waving his arm toward the door, "you—go down Mr. Wright, go superintendent office with catechism. You open up, show him. You say: 'Mr. Wright, Boss, I'm show you somet'ing,' you say like you say to Joey, and you show in book, 'Here,' you say, 'dis Seventh Commandment, you see! What *is*,' you ask Big Boss. 'What say? NO STEAL,' it say. 'No steal worker's house! No steal, somnabitch!' you say. 'God say no steal house! Give back workers him house, give back him job, give back life, Mr. Wright, Big Boss, Company Boss!' You say him, Benediktas, to Company," he cried passionately, his chest heaving. "Then come tell me what *Company* say!"

"It's different," Benedict replied, not looking at his father.

"You tell me, Mr. Fine Teacher," he asked respectfully.

Benedict turned to Joey. "What was the answer?" he demanded.

Joey opened his mouth, his eyes on his father.

"Ah, Joey," his father cried, raising his big hands and lowering them tolerantly, "you take rest!"

Joey's mouth closed obediently. Rudolph began to crawl under the stove pulling the cat by the tail.

His father caught the little boy by the shoulder and separated him from the cat. "Go, go," he said, patting him on the seat and picking up the cat and speaking to it, as he always did, formally, and in English: "Mr. Cat," he said, "maybe you tell me, no?" He flicked its ears with his finger and then put it back on the floor. "Take walk," he ordered. Benedict's mother entered the room on her way to the garden.

His father jerked his head at Benedict.

"What you got say?"

"Papa," Benedict said quietly, "don't ask me like that! You made Vince run away; don't make me!"

His father's face became deadly still for a moment, staring at him; then it twitched.

"What you say?" he demanded in a low, rumbling voice. "You say I make Wince run 'way! You say dat!" He leaned forward. "No, I no tell Wince run 'way!" He brought his fist down on the table with a heavy thud. "I tell Wince *stay home!* He t'ink himself run 'way! Long time t'ink about dat! Not today, not odder day— long time he t'ink!"

He lifted his finger and slowly shook it. His blue-gray eyes looked at Benedict sharply.

"He come back! You t'ink he find bread on ground, walk over, pick up? Pick up like dat? No, no! Work, work, work! Always work for bread!" He threw his arm in a big circle to include the world. "Everywhere work for bread! He find out. Smart American—he come home, say, 'Papa, give me eat, I'm hungry!' You see what I say!"

"I have to go," Benedict said. "Mama," he added as his mother re-entered the room with cut green onions, "I have to be at church."

"Benedict!" his father cried. "What priest say?"

"Eat something first," his mother urged. He shook his head.

"What say?" his father repeated.

"About what, Papa?" Benedict said patiently.

"About Company buy house, kick out everyones?"

Proudly, a little contemptuously, Benedict replied: "Father Dahr says he'll never sell the church. So," he shrugged, "the people don't have to sell their houses either."

"A--h?" his father cried, with his voice rising. "And what *young* priest say?"

Benedict was surprised. "What?" he asked. He answered slowly: "I didn't ask, Papa." He said confidently: "But he feels the same way as Father Dahr. You can't *sell* a church," he said simply.

His father shrugged. "Ah?" he cried, and tapped his forehead and tilted his head. "How you know?" He shook his head with a knowing smile, and then his voice going back to recall, his mother listening, wiping her hands in her aprons, her face softening at the tone of his voice: "Benediktas," he said in his own language, "I will tell you a story, and the story is about you. So it's been with you all your life. You will not remember it." He placed both hands along his thighs, lifted them and pushed his glasses back on his nose, and smiled a little sadly, wisely: "I remember this day, for you were five years old. I was coming home from work in the Mill, and it was raining. And as I am walking along, I see a little boy standing in the rain, and he's bitterly crying. What could the little boy be crying for? I ask myself, and I draw near. Then I see that it's you."

He stopped and looked, rather than at Benedict, at his mother; and she was gazing with a gleaming tear in her eye at the kitchen-stove. Joey was listening with surprise and awe to these remote and magical events, and a faraway look came into his eyes, and his mouth softly fell open. The cat had hidden under a chair, and Rudolph was reaching a fat hand for it.

His father smiled patiently, gently. " 'Why are you crying?' I ask: and you lift up your eyes full of tears and you point down to the puddle in front of you. 'It's dirty!' you said. 'Yes,' I said to you, 'it's dirty.' Then you pointed at your beautiful new white shoes that we bought for you for the Mill picnic, and you wept: 'If I walk through the puddle, they'll get dirty!' Oh, what a wise little boy!" he cried ironically, and Benedict felt his blood moving. "Oh, what a smart leetle American boys," his father relapsed momentarily into his broken English. "And you were right! But as you cried standing there and tried to make up your mind whether to walk through the puddle and spoil your shoes—the rain was melting your nice new straw hat!"

He spread out his hands and shoulders, and then lifted his head and laid it over his right shoulder. "That's a parable," he said quietly. His mother smiled, with a longing sadness, and put her hand on his head and stroked it. Joey's mouth hung open and he looked at Benedict with a long stare as though new depths had been revealed. And Benedict stood flushing.

"I don't remember that," he mumbled.

"Of course not!" his father readily agreed. His eyes clouded, and he turned, almost sullenly, away from Benedict, and resumed his whittling, brooding on the wood.

The story had stung him, but he didn't know why. He shrugged swiftly. The world of the Church beckoned as though in the next room, through which he could slip in a moment and be transformed. Already he could see *this* room, this kitchen, the tiny window, Joey staring at his bloody wart, Rudolph crawling after the cat, which hissed at him, his mother going with a bemused expression on her face to the stove and lifting the lid on the pot of soup—as though from some elongated distance of gentle benedictory hands and bowed pious heads. He saw himself *there*, suddenly through the eyes of his mother, standing tall and slim in a black cassock, detached from everything worldly, solitary, meditative, purified. He longed for that vision, his arms in his thoughts stretched out for it; he wanted that dark solitary form to lift its head and smile for him. He longed for it even more intensely since the events of the last days. "Oh, God," he pleaded, "let time pass fast! Let the day come quickly!"

"No," his father said suddenly, staring at all of them. "We won't move because we cannot move. We'll stay here!"

He turned his look then remotely on Benedict.

"What we do, Mr. Fine Teacher," he said. "Tell Fadder what we do?"

"Nobody's going to make us move," Benedict answered, with his head lowered.

"Who tell you *dat?*" his father demanded heavily, sarcastically. "Boss come write you letter?"

Benedict shook his head.

"Mama," his father said, turning to her from the stove and looking at her with a slightly-embarrassed, serious smile. "Mama," he repeated in English, "you want stay here?"

"What are you talking about?" she answered in their own language, looking self-consciously at him and avoiding Benedict's eyes. She turned back to the soup and said: "I only look from day to day. Today I'm here." She banged the wooden spoon on the pot. "Why are you frightening the children?" she said angrily.

"Joey!" he demanded suddenly so that Joey bumped, torn out of reverie. "You want to move?"

Joey nodded eagerly.

"See!" his father said mockingly. "Joey want go 'way!" He looked around for Rudolph but couldn't find him. He turned instead to Joey again and said: "You go Boss, and say, 'Joey ready to move to nice new house,' and Boss give you kick in ass!"

Joey looked startled.

He turned to Benedict and asked softly: "And you, you want to move?"

Benedict looked at him intensely and replied: "No, Papa."

His father jerked up his head. "You don't want to go? You tell me, now, how you gonna stay? How you gonna keep Company from kick you out?"

Benedict stared at his father and then said as profoundly as he could: "Papa, if the church tells the Company not to—they won't! Because, Papa, they are Christians and Catholics, too. The Church would forbid them throwing people out without homes——"

His father's eyes were heavy on him, and his voice faltered; he paled suddenly and turned away. There was a silence in the room. Then his father spoke again, and his voice had regained the same formal mocking quality it had had before. "Missus," he said turning to his mother, "you tell me, Missus, how long we live here?"

She looked at him and more angrily than before cried: "Go to sleep, are you drunk?"

He laughed; turned to Benedict and said: "No, not unhappy for us those first years," smiling as though Benedict would refute it. There was a gentleness, even an understanding in his voice, that brought Benedict back to him, to listen. He had been thinking of those burning shacks! His father's voice grew softer, and the language, in magical contrast to his English, came fluently and well; and he seemed, as he always seemed to Benedict when he spoke in his own language, to be an entirely different man, a man hidden away behind the tongue, full of feeling and a kind of odd, foreign wisdom.

"Some days were good," he said. "I worked 10-12 hours a day, but I saved money. I married." He stretched out a hand to Benedict's mother to show who it was he had married. "I placed the first payment on this house——" he slapped the wall and the sound stung on Benedict's ears—— "I soon had two children——" He paused; he looked at Benedict as though gathering memories from him. "You were born choking," he said soberly. "I breathed my own breath into you." His eyes clouded, Benedict looked at his mother for confirmation and she nodded her head. Joey stared hard at him again. "No, those first years were not too unhappy. I was young, I could lift a table with my teeth!" He raised an imaginary table with his hands. "During the flu epidemic everyone's children died but not mine. I thanked God for that; but I thanked secretly myself more!" He looked at Benedict at this, but Benedict made no reaction. He fixed his glasses and stared through them dimly. "In those days," he said, "in those days I had a secret thought about myself—a secret thought: it was this: that no matter what happened, where I found myself, whom I was among; if a house fell, if a building burned, if a bomb crashed, I, Vincentas Bulmanis, would always escape! That was my secret thought!"

His eyes flashed and he swung a fist through the air. His mother's head nodded bitterly and she said, almost to herself: "Ah, so, so. . . ."

"Where I got this feeling," he continued with surprise, "I don't know. In the Mill, accidents would happen all around me—a leg burnt off, an arm torn away—like a great calamity, only I would suffer no accident!" His face broke into a sudden innocent radiance that amazed Benedict. "The war," he cried, in the voice of Fate, "it ended just as my name came up in the draft; I didn't go." He opened up his arms again. "This was my feeling, then, this was what I thought: no matter what happened, what bad luck befell everyone around me, I would escape!"

He looked at Benedict's mother, his face pure and calm, but she shook her head from side to side and raised a hand to her head and leaned against it as though in woe. She closed her eyes and when she opened them again, there were iridescent stains on her eyelashes.

"I cannot explain to you why I felt this way," his father continued, in a lower, more somber tone. "I was young and could knock down a bull with my fist!" Joey looked at his fist, and his father, catching his eyes, raised it and shook it in the air. It seemed huge even to Benedict. "What was I thinking in those days?" he cried, lifting his eyes in a kind of agony, catching his breath, and recalling. "What was I thinking?" he repeated in a whisper. "It's hard now to remember. I had a house, wife, children; I worked— such work would kill me now in a week. In the Mill, to the bosses I was a greenhorn, but to myself I had my own thoughts. All I had was my—strength." He held out an arm and tapped it. "My work. In my arms, my back, in my legs—there it lay: work. With it, I had everything. Without it——" He stopped and again raised his eyes; squinted. Suddenly he leveled his look at Benedict and cried: "You! You remember nothing! Now, how did I live? How did the house come? By itself? Who keeps it? No, this is how it came, this is who keeps it!"

His mother stirred the soup; the Mill whistle throbbed, and they could hear too the sharp whistle of the hot-metal train coming around the bend. His mother brought a spoonful of soup for Joey to sip, and she waited with lifted eyebrows for him wisely to consider it, and then nod that it was ready.

"The first years," his father continued, almost to himself, closing his eyes. "The first years, I made a scale. If I worked all year, and we made $4 a day six days a week—how much," he demanded, "how much did I make?" But before Benedict could answer, he went on: "In a year I would make $1248." He nodded at Benedict. "Yes, yes," he said efficiently, "that's correct. I learned how to figure. First, on my fingers—Joey, you look!" he cried, nudging Joey who had come near. He held up thick strong fingers, black at the tips. "How much?" he demanded, and Joey whispered: "Five." "Good!" his father approved, slapping the palm of his hand. "You know from school, I learn myself! And then I learned to write. How?" he demanded, shrewdly, and Joey shrugged his shoulders. He pointed to the calendar and Benedict's eyes followed the finger, and then rose to the crucified Christ hanging above. "From there! I sat with a pencil and butcher paper, like a little boy, like Joey ——" He poked Joey. "And I copied the figures and I bothered the men in the Mill. I would say, 'Meester,'——" Here, not only did he adopt the broken English, which he now exaggerated, but he also put on an expression of a greenhorn, with an appealing, somewhat deaf, somewhat humble look, very eager to be pleased. " 'Meester,' " he whined in a tone that was nevertheless subtly mocking, " 'Meester, you help me, Meester Boss!' " He hunched his shoulders and crouched down with a big happy greenhorn smile on his face. " 'Meester, I forgot glass, no can read dis. You tell greenhorn fella what dis say?' " He laughed silently to himself and Joey laughed, too, and his mother laughed. Benedict alone did not. "And I show him," he continued in English, "my paper. And dey tell me what is, and I listen and I remember!" He turned to the two of them. "That how *I* learn read!"

He paused for a moment, thought, and said: "That time how beautiful it was in the valley! Artists came from all around to paint it. Not like now. I save up money, buy this house. I dig cellar for it, I paint it, I set concrete, I dig a garden. And I pay; every year I pay on time: interest I pay, and I pay for house, too. Pay, pay, alla time pay," he said in English. " 'Denk you, denk you,' Bank say. 'Denk you, denk you.' "

He dropped his hands in his lap, and as though he had grown tired of the story, said: "And now Bank say, 'Move away!' "

There was silence in the kitchen. Benedict turned to his mother. "I have to go," he said. "I'm late."

His father nodded. "Yes, you late," he said. "Good-bye," he said formally, "Denk you, too." And he inclined his head.

As Benedict reached the door, his father said: "Ask priest what I'm gon' do now?"

"I'll be back for supper, Mama," Benedict promised.

3.

Benedict didn't go to church right away. Ever since Vince had disappeared, he had been searching for him; his thoughts had

148

never entirely been free of him. He felt that if he could only find Vince again he'd be able to convince him how to live peacefully at home, how to find some kind of harmony between him and his father—or, failing that, to find it in the Church, as he did. Somehow, he felt that he could show Vince what he had found; bring him, some evening, into the empty church where only the two of them would be, and where in the tallow-candle silence, kneeling underneath the tortured countenance of Christ, Father Brumbaugh would come and speak to him in his quiet silver voice of God and of His Son, who had passed among common men, Himself born into a carpenter's family.

Father Brumbaugh would show Vince how all of them were sons of God, all were Jesus, mortal and immortal, doomed to live on earth an appointed length of time before once again rejoining the jubilant Holy Family at the Godhead. God's work, and the work of His Son, was the work of the Church on earth: was their work, *his* work, Benedict's work. He longed to explain to Vince what his most inmost dreams and aspirations were, so that he would see how wrong he was to mock him; he would show Vince a way of life that would return both of them to the family, change their father, change the destiny of the whole family, raise them again to God, where they would find peace and love for one another. Vince would surely respond! Once shown the glory of God's work, he would repent the life he had been leading; return to the Church, come to confession and communion every week, renounce those who would try to reclaim him to the old ways of life. Everything would change. Benedict was sure of it; he wished and prayed for it so deeply.

Behind the old barn, where Benedict had sold the candelabra and other junk to two old men, brothers, who conducted the junk business, he located the first dice game. A circle of young and older boys, some squatting, some standing, was attached like a blister to the back wall of the barn. There was an air of wariness about them—of the illicit; for among them men with good suits and spotless hats, on whose wrists gold glinted, also mingled. Their voices came hoarse and muted: and they looked as if they could vanish like shadows at the first warning.

149

Benedict approached them diffidently. It had taken him a long time to make up his mind to search out Vince's old haunts. His pulse was beating rapidly as he drew near. Naked curses curled out of the parted mouths of the big boys with thick cigarette smoke. Sexual images moved in and out of their talk, so that he tightened as though he had stepped into an electrified zone. Their faces were tense, and their eyes implicated. On the cold ground the nimble white dice danced.

If he had seen Vince there at that moment, he would have felt sick. He moved to the outer rim of the circle and stood mutely by. He had recognized Pogy, Vince's friend; he was a broken-nosed boy, a little older than Vince, with narrow slant eyes, and full-blown baby mouth. He was begging huskily: "Come on, baby, do right, now!" He huffed on the dice and rolled them: "Eight!" he cried. "Goddamn," he rubbed the dice between his palms. "Buck says he makes it," an older boy remarked without removing the cigarette between his tight lips. "Covered," somebody else replied.

Pogy caught sight of Benedict.

"Come here, kid," he ordered, knocking the dice against his ear.

Benedict drew reluctantly near, conscious of the outlaw eyes on him. He started to say: "Where's——" but Pogy pressed the dice suddenly against his lips and yelled: "God*damn!* They're all right *now!*" And he threw the dice and two fours turned up. The boys mumbled and gave Benedict a stare—half-hostile, half-superstitious. Pogy raked the money in and grinned at Benedict. "Can't lose now," he said jubilantly. "You took the curse off 'em," he explained privately to Benedict. "Kiss 'em again." But Benedict dodged back.

Pogy rolled and snake-eyed. He grunted, cursed, and duck-walked through the circle and took Benedict's arm. "See what you done?" he said, his slant-eyes full of indignation. "You queered me!"

"I'm Vince's brother," Benedict said in a naked voice.

"I know," Pogy replied. "That's why I had you kiss them dice!"

"I'm trying to find out where Vince is," Benedict said, staring at the ground. "Do you know where he is?"

"Nope," Pogy replied.

150

"You're his best friend," Benedict said accusingly. "You know where he is."

"Didn't even know Vince was gone. Where'd he go?"

"I'm asking *you!*"

Pogy scratched his stomach passionately for a moment, and then said: "Vince said you going to be a priest?" His voice was cautious with respect, and Benedict flushed.

"Maybe," Benedict admitted gruffly.

Pogy pulled out a bag of Mail Pouch and stuffed his cheek, till there was a hard knot in it.

"What you think I am," he demanded, " a stool-pigeon?"

"Vince didn't do anything," Benedict said. "And I'm his brother. I want to tell him he can come home. We want him home."

Pogy's yellow eyes pondered for a moment, drifted to the dice game, he spit, and then said decisively: "Don't know a thing! He didn't tell me nuttin'. My dice coming up." He wove himself back into the game. Benedict followed.

Money fell into the ring; Pogy rubbed the dice between his palms, prayed to them and rolled. A five came up. More money fell. He rolled and a seven came up. He swore. "Buy the dice," he said fiercely, throwing down five dollars, and the boy beside him picked it up, nodding his head.

He threw and a three came up. Money fluttered. He rolled and a five showed; rolled again and a nine showed; and then came a seven. He cursed bitterly. He picked the dice up between taut fingers and turned to Benedict, holding them up to his mouth. "Go ahead, kiss 'em!" he said. "Sonabitch! Vince's shacked up with Goldie Perhach," he said, "go down across the Railroad. Get 'im out of there. He don't like it none nohow."

Benedict stared at the white cubes before his lips. He looked into the bitter anxious eyes of Pogy. He held his breath, shuddered, closed his eyes—and kissed.

He heard Pogy's happy voice behind him as he pushed himself through the gang. His blood had rushed to his head and his lips felt cold, as though ice had been pressed on them. "Seven!" he heard. "God*damn*, made it!"

He ran and didn't stop until he had put the game far behind

him. He shuddered a little, but cried once under his breath: "I don't care!" A truck groaned past him as he made his way up the street to the City. It was loaded with furniture, and he went to the side of the road to let it pass. The day before the Duseks had moved out of the Hollow, and already wreckers were tearing down their house. Benedict had seen the naked girders and stripped walls, and he had watched with a cold feeling of depression as the long, secret chimney was uncovered foot by foot. And then they had knocked that down. He wanted to hurry the truck out of sight, to cover it up, so that when Vince came back he would see everything as it had been—the Hollow *had* to be there!

But the truck dragged and he followed drearily after. It churned up dust and strained as it tried to make the hill; a pot fell out of it and rolled down the road and settled in the ditch hidden by daisies. Nobody in the truck noticed that it had fallen.

He stopped at last and waited resentfully until the truck was out of sight, as though it took his arguments for Vince with it; as though, in some way, it went in an atmosphere of desertion. People who had long wanted to leave the Hollow had taken this chance, he knew. They had sold to the Bank houses nobody in their right minds would buy; only *they* had bought them, under pressure, but years ago, from the Bank—and how often in one's life did one get the chance to sell on decent terms back to the Bank? Those whose houses had almost been paid up sold gladly and bought new houses in the City. They had been leaving the Hollow every day, and behind them in a few weeks appeared the wrecked skeletons that had sheltered them; and the old musty air of their lives, an atmosphere of dried plaster, faded wallpaper, dead paint, opened-up cellars, shattered cement, faded lime hung about the empty hole in the earth for days. Bit by bit, like a subtle disease, the odor of departure had begun to creep up on the Hollow. More and more broken foundations, their houses bitten off as though by some monstrous tooth, appeared among the other still-standing houses. And in the morning, instead of finding Mr. Petronis in the yard bent over a row of tiny green ears sticking up from the loamy garden, his neighbor saw only the gigantic empty hole, the disaster of the nightmare, and a brown puddle growing larger day by day.

The truck turned right as it left the Hollow and Benedict continued to the left, down toward the Mill and the railroad tracks. A huge red cloud rose like a mushroom in the sky and floated gigantically across the horizon. It was an ore-dust "slip" from the Blast Furnaces. The sky over the Mill was a long ridge of buffalo mountains, as the smoke rose and fell from the stacks, and hung motionless along the horizon for a mile. Constitution Avenue led between the two sections of the Mill, straight to the river; but between the Mill and the river, between the tracks and the river, was Smoky Bottom.

Benedict prayed nobody he knew from the City saw him there now!

He hunted up and down the alleys and streets, jumping over gutters, getting out of the way of men staggering out of saloons, or stepping over men lying in and out of the alleys. Voices rang hoarsely from house to house—always the wailing despairing cry of a woman, always the heavy hoarse cry of the man. And Benedict staggered as though beaten from house to house. There didn't seem to be a whole window in any house he passed; they were all stuffed with rags or paper, or just gaped, ragged-edged, open. Some doors were left ajar, and from one of them he saw a pair of feet dangling, as though somebody had just managed to get so far home and had collapsed, half outside the door.

As though it knew that he wasn't from Smoky Bottom, a dog leaped at him from an alley way and nipped his knee and then went careening down the road, yelping hysterically at the top of its voice. Benedict paled and sat down on the curb. He pressed his legs close together with his knees touching each other. The bite stung like a burn. For a moment he couldn't breathe and he twisted silently on the curb with his mouth open and sucking air, and his eyes slightly sprung; and then the air burst out of his lungs like a shot and he doubled over into his knees.

He sat still for minutes; and when he lifted his head finally, he felt blinded. He rolled up his pants leg to look at the bite. His knee was red. He got up from the curb and limped down the street.

He stopped a Negro man, who was on his way to work. "Where does Goldie Perhach live?" he croaked.

The man looked at him gravely. "You don't want to go there, boy!" he said, putting his hand on Benedict's shoulder and staring into his eyes.

"I have to go," Benedict answered, averting his eyes.

"You're too young, boy," the man said roughly, pushing him back toward the City.

Benedict shrugged his hand off his shoulder. "I *have* to go, Mister!" he cried, lifting his face, still pale and tear-stained.

The man pointed. Benedict broke away and stumbled toward the corner house; there was a porch in front of it, with morning glory vines climbing up strings to the roof. All the windows were shuttered: it looked abandoned. He knocked with knuckles that felt all bone, and waited. And then, in a moment, a hoarse voice cracked from behind the door: "Go around back!"

He stumbled loudly off the front porch and walked stiff-legged, as though his knee had locked in its socket, around the side of the house, along a little walk, bordered with white and yellow irises and decorated with little Dutch-maid wooden cutouts. The yard at the rear of the house was hidden from view by a wall of enormous snowball and privet bushes. A white door, covered with seamy cream paint like an old skin, was loosely shut, and he pushed it open, calling at the same time in a small voice: "This is me, this is me."

He was in a kitchen: a kettle was steaming on the stove; an icebox door hung open and the shelves were stacked with bottles of beer and slabs of bacon. On the wall a gilt-frame Christ was bleeding, and behind it was tucked a crossed faded pair of Easter palms. On a clothes line stretched across the kitchen, pairs of long silk stockings hung shrunken beside pink and yellow chemise and underpants. A sickly-sweet odor, mixed with something sharp and medicinal, in which, too, he could smell orange pekoe tea, filled the kitchen. He sat down on a white-and-red painted chair and waited.

On the other side of the room, facing him, was a closed door leading to the rest of the house. He sat stiff, as though he was waiting in an office, upright in his chair, his knees pressed together and his feet side by side on the floor. His hands found themselves palm to palm in his lap; he closed his eyes, and without forming words or images, prayed against his brain. He pressed his teeth together and breathed in and out through his nose: and he looked, sitting on the chair, as though he had been running.

A door in the front of the house closed, he heard a girl's high-pitched voice, he heard then soft steps arriving; he sat back in his chair, his hands pressed stiffly against his lap: and the door opened and through it, as though she was just coming into the kitchen for morning coffee, stepped a naked red-headed girl.

She hardly glanced at him. "How'd you get into the kitchen?" she said petulantly, with a sleepy expression, her eyes a little puffed. She went to the line and pulled down two stockings, turned, and shrieked indignantly: "What are *you* doing here?"

Benedict's hands flew to his mouth and eyes, and his elbows knocked against his sides.

The girl's face had turned an angry red; she came to him and slapped him across the face, and then ran crying through the door. Behind it, she sobbed: "Get out of here, you filthy dirty boy! I'll call the cops! Goldie!" she cried. "Goldie!"

Benedict's face was soaked; his soapy palms slipped off his wet face. The girl behind the door was hysterical. She swore at him now: "You'll pay for this, you dirty stinking hunky! You'll pay for this!" And then called again: "Goldie!"

Benedict heard other steps running; and then the door flew open again and now a deep husky voice, almost like a man's, yelped at him: "Who are *you*? How'd you get in here? Who left the door open?"

She took a handful of Benedict's hair and lifted him by it off the chair. She pulled his hands off his face, but Benedict kept his eyes tightly shut.

"A-h-h!" Goldie took a deep inhaled gasp, and held her breath with her enormously bloody mouth wide open. She pulled Benedict's head up still further, till his lips parted in an agonized involuntary grin.

"You want to get me pinched?" she cried in an outraged voice, breathing heavily.

Without opening his eyes Benedict cried hoarsely: "Where's Vince?"

She jerked his head and his teeth bared themselves into a more violent grin. "What Vince?" she yelled. "Your old man? Tell your old man to stay home where he belongs after this!"

"No, my brother," Benedict whispered huskily.

"I don't know your goddamned brother!" she cried, twisting her grip of hair. "And you tell him for me if I ever *do* see him, I won't let him into the yard! I'll have my girls spit on him! Now, get out! And if I ever catch you hanging around here again, trying to peep in through the windows, you little snot-nosed kid, I'll get a club and beat your clappy head in! For God's sakes, what kind of mother you got?"

She dragged him by the hair through the open door and heaved him into the yard. He fell among the irises. The door slammed shut, and the bolt shot decisively into place.

Benedict had not opened his eyes once.

4.

Benedict trembled. He didn't know how he got out of Smoky Bottom, what the road back to the Hollow was like. The sun was still shining, but it seemed like midnight: he had sleep-walked with his wide open eyes staring at his feet.

The drowsy complaining creak of the gate roused him, and in the middle of the yard he turned to watch the swinging gate die down again. And then he shuddered. A cat slid into the broken lattice-work under the porch. He mounted the three wooden steps and knocked. He pulled the screen door, which had been newly painted, wide open and pushed back the door. No one was in the kitchen: all was serene there, a white cloth covering the table, the cupboard doors shut, the curtains drawn; on the window sill a red geranium bleeding in the pale sunlight.

"Father," he whispered through flaky lips.

He passed through the twinkling hallway and knocked softly on the door. When there was no answer he pushed this open too. It was the room in which he had found Father Dahr: but sitting now near the window, in side view, a book spread open on his lap, his delicate profile penciled by the light, was Father Brumbaugh.

"Father," Benedict again whispered.

Father Brumbaugh lifted his head with a startled motion and a half-suppressed cry.

Benedict moved, knees turned inward, half into the room. "Benedict, Father," he explained in a hardly audible voice. He advanced further, his eyes turned upward, his mouth slightly open.

Father Brumbaugh placed the book on the window sill and turned toward him. His eyebrows contracted, and he asked: "What's the matter, Benedict?" Then he gave a short embarrassed laugh: "You surprised me!"

Suddenly, as though they had been rooted in him and now were violently pulled out, his sobs broke free of him, and he rushed toward Father Brumbaugh, stumbled and fell to his knees. Father Brumbaugh let forth a startled exclamation. Benedict lowered his head on the young priest's lap.

"Take me away, Father," he said, in a muffled voice. "Send me away to the seminary—send me away now! I'll die if I have to live here anymore! I can't live here anymore!"

"Oh, what's happened?" Father Brumbaugh cried nervously, lifting Benedict's soaked face from his lap and staring down into his exhausted eyes. "Tell me what's happened? What did you do?" he demanded, searching through Benedict's eyes and face. He lifted his head and looked around the room with an expression of harassment, of added complication, breathed sufferingly and added: "Tell me what you did, Benedict, and I'll help you!"

"I want to die, Father," Benedict sobbed.

"What are you saying?" Father Brumbaugh gasped, frightened and offended. His own pale face was now as stricken as Benedict's. "How unhappy you look!" he whispered with a soft moan. He let Benedict's head fall back into his lap; he caressed the bent head ab-

157

sently, and searched the room with distressed eyes. He looked down at the shaking shoulders, and felt Benedict's hot hand as he touched it with his own. "Oh, Mother of God!" he implored, half aloud. "You've got to tell me what you've done!"

He sat helplessly while the wretched noises continued. He could feel the tears soak through his cassock and stain his thigh. He lifted Benedict's head again gently by the soaked hair and examined the half-closed eyes as if the secret lay in them. "What is it?" he repeated. "Death?"

Benedict shook his head. His eyes, as they had been before, were closed; he could smell the odor of the tea and something else —something sweet and strong: and he pulled his head out of the priest's hands and pressed his hands like lids over his eyes.

"An accident?"

Slowly, then, Benedict removed his hands from his face. The palms were stained with tears: they burned like stigmata and seemed alive. He drew a deep breath, dragging his unwept tears down his throat harshly, and then laid his head back on Father Brumbaugh's lap, turning his face to the window. He remained in that position without speaking, feeling Father Brumbaugh's hand on his hand and the quickened motion of his breath.

"Father," he said finally, in a distant, bloodless voice. "I hate the Hollow now, too. I know you do. It's dirty and ugly, and I hate everyone in it." He stared out of the window: an empty truck passed by, and he thought of the other truck that had worked so hard to leave the Hollow, straining like a turtle. Again he saw Father Brumbaugh standing on the wooden steps staring over the Hollow with tears in his eyes; remembered his vanishing form while Father Dahr's voice vainly called to him to meet his parishioners.

"Forgive me for coming here, Father," he said, his mouth pressed against the black cloth. "I didn't know I was coming here. I don't know why. I came."

There was a long pause before an answer arrived from the young priest. In that moment Father Dahr's mocking voice intruded, almost as though he had entered the room to take part: "Have you come for secular advice, too?" He turned his head as though not to listen. "I'm *glad*," Father Brumbaugh said slowly, "when you come to me with your troubles, Benedict." Benedict shut his eyes and smiled in the knowing darkness.

"I want to leave," Benedict said. "Father Dahr has told me a hundred times I could go to the seminary when I chose. I want to go now! *Now!* Please ask the Bishop!"

"You're still too young," Father Brumbaugh said, softening the words with a reassuring pressure of his hands. He added suddenly: "This is a wonderful moment for me, Benedict."

"Will you help me, Father?"

Father Brumbaugh again pressed his head. "Yes," he said. He closed his lips and waited a moment and then said gently: "Will you tell me in a little while why you decided now?" He inserted his fingers under Benedict's chin and raised his head. "In a little while," he repeated, lifting Benedict to his feet.

Benedict turned and with his back to Father Brumbaugh, he said: "I was down in Smoky Bottom, Father."

Father Brumbaugh rose from the chair, looked down, took out a handkerchief and wiped away the tear-stains on his trousers. Benedict did not see him.

"What?" Father Brumbaugh said, wetting the handkerchief with his tongue and dabbing at a spot.

"I was hunting for my brother," Benedict said in a flat, unstressed voice. "Somebody told me he was there." He stopped and licked his dry lips. "I . . . committed a sin to learn where he was. I went there, I went inside." He turned to Father Brumbaugh and said, painfully, his face tightening: "I know how you *feel*, Father!"

Father Brumbaugh tucked his handkerchief away.

"Well," he said with a bright relieved smile. "How you worried me!"

"I think I sinned, Father," Benedict said dully, looking away from him. Father Brumbaugh looked at him sharply.

"Sinned?" he repeated.

Benedict said, hs face still turned: "I *wanted* to go in there, Father. It wasn't just for Vince's sake. I wanted to *see!* I *hoped* I would see!"

"See what?" Father Brumbaugh inquired.

159

"Them!" Benedict cried, lowering his head stiffly and closing his eyes. His chin trembled. He *had* seen—even his hands over his eyes had not prevented him from seeing. "The girls, Father!" he cried passionately. "The naked girls, the hoors down in Smoky Bottom!"

He stood still, the words all out of him. The room rustled in a soft sleepy way. The Hollow outside the window coughed hoarsely, shook gently.

Father Brumbaugh's voice came finally. He turned around to hear. The priest now had turned his face, and when he spoke, his voice was uncertain: "I don't understand what you're telling me," he said. "But if you've done anything sinful, Benedict—" and his voice faltered. He turned his eyes on Benedict. "You didn't——?"

Benedict looked at him. He flushed and lowered his eyes, and repeated: "I mean, you yourself didn't, Benedict—I mean——"

He understood, and the blood rushed to his head. A profound shame engulfed him. He lifted his head and said coldly: "No, Father!"

Father Brumbaugh laughed nervously. "I just mean," he said, his face very white, "that I didn't understand. And you——" He smiled gravely at last, and took Benedict by the elbow. "Come on," he said. "Let's go into the kitchen. We'll talk there."

He led Benedict out of the room, and Benedict followed morosely behind him, back through the hallway saying, in a voice louder and gayer than before: "You know Mrs. Rumyer's left us at last? Do you know of anybody else who might serve, Benedict? Have you any relatives?" Benedict shook his head mutely behind the priest's back. "Doesn't matter too much, though! We'll manage for a time." He opened the icebox and brought out a bottle of milk and placed it on the table. Then he brought a cake, one-fourth gone, out of the cupboard and placed it beside the milk. "I like to come down here and have cake by myself," he said. "There," he added, avoiding Benedict's eyes.

He picked up a slice of cake and bit into it. "Now," he said suddenly, looking at Benedict, "talk to me. Open your soul. . . ."

But Benedict could not. "There's nothing more to say," he mumbled.

"Think of me not only as your priest," Father Brumbaugh said, "but as your friend."

Benedict flushed. He stared at the cake on the table, and said finally in a dry voice: "They're tearing the Hollow down, Father. Maybe we'll have to move." He built his fingers into a wall, one on top of the other. He felt Father Brumbaugh's shadow cutting off part of the window. The red geranium bled in the sunlight. "I feel weak, Father," he said, his thoughts slowly forming themselves. He felt the receptive interest of the young priest, and in a sudden rush of complete trust said: "I feel more and more weak, Father. I used to think only a little while ago that the older I grew the stronger I'd grow; but I've only grown weaker, Father. I used to think that everyone—all *good* people—must hate Evil, Father——" He lifted his eyes to Father Brumbaugh's. "——and now, Father, evil things tempt me! My thoughts are evil. I don't know how to resist, I call and call on Christ, but I grow weaker every day. I'm very sick at heart, Father, and have lost my way. I sometimes think I no longer know what is good and what is bad. Is my father bad, who hates the Church, and are the Catholics in the City who sold the Church to the Bank—are they good? Is my brother Vince evil—but he's so good to my mother! I met a man whom they beat in jail, Father, and they call him a Communist. But he wants to save our homes and to build a union—is he evil, Father? And are those who beat him so and want to make us give up our homes good, Father? What is good, Father, what is evil? I try with all my strength but I can't stop anything!" He pressed his hands against the table. "My faith," he cried from the depths of his heart, "my faith is weakening, Father! I want to go away for awhile! I want to go into training. I want to live somewhere in retreat alone for a long while so that I can study, so that I can strengthen my faith, restore my soul!"

He lifted his tormented face to Father Brumbaugh who was listening with an intent pale smile on his face. "Help me, Father!" he implored.

Father Brumbaugh smiled quickly at him, wet his lips, and said: "Don't voice it again, Benedict—don't say that your faith is weakening! We value you so much!" He looked at Benedict. "I don't *want* you to say it again!" he cried, with a note of earnest entreaty and even command. "You mustn't!" A train of sweat beads had formed on his forehead, and Benedict stared at them. Sweat, too, had formed on the blond hairs along his lips. His eyes concentrated on a point beyond Benedict. "These thoughts trouble all of us," he began in a nervous voice, now a little hoarse, "at one time or another. But they pass! They are settled. The nature of Evil is that it often passes unseen into the Good: it assumes the face of Good: and it is particularly the power of Faith that penetrates beyond the appearance into the black soul of Evil! Faith, Benedict, absolute Faith in the Church Triumphant! Such profound periods of anguished spiritual struggle are the valleys of shadow through which the greatest saints of the Church have gloriously passed! Turn to *Him*, Benedict, in such moments! Deliver your soul to Him —He will not fail you!"

He paused for a moment, his voice exhausted; he leaned over the table toward Benedict and his entire body seemed to be gripped like a fist.

"Never, never weaken!" he suddenly cried again, pushing with both hands against the table. "Come to me when you feel temptation! Together we'll pray against it, together we'll fight it off— the evil, the monstrous thoughts, that come even in dreams to torture us so that we wake bathed in the sweat of our fears, the heat of our dread, feeling on us the breath——" He drew in his own breath so deeply that his chest moved visibly out—— "of darkest temptation!"

"I will, Father," Benedict said in a lowered voice, casting his eyes down so as not to see the priest's face.

They fell into a momentary throbbing silence, and Benedict was conscious of the other struggling to control his breathing; and he kept his head lowered.

Then Father Brumbaugh's hand touched his, and when he lifted his eyes, he saw that Father Brumbaugh was now smiling, his eyes elevated beyond Benedict. His face wore a thin veil of moisture on it, and his lips were specked with tiny flecks of foam. His eyes gradually focused on Benedict, his smile found him, and he said: "Later, we'll go into church, you and I, and we'll pray together."

"Father," Benedict said in a low whisper. "Father I feel wonderful now—when I'm with you—here—in the church. I feel good, and just, and peaceful." He smiled wanly, and added: "But when I leave the church, when I go out there——" His elbow twitched slightly toward the door. "It's different."

Father Brumbaugh did not hear him. The sweat was slowly evaporating from his face, and his eyes stared at Benedict without changing.

"I know, I understand," he said.

"The other day," Benedict said, wanting to talk now, casting a look at Father Brumbaugh and then lowering his own eyes to his hands again. "The other day, remember how they threw out the colored people from their houses?"

Father Brumbaugh shook his head.

"The troopers came and threw them out," Benedict said, looking sidewise down at his hands. "They came to Mrs. Burns' house, and I tried to keep them from throwing the furniture out on the road. I told them——" He lifted his face appealingly to the priest. "I told them," he said, with a helpless rush of words, "that I served here, to ask Father Dahr about me: I begged them to wait until Mother Burns came home; but the——"

Now Father Brumbaugh's smile was warm, clear. His face had become calm, uncomplicated.

"Oh, Benedict," he said gently, "you try to carry the whole weight of the world on your shoulders! You shouldn't have resisted the officers. You should have come here instead."

"I know, Father," Benedict said humbly, "but that's what I mean. I couldn't remember the Church, and prayer, then. They were evil, and I wanted to kill them!"

"But the colored people probably didn't *mind* leaving those shacks," Father Brumbaugh rebuked him gently. "They'll live in better places now," he said. "Perhaps it'll turn out best in the long run."

"They're living in the woods, Father," Benedict said.

"Woods?" the other repeated.

"Mother Burns, too."

"What woods?"

"Back of the Flue Dust. They built little shacks there, and are living there. You see, Father," he said kindly, "some of them are out of work and can't go anywhere else."

Father Brumbaugh sighed; a slight look of vexation crossed his transparent face. "I've never had to deal with such problems," he said half-complainingly to himself. "I'm not really suited to them."

Benedict lifted his head hopefully.

"If you'll come," he said, "to the woods with me——"

Father Brumbaugh closed his eyes and shook his head.

"No," he said, "they'll have to come to church here."

"Maybe if you sent a letter to the Company?" Benedict said.

With his eyes still closed, the priest's head shook back and forth. "No, no, no, Benedict," he said patiently, "I can't mix in these things, even if it did good, which I doubt. I don't know anything about the Company, but, Benedict, both rich and poor are equal members of our church. We can't put ourselves on one side against the other. Our concerns," he said pointing to his breast, "are here."

Benedict stared at the point Father Brumbaugh had touched on his breast. The unquiet Mill coughed. Still staring at his fingers, he asked: "Will you write to the Bishop?"

Father Brumbaugh nodded with his eyes.

"I would have done it even if you hadn't asked," he said, his eyes passing over Benedict. "You see, Benedict, the Church cherishes such as you." He smiled at Benedict; then at a noise raised his head, his body stiffening. Benedict turned. Leaning against the door jamb, his heavy woolly head fallen over on his arm, in his bare feet, suspenders over his winter underwear, his trousers half-buttoned, was Father Dahr. He was gazing at them with a shrewd smile, his damaged face puckered into painful patches of discolored skin. His eyes went over the cake and milk, and he cried, with heavy gusto: "Ah, a party!"

He stepped into the room, his large square toenails blue and cracked, and put his gnarled hand on Benedict's shoulder, and shook him reassuringly, and then waddled to the icebox.

He stooped painfully down to peer into it, opened the top to look at the ice, and then said, turning his head, into which the blood had rushed: "All gone?"—studying suspiciously Father Brumbaugh who had turned his face to the window and was sitting with his lips tightly compressed.

Father Dahr shrugged, dug into his pocket and pulled out a dollar.

"Benny, boy," he said ingratiatingly, "run down to the corner and get your old Father a bucket of beer."

Benedict reluctantly began to rise.

"Stay where you are!" cried Father Brumbaugh, his voice snapping like a whip, turning suddenly in his chair.

Father Dahr's heavy bush head lumbered around to study Father Brumbaugh.

"You'd deny me a bucket of beer?" he asked portentously, starting to pant. Father Brumbaugh didn't look at him, but crushed his fingers in his lap. Father Dahr turned to Benedict: "Benedict, my boy," he said, in a low, wheedling voice, "just jump off your chair for me, and do this little errand for an old man. It's just around the corner. Here's the money." He extended the dollar. It hung like a limp leaf in the accented air. Father Dahr's panting voice came like an exhausted animal's lying in a bush. His eyes turned from one to the other. He spoke to Father Brumbaugh, his voice lowered to a jagged whisper: "What are you up to? Setting the boy against me! Where are my clothes?" he demanded.

"You know perfectly well where they are," the young priest said, glancing briefly at Benedict.

Father Dahr turned to Benedict. "He hides my clothes," he complained, and laughed ponderously. "This is all I have!"

Benedict stared at him, then his eyes turned to Father Brumbaugh. Father Dahr, catching the expression, coaxed eagerly: "Tell him, Benedict—tell him, my boy; tell him what the workingman does when he comes home from work. Would he deny *them* their bucket of beer after slaving eight and ten hours in the burning gates of hell in the Open Hearth? Haven't *I* served eight and ten and twelve hours a day, year after year, in the same flaming gates of Hell—and don't I deserve a little bucket of beer from time to time to dull my brain a little? Tell him, Benedict."

Benedict was silent.

Father Dahr looked at Father Brumbaugh, and the young priest unexpectedly said: "Are you trying to make a criminal out of the boy?"

Father Dahr was startled; his heavy head moved slowly in an uncertain arc. "A criminal?" he repeated.

"You'd send him to the speakeasy," Father Brumbaugh said, pronouncing the word squeamishly, dropping his voice, "you—a rector of the church——"

A heavy, dragging silence followed this. Father Dahr stared without blinking, repeated the word criminal several times as though rehearsing it; looked at Benedict, back at the curate, and shook his head.

"Am I?" he demanded suddenly of Benedict. "Am I?"

Benedict turned his eyes away; the old man clutched his arm and pulled his face back. "Am I?" he cried. Benedict shook his head mutely.

Triumphant, Father Dahr stood back, and surveyed Father Brumbaugh. "You're young, Father," he said with heavy tolerance, "and there's a lot for you to learn here. One is that you shouldn't fly in the face of custom. Another is," he said grimly, "that you shouldn't run away from your people." He measured the young priest with his brooding eyes. "Tell him, Benedict," he said, poking Benedict. "You back me up. Why, the people here send me their own beer whenever a barrel is opened, knowing that I'm one of them, in a manner of speaking, with them at the Mill, in the pits, sticking my old nose into the furnace with them, being scorched on the seat of my pants just like them! Tell him, Benedict," he commanded, "tell him if that's not the God's truth, boy! You know, you were born here, you'll tell him!"

Benedict nodded, his eyes downcast.

Father Dahr walked up to the table and leaned far over it, shaking his finger at Father Brumbaugh, whose set face showed nothing but an ironic patience. "They *want* to know that my habits are the same as theirs!" he cried. "They appreciate a man who likes their beer, has been burned in the same way, with the same sins, as they, and, if the truth be told, spends as much time in the confessional as they! Tell him," he almost shouted appealing to Benedict. "You know the truth! The very water I baptized you with, child, was gray from the smoke of the Mill! The truth is in your bones."

Father Dahr tapped him on the shoulder, leaning his mammoth face into his, so that Benedict looked directly into eyes that seemed clouded with blood. "You've got to instruct the curate here, Benedict," he said solemnly. "Not everything is learned at the seminaries nor in the books!" He hoisted his trousers up and bent down again to re-examine the icebox. "But I left at least two bottles here," he complained. Then he rose again with a heavy flush, and roared: "Ah, Mrs. Rumyer! The old biddy took them with her when the young Father here gave her the boot!"

"I asked her to leave," Father Brumbaugh said coldly, almost officially, "because I caught her drinking in the kitchen. Because she was drunk!" He looked at Benedict, as though the explanation was meant primarily for him.

"Why," Father Dahr roared, "for all the wages she got, would you begrudge her the solace of a drink or two?" He stared at the priest and then shrugged. "If you took a nip yourself," he said, "you wouldn't notice others." Then he leveled a closed eye on Father Brumbaugh and added with heavy conviction: "And in a few years, you, too, will begin to add drops to the wine Mass by Mass!"

Father Brumbaugh's face shot up. "Benedict," he panted hoarsely. "You heard that! Did you hear that?"

Benedict's face was scarlet. "Father," he said, wrinkling his brow. "Let me help you upstairs!"

"Where did he hide it?" Father Dahr complained again. "He plays games with me. A Jesuit—he should have been a Jesuit. Do you know, Benedict," he said in a lowered confidential voice, quite audible to Father Brumbaugh whose pale face was bowed, "we've a casuistical Jesuit with us? A politician, a diplomat, a conniver? Down he comes from Boston with his educated accent: comes here, *here*, Benedict," he emphasized significantly, tilting his head. "In this pest-hole of the country, where the very souls are stained with smoke and dust and are unrecognizable in heaven! Why does he

come?" he demanded, narrowing his eyes, and almost falling off
balance, and as though Father Brumbaugh were desperately trying
to hear, lowering his voice. "Who suddenly remembers Father
Dahr exiled here for twenty years, ever since the miners' strike,
when he did his little bit with the miners against the Company,
buried all these years in a rotting church sinking down into the dirt
like a grave? The smell of the Bishop is on him!" he cried standing straight up and lifting his hand high above his shaggy head.
"The smell of intrigue comes along with him! Dark deeds are in the
making! Does he come like a priest to his parish? Look, look at
him, Benedict, and tell me what you feel in your heart!" He turned
Benedict's face, holding his cheeks between his yellow-stained
fingers, so that Benedict was helpless in his grip and faced Father
Brumbaugh with his mouth wide open, like a fish. Father Brumbaugh stiffened and looked away. "Look him in the face!" the old
priest ordered, his hands shaking and his fingers pressing painfully
on Benedict's cheeks. "Does he look like a man who's come to live
his life among these poor downtrodden miners and workers, men
who come stumbling into church to snore through the service, sunk
in the death of exhaustion, with bodies that smell to high heaven
from the pits of the Mill? Does he? Ask him, Benedict, if he can
stand to hear the broken language of our people here, their broken
minds, too; warn him, Benedict, for you can talk to him, warn him
how he will be forced to hold his pale white nose as he goes among
these souls already doomed to Purgatory of poverty and labor!
Let him go—beg him to go, Benedict—to the Moloch: let him go
to the Mill and throw himself before it, and beg it to give back the
numberless souls it already has eaten up: the broken bodies on the
wheels, the bodies burned to ash, the bodies cracked bone by bone
until they lie a soaking heap on the floor! Tell him, Benedict,"
he begged, tears suddenly streaming down his face and his voice
coming huskily through his mouth. "Tell him, Benedict," he cried,
in a half-broken, almost whistling voice, with his eyes fixed strangely on Benedict, "tell him when he is called to administer the last
rites—ask him how will he recognize the human being who is
handed to him on a shovel, scooped up from the furnace floor;
or how will he bless the box of ashes with confidence, or pass his

blessing hands over the ton of pig-iron in whose heart is fastened the body of some poor human soul sealed forever in this iron prison that not even dynamite but only the flames of Hell could loosen again!" His voice was rising, and he shook both hands at Benedict. "Tell him all this, Benedict," he throbbed hoarsely, "and then ask him if he is the man for these men and these parts!"

He poked Benedict a few more times, breathing heavily, his lips wet, jerking his hand toward Father Brumbaugh who had not moved. Then he went to the cupboard and opened it, shuffled back and pulled a letter out of his pocket. "Here it is!" he said, tapping the letter, and watching with satisfaction as Father Brumbaugh's eyes turned irresistibly toward it. "Do you want to read it?" he asked Benedict. "Do you know what's in it? No? *He* knows what's in it," he said, mysteriously nodding toward Father Brumbaugh. "But I'll tell *you*. This little letter, Benedict," he said, tapping it with his forefinger, "will make us all rich! Make the church rich! I'll tell you, Benedict, do you want to know why our Jesuit suddenly appeared in our green valley?" Again he tapped the letter. "It's in here," he said significantly. "A fortune. A new church, Benedict—a new, bright new church! *He* knows," he said slyly, looking at Father Brumbaugh and nodding confidently to Benedict. "He knows what's in the letter! He knows all right!" he said, nodding his head three times decisively. He narrowed his eyes at the priest and lowered his voice again. "They stuck me down in this hole and forgot me—I fought for the miners' union, Benedict, and this is where they sent me to die forgotten. And now—luck and the Company have found us out; and the Bishop has once again remembered my existence. That's why this young spy is down here—to see that my old affliction, my worldly love for my parishioners doesn't overcome their superior love for——" and he tapped the pocket— "gold, my young friend. A fortune, Benedict," he repeated. "A sum to stagger the imagination! A new church! And," he added finally, again nodding, "he knows all about it. The news travels far; he's come like a buzzard to the feast." He poked Benedict very hard in the shoulder and said, rumbling in his throat: "I'm a prisoner, Benedict, in my own church, in my own house. But tell him, Benedict, that the others stick with me—the church will stand;

and they'll stand by me. No, we say to them——" He pulled the letter out of his pocket and raised it above his head—— "No, we say to the Company—no, no and no!"

And he tore the letter in half, and again in fourths, and threw the pieces into the air, looking triumphantly at the young priest who had half started from his chair. He turned to Benedict, his eyes flashing, punched him on the shoulder and cried: "You see, Benedict! You see! Riches!" Then he almost staggered over to the icebox again and looked once more inside. "You wouldn't do that favor for an old man?" he said plaintively. He pulled himself up again and, without another word or look at them, drove through the door and they could hear his wheezing breath pulling up the stairs.

They waited for a long jagged minute in the kitchen, which seemed somehow to be upset, as if a wind had knocked the furniture over. Benedict turned burning, humiliated eyes to Father Brumbaugh, who sat like an image in his chair, the delicate blue veins in his cheeks pulsing.

The young priest turned to him at last and said: "Did you hear him?" His face was cold and white as alabaster. Slowly, in a voice icy and low, he pronounced: "What you just heard, Benedict, was blasphemy!"

Benedict stared at the face in which a trace of fear, a kind of repulsion, still lingered. It seemed to Benedict that it was not so much Father Dahr's blasphemy which had moved him, and it was not anger that he showed in his face: it was a kind of squeamish disgust as though the old priest had come with a bad odor.

Father Brumbaugh sat and brooded with his lips still slightly curled.

"That old boor!" he suddenly burst out; then turned to Benedict and added with indignation and still a trace of sincere incredulity: "'My people! My people!' he's always saying! And he's just like them. What's so special about these people I'd like to know? They're all foreigners—and colored! Why, most of them have no education, and you know they hardly know how to speak English! They're just common laborers. What's so marvelous about them?

170

All they do is work! Why, my father hires and fires people like them every day!"

5.

Joey came padding down the dusty road toward them. His bare feet kicked up a cloud behind him. Benedict and his father were hoeing their "farm." Joey began to shout the message before he arrived. His father, wearing an old crushed straw hat that hung in shreds around his ears, looked up. When Joey arrived, he had to stand still, panting with a pale eye, unable to speak: and then he blurted out: "Mr. Draugraubaus! Mr. Draugraubaus!"

"Cath breath, catch breath," his father advised, taking a pint bottle out of his back pocket and tilting it up to the sky.

Both watched him in silence, followed with their eyes the hard knot in his throat which jumped like a frog; and when he was through, Joey still stood staring at his throat where the knot had vanished. His father poked him with his thumb. "*Nu*, cloud-gazer?"

Joey spoke in English to Benedict and Benedict translated not so much the English but his brother.

"Benny, they're doing it! They're doing it!" Joey cried, pumping his arms and shoulders. He started pounding the air with his fists. "Hitting them, hitting them!"

"Who? What?" Benedict laughed, trapping Joey's flailing hands into his.

"Them, them! O-o-o!" he moaned, pulling his hands away and flattening them against both cheeks, his eyes rounding with horror.

"What's the matter?" his father asked with impatience.

"The Sheriff," Joey panted. "He done it!"

Suddenly he grew pale, and he turned away from them and walked off into the daisy field and would not come back.

Benedict and his father slung their hoes over their shoulders and started homeward down the dusty limestone road.

Long before they arrived, they could feel the crackle of tension in the air. A kind of force drew them to the center of the Hollow. They could hear catcalls. And then when they were there, it was as if they had come on a field of battle. Blue-uniformed troopers with rifles cradled in their arms, some on horses, some on foot, stood facing the crowd which had gathered in a half-moon across the valley. The familiar red face of Sheriff Anderson, who was standing with two Company police, loaded with brass bullets in a curving belt around their stone-hard bellies. In the alley there was already a kitchen table, a stove and several chairs.

Mr. Draugraubaus' wife, a little brown woman, stood with her apron flung peasant-like over her head and face, while another woman had her arms around her, glaring over her shoulder from time to time at the troopers. That woman was his mother, and Benedict went over to her.

"Mama?" he begged, half-question, half-fear.

She drew in her breath when she saw him, as though now with him danger had materialized, and she pulled him into her embrace, in which Mrs. Draugraubaus still stood, moaning; and Benedict thought that she was going to throw Mrs. Dragaubaus' apron over him, too.

At her feet was a patch of blood, in the shape of a crab.

Benedict stepped around it, staring.

His father came: and, as if with his appearance she was released from courage, his mother dropped her head on the woman's shoulder and her own shook violently.

Suddenly, white rocks like a hard snow fell on the troopers. His father moved all of them back into the crowd, pushing Mrs. Draugraubaus who stumbled childishly. Shots exploded behind them; a horse reared; Sheriff Anderson's booming, and grotesquely public voice was saying: "Over their heads, over their heads. . . ."

The crowd fell back on itself; and Benedict thought how different the faces looked now: "N-----s first," he remembered, "hunkies next!"

Whose blood was that?

Lena suddenly appeared in the crowd; she stood as though she alone were on the street. He remembered her taunting words when he had come to sell her father the moonshine, and his eyebrows jerked nervously. "*You* won't be. . . . !" he heard the words in his brain; and then, somehow, he knew that the scarlet crab on the sunny road was her father's.

The faces of the crowd were like faces in a pit watching their own execution. Some snarled, some held their breaths, some were ashamed as the visits of police were always shameful; and some were bitten with fear. A constant sound, as though a mean wind were rising, wound in and out: but nobody was speaking aloud.

The shots, as if they had traveled around the world warning workers everywhere, now came echoing back, exhausted, and died at their feet.

And then he was not surprised at all to see her dark face beside him, a bitter remembering look on it, which only clouded a little when he exclaimed: "Mother Burns!"

She stared through him and his blood hesitated: her eyes had not answered him. She pushed out of the crowd again, and he followed her, disturbed by some fear he couldn't name. He caught up to her and took her elbow: "Mother Burns," he said with anxious reproach, "it's me, Benedict. Don't you *know* me?"

"Go away, boy!" she cried, her eyes impatiently pulling away. "Can't you see I'm going?"

She broke from him, and pushed forward through the yellow dust, swinging her sharp elbows behind her as though pumping her way along. He stood rooted in the road, staring after her.

Again there were sudden shots behind him. A horse screamed: he turned to see it rear in the air, its trooper frantically holding on and then flinging up his arms to fall backward; and then the frightened horse plunged into the horse of a second trooper, and galloped down the road. People broke from the half circle and pushed forward. Sheriff Anderson's official voice rang over them all: "Keep back! Keep back!"

Shots.

And then, suddenly, there was nobody there. A tart dust hung in the air, turning lazily over and over. On the ground a man was crawling on his hands and knees, and trailing behind him, like a red snake, was his heart's blood.

6.

Benedict watched his father carefully spoon up the last of the cabbage soup, wipe his thick mustache with the back of his hands, first with the left and then with the right, refuse more, look suddenly up as though he had just been reminded, and then rise from the table.

He sighed, gave a stretch, and said casually: "I'm going to see Jacobis."

It was dark outside. A train of hot-metal cars had dumped, and the leaning side of the slag hill lay burning and quivering under the starless night. The shambling shadows of cows coming home late from the meadows crossed the street, and the pale light from the street lamps drenched their bony spines. They lowed and their heavy udders swung ponderously. Dogs shot like lightning out of an alley and disappeared as quickly between the houses. Never still, the Mill roared hoarsely.

Shortly after his father had left, Benedict also rose.

"I have to go to see the Father," he announced, also casually.

His mother turned. "So late?"

Benedict nodded. Joey hurriedly packed his soup away and jumped up.

"I gotta go, too," he declared.

"You stay!" Benedict cried, fiercely.

Joey withdrew with an injured look, but set his lip rebelliously.

All day rumors had spread through the Hollow. The streets had been unusually deserted, and pairs of troopers had patrolled them on horses. Mr. Draugraubaus lay peacefully in a hospital. The other man, Peter Janicki, had died; he lay at home.

Outside he could sense shadows moving in and out of the alleys. Doors softly opened, revealing for a brief instant the yellow outline of a workingman; then shut like a sigh. Children were off the streets. Homeless dogs, frightened by the stillness, fled with no one chasing. Clouds, darker than the night, scudded across the sky; a sudden chilly wind rose and careened across the hills.

Behind him he caught sight of his little brother, following like a leaf, and he hid behind a pole. When Joey came by Benedict reached out his arm and dragged him over by the neck. Gruffly he shouted into his ear: "Go home!" and hit him with his knuckles over the head. "You can't come!"

Joey fell back—but when Benedict moved, he moved, too. Benedict shook his fist at him, and then suddenly turned and ran. Soon there were no street-lights: only the faint gray of the road to guide him. He felt that he was no longer alone. There was a soft shuffling tread along the road. He stopped to listen and sensed shadows passing him by. Someone touched him, but moved on without speaking. He smelled the incinerator; he smelled the choked odor of the dump, and his shoulders jerked.

The road turned sharply off into the scrub of the hills. They could smell carbon from the opened and abandoned eternally-burning pits. Rabbits fled before them: and suddenly a shudder of wings rose at his feet and a dark bird stumbled drunkenly through the sky. He sensed where to go without knowing. The road had disappeared. Now branches suddenly snatched at him. He smelled crabapple trees whose lingering blossoms fell on his hair as he brushed by.

Now he felt more and more men around him. The darkness congealed. They were moving elbow to elbow now. And suddenly they stopped.

He was shivering. He heard his teeth chattering lonesomely. There were muffled uneasy curses; choked-off laughter: a feeling of violence hid behind the darkness. Benedict remembered Mr. Janicki crawling along the yellow road, trailing blood: and he shuddered more. He remembered Lena's chalk face as she staggered after her mother. He remembered that other, suddenly stranger's, face; the masked but hostile look she had turned on him. He longed for his father.

A mutter began to rise. It moved quickly through the packed men. There was a hollow whistle. Somebody laughed nervously. He shivered again and almost dropped to his knees. He stood stiff, cold, as though on the edge of a cliff. Something—a dog—whined and pushed between his legs. More whistles. "Well, where is he?"

That was the first voice Benedict heard. It sounded so clear and normal that he jumped.

Then a voice ahead of them responded from the dark.

"Everybody here?" it asked.

"Yes, yes," voices responded from all around; and suddenly Benedict sensed the organized quality of the arrangement of these replies. He could feel too how big the crowd was.

"All right, boys," the same confident voice that spoke as though in a lighted room returned from the dark. "Take care of our uninvited guests!"

There was an immediate scuffle and shuffle at different points in the darkness; a startled cry, choked off; a half-curse; a body thudding to the ground; grunts; a naked fist hitting on a bone. Then absolute silence again; followed in a moment by quiet satisfied laughter. A man beside Benedict lunged and knocked him over. Hands reached for the man, Benedict caught the white flash of teeth, a frightened upturn of the silk of an eye. Someone clambered over the fallen one, pinned his arms together, hissed in his ear: "You Drubak—spy!" Pushed a gag into his mouth, whipped rope around his arms and tied a red workingman's handkerchief over his eyes. He rolled him over on his face into the coal-specked ground.

"All right, brothers?"

"All right!" someone answered from the right. "All right!" "All right!" voices came from behind and ahead, from the left and from the right again, as though posted, as though possessing and organizing the darkness. Benedict felt a strange sense of penetrating eyes, though he could see no one.

Nor could he see the man who had been issuing the orders in that calm, matter-of-fact voice. The voice came out of the dark somewhere ahead. Benedict pulled himself to his feet. The caught spy lay writhing gently on the ground. Benedict suddenly wanted to kick him. Suddenly, too, his fear left him. He felt a strange shaking thrill: the darkness had erupted with strength. The voices he heard were all somehow familiar, the tones of his people: and the voice rising out of the dark, speaking almost carelessly—this, too, sounded hauntingly familiar.

It came again: "Brothers, the stoolies, company spies, FBI men, finks and rats have all been removed, I hope, from the meeting." Quiet laughter. "Now we'll get started."

A match suddenly flared up. Benedict jumped. "Dobrik!" he cried, astounded. There was more laughter. The same broad humorous face, the same grin as though he was always surprised to find that people listened to him: it was Dobrik from jail! Dobrik crawling along the stone floor for a pencil-stub! Dobrik telling him that they were both alike—because they refused to give the police names! Smiling ruefully through the blood on his face and scolding himself for having let himself be caught! It was Dobrik!

He strained toward the image held in the match-light, and then the light went out.

"Joe Magarac," someone said knowingly, laughing softly.

Benedict was quivering. The memory of the bitter night rushed back to him. *What was he doing here?* "Why, you're the union man!" he had said with surprise. "Son, that man's a Communist —" but he remembered the bloody hand coming through the frenzied air to settle on his head. He shuddered.

"Well, brothers," Dobrik's voice came again, speaking as though he were sitting on a chair across the table from everyone. "I've been to the Amalgamated Iron and Steel Workers and they don't give us any satisfaction. No hope at all. They won't touch us."

Murmurs.

"We'll go without them!" a voice cried.

"Yeah, we can do that," Dobrik continued. "They're against any strike, Boyle tells me: but when we walk out, we're going to bring the Amalgamated craft boys out with us, too!"

"You tell 'em, Doby!" somebody yelled—except that his voice was muted and could not be heard beyond those there.

Dobrik continued in his easy, informal manner, except that his voice was also in deadly earnest. "It's got to be fast, got to be secret. No names, no leaders. *Everybody* is leader this time. We'll be in the woods. You understand. *Furstay?*"

"*Furstay,*" they laughed.

Dobrik's voice got serious. "Those of you in the Hollow— what's the matter? What happened?"

"They're kicking us out now, Doby!"

"I know that," Dobrik said impatiently. "That's not what I mean." They sensed that he leaned toward them in the darkness. "You let them throw our colored brothers out without lifting a finger!" he accused.

"They was scabs, Doby," someone complained defensively.

"They're n-----s, Doby," somebody else chimed in. "They don't understand union talk!"

Silence instead of Dobrik's voice. Finally, it said: "Look around you." Benedict looked. There was solid darkness. "Now," Dobrik demanded, "tell me: who's white, who's black?"

Muffled laughter followed this.

"You willing to take your chances," Dobrik cried, "with the guy next to you *whoever he is?*"

"Got to, Doby," they cried.

"Tell me," he demanded cuttingly again, "is he white or is he black?"

Again there was laughter, some sheepishly.

"Can't tell, Doby." And then a voice picked up. "But they're still scabs, Doby! How do we know they ain't going to scab on us again?"

"Company brought a lot of colored up from the South to break the 1919 strike," Dobrik began. "They didn't know what they were coming for—they were packed in freight-cars and first thing they knew—bang! they were inside the Mill, scabbing! Who the hell did that?" he demanded furiously. "You going to keep them responsible for what the Company did to them too?"

He waited in the darkness, and then said: "Light a match." Again a match flared up, and this time, instead of Dobrik's face, there was a Negro man's. The workers laughed, and cried: "Hi, Cliff, how'd you get up there?" (Benedict jumped—the long fingers on his throat! "He's a union man," Mother Burns had explained, as though it unpuzzled his strange and even threatening behavior.) Clifford waved his hand, and suddenly the match went out.

"You all know him," Dobrik said from the darkness. "You didn't know it—you couldn't see—but he's been up here beside me." He paused and when he spoke again his voice was chiding them: "You let 'em throw your colored brothers out, and what happened yesterday?"

Benedict whispered the names to himself: "Draugraubaus, Janicki."

"*Everybody* walks out this time!" Dobrik said sharply.

"We're with you, Doby," answered a voice. "Anything you say, Doby!"

"A few weeks ago," Dobrik resumed in a softly mocking voice, "you all got a letter." Wry laughter burst out, in which Dobrik softly joined. "You from the Hollow, know what the Company wants you to do? Sell out, or starve out—and the Company will take over the whole Hollow—millions of dollars of property—to build a new Mill on! A new modern Mill—with new chipping machines and electric furnaces—take half the men they got now to do twice the work!" Wounded angry cries. "We can't let that happen!" he said indignantly. "Where we going to go? Don't sell at Bank's price; hold on. We'll fix 'em!" To the others he added: "You see: they fired our brothers living in the Hollow. Why, do you think?"

"Company thinks they work too hard. Give 'em a rest!"

Appreciative laughter.

"Of course," Dobrik said, broadly sarcastic. "Big vacation. With no pay!"

The crowd enjoyed him: they loved to throw remarks up and have them come back pointed with bitter wit. And all during the exchange Benedict felt thrills bursting over him—a strange fantastic sense of freedom; of a restoration of liberty he had never known was absent. There was a flow of spontaneous power that ignited the darkness.

"Company fire the men to *make* them sell!" Dobrik cried angrily.

This was the first time his voice had shown anger. Benedict felt himself getting hot, as though the anger had burned him. Strange, too, he felt as though he anticipated every remark of Dobrik's, and that the passion was his own expressed passion, and it was *he* speaking in a tumultuous voice over the rolling darkened hill.

"Now: some of you: you hide out in the hills. You know where."

179

"They'll come after us, Doby!"

"We'll take care of them!" another voice from the crowd replied confidently.

"We'll send a committee in a few days with your demands," Dobrik continued. "Ten cents an hour from laborers to blowers. Recognition of the union. No yellow-dogs. Grievance machinery."

"Fire the spies!"

"We'll take care of them ourselves," Dobrik replied.

"These?" someone begged.

"No," Dobrik said contemptuously. "They're no use to the Company now. The Company'll fire them!"

Happy laughter greeted this. Benedict, too, found himself laughing. The mysterious, the frightening darkness was gone. Darkness now was safety. No one saw them there, not even stars. And in this profound darkness they could speak the truth they had kept hidden in their hearts. The voices were warm—and for the first time it seemed to Benedict—*all* of them underwent that mysterious change, as his father did when he changed from English to his own language, as though they lurked behind their citizens' cloak of humility and obedience, ignorance and even drunkenness, for moments of freedom like this. How confident they were, he thought with surprise, how free they were—how different from the way they came to church!

His teeth were bared in an unconscious grin as he pushed through the darkness to Dobrik's casual, firm voice. He felt as though Dobrik was bound to know he was there: that, if he caught sight of him, he would say: "I remember you!" and smile at him. He shuddered with pleasure.

"So they fired you!" he heard Dobrik's dry comment. "Fired you before the next payment was due. What you going to pay the Bank with—beans you grow out on the hills? When you lose your house—then they'll hire you back again!"

"We'll tell 'em to go to Hell, Doby!" sounded an uncertain voice.

"Bank and Company are one!" Dobrik went on. A match lit magically and up in the darkness they saw two hands tightly gripped together. "What Company say, Bank do!" he said.

180

Grumbles and muffled curses followed this.

"But——!" And here his voice had an arresting command in it. The murmurs went out as if cut with a knife. "But, workers are one, too!" Again the match flared up, and in the fantastic light a dark and a light fist, gripped tightly together, knocked the Bank and Company down with one blow. Hushed cheers rose from the packed audience as though it was the climax to a Punch and Judy show. Benedict swayed: his heart pounded. Across the shadow of his mind flashed the frantic memory of Mother Burns rushing to her empty cabin, kicking her skirts into froth. A pang shot through him: and he regretfully longed now to follow her.

"Yeah," cried the same skeptical, cynical voice from somewhere in the darkness. "They'll bring in the n-----s—you'll see. We gotta keep 'em out *now!*"

There was silence again at the head of the meeting. The men waited in the darkness.

Again, but this time from a flashlight, a circle of light miraculously appeared. They could see the shadow of Dobrik's head. Suddenly he pulled a white hand into the bright light, shaded by someone's cupped hands. Then he brought with frightening quickness a knife into the light and snapped open a long steel blade. There were involuntary gasps from the workers, followed by short laughter as the men pushed forward with fascination. Benedict controlled a shudder, giggled, and strained against the man in front of him who himself was straining. Dobrik now brought the knife, sharp blade down, on the white wrist, whose raised veins seemed to be quivering with moving blood. The wrist attempted to jerk away but Dobrik held it in a grip of iron.

"If I cut," Dobrik's angry voice came to them all, "what color's your blood going to be?"

"Red, Doby!" the owner of the hand blurted out. "But for Christ's sake, Doby, don't do it!"

Men laughed. Benedict shuddered deliciously.

Suddenly from the opposite side of the lit circle another hand shot—this time a dark hand. Dobrik gripped it firmly around the wrist and brought the knife down on it.

He turned to the shadow where the white face would be.

"What color?" he demanded sternly.

"Red!" the other gasped, quickly, as though he had no time to dally.

Everybody on the hill roared, and the laughter—itself somehow controlled and disciplined—swept up and down like a joyous wind.

Dobrik lifted his head and looked out into the darkness from which the previous voice had come.

"Anybody want to *test* that?" he cried. "Come on up here!"

Profound silence.

He waited as though to give the doubter every opportunity; then when it was clear that nobody was going to come up to challenge whatever he was proving, he said to the men in a grave, measured voice:

"Yes, that's what I mean. His blood and your blood, they got but one color, and that's the *same* color: red. It don't matter to me what the color of your skin is as long as you got red blood in your veins! And if you got the heart to go with it, and you're a union man, then I'm here to defend your right to be my Brother—" and he shook his own gripped fist in the light—"till there's not a drop of my own blood in these veins!"

They laughed and they cheered, but carefully and mutedly. Benedict's cheeks were burning with an extreme excitement.

A man pushed his way through the crowd, like a wind going through wheat. There was an intense silence at the point where Dobrik was speaking; the flashlight went out, and the great darkness returned. Then, in a voice as calm as the one he had used all evening, Dobrik said: "The State Troopers are on their way out on the hills. I guess we finished up our business here. So, we'll call this meeting adjourned till you get word again. Keep in touch with your stewards. Follow out everything. Goodnight, brothers!"

And immediately it seemed the darkness moved in deeper. The squirming man, trussed on the ground, jerked like a dying fish. Benedict squeamishly stepped over him and hurried back over the hill.

Again, as he walked, he sensed shapes passing him in the darkness. But now, instead of the sinister he felt the friendly movement of men he knew. He was satisfied to let the darkness that included him include them. The burning mines wafted the sharp carbon odor across the hill. He smelled cow dung soon: and then the incinerator. The gray road curved like the thumb and forefinger around it. Now, a sudden wind brought the sour smell of the Ditch that remained uncovered at this far point and entered the concrete culvert only at the place where the houses began. The same wind brought a grain of pig-iron, still hot, and nicked his cheek.

With a rush of wind two horses suddenly charged around the hill and galloped up the road. He threw himself into the thick grass beside the road and shook as they thundered by.

He walked stooping through the tough grass along the road: and suddenly stumbled over Joey squatting in the grass like a bird on a nest. They both cried out with fear, and then Joey's teeth began to chatter. Benedict rolled him over and clamped his jaws together to stop the noise. In the silence it seemed to carry through the night. Then he took Joey by the hand and led him through the back alleys home.

There was no light in the house, and when he entered he lit none. Both sat in the dark kitchen, trembling. When they heard footsteps on the porch, they froze. The door softly opened and they sensed their father entering: and in a moment he was climbing upstairs; and then they heard the springs, and then the shoes come off.

Benedict punched Joey on the head.

Joey understood.

7.

Never had St. Joseph's been so filled. Never had a funeral been so well-attended. Hundreds of workers came from all over the Hollow and the City to Janicki's funeral. Few outside the Hollow knew him, but they came. The Mill faltered, staggered, telephones rang from department to department: "What's going on? Where're the men?"

The men were at the funeral. They stood outside the little church; those who could get in squeezed into the benches. The church was lit with nothing but a few dying candles offered for souls in purgatory: with the gray sun that shone through the ruby robes of St. Peter and flooded the pews with a wine light.

Benedict was garbed in black. He waited with another boy in the sacristy. It was cold and they had not turned on the lights. The other boy, Anthony, whose dark shining hair was wet, sat chewing his finger nails.

They were carrying the coffin down the aisle, and Benedict sent the other boy after Father Dahr. He waited anxiously. Outside, the breathing of the congregation was like the soft moving of a sea.

Minutes passed and Anthony failed to return. There was an impatient scraping and coughing in the church. Finally, Benedict slipped out of the sacristy and made his way to the back door of the parish house through the garden that was still wet with dew. The other boy was leaving by the gate.

"Anthony!" Benedict called indignantly, and Anthony half-turned with a look of fright, and replied: "Father Brumbaugh told me to go home!" and he let the gate bang behind him.

Benedict knocked on the door. No one answered. He turned the knob and entered the kitchen. He heard muffled angry voices in the front room and cried uncertainly: "Father? Father?"

He pushed his way through the dark hall and hesitated at the door. The voices inside had died down but he felt the tenseness. He called again: "Father?" Then knocked gently.

The door opened. Father Brumbaugh, his face tight and pale, said: "Yes?"

Beyond him Benedict could discern Father Dahr half-crouched with his head hanging; he was pulling himself to his feet with the help of the back of the chair.

"Benedict!" he cried in a hoarse, choked voice, lifting his hand and pulling Benedict to him desperately.

"Father Dahr?" Benedict said questioningly, turning to stare at Father Brumbaugh.

Father Brumbaugh let him pass his arm. Benedict rushed to Father Dahr and helped him upright. Sweat stood like blisters on his purple cheeks and yellow waxy forehead. He nodded into Benedict's face gratefully with his leaking blue eyes. "Good," he gasped.

Father Brumbaugh remained standing stiffly at the door. Benedict turned a frightened and begging glance to him.

His eyebrows were arched, his lips were pursed.

"Father?" Benedict asked.

His eyelids moved. "You've got to convince him, Benedict," he said, in a low intense voice, though completely composed. "He mustn't go out there. He mustn't try."

"But the Mass!" Benedict cried, astounded.

Father Brumbaugh lifted his head. "There'll be no Mass!" he pronounced.

Benedict stared wordlessly at him. Father Dahr was reaching a trembling hand toward him, and he felt it fall, at last, on his shoulder.

Father Brumbaugh's shoulders seemed to rise. "The police," he said, in a quiet, certain voice, with the firm touch of authority behind it, "have been here. They've asked me not to perform a public Mass for——" He nodded his head slightly toward the church. "Those men out there haven't come for a funeral. They've come to avoid going to work—pretending *this*. It's really a plot. If I serve Mass, I'll be part of the plot. Therefore, I forbid anyone to! We must empty the church of all but the immediate family before we proceed. Do you hear?" The question he directed to Father Dahr. "Do you hear?" he demanded again.

Benedict heard Father Dahr's enormous wheezing rumble in his ear. "Help me, Benedict, my boy," he said gently. "Just let me have a little of your strong shoulder to lean on," he coaxed.

He placed more of his purpled hand on Benedict's shoulder and Benedict's knees buckled.

"Good, ah, good," the old man's voice came hoarsely, but lightly, too. His brows, fruited with sweat drops, were knit, but his eyes were concentrated on some other further point to be gained, and he labored gasping, but also congratulating himself, and encouraging Benedict: "Oh, fine! There, we did that! A strong fine boy! Now, next!" He pulled himself forward. "See, we're making it; it's not so far."

Benedict stood wavering; his shoulders sank and rose, and the old man supporting himself on his shoulder sank and rose with him.

"Easy, easy," the old man advised him. "And now—now we're off."

Benedict sought Father Brumbaugh's face. There were two red spots slowly deepening: the eyes were almost black.

"Get away from him, Benedict!" the priest cried in a deep shaking voice. His body shook also. "You can't go out there!"

"On, on," Father Dahr urged, lightly, doggedly, into his ear. His lips were wet and Benedict felt the spit fleck his ear. He moved a step forward. His eyes had not left Father Brumbaugh's face. His own had grown pale; his lips had dried and his mouth was sticky. He felt sweat swell to his pores and bounce down his thighs and soak his knees.

"Father!" he cried again, his face uplifted imploringly to the priest. His voice sounded horrible, like a croak.

Father Dahr's body pushed him forward.

"I've got to go, Father!" he cried desperately.

Father Brumbaugh leaned forward; his eyes burned. "Don't forget what you've got at stake, Benedict!" he warned. "Your whole future! Your whole future will depend on whether you go out there now! Those men are Communist-led and desecrate the church. You mustn't let them make use of you! Don't throw your future with the desperate men—they're disobeying the law. They're criminals— the police are after them!"

"But the *police* shot him!" Benedict cried.

"It was provoked, Benedict," he answered intensely, his eyes flaring. "*This*, too, is a provocation. I've been told the whole story, and I'm warning you!"

Benedict staggered forward, his knees wobbling. He moved, propelled by the old man's weight upon him. He cried as though through pain: "I've got to go in, Father! They're waiting for the Mass! *We* cannot deny God's word for the dead!"

"Stay, Benedict," the young priest cried. "For the last time, I order you, Benedict, not to desecrate the Holy Mass!"

Benedict sobbed out loud and stumbled forward. "I must go!" And the old man pushed him through the hallway, the screen door flew open, and they fell into the yard. He pulled the old priest up on his arm again, and pushed and pulled him to the sacristy door. The old man clung greedily to his arm, talking to him in broken, exultant, half-articulate words, while his cheeks beat together like bellows. "Good boy," he cried, nodding his head rapidly, chortling through wet lips. "Fine boy, church militant and savior all . . . and now we're there, and God be with us, and God be praised . . . and now we're closer, and now Golgotha is ours. . . ."

He collapsed on a chair in the sacristy, and closed his eyes for a moment. But almost immediately they were open again; the light in them was sharp and active.

"Are you——?" Benedict asked, frightened.

The old man breathed heavily. "Go, go," he directed harshly, and Benedict ran for his vestments.

He helped the priest don them, wiping away tears from his eyes. Meanwhile, the people were audibly more impatient. Police appeared outside the church.

They rose together, the old man wavering. He put his unsteady hand again on Benedict's shoulders, and they moved slowly through the door. The golden bell tinkled and a great shuddering sigh rose from the church. Slowly, they moved out before the altar. Father Dahr's bright eyes were sheathed, his feet shuffled as though searching for a path; his face was drawn, long white lines were carved deeply in them, his eyes were closed, his eyelashes were gray. Benedict moved with infinite slowness. At the altar he waited nervously while Father Dahr slowly lowered himself to his knee. He, too, then carefully genuflected, and then bore the priest's biretta to the sidelia, a wrought bench to the right of the altar. The black coffin stood outside the communion rail.

Father Dahr painfully ascended the steps; and now he turned, and looked upon the church as though stunned; his face was a dreamer's lost face; he wavered momentarily and then descended. He shook as he knelt and Benedict knelt again with him, suddenly smelling the old man's faded smell of tobacco and whisky, and the smell of moth balls in his clothes. In a low grating voice the old man began: *"Introibo ad altare Dei."*

"Ad Deum qui laetificat juventutem meam," Benedict answered.

"Judica me, Deus, et discerna causam——"

"Father," Benedict whispered at these words. "This is Mass for the Dead!"

Father Dahr did not hear him. Benedict tugged his robe. "Father," he repeated, more urgently, "this is not——"

". . . meam de gente sancta: ab homine iniquo et doloso erue me."

There were murmurs in the church. These were not the words for the Dead. Benedict rose to his feet and leaned over into Father Dahr's ear: "Father," he cried, "you've forgotten that this is *not* right. We must say the Mass for the Dead!"

Father Dahr turned his heavy head toward him and said hoarsely:

"Get back!" His lips moved then and he continued: *"Emitte lucem tuam et veritatem tuam; ipsa me deduxerunt et adduxerunt in montem sanctum, et in tabernacula tua."*

"Do not insult the Dead, Father!" a voice cried from the audience.

Father Dahr paused; his voice began, then trembled, and he turned, his eyes drawn to the voice. Benedict pulled at his robes, then placed his clasped hands against his throat.

"What? What?" Fathr Dahr stammered hoarsely.

Two troopers entered the church through the front door. A profound silence settled on the people. They moved down the aisles searching through the crowd.

"You've forgotten," Benedict whispered.

The troopers moved through the benches, tapping men on the shoulder with sticks and jerking their thumbs to the door. The workers' heads lifted and they glanced nervously about them, and one by one rose and made their way through the crowd to the door. A woman started a chanting wail, fear and mournful keening combined in it, an elegiac protest against death and oppression, so old, so traditional it filled the church with the oppressive memory of history.

Father Dahr rose unsteadily and crossed his hands over his eyes. Suddenly, in front of the church, leaping up from the kneeling worshippers and rushing for the sacristy door, a man burst toward them. He pushed through the communion rail gates. A trooper shouted after him. Benedict caught a glimpse of his white face, grinning tensely, as the man rushed past him. Shouts now rose from everywhere, drowning even the wailing of the old woman; and the men rose from their benches and began to surge toward the doors.

Outside they heard a shot. Screams, though from outside, still piercing, followed the cries in the church, and all of a sudden they were in a panic, climbing over the benches, falling down between them, crushing against the wall. Glass tinkled, and grotesque hieroglyphs appeared in the unstained windows, showing fantastically the blue sky. They burst up the aisle of the church, through the railing, through the sacristy and into the garden beyond.

Father Dahr had stood watching, his hands by his sides, his face strangely calm. Benedict's hands were gripped together palm to palm, his wrists ached.

The church was in a dense uproar. Women were screaming now, abandoned to fear, and children were shrieking. The men were breaking out in every direction—through the side doors, through doors leading into the cellar, through an open window. The two troopers had meanwhile been joined by others, and they swung up and down the aisles through the screaming crowd, their clubs rising and falling: and outside on the street the crowd broke and ran for their homes, or for the hills.

Almost as soon as it began it was suddenly over. The church was clear. Benches were overturned, books were lying in the aisles, hats and bonnets, a shoe, a package of tobacco. . . . The coffin remained undisturbed at the foot of the altar.

Father Brumbaugh appeared at the door, gazed at them with a bitter, yet mocking, expression, and then disappeared.

The old man sat down on the altar steps.

Outside Benedict could hear the faint sound of running, the sound of a motorcycle. Across the red carpet, as clear as though it had been printed meticulously there in black ink, was the exact outline of a single foot. . . .

It was like midnight on the streets. It was only noon, but the streets were deserted, the Hollow had the blind look of a sleeping town . . . as though the covering night had suddenly been ripped away. The Mill, whose boom was like the beating of a heart, unnoticed, was still: and Benedict heard the stillness now. An uncanny waiting silence followed.

Benedict came along the road at the foot of the Hill until it reached Washington Avenue and followed it down to Shady.

He had led Father Dahr back to the house and had dragged him upstairs and put him to bed. Then he had called a doctor, but had not waited to learn what the doctor had found. Father Brumbaugh was gone. His head had begun to ache; there was a roar in his ears: he clapped his hands over them and rocked back and forth.

The coffin remained alone in the church.

He could see, lifting his eyes to look at the sky, men on horses galloping over the red dunes on their way to the hills. The taste of murder was in the air.

The blinds had been drawn at home, and they were seated around the kitchen table in the darkness.

When he entered his mother burst into tears.

"I'm all right, Mama," he said in a tired voice.

His father took off his glasses and began to wipe them. New sweat appeared over the gray shadow of old sweat: fear over fear. He wiped his face, too, with the same handkerchief.

"I was there," his father said, hardly above a whisper, and Benedict stared at him and realized that his father had been worrying about him ever since the riot.

"I helped Father Dahr into the house," he explained to his father, and his father nodded. "I called the doctor for him."

His mother, who would have reacted to this, only looked at him—at his hands, at his head, as though somehow these repossessed him.

190

"But I'm all *right*, Mama!" he repeated.

She put both hands on his head, like a benediction, and then laid her face on it. He felt his hair grow wet. His father stared at them blindly, and Joey, as though this affected him more than anything else had, grew pale, and stared at them with a fixed forgotten smile. Benedict patted her shoulder and whispered in her ear. "Mama, you see, I'm all right." She turned from him finally and went to the stove and brought him a bowl of beet soup. He ate it obediently.

They seemed, in that darkness, to be entombed. They could hear, as if it came from miles above them, sounds—sounds distorted and sinister; once, too, the sound of a shot, and Benedict, who had never heard gunshots before, only raised his head for a moment and then returned to his soup.

"But Papa——" he finally said, and his father raised his head and read his eyes.

"I don't know," he answered with a heavy shrug, his eyes turned down. Only his father understood that his unspoken question referred to the promise of the men who had gathered on the hills the night before. His mother seemed not to hear anything—she sat and gazed at his face following every move of his lips and his head.

He looked at his father and their eyes met, and in the semi-darkness they clung together: and they exchanged knowledge with sudden clarity, and they joined in conviction.

"But why did they come?" Benedict asked, and he was speaking only to his father now in that low, understood tone that had come into his voice.

His father shifted on his chair; and then for some reason spoke in English. "To take mens back to Mill!"

Benedict stared at him with remorse.

"Papa," he said in Lithuanian, "speak to me——"

His father looked at him and repeated stubbornly: "Take mens to Mill! You see, you see!"

Benedict lowered his eyes.

"Back to the Mill?" he echoed.

His father nodded. Benedict looked at him again, and his

father turned his eyes away, and getting ready to speak again in "English," the "hunky" expression he wore for the American world returned to his face, returned for Benedict: "They come ask: 'What you name? How come you no vork today? You vant vork? You come by me.'"

"But in church, Papa!"

His father shrugged again cynically, looking at him as he shrugged. "Best place—come church! All workingmen in church—they know! Come church and find. No hunt hard!"

He shook his head with bitter laughter, and Benedict felt the sting of that laughter.

"Don't go out on the street again!" his mother suddenly cried, as though waked from a spell, rapping Joey across the head.

Joey ducked and slid off the chair under the table, rubbing his head.

She lifted her apron to her eyes and wept in it.

"See?" Joey said from under the table. "You started to cry!"

They stayed in the house all the rest of the day, except that in the evening Benedict returned to the church to inquire about Father Dahr. The doctor, who had come back a second time, reported that Father Dahr was sleeping and would recover from a slight stroke. Benedict asked for Father Brumbaugh and learned he had not come home since morning.

The Hollow remained tense all the rest of the day. Troopers came to the homes of individual workers and if they found anyone at home forced him to go to work. But there was no violence. They put no light on, ate supper of bread and soup, and went to bed.

Still, curled next to Joey's warm bony body, Benedict was jerked roughly awake by heavy pounding on the door. The dawn was graying the windows. He lay still so as not to wake his brother who breathed serenely beside him. The door under his window opened and he heard his father's morning-husky voice, and then the familiar police-voice demand:

"Are you Vincentas Bulmanis?"

"Yes, Boss," his father answered humbly.

"Do you know where Dobrik is?"

192

"No, Boss."

"You're lying, you greenhorn son-of-a-bitch! Why ain't you at work today? Sick?"

"No, Boss," his father replied. "Mill fire me."

"Oh, is that so?" the trooper said. "Well, you're hired back right now!"

8.

This was Benedict's first train ride. He'd never been on a train before, and yet he felt no thrill. When Father Brumbaugh said to him, "You and I are going to see the Bishop, Benedict!" he had nodded without speaking.

They left at noon. It would be a two hour trip. His father had not come home the night before: he had stayed in the Mill. Some of the workers had been induced to remain in the Mill where they were fed and where they slept. A large group of Negro workers had been run into the Mill in closed box-cars. They had been rounded up in town and from out-of-town, and didn't know where they were bound for until they got there. Then they stayed. Some had been able to escape by climbing the high barbed-wire wall separating the Mill from the river and swimming across to the woods beyond, dodging bullets. There were no grown men left in the valley, or in the workers' section of the City. It was as if a strange disease had taken the male population off—or a war had started.

Now he sat brooding on a green plush chair. Father Brumbaugh sat beside him, with a restrained, but excited, smile on his lips, exclaiming: "Look at that marvelous lawn, Benedict! Those are Lombardy poplars—they must be a hundred years old: They remind you of an Old Master's painting, don't they? That's Old English —that house we're passing—we've so many of them outside of Boston. . . ."

He could not feel as excited as Father Brumbaugh. He had not seen Father Dahr before he left, but he had learned that the old Father was on his feet again. For some reason he had not wanted to see the old man. Nor had he wanted to see Father Brumbaugh immediately: Father Brumbaugh had sent a messenger to bring him. Somehow, he had wanted to get away from both of them. He was tired of being pulled.

The image of the black footprint, clear and distinct on the altar carpet, haunted him: it had come back to him that night in his dream, multiplied by a thousand others, running up and down the altar steps, across the altar itself. Obscenity and sacrilege: and then Father Brumbaugh's passionate face watching them from the doorway, oblivious to the dark footprint, staring only at Father Dahr with such an expression of triumphant fury that Benedict, in his dream, had been shaken awake.

He turned willingly from this memory to the vision of his father's face in that moment of poignant confidence that had passed between them . . . or had it been a dream, had he imagined it? He felt an anguish of fear and doubt—and he reached for certainty in his mind and could not find it.

Now his father was gone! The Company would never give in to the strikers—it never had; the workers had never been able to keep a union going, and the Company had always managed, through stoolpigeons and spies, to break it up every time it got started. It would send troopers into all the hills and woods and drag the men out, one by one, and break, as they broke a man's bone, this hopeless strike.

The young priest sitting beside him didn't understand any of that, he thought. He was now staring out of the window and crying: "But that's a red maple!" It seemed the farther he got from Hunky Hollow, the happier he became—welcoming even trees as though welcoming a lost world.

"Father?" he said.

Father Brumbaugh turned his glowing eyes on him. Benedict flushed uneasily. Again a flash of remembered affection passed out of him for the young priest—of a strange gratitude for his purity, for his very difference from everything ugly in the Hollow —his gentility, his musical tone of voice, his air of being used to beautiful things—as though these things brought him closer to the purity and nobility of religion. It made him weak and gentle, too, and Benedict felt the same protective feeling rise up in him again.

"Father," he said, with deep feeling, "when the trouble's over, I want to come to the Church with you and never leave it."

Father Brumbaugh tore his enamored eyes from the distant estates that stood like Christmas cards behind screens of great fir and maple trees, and smiled with approving surprise.

"But, Benedict," he said, "that's our secret—that's the reason for our trip."

Benedict's heart leaped.

"You mean——?" He hardly dared speak.

Father Brumbaugh nodded happily, and brought out a letter. "He asked me to bring you. He wants to interrogate you."

"And then I can——"

"Enter a seminary?" Father Brumbaugh nodded with a gift-giving smile. "As soon as you're old enough."

Benedict sank back into his seat. Hot and cold waves burst over him. For a moment the pounding of the train sounded like his blood that had broken free and was roaring in his ears. Tears rose to his eyes and he shuddered them away. He felt that he would begin to shake all over and not stop. There seemed to be an enormous light in the train, as though the sun were screwed to the ceiling. He bit his lip and pushed his soaked face into the back of the seat. He felt Father Brumbaugh's comforting hand on his shoulder.

It seemed to Benedict as though it had already taken place, and he was now leaving home. This was the train taking him. Home was past now: mother, Joey, Vince, Rudolph, Father Dahr, the old church, the smell in the Hollow, the troopers, the guns, Mother Burns—all these were gone, he was delivered from them. When he returned it would be with power to set them right. He prayed with his wet lips pressed against the dusty seat. He moved among his prayers with his hand uplifted over the heads of workers, over the heads of the Company officials. Both would kneel before him. They would rise again brothers. The church would be crowded:

he could hear the music now; the brilliant lights, the thunder of celebration: *Kyrie, eleison!* throbbed in his mind, *Christe, eleison!*

"I want to come back to the Hollow when I'm ordained," he said with brimming eyes.

Father Brumbaugh replied, with a slight shadow on his face. "You come from the lower class, Benedict, and the lower class needs priests who rise from them and understand their problems. The Bishop will be glad to hear you say that!" His eyes clouded. "The last days!" he cried.

"I wouldn't have failed the way Father Dahr did!" Benedict cried painfully.

The little blue lines around his lips creased, and Father Brumbaugh said, with restraint: "Father Dahr was responsible for a great deal!"

"Can I learn, Father——" Benedict asked earnestly, searching his face. "Can I learn how to work among my—my people, Father? Will the seminary——"

"Especially that!" Father Brumbaugh said happily, and with a decisive nod of his head.

Benedict was silent. He watched the unrolling landscape for a moment and then asked softly: "Are *you* going to ask the Bishop——" He hesitated.

Father Brumbaugh studied him.

"Ask the Bishop," Benedict resumed, "to—to send you—away—somewhere——"

"No," Father Brumbaugh answered firmly, his lips tightening. "I planned to—but no, not now!"

The shadow of anxiety cleared from his eyes and Benedict sighed deeply.

"Father," he said shyly, looking at his fingers, "I was very glad when you came to the Hollow."

The priest looked down at him with surprise.

"You were, Benedict?" he said, moved.

Benedict nodded. "I thought you'd leave again," he went on with difficulty, "when you saw how——" He swallowed and wet his lips. "——how we lived. I mean—everybody in the City hates us," he said.

196

"They're just afraid, Benedict," Father Brumbaugh told him kindly.

Benedict looked up. "Why?" he asked with a perplexed expression.

Father Brumbaugh was surprised. It was so obvious why! "Well," he laughed, a little helplessly, "I don't exactly know why. *We* were always for some reason afraid of the poor—I mean at home, our family and friends. Why, I don't know. We weren't *really* afraid, of course—there were police to protect us and so on; but we *were* afraid . . . in an odd way." He chewed his lower lip thoughtfully, frowning. "Well—just look at what's happened in the last few days here!" he cried. "The riots! The violence! The strikes! The better-class people don't act that way, Benedict; they've been terrified; they've complained; they've demanded that the police force be increased." He shrugged nervously. "Why, it's been nerve-wracking," he said.

"But, Father——" Benedict gasped.

"Resisting police," Father Brumbaugh went on. "Like the anarchists in Boston. Have you heard of Sacco and Vanzetti?"

Benedict shook his head.

"Well, that's the same thing. Foreigners! If you'd been in Boston—and now here!"

"But, Father," Benedict said painfully. "The workers *had* to strike!"

"*Had* to, Benedict?" Father Brumbaugh asked reprovingly. "All of them?"

Benedict hesistated. "All of them?" he repeated, thinking. "But— they had to, or the Mill would have——"

"Who put the idea in their heads, Benedict," Father Brumbaugh went on gently. "Themselves? You know that's not true. An agitator —a Communist agitator—was there. *I* know about that meeting on the hill!"

Benedict went pale. Then he flushed guiltily and his eyes fell. For a moment he felt scaldingly exposed: his mind completely opened and revealed. He dropped his eyes to his fingers and gripped his hands together. The train bore forward, and day snapped on and off.

"Father," he said, after a long slow time, without lifting his eyes. "Father if you knew something—something like where the leaders of the strike were hiding, would it be a sin not to tell the police?"

Father Brumbaugh's face turned swiftly on him. "Do you know?" he demanded excitedly, leaning his head down to look into Benedict's eyes.

Benedict lowered his head further. "No," he said. "But, would it?"

"Of course!" the priest cried. "Do you know what Dobrik is? A Communist! A criminal, an enemy of the Church! Wouldn't it be both a civil and spiritual sin to protect a criminal?"

Benedict nodded. Anguish tossed in him.

"But my father——" he began again, and then stopped.

Father Brumbaugh turned to him with new surprise.

"Is *your* father one of the strikers?" he asked with a disbelieving smile.

Benedict couldn't answer. "I don't think so," he mumbled.

"Oh," Father Brumbaugh said, pleased to have remembered it and offering the memory to Benedict to show that he had had no real lack of confidence in him and his family. "Of course! Your father was discharged by the Mill: so he couldn't have been on strike."

Father Brumbaugh put his arm around Benedict and whispered: "I know how you've suffered, Benedict. I'm not blind. You've gone without proper food many times, haven't you? That's why I wanted you to eat with me as often as possible."

Benedict remembered the cake in the kitchen and Father Dahr standing portentously in the open door. *He had not eaten the cake after all,* he thought.

"We eat," he said gruffly.

Father Brumbaugh pressed his shoulder reassuringly, and then removed his arm. "I understand," he said warmly.

He began to tremble a moment later, as Father Brumbaugh's eyes returned to the scene outside. *Suppose the troopers knew?* he thought wildly. *Was it a sin?* He pressed his hands over his eyes, and the broad brown face of Dobrik rose up, and he heard the calm voice saying. *"What's your color going to be?"* *"Red,"* the

198

voice had answered quickly. *"As long as you got the heart to go with it, and you're a union man, I'm here to defend your right to be my Brother!"*

Benedict shuddered violently as though only now he realized how close to great danger he had been. As if he had almost blurted out the name, Dobrik, under the influence of some treacherous spell! Sweat oozed up through his skin and he "watched" it cautiously roll down his side.

He turned to the window and cried: "Rich people live in those houses, don't they, Father?"

Father Brumbaugh studied the passing mansions with a tiny smile, his lips slightly pursed, and estimated: "Not so *very* rich, I'd say. *We* could have lived in any of these!"

Benedict exclaimed: "Your family?"

Father Brumbaugh nodded tolerantly. "Oh, yes," he said casually. "Our home was——" His eyes filled with nostalgia. "——much finer. . . ."

"Than *these?*" Benedict cried incredulously, staring out at the castle-like mansions.

"But, oh, yes," Father Brumbaugh replied mildly.

He heard Joey's indignant voice: "Oo, what a *big* lie!"

"But——" Benedict wanted to protest, and then stopped, not knowing what it was he wanted to protest.

"My father," Father Brumbaugh said, his eyes narrowing into a reminiscent and slightly bitter mood, "was an important man in his day. When you think of Boston," he went on, with a slightly embarrassed smile, "you perhaps think of beans, or Bunker Hill. But when Bostonians think of Boston, they think of Brumbaugh, of fine fruniture. In fact," he said with a deprecating laugh, "that was my father's business slogan. He had it painted ten feet high on his factory, 'When Boston thinks of Brumbaugh, it thinks of Fine Furniture,'" he quoted. "Mother, of course, didn't approve," he added. He fingered his lips delicately as though to trace the faint smile he had on them. "Father didn't want me to enter the Church," he confided. "Mother did." He turned his eyes again to the outside. "Oh, yes," he said lazily, "our place was much nicer!"

"Then," Benedict said, with a kind of understanding coming

home to him. "Then, our place must seem like——" But he didn't finish.

Faher Brumbaugh turned a pale smile on him.

"You see, Benedict," he said in a simple quiet voice, "I was prepared to live and suffer in a tent if need be."

Benedict stared at him, thinking of the tents in the woods. . . .

Their destination was Morgantown. It was the biggest city Benedict had ever seen. It had the tallest buildings. Taxicabs swarmed up and down the streets. A vague but familiar fear welled up in him, as though these people, too, somehow, in some mysterious way, would detect at a glance that he came from Hunky Hollow. The city looked Protestant. He felt that he wouldn't talk, wouldn't meet people's eyes squarely; he would let Father Brumbaugh do everything for him.

Father Brumbaugh hailed a taxi, and this was the first taxi ride Benedict had ever had.

They rode through the city and into the green suburbs. Benedict stared, the window rolled down, at the great homes, always discreetly set back among lawns and unfamiliar trees. He was struck by the uncanny stillness here, the strange absence of children, the so-quiet and almost sleepy quality of the restful green vistas.

He turned, at one point, to Father Benedict with his nostrils distended: "What's smelling like that?"

Father Brumbaugh gave him a puzzled look.

"I don't smell anything," he said. Then added as an afterthought: "Unless it's the air, it's fresh."

But Benedict didn't believe it was just air he was smelling. . . .

The Bishop's mansion was set among a grove of elm trees. To Benedict's surprise there was a large pool in the front lawn, and gold fish swam among the green-padded lilies. A bronze sun dial stood beside it. Farther on, he could see a row of dog kennels and near it a man leading a huge greyhound. There were great flaming-leafed bushes bordering the gravel-covered driveway leading up through the grounds.

The taxi came to a stop underneath a stone arch, in the keystone of which was a carved coat-of-arms, a great cross, and in Latin the inscription: *In hoc signo vinces* The mansion was ivy-covered from top to bottom: blinking windows stared out from behind the shaggy greenery; copper, brass and bronze gleamed dully from windows and doors and cornices. Over it all rested a peaceful, shining calm like a dream.

They rang the copper bell, standing between two copper-bound carriage lamps, which hung on each side of the door, while the taxi which brought them there crunched through the gravel on its way back. And Benedict felt as though it had brought him miraculously here and left him stranded on the unreal side of sleep.

And then, as though it opened like an eye or a mouth, the door parted without a sound, and a young man was showing them into the library.

Father Brumbaugh spoke casually and smiled at Benedict whenever Benedict caught his eye, as if to say: "See—didn't I tell you?" without explaining what. The library was furnished with dark leather chairs, a broad walnut desk, dark reading lamps with rose-colored shades; and the walls were covered with calf-bound volumes whose gilt titles flickered in the dim light. When Benedict stepped into the room, he felt cocooned, as though the noise of his feet and even his breath was suddenly absorbed into the carpet. He almost stumbled in the sudden softness. His knees wobbled: he felt as though he were not walking at all, but somehow floating. The booked walls shut him in with their leather solemnity and the air he breathed seemed like cotton that packed itself around his nose and throat and gently suffocated him.

Father Brumbaugh indicated the chair he was to sit in, and himself sat, with a slight flutter of his eyelids, down in one of the dark leather ones that sighed luxuriously as he sat, as though it were proud of it. Benedict's chair just squeaked a little; he didn't dare to put his whole body down. Father Brumbaugh offered him a ghostly smile from across the room, but Benedict could not smile back. He did not think he had the strength to push one through the steeped air.

It was not too long before the same reserved young man, with very dark wet eyelashes, returned and said something to Father Brumbaugh in a voice so soft and melodious, and pitched in a

201

tone Benedict never heard before, so that, although it carried to him, he failed to understand what he had said to Father Brumbaugh.

"Thank you," Father Brumbaugh said gravely, and rose and followed the young man out of the room.

And now Benedict felt as though his last link with his past life had totally disappeared and he was at the mercy of this. The Hollow was as remote as his birth; he couldn't return it to mind, as though the very magnificence of the room refused to accept such images. He stared at Catholic medals and pictures on the walls—examined them without connecting them to himself, to his religion, as though they were things in a store window. And this was because he had taken it for granted that "Catholic" and being poor and a worker were the same thing: what was "rich" belonged somehow always to the Company.

He sat stiffly in the chair, therefore, a little on guard, unable to move his legs or arms. When his haunches grew sore, he moved them stealthily, letting the leather creak bit by bit. A long row of framed Popes looked down from the walls at him, culminating in a large Pope Pius XI, in a gilt frame, who with Pope Benedict XV flanking him watched him placidly as he squirmed. Benedict wanted to nod, as though he owed a certain respect to them, and explain himself away—he felt uncomfortable that the Popes had only him to watch in the great silent room. Benedict longed for Father Brumbaugh to return.

As time passed he felt himself dwindle more and more. The room was too powerful: two long drapes showed martyrs being burned and stabbed, and blood fell in huge dark crimson drops from ceiling to floor. An enormous cross held his eye; the wood was a dark highly polished walnut, and the spikes penetrating His hands and feel were gold: and it seemed to him as he watched that Christ moved.

He shuddered and turned his eyes deliberately away. Fantastically he had been carried into another, unbelievabe land. Voices here were so soft and muted, and sounded tones so sweet, so different from home, that he could not believe they were human. So Father Brumbaugh had spoken; and he remembered how fascinated he had been by his voice that first meeting.

202

He was an interloper here. He wanted something important to happen so that the room would have more than himself to honor. He felt that what the room expected was for him to sneak around in it, filling his pockets with pens and pencils and the money he could see lying on the walnut desk. Sweat gathered under his haunches and he turned cold at the thought that he would leave a wet spot behind him on the fine leather. He commanded himself to stop sweating.

The same, almost catlike young man, was at the door again. Benedict stared guiltily, and helplessly hid his hands behind him. He brought all his senses to bear in case the man spoke to him so that he would not fail to understand.

But the man only lifted his head sharply. It was a command, and Benedict slid off his chair. He felt his haunches unpeel from the clinging leather. His hightop shoes, his long black stockings and knee-pants, patched but the patch hidden, which had been put on with such care, now seemed to him like wood. He walked stiff-legged across the yielding carpet, while the young man waited silently until he was within range: and then he turned and Benedict followed him out of the room.

The hall, for some reason, seemed to be under water: it was shadowy green. Then, a door opened, and Benedict saw Father Brumbaugh standing modestly in a corner, petting a tiny smile on his face. Benedict's face was like a white streak of chalk. He couldn't take his eyes from Father Brumbaugh until a voice said: "So you're Benedict!"

And Benedict whirled, for it was Father Brumbaugh speaking, he thought: the very words he had greeted him with that first day. But Father Brumbaugh's mouth hadn't opened. Instead, sitting behind a dark desk, which seemed somehow, like the hall, to be moss-green, sunk in a green shadow, sat the Bishop. He was watching Benedict without a smile, his very clear blue eyes abruptly separating from his full, cream-smooth face. His head was covered with white hair, although his face was youthful: white hair that grew like silk. A pale yellow shade ran through it. Benedict thought he must have been born in the house, and grew in it like a mushroom.

"So you're Benedict," the Bishop repeated.

Benedict nodded, and lowered his eyes.

"What are you here for?" he was next asked.

Benedict looked up startled; looked from the Bishop to Father Brumbaugh, who closed his eyes slowly, and then slowly opened them.

"You——" Benedict began abruptly. "You wanted to . . . question me?" he said.

"Oh, yes," the Bishop said carelessly, "we'll come to that. But, tell me, Benedict," he said slowly, leaning his head out of what only then Benedict saw was a shadow, so that his eyes looked pale, almost transparent. "Tell me, Benedict, what do you know about Father Dahr?"

"Father Dahr?" Benedict repeated between dry lips.

"I've had letters," the Bishop said, "from both of them."

Benedict looked at Father Brumbaugh, who stared only at the Bishop.

"From both rector and curate," the Bishop added. "Both speak well of you. Both have highly recommended you to me." He paused. "Tell me," he said, leaning slightly forward, his voice tinged with a faint, almost ironic, curiosity, "how do you manage to win such a high opinion from both of them?"

Benedict could not reply.

"Tell me in your own words," the Bishop went on, after studying Benedict for a moment but not pressing for an answer, "tell me what would you do if you were the pastor of St. Joseph's?"

Benedict licked his lips. "I don't understand, Fa—Your Grace ——" He flushed.

The Bishop ignored his confusion.

"Haven't you dreamed of being?"

Benedict nodded dumbly.

"Tell me your dream."

"I would——" he said impulsively, and stopped. He looked at Father Brumbaugh and Father Brumbaugh nodded encouragement to him. He laughed suddenly, then clapped his hand to his mouth.

"Go on," the Bishop directed. "Would you continue the church as it is?"

"No!" Benedict cried.

"Go on," the Bishop said, "what would you do? What would you do first?"

"Oh, Father," Benedict breathed, his eyes shining, "I would *live* in the church! It would be my real home! I would make it clean and spotless. I would paint it, and decorate it. I would have the workers come and fix it for me—they'd come if I asked them to! Even my father! I know they would!"

"Does the church need much repair, then?"

"Yes, Father," Benedict replied.

"Why haven't repairs been made?"

"I don't know, Father," Benedict said slowly.

"Has there been enough money?"

"No, there has not been."

"Then that's the reason why there have been no repairs? Is that right?"

Benedict hesitated. "No," he replied slowly.

"No?" the Bishop repeated. "Why, then?"

"The church *could* have been kept beautiful," Benedict said fervently. "*I* would have kept it beautiful."

"Because you cared so much?"

Benedict nodded.

"When do you get up to serve Mass?" the Bishop asked.

"Four in the morning," Benedict replied.

"Four in the morning?"

"Yes, Father—I—have to do other things before coming to church."

"Other things?"

"Yes—I——" Benedict flushed. The vague idea of confiding in the Bishop about Mother Burns fled across his brain. "I—I—pray," he ended huskily.

"When do you arrive at the church?"

"At five."

"And Mass is at——?"

"Six."

"Why so early, then?"

"I—I like to come early," he said.

"Is Father Dahr waiting for you when you arrive?"

"No," Benedict replied.

"Where is he usually?"

Benedict's lips worked; his throat choked. "I don't know," he whispered.

"Don't know?" The Bishop smiled. "Is he downstairs, in church, waiting for you?"

"No," Benedict replied in a low voice, looking off to the floor.

"Where do you find him, then?"

"Sometimes," Benedict said slowly, without lifting his eyes, "he's sick, and he's asleep—and I go upstairs, and wake him," he said.

"Is Mass ever late because you have to wake him?"

"Once, but not much," Benedict said painfully.

"Because you had to go upstairs and wake him?"

Benedict nodded, and said in a whisper, "Only once."

"Only once," the Bishop said, and watched as Benedict nodded. "And what was he sick of, do you know?"

The Bishop looked at him over the desk, and the room seemed very lonely. He wanted to go away now. His heart had been beating recklessly in his chest; and now it suddenly stopped and his head seemed to echo with its silence.

"What is happening in your parish?" the Bishop asked.

Benedict didn't want to answer. He felt tired. The Bishop had to repeat his question.

"I don't know, Father," Benedict replied distantly.

"But the church was invaded," the Bishop said.

Benedict nodded. He saw the footstep on the red carpet. Only now it was an inky bare foot: the toes and heel were acutely marked.

"What is happening in your parish?" the Bishop asked.

Benedict shrugged. He lifted his eyes finally to the Bishop; they were filmed with tears that had somehow formed there: he stared blindly for a moment, appalled at the sudden loss of his sight.

206

"I can't see," he said simply; then he brushed the tears away. "They're striking against the Company," he said.

"And the funeral?" the Bishop asked.

Benedict gasped. They had forgotten the coffin in the church! Late that night men had come secretly into the church and had taken it away and buried it.

"But it was wrong," he said suddenly.

"What was wrong?" the Bishop asked.

"To kill," Benedict said softly.

"But Father Dahr?" the Bishop asked.

"He forgot!" Benedict cried, lifting his stricken face to the Bishop. "He forgot!"

"Forgot what?" the Bishop asked, peering at Benedict.

Benedict brought his hands against his cheeks, and his mouth was opened in a rigid O.

"Wasn't Father Dahr warned not to hold Mass?" the Bishop asked.

But Benedict didn't hear him.

"*I* warned him," Father Brumbaugh said respectfully, but his voice did not seem to penetrate the two.

"They came into the church," Benedict said, closing his eyes and his face growing pale. "They came into the church and they yelled: 'Come out! Come out!' "

"Who, Benedict?" the Bishop asked.

"The troopers," Benedict replied, shuddering. He looked around the room and lowered his voice. "They came for the strikers," he confided.

"And didn't Father Dahr know they'd come?"

Benedict shook his head until his cheeks blurred. It wasn't in reply to the question, however: the memory shook in his head until it was lost.

The Bishop was silent. He studied Benedict, and his lips moved. He lifted his hand, and Benedict stared at the ring on it. "Kiss it," the Bishop urged, and slowly Benedict came forward, fell to his knees, and the Bishop leaned far over the desk to lower his hand. Benedict heard Pogy's foggy voice. The hand tasted sweet as it touched his lips, cool as the remembered dice.

"When would you be ready to go?" the Bishop asked.

"When?" Benedict repeated, raising his wondering face.

"To St. Thomas' Seminary?"

"Oh," Benedict said. A silence followed and he let it go on, not understanding that he was to reply to a question.

"You'll be informed," the Bishop said and raised his hand and extended it with two fingers elevated.

Benedict lowered his head.

"In the name of the Father, and of the Son . . ." he heard the Bishop say.

9.

He carried an aluminum bucket, which was divided into two sections: the bottom half was warm with coffee, and warmed his thigh gently as he walked. The Mill was quiet: smoke was coming thread-like from the high stacks, as if there was work inside, but it was quiet. The Hollow was deserted. Old women, wearing *babushkas*, darted down the narrow alleys, with handkerchiefs clamped to their mouths. Dogs whimpered uneasily in the corners; and watching him as he passed, from under the porches cats sat with their tails curled around them. It was almost noon.

Troopers, with the shallow steel helmets of the World War, stood at the steel mill gates. Around the Mill the high brick wall was topped with barbed wire, and at certain strategic points men in khaki uniforms sat sullenly in the sunlight, cradling rifles in their arms. High above the walls, in a wooden tower overlooking the City and Hollow, sat other guardsmen behind machine-guns. There was nobody else in sight. He had to cross the railroad track to get to the gate.

The tall trooper looked down at him. "Whaddye want?"

Benedict stared, unable suddenly to answer. The soldier prodded him lazily with the barrel of his gun. Benedict started: the soldier's lips parted slightly. Benedict lifted mutely the work bucket up to the trooper.

The soldier glanced at it.

"My mother," Benedict said painfully, "told me to bring my father his lunch."

"What's your father's name?"

"Vincentas Bulmanis," Benedict replied.

"Oh, a hunky!" he drawled; stared at Benedict and pondered. "He in here?"—jerking his head behind him.

Benedict gazed past him: the iron gate was closed. It was like a prison gate, solidly barred; a little door, only large enough to let a man through, was cut into it. He nodded.

"What was his name?" the guardsman asked again, and concentrated his face to receive it. Blinking with the struggle to speak normally, Benedict repeated it. The soldier looked at him sourly, then took the bucket from him. He opened it and brought out a sour-dough sandwich, separated the slices of bread and sniffed at it. There was nothing but fat drippings on the bread. He looked into the coffee container and dipped his whole finger into it. "Warm," he said suspiciously.

"I live near here," Benedict explained.

The guardsman put the bucket together again and said: "If your old man's inside, he's getting fed all right. Scoot back home."

Benedict hesitated.

"Git!" the guardsman ordered, taking a menacing step forward. Benedict whirled and ran, and the guardsman broke into laughter.

"Hey, kid!" he called, "come back here!"

Benedict stopped and looked back cautiously. Suddenly the noon whistle, gigantic against his ear, roared; all the muscles and nerves of his body stood up to answer it. The roots of his hair tingled.

"Come on!" the guardsman commanded.

Benedict advanced warily, keeping an eye on the man's mouth. He stopped just out of reach. The guardsman crooked his index finger and beckoned him onward playfully. Benedict took another step and now the guardsman leaned over and took back the bucket. He opened it again. He took out the sour-dough bread sandwich, looked at it, bit into it, made a disgusted face and spat it out on the ground. He sniffed, then, at the coffee, took a mouthful, swabbed his mouth with it, and then spat it out, in a thick brown stream; then he poured the rest on the ground.

He handed the bucket back. "Okay," he said. "You can go in."

He knocked on the iron door with the butt of his rifle, and the little door opened, and Benedict stepped through.

A yellow brick road led past the brick time-shanty where blue-coated Coal-and-Iron police sat on benches playing checkers. The steam of whisky rose from them. Rifles stood stacked against the walls, and revolver butts stuck out of black holsters. One man laughed and turned his slightly bitter eyes from the checker board and caught Benedict in his sight as though he was a quarry. Benedict froze. For some reason he grinned, and his skin crackled; he lifted his bucket up to show. The policeman's expression didn't change; he spat tobacco juice on the ground, and rubbed it out with his shoe.

Benedict had often taken his father warm lunches. His father worked in Number 2 Furnace, that looked something like a gigantic pot, and towered, tangled with pipes, tubes, catwalks and lines, high above the rest of the Mill. A skip hoist leaned against the furnace. Little cars moved up and down it—coming down to get filled with iron ore, limestone and coke, and then going back up to the top of the furnace and dumping this in. Slowly then this sank to the bottom of the furnace, heated by a roaring gas, and finally melting into pig-iron that flowed from the furnace through a hole in the bottom like a living sea. Only now, the cars, though they moved busily, were empty: empty they rode up the incline to the top of the furnace and dumped this into the empty furnace, and then clattered down again to be reloaded with nothing. Benedict· felt a ghostly stillness underneath the synthetic noise: only the machinery went through the motions of working. A huge shears roared and pounded —cutting air in half. Smoke, from oiled rags, curled out of the chimney stacks.

He entered the little shanty built around the hearth of Furnace No. 1. The squat base of the furnace sat in the center of a brick yard, its top jutting up through the roof and lost to view. Men were banking the furnace, and stood around the open tuyere holes dressed in heavy blue shirts, goggled so that they looked like frogs. They wheeled clay into the yard, and took the tuyeres out and packed the holes with clay. There were only a few of them—men who had been brought in from the office as well as regular furnace workers. Some men sat on the worn and shining benches, holding a hand of greasy cards: they had bottles of whisky beside them, and didn't notice him as he went by, as though lost in a dream of cards. Soft, minor curses followed him.

He passed through the No. 1 yard, out into the brick sidewalk going to Furnace No. 2. An iron railing separated him from a huge slag pit into which hot slag had been poured and then blown into popcorn with a water hose. Here, the silence seemed more deliberate, more candid. From here, too, because of a trick in the angle of the walk, he could see over the mound of red dirt that ran like a tiny mountain range beside him, across the barbed-wire fence to the City. It lay crouched against the hill, as though conscious of being caught in the sight of the machine-gun in the tower, staring with unblinking calm down into the barricaded Mill. It seemed to Benedict to be not space but time away, as though his childhood distant. He felt suddenly cut off from it: and for a moment he stood still on the brick path, feeling as though he had walked into a trap, and silent iron doors had closed on him and on his boyhood forever. Chills turned his shoulders in a slight dreaming shiver. He ran down the path and burst into Furnace No. 2. Again the same foggy stillness hung over everything. Water dripped from pipes high up on the furnace. The furnace itself was cold: its cold breath touched him as he passed, and this gave him a feeling of having touched death. He stared at it with slightly fearful eyes. This gigantic stove, this fiery oven, where men worked so hard to keep it burning, where they sweated day in and day out, coming home like cloth wrung out by an enormous hand, where they gave up their lives regularly as though steel were made with human flesh and bones as well as coke and lime stone, was dying down into cold ashes. The silence was cold; the yard was lonely.

At first he could find nobody. Benches, like the benches in church, gleamed with grease where bodies had polished them. Only on the other side of the furnace's belly, in the yard where

211

a solitary man was making moulds in a sand bed, he found them grouped around a pig-iron billet silently playing cards.

His father was not playing. He was off to one side, sitting on a wooden block.

Benedict approached.

"Papa," he said indistinctly.

His father was whittling. Benedict recognized, with a pang, that he was whittling a flute out of a piece of ailanthus branch, as he used to do at home.

"Papa," he repeated, and his father looked up.

There was a blinded expression in his eyes when he raised them, and Benedict moved forward. "Papa," he said, seeking for the gentle Lithuanian, "it's me, Benedict!"

His father's eyes focused and cleared. Benedict smiled: his heart seemed to crumple. He cried, hoisting the bucket high in front of his brimming eyes: "Papa! I came to bring you food but the guard took it away!"

He swayed back and forth, and his father laid his flute aside and said: "Sit down, Benedict."

Then, when Benedict was seated beside him on the huge wooden block, asked: "How is your Mama?" as though she belonged first of all to Benedict, and only secondly to him.

"All right, Papa," Benedict replied.

"You tell her I'm all right, too," he said.

"Yes, Papa."

"You'll tell her?"

"Yes, Papa."

He fell silent, and Benedict said: "And Joey's all right, and Rudolph, too."

He didn't dare to look at his father after the first glance. He was ashamed of the pain in his heart, which had come suddenly. He spoke, looking at his feet, which stood amidst parings of steel like apple peels on the iron floor. "I was in Morgantown," he said, "with the Father. We went to see the Bishop, and the Bishop says I can enter school, Papa, to be——" He licked his lips, and added almost silently, "—a priest, if I want to be." He felt nothing lift in himself as he uttered the words.

But his father said: "Good, good. . . ."

He looked up at him surprised, but realized that his father had hardly heard him.

"Papa," he said, "can't you come home?"

His father looked down at his upturned pale face and could hardly smile. He shook his head. "Pretty soon," he whispered.

Benedict dropped his hands in his lap and twisted his fingers. He kicked the iron spirals at his feet. The men with the cards cried—and it was all in a different language—as they played their cards. His father picked the flute up and stuck his knife blade in to carve out an air hole.

"You don't need a dry pea," he said, "to put in." He raised it to his lips, and blew. A low warm note came out of it. "I'll make another hole," he said, "and it will give another note."

Benedict sat and watched him carve in silence. Over their heads a motionless crane sat parked. From it hung a long cable, and beneath the cable a huge electrical iron platter also hung. Beside them, with two handles sticking out like outspread legs, was a 20-pound hammer.

"Did you go to the garden?" his father asked.

"What, Papa?"

"Did you go to the garden?"

"Yes, Papa," Benedict replied. "Mama and me and Joey go. The peas are coming up and the corn is coming up. We already have onions and lettuce. The police——" he said, "rode through Mr. Tronis' garden but they didn't ride through ours."

His father nodded, and Benedict was glad that he could tell him such happy news.

He recalled again: "The guard outside the Mill took the bucket from me, Papa, and threw away the sandwich and spilled out the coffee. Mama *made* you some sandwiches!"

"I understand," his father said.

Now he put the flute again to his mouth, and his gnawed hard fingers moving awkwardly over them, yet with a delicacy Benedict was surprised to see, he blew back and forth on his two notes, low and high. The tip of the flute was wet when he took it out of his mouth. He handed it to Benedict, and Benedict put it into his mouth, tasting his father's pungent cigarette-stained spit, and blew. The sound trembled all through him. He turned to his father and raised the flute, smiling, and blew the two notes proudly back and forth. His father nodded his head and turned him an ear. Benedict took the flute out and laughed.

"Take it with you," his father said.

"Papa," Benedict said, "nobody else *wants* to sell their houses now!"

Suddenly his shoulders began to shake and the horrible tears came up. He folded his arms together and brought his face into them and wept hoarsely through his mouth and nose. He felt his father's great hard hand touch him, then pull him over so that he was lying in his lap, sobbing against the acid, steel-and-coal odor of pants, saturated in an old salty sweat, rancid and keen.

"Papa," he said, his voice muffled on his father's thigh, "what are they going to do to you?"

His father pressed his head and said nothing.

"Papa," Benedict cried, turning his face over, "why don't we all leave the valley and find another place to live?"

His father looked down on his upturned face and his face seemed first hard, and then cold, and then it saddened, and he said: "Where do you think you can go where there are no bosses?"

"God will help you, Papa!" Benedict cried wildly.

"Now lift your head up," his father commanded. He cupped Benedict's chin into his calloused hands and raised him gradually up again. "Tell me, Benedict," he said gravely, "can you keep your mouth tight?"

"Yes, Papa," Benedict answered. He remembered that sharp moment on the train with Father Brumbaugh and he shuddered.

"If I give you a secret to carry?"

Benedict nodded. "Yes, Papa, I swear."

His father looked at him seriously, then put his hand on his head and drew him near. Benedict shut his eyes against his father's heavy shirt, hearing the thunder of his heart, and swallowed the sour salt smell of his body, and his eyes closed tighter with aching tears of love.

214

"When you go back," his father, touching him gently, said, "tell them we'll find a way to come out."

Benedict lifted his head and stared.

"But Papa——" he cried. He looked about the Mill. "But, Papa, the guards!"

His father put his finger to Benedict's lips. "The guards will guard," he said.

"But, Papa——" Benedict began, his lips trembling.

"There's a way," his father said. "Don't fear for me—don't I think always of you? So go," he said, shoving Benedict by the seat of his pants, "and tell Mr. Tipa to come with a boat at midnight outside the No. 2 furnace pipe that goes out into the river."

"Papa, will you go through——?"

His father pushed him gently.

Benedict took a few steps away, turned, and made as if to speak.

"Go, go!" his father cried impatiently.

"Papa," Benedict wailed, "are you hungry?"

His father pushed him away with his hands. Benedict turned mournfully and shuffled through the yard, passing the clot of men covering the cards as though the cards were a living fire and they were hunching over them for warmth. When he stepped out of the gate the trooper looked at him sourly but said nothing. Benedict crossed the tracks and climbed the rough round road through the City home. Half way there he remembered that he had forgotten to bring along the flute.

10.

With the Mill shut down the hot-metal cars stopped coming, and the slag dump hardened into flinty rock, shining in the sunlight from exposed silver bits of steel lodged in hunks of slag. The huge moving monster held what were once the houses and the Ditch in its hard bowels; it had moved on fiery feet along the bottom of the Hollow, meeting the ridge down at the eastern end and moving slowly up the hills and woods in the west. More houses had gone up in flames, had melted in the sudden heat of the inferno: morning showed nothing but a field of gray, pulsating softly with wicked eyes of flame, while underneath, the rusted iron beams and chalky foundations of the houses were locked forever in a grip of iron.

To the west a wall of rock faced the ore dunes, and the sour creek ran down into it, pausing at the mouth of the culvert which had been built to receive it and backing up into a sluggish pond. The creek was low now, but still it formed a growing pool at the mouth of the concrete pipe.

Benedict had not even gone home. When he left the Mill behind, he had skirted the City and taken the road out to the flue dust dunes that led off into the woods farther on. He followed the same road he had walked that night when he had seen Dobrik again; it had barely been visible in the moonless night: but now it was rough with limestone and the dust rose and choked him. But he was half-running and half-walking, his head raised like a prow ahead of him, breathing in the stinging dust and swallowing it.

No one had to tell him how important the message he was carrying was. He would have flown, if he could have. The tall stack of the incinerator guided him; it stood like a lethal finger poisoning the sky, but it also showed him where east and west were.

Over the rise of the hill, from which he could see the other folds of the receding hills fall away, he stopped with fear, and sank down on the curly grass to keep from sight. In the distance a trooper on horse was dragging two men behind him. They were tied together with rope, which was knotted to the saddle. The trooper had found them hiding on the hills. They ran stumbling on stiff feet, holding up their knotted hands in front of them, in an involuntary attitude of supplication. And as he watched with horror, one stumbled against the other and both lost their feet, and the horse dragged them bounding along the road for fifty feet before the trooper turned to look at them. Benedict could hear faintly the curse he flung out at them. The horse turned and flared its soaking nostrils. Benedict could see its distorted white eye, the way it lifted its black hoof and hysterically pawed the ground. The two dragged themselves to their feet, leaving behind a pink path through the dust, and again the horse started, and they ran behind.

And yet even this couldn't stop him. He had watched with horror, but also with impatience. When they were hardly out of sight, he was skimming over the hill and climbing the first red dust dune. The Flue Dust Mill slumbered in the red air as though caught in a spider's web. He pulled "horse's tails" to help himself up. The red dust rose around him like a cloud, got into his mouth and nose, and settled on his eye lashes so that he looked out through a crimson haze. Nothing was ever in sight when he reached a peak. Even the Flue Dust pond lay red and empty, like a stagnant pool of blood. He would have cried with joy to see Joey's skinny white body jumping up and down.

The woods, dark green, almost gray, huddled in the distance beyond the red earth. He was already red from head to foot. But no one came this way, and he met no other troopers, who were still out in the hills trying to find where the men were hiding. He had to get there and come back and see Father Dahr, too. He had not gone to see him, as he had promised the old man he would do; and Father Dahr *wanted* to see him: had asked for him.

A patch of low-growing sumac trees took over where the red dust ended. Then he had to pick his way through thick elderberry which later would bear the white fan of blossoms that his father made into wine (and still later would be turned into jelly by his mother); and then came blackberry bushes, with pink thorned runners that clung to him. Old mines had sunk here and the woods were dotted with deep holes, sometimes covered with vines and bushes, so that he had to go cautiously. He was following an old mule trail that led once to a mine; overgrown now with grass and bushes, he could feel under his feet the rusty remains of a narrow guage track, which had led to the pit. Underneath the snake grass and brambles a tiny creek ran, laughing giddily to itself: for it was sour and nothing lived in it, and not even snakes drank from it. The bushes gave way to ash trees and maples and the golden mulberry, mixed with the apple-green of sassafras trees. The road sank suddenly in front of his feet, and he made a detour around it, looking down into the slanting side of the pit from which a mordant odor arose—from the carcass of a fox, perhaps, or even one of the few deer that came so close to town. It was harder to find his way now. Suddenly a ridge of orange-stained slate rose out of the green bushes, and he climbed it on his hands and knees, sending slate rolling crazily down the hill to plunge into the pit at the bottom. There at the top of the ridge he was challenged.

"What in the hell are you doing here, Benedict?" somebody demanded with exasperation, and, gasping, Benedict raised his sweating head. He was so relieved to hear that raw "hunky" voice, he started to laugh: he wanted to grip him by his arms and feel him real. The guard was a nineteen-year-old boy, one of the young workers in the Mill, Peter Grauzauskaus, whom Benedict had never seen do anything before but gamble in the alley. He was leaning, long and raw-boned, with a hank of yellow hair over his eyes and an air of disgust, on his shot-gun.

Benedict stood panting, trying to smile out his fatigue. Finally he gasped: "I got to see Mr. Tipa!"

The guard was not impressed. "What for?" he asked. Even in the woods his shirt was clean, his hair had been combed; he had a red handkerchief knotted around his throat.

"I *have* to see him!" Benedict repeated.

"Yeah?" the other said. "What for?"

"I can't tell *you*," Benedict replied.

"No?" the young man said. He narrowed his eyes with heavy suspicion. "Who sent you?" he shot at Benedict.

"My father," Benedict said with exasperation.

"The Father in the Church!" Peter Grauzauskaus cried. "Father Brumbaugh!"

"No!" Benedict recoiled with horror. "He don't know I've come here! *My* father—my own father, he's in the Mill."

"What's he doing—scabbing?" Peter said contemptuously.

Benedict closed his lips. He flushed.

"Take me to Mr. Tipa," he demanded.

The guard raised his rifle and patted it. "See this?" he said, and went on: "If you try anything funny, I'll give you both barrels!"

Benedict scoffed: "Just don't run when the troopers come!"

The other said darkly: "I'll be waiting for them, don't worry!"

He turned around and started skidding down the other side of the heap. Benedict followed him, thinking resentfully: "If I had been somebody else, look what I could have done to him!"

There were just pits and hills from there on. A narrow trail led around them: a trail that vanished from step to step. The young guard didn't say anything, but walked rapidly, and Benedict had to hurry to keep him in sight. Now they came to an area that seemed to have been burnt from the face of the earth, and little warts of rock and slate stuck up from the soil; a noxious smoke rose from holes in the earth—where Benedict used to think Hell was and expected the Devil to issue forth in smoke and flame—and the ground was hard and hot, so that they walked across it rapidly and delicately like dancers. Red hot earth glowed in mounds near them, and underneath them, not too far beneath their feet, an old mine burned month after month and year after year gutting the soil and then collapsing in a weary heap from time to time.

But they were back in the woods again—darker, denser woods now. The troopers, Benedict exulted, could never find them here: no horse alive could get through that jungle and around all those treacherously covered pits! And yet the Hollow was only a few miles away: the men slipped back into town at night to see their wives and eat whatever they could, and sometimes stayed till dawn, escaping before the sun came up. And some did not escape.

And then, suddenly, as they rounded a slag heap, there was a little group of huts, half-hidden among the maple and ash trees, before them. He recognized immediately the men and women who had been evicted from the Company houses that had lined the Ditch (all gone now)—they had moved here first and built these huts—and his eyes searched back and forth among them.

Peter led him through part of these flimsy lean-tos, and plunged beyond to another part of the woods, and again tiny huts of green wood appeared. These had been built later, since the strike. They had been made out of newly-cut saplings, many of them still with their dried leaves on so that the wind shucked through them, and covered with flattened-out tin oil cans. The uprooted earth of the woods smelled rich and full of worms and beetles. Men sat around on rustic benches they had already made, and two of them were pitching horseshoes, while the others watched. A couple of Italians were beating out a level strip of ground with their feet to flatten out a *bocce* alley. The heavy silent hum of the woods covered their work like a dream. Benedict heard their voices muted and low as he passed.

Under a black walnut tree, dotted along the branches with the green unripe walnuts, the men had built a long picnic table, with smooth-planed benches nailed to the legs. Five men were seated at the end of it—three white and two Negro. A big brown pitcher, half filled with foam, stood before them on the table. Newspapers, and a big map, drawn crudely by someone in pencil, were spread over the bare boards and the men were studying them.

Benedict's guard hesitated, looked again at Benedict to see whether he was really worth interrupting a conference, spat, and turned back to the men. Someone was speaking. Benedict could hear him. The two of them moved closer.

"You take a close look at that," one of the Negro men was saying, pointing his lean finger at some spot on the butcher-paper map, "now they ain't got but a couple men there, and they're mostly drunk. I could sneak past them any old dark night and——" Benedict saw his face now, and at the same moment the speaker raised his eyes and looked right into Benedict's—and gave him a wink! Benedict jumped! Those hands had once been at his throat, and those eyes had glared down into his, and that voice—now intense but calm—had been against his ear!

"But Cliff," one of the men interrupted, "you can't get into the goddamned place, and even if you do, so what? Leave them there! Let the State feed 'em!" He laughed cynically, pushed back and raised a mug of beer to his mouth.

Clifford leaned closer to the map.

"We get 'em out, we break it up! We got to show 'em we can do something they can't stop! We get those men out—why, *nobody* will go back to the Mill again. . . ."

220

"You worry about the men in the Mill! What about us out here?" another one interrupted again. "How we going to keep going? Suppose they come out after us?"

"But you don't see something," Clifford said intensely. "We got to get the colored workers out, and show 'em we can do it. Man, they *want* to get out!"

"How do you know?"

Clifford looked at the last speaker. "I know," he said softly, bitterly. "Tipa," he said, "what do you say?"

Benedict looked at the man whom he had been sent to find. He was little and dark, with a tiny straight mustache along his upper lip. He shook his head now, unsatisfied.

"You take too much for granted," he said almost sharply. "You're not *them* in there, Cliff," he said. "I can't believe they want to come out. They're comfortable in there and they're getting paid. They've been promised permanent jobs. . . ."

"Man," Clifford interrupted passionately, "what are you saying? They took 'em in there in sealed boxcars, and you saying they want to stay? Tipa, a man ain't always what he looks to be! Didn't they fight those bastids when they come to burn up Ditch Row? They fought for those damn shacks like they was palaces! Sheriff thought all he had to do was say, Shoo! Don't let them 'happy' faces of my people fool you, Tipa! We're smiling, but we ain't happy! We're looking right hunky-dumb when the Big Boss comes around—but we're *thinking* to ourselves! Now, I'll bet my last dollar I ain't got that the colored folks in the works have been doing a heap of thinking these last couple days, and they're ready now for the right voice to come along!"

"No, you'll get yourself caught——" Tipa began. He shrugged. "You'll be lucky—even if you *could* find a way to get in yourself— if they don't turn you over!"

"I'm willing to bet my skin on that!" Clifford cried.

Peter now went up to the table and leaned over and said something. The men raised their heads and looked over to him, and Benedict felt tight for a moment, and reviewed his message in a little panic. Then one of the men waved him to the table, and he walked across the cleared ground tensely, as though on a fence railing.

"What do you have to tell us?" Mr. Tipa said sharply.

Benedict swallowed, and answered: "My father's in the Mill. He sent me to tell you——"

"How did *you* get in the Mill?"

Several of the men laughed. Benedict flushed slightly before the hostile question. "I—I took my father his lunch bucket."

"What's your father's name?" Tipa, his dark eyebrows pointing at him, demanded.

"Bulmanis," Benedict replied.

Now one of the men at the table lifted his head, which had remained buried in a newspaper, stared at Benedict, his big face parted in a grin, and said laconically: "I know this boy, Tipa!"

Everything he did seemed somehow a miracle to Benedict. Joe Magarac! Now everybody turned to him, turned to Benedict, their faces changed, relaxed, and they laughed.

"I'm thinking I know him, too!" Benedict turned to Clifford who looked slyly at him and then burst into ringing laughter. "He's old Mother Burns' boy," he said, and Benedict smiled sheepishly, and Peter, his guard, laughed with relief and looked confused. Benedict's tight heart relaxed, the woods and the village, which had been sunk in silence, awoke with sounds of men, the dream-silence departed, and it seemed as though his hands and feet were working again and he was no longer conscious of the muscles in his face. The big brown hunky face was as natural and honest as sunlight—it set things right by just looking at them.

"And where do you think I met him?" Dobrik demanded, regarding them all with a big, promising grin. He gave them enough time as if they had three guesses, and then with a huge dramatic spread of his arms: "In jail! In *our* jail!" he cried, hunching up his shoulders, stretching his arms out further, as though who could understand the crazy world? Benedict flushed and glowed at the same time. Dobrik got up and walked around the table. "Sit down," he ordered, taking Benedict by the shoulder and seating him on the end bench. "Do you drink beer?" he demanded.

Benedict mumbled and shook his head.

Dobrik, however, poured himself out a mugful, and drank: and it seemed as if the beer could be traced going down his throat and settling with gusto in his stomach. Some of it appeared on his chin and trickled down. He swabbed off the white mustache, stared down at Benedict until Benedict reddened, then slapped his hand down on the table and roared. "I scared the old priest out of his pants!" he shouted, laughing, and everybody around the table couldn't help but laugh, although they didn't yet know why. Only Tipa kept a frowning face. "Look," Dobrik cried, stepping back from the bench, so that he would have plenty of room to demonstrate—"Look, here I am, squatting in the bushes—they just run me out of town, but I come back"—he explained in an aside. He got down on his haunches. "I'm looking right, looking left——" he shaded his eyes and turned right and left—"nobody in sight; the police cars are uptown. They think I'm on my way to Dravosburg, where they got another delegation waiting for me. But no, here I am in the priest's garden——" He looked sternly at those who snickered. Others seeing him from afar had come running, and already he had an audience. "I jumped out of the bushes, knocked —uno, duo, tres—on the door, jumped back in again—like a girlie on a cold Sunday morning. Pretty soon I heard a rattling at the door, and finally the door opens, and the old man stumbles down off the steps——" Dobrik staggered fantastically for a moment, caught his balance, and looked around him, muttering what could have been curses. The men at the table watched him with fascinated smiles. The people around had their mouths open. Benedict could see Father Dahr, conjured up this way, and he, too, smiled, though a little painfully. "The old man isn't sure he heard the knock. He goes back to look at the door. He's got only his pants and winter underwear on, and sitting down in the bushes I can smell him like a brewery. From behind that bush, I say——" and Dobrik lowers his voice to a hoarse whisper——"'Are you Father Dahr?'" He aimed a finger at Benedict. "That's his name?" Benedict nodded. "The old man jumped back like he was bit——" Dobrik jumped back with a wild twitch of his legs and his arms upflung—and crossed himself in a gigantic cross—stumbled against the steps, fell down on the boardwalk, and started crossing himself, where he was sitting. "I jumped out of the bushes to help him—you under-stand—and he let out a wild yell and poked me in the eye with his thumb!"

Dobrik had to stop to mash the tears in his eyes. Everyone was laughing helplessly, holding their stomachs. Dobrik had ended up by sitting on the ground jabbing the air with his thumb and the men on the far side of the table had climbed on the table to see him. Benedict winced, but laughed in spite of himself. Dobrik fought to catch his breath but roared again: "He said he only had 63 cents and I was to take that and leave his soul alone!" There was a new explosion of laughter at this, and Dobrik pulled himself to his feet, explaining: "I helped the old man up, while he kept hitting me on the head. We tripped over a cat that came out from under the porch, and the cat gave out a scream, and the old man took hold of my ear and cried: 'Holy Mother of God, what damned soul in hell is that?' 'A cat, old man,' I said. But he didn't believe me, and looked me over for horns!"

"Did he find them?" somebody jeered.

"So I sat the old man down on the step, held him there until I told him——" he explained to the others—— "I told him to go back and look up his altar boy who was in jail!" He ran his square hands through Benedict's hair, pushed his head toward the table, and grinned at him and the others laughing; and then suddenly he said: "Now, what's all this about Vincentas?"

Benedict started.

Dobrik nodded. "Yes, yes, I know your father!"

Benedict told, then, what had happened, conscious of the serious attention they gave his story.

As he talked, Dobrik leaned his broad brown face toward him, nodded, drank again from his mug when he was finished, and wiped the suds from his mouth with a wide sweep of his hand and an, "Ah!"

"Now, show us," he muttered, pulling the butcher paper over to Benedict, and with his stubby finger pointing out to Benedict a pencil-drawn picture. "This here is Furnace No. 2. Now show us what he said?"

Benedict chewed his lips.

"My father said there was a pipe leading out to the river——" he began, and all the men bent their heads over the map, and Dobrik picked his pencil up and drew a line jutting out into the "river."

"Here?" he asked not Benedict but the others. Clifford nodded. "Why not?" he said.

Dobrik played with the pencil, studying the map; then muttered: "Good, good." His eyes lighted craftily, and Benedict thrilled a little, feeling that he had contributed something of great value.

"How did you find us?" Dobrik asked him, suddenly.

"I——" Benedict began and then stopped shyly. "I was at the meeting on the hills," he said. "I saw *you* there—I knew you were the man I met in jail."

Dobrik eyed him.

"How did you know about the meeting?"

"I knew," Benedict replied significantly. "I also followed my father."

Dobrik looked at the others.

"And how did you find us *now?*"

"Oh," Benedict said confidently, "I know these woods!"

"Oh, you know these woods?" Dobrik mimicked. "So that's how you knew how to find us?" He looked at the others and muttered: "It's a good thing he's one of us!"

Benedict reddened.

"I walked," he said. "I walked through the woods until I met— Pete."

"That's all?"

"Yes."

"You knew Pete was——"

"No," Benedict said. "But I thought I'd keep walking till I met someone."

Dobrik chewed on this. "Did you see any troopers, any deputies on the hills?"

Benedict nodded.

The men leaned forward. "Where?" Dobrik demanded.

Benedict thought he had to be accurate.

Slowly he said: "About one hundred yards west of the Flue Dust Mill."

Dobrik smiled. "How many?"

"One," Benedict said precisely. "He was dragging two men to jail."

"Rudnik and Piet," Tipa said.

"Rudnik and Piet," Dobrik echoed. But he smiled a moment later, and said suddenly: "Isn't he a smart boy?" And Benedict startled, paled, and then burst into flame, and the others stared at him and some laughed and some still thought of Rudnik and Piet.

Tipa, his dark eyes glowing, said: "What do you say to Father Dahr and the other one, the young one, Father Brumbaugh?"

Those who were laughing stopped suddenly, and Dobrik cast a glance at Tipa. Tipa's hair curled from his head like a fan; his dark eyebrows seemed alive on his face and moved with his every word and "listened" when one talked to him.

And now Benedict remembered the trip on the train, with the young priest sitting beside him, and the question he had asked then. "Would it be a sin not to tell?" And the young priest had looked down at him as though it would not only be a sin but a mortal sin—a crime—not to reveal the whereabouts of the arch-agitator, plotter and godless Communist, Dobrik. His face had shown only a terrible eagerness to know; it was an expression that followed his look when he mentioned Sacco and Vanzetti who were not only anarchists and criminals but foreigners as well.

He said in a low voice, turning his eyes into Tipa's: "I wouldn't tell Father Brumbaugh anything!" He added in a shaking voice: "Not even in confession!" His hands trembled, but he cried: "It's *not* a sin!"

"Aren't you going to be ordained a priest?" Tipa demanded.

"I'm too young," Benedict replied.

Tipa shook the answer away impatiently. "I mean—later. But now, aren't you planning to study for the priesthood?"

Benedict hesitated; he nodded his head but kept his eyes lowered.

"Then do you know," Tipa said harshly, "that your Father

Brumbaugh has met with the police and the sheriff in the City and has agreed to supply them with names of our men and information about where they are? Do you?" he cried.

Benedict shook his head, lifting his eyes brimming with hot tears.

"Do you?" Tipa shrieked at him, leaning his dark face far over, his eyes bright and smoldering on him. "*Who's side are you on?*"

Dobrik stood up. "Ours!" The strong arms that fell around Benedict's shoulders were like an embrace. His blood surged up and flooded his body with warmth—like an opening fan, shedding sunlight. And the voice was calm and very certain. "And now you—you will have something to eat! Mother!" he cried, and out of the lean-to an old Negro woman came and said: "Food's all ready!"

He sat and ate with them on the bare table, not hearing their talk, his food mixing in his mouth with unshed grateful tears. He realized only later as they took the dishes away, that the food had tasted familiar and that the woman who had served them was someone he knew.

11.

After Benedict had left him, forgetting the flute and taking the empty lunch bucket back with him, his father had sat a long time brooding. The Company had given the men whisky. He had not refused it; it had not been offered—it had been ordered. He had long ago learned how to live with the "Americans"; so he had accepted the bottle, popping his eyes a little, smacking his thigh with his hard hand, and crying: "Long time vant dis! Okay—boss!" And he grinned his "hunky" grin, and the foreman who had handed the bottles around slapped him on the back and said when he got back to the office: "Them greenhorns'll do anything for a slug of moonshine!"

But he had drunk nothing. The whisky had looked not only like poison but like betrayal. His throat was dry, but not from thirst. He had watched Benedict leave with sadness, and had sat on the stump brooding long into the evening. The furnace yard, which had been as familiar to him as his own kitchen, seemed strange and hostile. Not to be working, but sitting among the rusty bars, watching the long shadows fall like beams from the darkened slits high up near the roof—was weird. More than the native-born he had been conscious of the forced character of his labor, and had never had illusions. No choices were offered him. The "Americans" had made everything plain to him almost as he stepped off the boat—that he was here to work, and nothing else. To endure, somehow to escape the eye of boss and oppressor: this was the skill of living. But perhaps, like the Eye of God, it was useless to try to hide from it: it had found him, dragged him out, and chained him with all but real chains to his work.

The Negroes, brought into the Mill at dead of night like cargo, sealed in boxcars, were then opened out into the empty Mill—the Negroes were kept separate in the shipping department. There had been a few flurries of struggle, quickly put down, at first when they realized how they had been tricked: but now all was silent over there, and the whisky, as here, remained undrunk.

But the troopers were not so troubled. They had begun to drink days before and were still drinking. The Company had sent trucks over to Smoky Bottom and brought them back with some of the Smoky Bottom girls who had entertained the troops in their own fashion. Vincentas recalled the horror with which he had looked into the mascaraed eyes of a "beauty" who had been brought to him, with the compliments of the Company: and he had angrily lifted his arm to strike her until he saw the black-smudged tears in her eyes.

He had always believed that the "Americans" were at heart unfeeling barbarians. The bosses, always Anglo-Saxon, stalked through the Mill and distributed "funny" quips at them, at himself: "Hey, greenhorn, poosh, poosh 'em up—like you poosh up for Missus!" Or: "Hey, Hunky John: what'sa matta? No got 'em poosh? Too much you give heem old lady!"

They had grinned back, more than glad that the boss was in a happy mood: but a sullen cloud had come over his brain, and drenched it, all these years, in humiliation and pain.

He shook himself free from his somber thoughts and joined the card game so that he could talk, as he did in bits of Polish and Slovak, to the men playing. The high shrieks of laughter, that was so like pain, came from the outside shanties where the troopers were gathered. The men looked up, their cards motionless, whenever this occurred: and when the high shrieks died away in a bubbling sob, they resumed their playing. From the shipping department a revolver shot came, and their hands jerked and then a Negro worker came running wildly through the yard, diving down under the railroad track for safety. The guards amused themselves with pistol practice, shooting at bits of steel lying on the floor and anywhere near the men.

Vincentas shook his head.

"We can't stay here," he said, slapping down a card. "We've got to find a way!"

Nobody answered: the slap of cards was faint.

Then Jozuos Porvaznik, an old man with steel gray hair, cut in military fashion, and gray leaking eyes, said staring down át his cards: "There's no way out. Stay here and mind our business. It will end itself. Play cards."

He squinted at this, and played a card blindly. Noises came from the shipping department.

"But perhaps," he remarked at last, "there is a way." He nodded his head: "There's always a way."

The other three in the circle kept playing.

"What would it matter?" Antanas growled, his face wiry with a two-day beard. "We would be caught again—and then what? Blacklist!"

Vincentas nodded his head slowly—not so much because he agreed but as though he was aware of this serious objection. Sounds of equivocal revelry came from outside.

"The troopers are happy," he remarked ironically.

"Even if we do go," the first old man said, rubbing his leaking eyes. "Even if we find a way out, there will still be left the *juoduku,* colored workers."

Vincentas didn't answer immediately; he wanted them to know he had pondered the problem.

"Perhaps," he said slowly, "they want to be free, too. . . ."

The other laughed shortly. "Don't you understand?" he said.

Vincentas stared moodily into his cards. "They, too, work like us," he said stubbornly.

"No, but you are wrong," the younger man snapped, lifting up his head, his eyes bitter. "They're not like us! They came willingly!"

"Did they know?" Vincentas demanded.

The other shrugged. "Does it matter?" he asked.

"But one should know," Vincentas said.

"Speak to them," the young man said harshly. "They'll laugh, will they not? Why should they go out into the woods and freeze and hide until they're caught?" He stopped to send a bitter look at the yard, where the furnace was dying, at the coke-fire they had built to cook on, at the cots the Company had set up—army cots with khaki blankets and army insignia. He returned to Vincentas and said: "They'll laugh at you!"

"But if we can show them that it's possible," Vincentas began. "They must believe in us— that it's possible to win——" He paused and frowned. "There must always be the hope of success."

He spoke the last phrase almost to himself, and without confidence. What hope of success? He had sent his son off with a message, but he had not seriously believed either in the message or in Benedict's arriving with it. When it was quiet, yes, he would go through the great pipe leading down to the river, and so escape; but this would mean nothing.

He was silent. He had been playing without attending, and now with surprise that was slightly mocking he discovered that all his moves had been the right ones. What were they playing for? The whisky the foreman had brought into the yard for them was piled up before him. He laughed.

There was a commotion at the southern end of the yard and two troopers, bareheaded, their blue shirts torn open or unbuttoned, their trousers soiled and sagging, came staggering into the yard, their arms around each other's neck and carrying bottles in their free hands. They were singing some obscene song, and swayed back and forth, coming upon them in a crazy dance, crashing through their cards which they scattered aimlessly, and then going on down through the northern exit.

They were young, both of them: the pink of their cheeks had hardly been razored. What a shame! he had thought, watching them with profound sadness. They had looked to him like the children of Slovak or Polish parents. They use our own children against us, he had thought bitterly.

They had been turned into *Americans*—these children exiled from home, these children who had come from their blood and bone—into *Americans,* he thought, into killers, into barbarians, neither remembering nor wanting to remember their parents, their language nor their past. . . .

He thought of Benedict, and a fresh pain shot through him, but he was not certain exactly for what.

The noises in the shipping yard were rising and growing more menacing. By climbing half-way up the ladder to the parked crane, he could see through a space there into the shipping yard next to them and below. The yard was vast and dark, and in it were piled, in various sizes, shapes and lengths, rows upon rows of steel bars, ready to be loaded into cars and taken away. He could see nothing—except that as he watched there was a flash from a gun and the bullet skipped across the top of the bars and screamed like a demented thing until it flattened out against the steel wall.

He climbed down the ladder again, and there standing at the foot of it watching him come down was a Negro man, his face already smiling as he anticipated Vincentas' surprise.

"Cliff," he cried.

Clifford nodded and smiled and held out his hand. "Your boy sent me," he said.

"Ah!" Vincentas breathed, lifting his glasses back on his nose.

"And Doby," Clifford added.

"How you come?" Vincentas asked.

Clifford showed him his shoes. They were ankle-wet with muck.

"Ah?" Vincentas whispered, understanding.

Clifford drew him off behind a pile of bricks and asked: "What do you think?"

Vincentas shrugged.

"To go through pipe—if all okay——"

"Can't go through the pipe!" Clifford said.

Vincentas drew in his breath.

"Too many," Clifford said. "We only got one skiff. Can they swim?" He laughed.

"Maybe no vant go?" Vincentas asked.

"They'll go," Clifford whispered. "Show me where they are."

Vincentas jerked his thumb. "There."

"Troopers?"

Vincentas nodded.

"Okay!" Clifford cried. "We got to find other way of getting out." A shot ricocheted among the bars in the yard next to them.

"What was that?" Clifford cried.

"Soldier boy!" Vincentas spat.

"They'll come!" Clifford said, his eyes flickering.

"How goin' do?"

"Don't know yet—but we're goin' to find a way! Come on!"

Vincentas was not so sure. He was afraid of recklessness! "You watch step!" he advised sharply.

"Don't worry none!" the other replied, suppressing laughter. "Cliff's on the job!"

Vincentas shrugged. "You on job, but what is job?" he asked, and shrugged again.

Clifford wanted to get into the shipping yard and speak to someone. Vincentas took him on a roundabout way, out through the yard and over a wall separating the furnace from the railroad below, and below the railroad were the loading yards. They slipped down through the shadows, keeping to the wall, until Clifford suddenly stopped and grabbed hold of his arm. He was pointing.

"What's them?"

Vincentas looked.

"No *furstay!*"

232

"Look," Clifford said intensely. "What's them?"

"Boxcars," Vincentas replied.

"You see them, too, then! No joke!" Vincentas felt the kindled passion in the other. Clifford slapped his thigh sharply. "What goes in can always go out," he said mysteriously. There was glee in his voice, low as it was, and his body seemed alight with fire. Vincentas took him around the rear of the shipping yard and watched as he climbed up a ten foot bank and disappeared into the darkness from which shots still came but almost lazily.

Clifford had told him to wait. He waited on the deserted railroad tracks wondering what plan Clifford could have in mind. Of course the pipe was no help—it led nowhere but into the river. A man could go in or out—but only one.

The Mill had never been so still before. Its uncanny quiet, monstrously interrupted by the boom of a gun, which, however, came to him here dimmed somewhat by the vast, the profound, stillness, provoked thought. Always he had been conscious of these guns lying behind the facade. When hunger failed in its work, then there were jails; and if jails, too, could not hold struggle in—then there were guns. In his ignorance of precise English he had never learned the refinements in the meaning of the sound, "democracy." It had meant being paid every four years to vote for somebody (whose name he could barely pronounce). They would march him out of the Mill to the polling booth and help him mark his X beside the right name. The workers had all shrugged during these comedies, and had not understood what was intended by them. Everybody knew—come mayor or go mayor—the Mill went on forever, and the bosses dictated every wind and whistle.

He had not realized that democracy meant that by putting a folded piece of paper in a box he had given the Mill the right to hunt them down with guns!

Perhaps if they had marked the X in the wrong column? This thought amused him, though his smile in the darkness was sad.

How raw the wind from the river was! Over on the other side the steep bluffs, covered now with red and white flowers, small trees and thick bushes, climbed to the night horizon: and beyond were hills untroubled by all but rabbit and fox and sometimes a quivering deer who came to the cliff edge to look down with brown frightened eyes into the Mill below. Freedom was the freedom of animals. If he could swim a river, and run through woods, he could live like that in deer-like freedom—until he died a hungry unfree man. Birds flying above the smoke had never ceased to call to him. The wind from the river had never ceased to stir him.

Clifford had been gone a long time. He had hidden his doubts when he spoke to his buddies back in the yard; now they came out, bare and bleeding. Decades of struggle that had always been crushed had taught him to believe only in the real; only in power, only in strength. Simple men did not rush into martyrdom. There always had to be lifted some measure of hope of success. What could Clifford tell them? To rush the troopers? Scale the walls? Go, one by one through the pipe, only to be caught at the other end? He had sensed a passion in Clifford that was too much like recklessness. The Negro workers were insulted and persecuted even more than they, the foreign-born—and he had seen a Negro worker, goaded by white foremen beyond endurance, go insane with hatred and pain and throw himself on the foreman and on all others who came with clubs. Negroes had more justification, he felt, for extreme and doomed attempts to free themselves. What was needed was coolness, careful planning—and success.

The two troopers in the shipping yard saw nobody. Even if there were anybody to see, they had been drinking between pot-shots so much that they shot through a dense cloud: but Vincentas could hear their guns going off, and this meant that they had seen nothing.

He suddenly became conscious of a shadow dropping over the bank onto the railroad track, and seeing him, suddenly start and look as if he was about to run.

"Okay, okay!" Vincentas said.

Another shadow dropped over the bank, and another, and more came; and they gathered around Vincentas, until Clifford appeared. There was a tense smile on his face, and he walked with muscles poised.

234

"Follow me," he whispered, and the command went down the line.

Then, snaking down the railroad tracks, keeping in the shadow, he brought them to the boxcars standing on the track at the end of the vast yard. He pushed open the boxcar doors and one by one the men climbed in. Then, shoving a long pinchbar into Vincentas' hands, he went to the back of the car and fitted the lever of the bar underneath the great iron wheel. Vincentas fitted his underneath the other wheel. Then, pushing with his arms, he "pinched": ever so slightly the wheel moved, groaning a little; and this infinitesmal advantage they followed up with the bar. Again they "pinched," bearing down the bar, and again the huge boxcar moved; and they pushed forward with what they had won. Now with a kind of whining, the car moved out of its bed: and they pushed together, pinch by pinch, and suddenly the car was out of their hands and rolling silently down the long tracks, past the furnaces, past the rolling mill, past the soaking pits—on past the shanties where the guardsmen sprawled over the tables and chairs, bottle and girl in arm and hand: a gigantic silent shadow that fled past on through the long mill grounds out into the open.

While Clifford was loading the second car, Vincentas went back to the yard. They had been quarreling while he was gone. The cards still lay scattered where the troopers had kicked them.

"Come," he said; and his voice and gesture were so certain, so imperious that they followed him out into the darkness and down the long track to the cars.

Daylight was beginning to break when he swung onto the last car as it fled with its human cargo into the free air. . . .

12.

Benedict wandered by himself in the woods afterwards. Dobrik had told him he could stay in camp, and then had gone away with some of the other men. Clifford had taken him aside and questioned him even more intimately about what his father had told him and where the pipe had come into the river. Then he had gone into the woods, following a tiny path that took him behind the camp into the deeper woods, which glowed with a glaucous light, striped with late orange beams from the falling sun. No one bothered him. He had seen Mother Burns working at a huge pot and oven, which had already been built in the side of the hill; seen the long pans of baked beans she had withdrawn, as if out of the earth itself, bubbling and steaming, with hunks of white pork swimming through it all. This is what they had had for supper. Only about twenty men ate within sight of him, but he sensed that other dinners were being served in other parts of the woods.

The Hollow seemed a longer way back than coming! As he thought of it he felt he'd never be able to make it through the pits and tanglewood; he'd be too exhausted when he arrived at the church to speak properly to Father Dahr. And he realized that he'd have to be prepared to speak properly. There was something else, too, something he couldn't quite catch: that it would be a wrench to change from thinking about things *here*—and Benedict looked about the green-glowing woods, with Dobrik's voice, that one word *"Ours!"* still challenging the air—to think about things *there*. It seemed very far away, and yet Benedict knew that if he could climb any tall tree right where he stood, he might just be able to make out the church's steeple!

But most of all, the conversation he had had with Father Brumbaugh going to Morgantown haunted him. Again he saw Father Brumbaugh's face. Exactly the same expression was on it when he spoke of the Boston police strike and of—of Sacco and Vanzetti: it was the face of Mr. Brill, the man in the City who had him arrested because he was from Hunky Hollow! That's what had confused him, his struggling oppression when he spoke of his childhood fear of the poor. The look he had when he spoke of the strike was the same look in his face when he spoke to him of mortal sin!

Benedict's face twisted. He remembered Mr. Brill all right! Mr. Brill's face was a familiar face: he had met it, had it look at him with its blank unseeing stare, as though he wasn't there—or with disgust, or irritation when he was a little snotnosed baby like

Rudolph, dragging along in a wet dress! Or there had been an amused tolerance, and women had called him "cute"! And when he had come to the City with his mother, the look they gave him and his mother—Mr. Brill's look—at the squire's office, or even at the Doctor's where Benedict had had to repeat everything the doctor said to his mother, and the others had stood by listening with a faraway smile waiting until the translation was done. He had felt the same thing with his father, too: the time the foreman had come to the house and his father had set the table with the best cloth, brought out the wine, bought a fine cake, and everybody had to stay out of the house till the foreman went again! Except that once his father had said: "This is my son, Benedict!" And the foreman had said: "A fine-looking boy. Bring him down to me when he's ready to go to work . . ." and Benedict had gone cold to the center of his heart.

The foreman left without touching the cake.

Poor Father Brumbaugh, he nevertheless smiled sympathetically, being sent all the way from Boston where he was used to rich people—all this way to *them*, to the foreigners who didn't understand him at all, and whom he didn't really feel at home with! That was a mistake, Benedict pointed out to someone lurking in the woods: the Bishop shouldn't have sent him. He was unhappy here, and too delicate: the workers just laughed at anyone—any man—who looked delicate. They couldn't help saying to themselves: "This one wouldn't last two hours in the Open Hearth!" So it was no wonder if Father Brumbaugh felt out of place, and even hated the workers in the parish. Father Dahr had no right to attack him—he couldn't help his feelings! Once, he had been reading Mass when snores began to rise from the early morning worshippers, and Father Brumbaugh's nerves had been unsettled by this: he didn't know whether to stop Mass or go on, ignoring the snores. Then Benedict had gotten into the habit of knocking on the altar and all around the walls and even on the steps before Mass to scare away the mice. Father Brumbaugh wouldn't touch the wine cup with his lips. Benedict felt sure of this. He just faked drinking—because he wasn't certain it hadn't been touched by something or someone before.

But he'd learn—he could still learn, couldn't he? he asked the indifferent woods. When he came to see that the strikers weren't wrong, that the Company was? Nobody wanted to give up his house! Father Brumbaugh would come to understand this, Benedict was sure: it just had to be explained to him, that was all. He was used to living in fine houses in Boston, and perhaps some of the old, and some of the rotten, houses in the Hollow didn't seem worth saving to him, let alone fighting for. Benedict was afraid Father Brumbaugh would say, why don't they move into *other* houses? But those houses were all the workers had, Benedict pointed out; they had bought them long ago and worked for years to pay for them—didn't he know that?—and they were still unpaid, and there *was* no place to go in the City where they could find houses even as bad as the ones they left. So you've got to understand, Father!

He found himself following a little fresh water stream. A smell like licorice was heavy here; there was a root he could dig out and suck its sweet flavor. Crabs swung their tiny scissor-shaped claws at the bottom of the clear-water stream, and tiny green frogs jumped off little rocks into the tangled grass of the bank as he approached. He found the ground strewn with unripe black walnuts, which a storm had knocked down, and he picked one up and tore its green shell open and painted the palm of his hand with its brown juice. The odor was pungent and dry.

The stream hesitated in a little pool, from which an old woman was coming carrying two buckets of clear water. Benedict stood still. He watched her toiling up the little path, still wearing those old-fashioned high-topped black shoes, with a million creases in them, like the creases on her face, and her black skirt was just as thick as ever and the tight bodice she wore, tightly buttoned to her chin, the strong broad nose, but wearing on her head now a simple black netted cap. . . . His heart stood still; and then he wanted to hide in the bushes on the side of the path until she passed. He watched her toil up the path with anguish, his arms hurting him, feeling the full buckets pulling the frail bones down: and he couldn't endure it any longer and shouted: "Mother, let me carry a bucket for you!" And he jumped at the surprised woman grabbing at a bucket and spilling water over her skirt and on her shoes.

She stod gasping for breath, her free hand on her bosom. "I almost bit my heart!" she cried putting the other bucket down and looking at him with a half-frightened expression, a look of being a-flutter, with her little netted cap coming askew.

He was filled with an inexplicable happiness that made him shout: "I'll race you up the hill!" But she only raised a protesting hand and said: "You shouldn't carry both of them buckets, Master Benedict!"

But he began to stagger uphill with them, trying not to wince as they beat against the calf of his leg, and throwing looks of joy behind him at the old woman who followed more slowly behind.

He was filled with an inexplicable happiness that made him want to laugh hysterically. It occurred to him that he had jumped suddenly out on her and taken the buckets *before she could refuse!* He jogged happily, and would have gone faster except that he wanted the old woman to keep him in sight, and he stopped to rest oftener than he needed. She drew up to him under a tree and said, "Thank you, Master Benedict, now I'll take them from here."

"No," he said frowning. "But why do you keep calling me Master Benedict?"

She looked at him in the same way she had done those Sundays he had come to visit her, except now her reply was more acid: "You ain't a Mister!"

He colored with some obscure humiliation, and without another word picked one bucket up, leaving one for her, and resumed his climb to the camp. She showed him where to dump the water in the huge copper kettle, which was already boiling. Then he left her and went off by himself to the side of the camp, feeling more lonely than ever, and sat down on a fallen tree. The evening had come, but it was still light enough to play and the *bocce* alley was ready and the men were rolling the black balls to a tiny ring covered with white paper. Nobody at the card game had changed: it was the same card game. The little huts, made of trimmed saplings, almost disappeared into the woods and shadows, as though they were still the growing trees they had been. Their dry leaves whispered.

The woods behind him were already dark, but the clearing was still awake with light. Red ants scurried along the fallen tree on which he was sitting. He blocked the busy work of one with a bit of bark, setting the bark down in front of it, letting it climb on and then suddenly transporting it up into the air, where it clung like a bead of blood, frozen with fear. He watched it as he twisted the bark idly in his fingers wondering what fate to bestow on it; and then he suddenly shuddered and threw the bark over his shoulder back into the woods.

He felt a hot line across his forehead. He pressed it with the tips of his fingers, covering his eyes and nose with the palms of his hands. He felt a sudden darkness come over him, darker than the palms over his eyes, and the muffled smothered feeling of his hands over his nose seemed more than that, as though his heart was being squeezed. "Help me, God!" he cried against his hands, his teeth digging into them. He began to mumble a "Hail Mary" in English; and then repeated it in Lithuanian: "*Sveika Marija, malones pilnoji, veshpats su tavim. . . .*"

"Help me, God," he cried again in a muffled voice, and pressing his hands hard against his face swayed back and forth on the tree.

Afterwards, he began to reason out loud: "But I can't go to see you *now*, Father! I've got to wait here until my own father comes, to see if he. . . ." He felt hypocritical and cried sullenly, "*I can't! I can't!*"

Nevertheless, he continued to see Father Dahr sitting in the same arm chair, wrapped in blankets, his lion's mane of hair now somehow tamed, less fierce, an orange wash through his eyes where tiny red blood vessels seemed like live things rising to the surface, waiting for him. He could see Father Dahr's expression: it was patient and confident, knowing that he, Benedict, would come, knowing he was there already because the kitchen door would tell him so. It seemed so inevitable to Benedict that he felt it would take no real effort—only the exertion of will: and there he would be speaking to the old priest.

Suddenly he grew sulky and shook the vision away. "No, Fath-

240

er," he said as though Father Dahr were within earshot. Then the look of regret with which these words would be received shocked him, and he bit his lips with remorse. How could he talk like that to Father Dahr? he asked himself reproachfully. Wasn't it Father Dahr who had come running that night to the jail and . . . Benedict smiled reluctantly as he saw Father Dahr again come wobbling down the streets with his short breath, sent there by a man who had risen spectrally out of the bushes and had frightened him almost to death. Then this vision, too, disappeared and he sat on the tree not daring any longer to think, any longer to dream. Automatically, in these moments made so certainly for dreams, *his* dream would have arisen: a full-throated organ throbbing, his white hands rising in a benediction: white, white all around, from the skies to the altar, to the lilies bank upon bank; and this quickly giving way to himself, tall and for some reason, thin (perhaps because he fasted?), in a black cassock, hurrying in the pre-dawn darkness among the shadows and smells (he went with Father Brumbaugh's nose now) of old houses and cabins where sick children wept in the morning and tired mothers sat at the window watching for his reassuring coming. And then this giving way to himself again, now dressed in practical business clothes, with only his turned collar (unrumpled and no dust) to indicate his calling, confronting the management of the Mill and with a voice that was inspired by the justice of God declaring that the Mill must raise the wages of the workers and grant large pensions to their widows and children; and coming out of the office then to where the workers waited in a dark group outside the Mill gates and kneeling on the snow-patched ground as he passed. . . . *I will be a saint!*

He saw the soldier at the Mill gate suddenly, spitting the bread out of his mouth. His hands trembled at the memory. He saw the bread still lying on the ground, and he wanted to pick it up again and kiss it, for it was bread, it was bread! Oh, that look—the way he looked! That look of disdain! That look on the soldier's face when he picked the sandwiches up, smelled them, tasted them, as though he was tasing their very lives, finding that they were only sour-dough and grease—with what contempt he had looked at

Benedict then! And suddenly before Benedict could stop it—happening helplessly in spite of himself—the soldier's face disappeared as he thought of him and in its place, with the same look of disdain, but now gently modified, appeared Father Brumbaugh's clean sensitive face! Benedict gritted his teeth; he hated himself for having let this happen. And yet, before he could rub it away, he remembered the young priest standing on the wooden steps of Honey Bee Hill, his nose arched, the slight look of pain and bewilderment that came into his eyes as he smelled the Hollow and turned to Benedict with the horrified question: "What smells so?" And Benedict had sniffed and not smelled anything; and had not smelled the Hollow, indeed, unaware that his life had an odor. . . .

Benedict's palms grew moist and he rubbed them over his face, wetting his face. He felt desperately the need to pray. He felt if only in the next few minutes he could get inside the church and kneel there for a while, he would be all right. He would get up again, cleansed and free of all the troubling thoughts that had assailed him. The well of religion, the depth of sanctity, into which he would let himself sink, as though into the layers of Catholic time, back into the medieval ages, into the age of the first martyrs, until he was remorsely drenched and stained, every cell and corpuscle, every inch of his brain, unalterably, infallibly, eternally Catholic!

He longed for his father to appear, as though somehow this would settle everything. He wanted terribly for God to permit time to telescope and now, *now*, for his father to appear, now that he needed his appearance most! Waiting for him had somehow frozen all other questions, suspended all other action: and Father Dahr would have to wait in his arm chair until morning, and Father Brumbaugh would have to find someone else to tell Mass with him tonight. His fingers ached to touch the flute his father had made and he had forgotten. As he thought of it, the pungent taste of his father's spit came back to him, and he felt him near by, sealed somehow in the granite darkness.

It was very dark now.

And finally he uttered it to himself: *I can't go to the church tonight to see Father Brumbaugh and speak to Father Dahr because*

—and he looked out into the dark woods where nothing but the uneasy trees stirred—*I could not tell them that my father is in the Mill, and that he will try to escape tonight and go hide in the woods with the Communist leader, Dobrik, and that I, Benedict, would rather die than reveal this to anyone! . . .*

He was asleep now. A hand touched him only once and he jerked awake, unaware of the faint dawn, crying, "Did my father come?"

And a voice answered, "Yes, your father's safe. He's here."

And someone kissed him on the cheek, and he dreamed he smelled old tobacco and the rancid odor of human sweat and human salt.

13.

How desperately they needed money! Benedict looked over the road to the fabulous garbage heap, remembering the candelabra he had found there. It had turned out to be worth five dollars. All they were living off now was what they could get from the gardens—their own and their neghbors'. There was even more lending and borrowing among families than usual.

Benedict was carrying a dead rabbit. Mother Burns had given it to him when he left in the morning. She was familiar with the woods and how to get food out of it in ways he had never dreamed. She had snared the rabbit. He himself would not eat it, he thought, but that was no reason why Joey and Rudolph shouldn't eat it. He debated for a moment with himself whether he might not even now take a quick trip over the dump, and maybe find something of value. He cast a thoughtful look at the huge dark mound, from which smoke rose and tiny flames poked among the derbis. He was strongly tempted to go: the dump held a deep fascination. But, no, he had to get home to see his father, who had been at camp early that morning, and then had left for home. He had to get home to deliver the rabbit. He felt its weight, and its cold touch against his leg, but he couldn't look at it.

No cars moved along the ridge. There had been no dumping on the slag dump all week. The slag boulders had rolled so far and no farther, as though a hand had drawn a line. Houses facing the slag dump were charred; their paint had curled and blistered. Nearest to the dump a row of houses was partially dismantled: even now men were wrecking it, and a truck stood by for piles of second-hand lumber to sell in the City. A wind had risen in the night and covered the slag dump with red dust. The roofs of the houses, the sides of the hills, the alleys and the people were dusted red, too.

As he crossed himself, passing the church, he stared curiously at it, as though he had been parted from it a long time ago. The doors were closed; the handle had been broken off, and someone had twisted a strong wire into a loop for a handle instead. He noticed a new crack through the face of St. Peter in the stained window. The old yellow bricks were discolored from rain and wind; a kind of green stain, like a faint moss, was already growing in the cracks and spreading over the bricks. The cross on top of the steeple was chipped at the edges and bleached an intense white. Pigeons flew in and out. Honey Bee Hill peeked over the roof of the church, like a green tassel hat, somehow rakishly stuck on top of the steeple.

He paused in front of the parish house wondering if Father Dahr was sitting in his arm chair behind the closed curtains and was watching him even now as he stood on the outside in the road. He swung the rabbit violently, then set off down Highland Avenue toward Shady Lane, crossing the street to the other side when he saw Sister Ursula and Sister Mary coming out of the convent.

Only his mother was in the kitchen and she began to weep when she saw him.

"Where's Papa?" he cried.

"Why did you come home?" she asked tearfully.

He put the rabbit on the table and said: "He came home, and I came to see him."

"He left," she said.

Benedict sat down. "Mama, I'm tired."

She picked up the rabbit and looked at it. He stared at her. Her dark hair was braided in two thick twisted strands, her yellow-gray eyes were estimating the rabbit, her almost yellow skin shone as though she had rubbed it. Tears were standing neglected in the eyes that were already absorbed by the rabbit. He studied her with an intentness he had never known before, and he was swept by a helpless poignancy he could not understand.

"Mama," he said.

She looked at him with still the trace of fear in her eyes.

"Mama," he said again, his voice aching. His lips were tensed. "Mama, Mama," he cried, and turned his face away, and she stared at him bewildered and frightened so that, with a wrench, he gave back his face to her, clear and smiling. "I got it in camp!" he said, pointing to the staring rabbit.

She sat down now, and brushed her hair absently with her hand, looked at him with dark eyes frightened, superstitious; then she said: "What is the matter with Joey?"

"What, Mama?" he said, smiling.

"With Joey," she repeated, and sat with her hands in her lap, and in her eyes a look so anxious, and almost bereaved, that he leaned over to her and poked her with his fingers.

"Mama!" he said, chiding. He smiled again for her before he asked: "Where is he?"

She brought her hands together and softly beat her bosom with them, and her face was filled with pain as though the blows pained her. "Under the porch," she whispered. Then she began to wave circles in the air. "He won't come out." She looked at him with wide, astonished and superstitious eyes.

"Why?" Benedict laughed.

She crossed herself. "He says he's going to sleep there all the time . . . until there's no more——" her eyes filled with fear—"fighting, till the soldiers go away." She looked at him. "Benedict," she whispered in a haunted voice, "did you see Rudolph when you came into the yard?"

"Yes, Mama," he replied. "He's playing with the chickens."

She sighed.

He got up and went around the house to the porch. The side of it was walled in, and the little board door was shut. Wood and coal were kept in it. He said: "Joey!"

There was no answer from inside the shed.

"Joey," he repeated, "it's me, Benedict." And for some reason he added: "Your brother."

Still there was no answer; only a subtle shifting of a breath inside. He knocked on the door.

"Whattya wa—ant?"

It was Joey's voice, with a slight whine, and Benedict suddenly felt such a surge of relief that he leaned against the door and let the tears come to his eyes. With his lashes wet, he smiled.

"What are you doing in there?" he asked.

"Nothin'," Joey replied.

"Why don't you come out?"

There was a moment of silence.

"Ain't you *ever* going to come out?"

There was a moment again of waiting, and then Joey's wailing voice: "No-o-o. . . .!"

"Joey," Benedict said, "you can't stay in there forever. You'll get hungry. Why do you want to stay in there?"

"Go away," Joey cried.

"But Joey," Benedict said, "what are you afraid of?"

"I ain't afraid of nothing!" Joey screamed.

"But what are you hiding there for, then?" Benedict cried.

"I ain't afraid of nothing!" Joey screamed again.

Benedict stared at the locked door. He chewed his lips nervously. He leaned against the door and closed his eyes, then said earnestly: "Nobody'll hurt *you*, Joey. The cops are all after the men. They don't hurt kids. Come on out," he begged. "I brought Mama a rabbit and she's going to cook it. It's for you."

"Go away," Joey cried, his voice breaking. "Don't tell 'em where I am, Benny!"

Benedict stared helplessly at the yard. Suddenly he shivered. His body was touched by ice. "Joey," he whispered, his whisper filled helplessly with fear, "come on out, you *got* to come out, Joey!"

He stared at the toilet: his eyes fixed on the crescent cut in the door. Now it came back: *The two men, with arms uplifted by the rope, stumbling and falling in the bloody grass; the horse turned its wet nostrils and its white eye and its black paw frantically kicked at the ground.* . . . He felt the cold fright suddenly, and cringed against the porch. His mother's superstitious eyes returned to him and he shuddered. *Joey would stay in there forever!* he whispered to himself flattening his cheek against the sun-baked board of the porch. *Forever in fear!* The threat seemed to move into the yard; he looked frantically about him and beat against the latched door.

"Joey!" he screamed, his voice sounding blunted and perversely unheard in his own ears, and he screamed louder: "Joey, if you don't come out, I'll break down the door and beat you till the blood comes!"

There was a sudden hoarse sobbing inside the shed. Benedict grabbed the door and began to pull, beating it with one free fist. He kicked with his feet, pounded with his hands, tore at it until the flimsy wood splintered. The door came loose and Joey screamed and began to scramble back into the coal. Benedict lurched inside the dark, web-sticky shed, groped among the wood and coal, panting hoarsely, and finally found him squeezed into a corner with a hunk of coal in his hands, which were shaking like beating sticks. He caught Joey's hand and twisted the coal out, and then holding him by the arm and hair dragged him into the blazing sunlight. Joey caught hold of the wooden sidewalk and screamed. His face, streaked with coal dust and tears, beat against the walk; then his toes pounded it. He tried to crawl back into the shed, but Benedict, crying wildly, beat him with both fists, shrieking: *"Don't go in! Don't! Don't! Don't!"* until he fell beside him on the walk.

He lay with his face turned vacantly toward the yard, his heart throbbing pitilessly, the sun shining into his eyes. His chin was trembling and his teeth hurt as though he had gripped them together in his mouth. Joey's sobs had died and he lay on the walk inertly, with his arms gathered under him and his legs crossed. His eyes were blank.

Benedict leaned over him and said softly: "Joey, it's me, your brother. The cops won't come! I'll never let them!" But there was no response.

He lifted Joey up under his arms and dragged him around the house into the kitchen. He stumbled toward his mother, and she caught him in her apron and stared at the coal-dust smeared face and the trickle of blood coming from his nose. She turned to look at Benedict, who stood in the open door gasping wildly.

"Benedict?" she cried as though she didn't recognize him.

"And if you ever go back there, I'll kill you!" Benedict sobbed in a hoarse ragged voice, and then ran out of the door.

It was six o'clock before he got back to camp again. His rage had subsided, but had left behind a bitter, tormented taste. He didn't want to see his father while the stain of sin was on him, while the taste of his furious rage and fear still remained with him, so he wandered about the camp with his hands tightly gripped in his pockets. He saw his father from a distance, talking to two other men: and he felt that sense of wonder and surprise that he had always felt whenever he had unexpectedly come across his father acting like an ordinary citizen of the country, unmarked by his status. Now he kept a distance away, refusing to go to his father, whom he wanted now more badly than ever to see; he waited, self-tormented, until he felt he had suffered enough, and then he approached his father, but obliquely. He stood silently near and listened to his talk—refusing now to feel any subtle humiliation that he always felt when he heard his father speaking in his broken English to people whose language was the language of the land. When his father's eyes fell on him, his heart unexpectedly leaped, as though he had really believed that he would be ignored.

"Go home!" his father cried immediately.

"But, Papa," Benedict said. "I just——"

"Go, go," his father said impatiently. Then he brought Benedict to him with a jerk of his hand. "Benedict," he said seriously, in his own tongue, "listen to me. This is no place for you. Go back home to Mama and the children!"

He wanted to cry: "Papa, talk to Joey!"

But his father said: "See! We're here; we got out safely. So go back home now."

"Papa," Benedict said, "I brought the message. . . ."

His father looked at him, and his face softened. "Did I doubt it?" he asked. Benedict's face glowed.

"Papa," he said, lowering his voice, "will there be——"

His father shrugged. "Nobody knows," he said. "But you go **home.**"

"I have to see Father Dahr tomorrow," Benedict said out loud, although it was a private thought.

"Yes, yes," his father agreed eagerly.

Benedict turned.

"Benedict!"

He whirled back eagerly.

"One thing," his father said. "If they come to ask you about me, you will——"

"Papa!" Benedict cried tragically.

His father smiled and put his hand on his head. "I know, I know," he muttered. "I didn't mean——" He pushed Benedict away. "Now go," he ordered.

Benedict raised his eyes toward him.

"Papa," he said, "Did you lose the flute?"

His father looked at him blankly; and then said impatiently: "Are you a child?"

Benedict walked away then without looking back.

It was a much longer trip home. He stayed on the hills, hiding in the grass, hunting for birds' eggs, and finding none. Darkness came hesitantly, groping its way, as though it had been hurt once here before. The wind was hot and the odor from the incinerator was like a bath. Benedict walked along, kicking at things: at stones and shadows and thoughts. He had sunk his hands into his pockets, feeling the taut thigh muscles with his finger tips, and he walked almost stiff-legged, only slightly bending his knees. Once he stopped and took his hands out of his pockets and listened. The sound had seemed like muffled hoofs, and he stood poised rigidly pointing in the darkness. He shivered, noticing the sudden darkness, as though it had closed in on him at that moment. It was far darker than usual: neither the Mill nor the dump was burning. They sky had not even stars: but ordinarily, either a flaming Bessemer or a new cast at the Blast Furnace would have lit the sky up in a huge arc of light, and the shadow that was swallowed now by the absolute darkness would suddenly show itself, long and inky behind him.

He stumbled on a tuft of grass where no doubt a nest was hidden for there was a hasty flutter of wings and a rush of air before his face. He walked around the spot, afraid he would trample on eggs. The memory of his search for Vince came unbidden to him. He had always been thinking of Vince—preparing to see his lanky body suddenly on the street, suddenly at the door, or even suddenly at his bedside at night, whispered, "Benny, is Pap home?" He had dreamed of Vince and searched over the whole country for him in his dreams. And now a sudden ache to see him returned, and he searched for him again—in the alleys, out on the hills, in other cities, along the docks and wharfs, in boxcars and in sheds and barns. He searched for him in Smoky Bottom, up and down the lanes and alleys, through shuttered windows where suddenly he found him sitting on a chair, dangling a cigarette, while a naked girl stood in front of him laughing, with her red lips making two oily half circles. Vince was laughing, too, but not as much; the cigarette was burning in his brown fingers, and casually he dragged one hand across his thigh, and the girl burst into laughter. Benedict, standing at the window, cried a warning: "Vince!" But the window was shut, and the darkness was like a deafness, and Vince reached out his long hand and lifted the girl's swollen breast, turning to look at Benedict at the window to catch his look of horror, and to laugh at him, wink at him, and then to go on with the girl.

Benedict followed the vision through, his heart pounding; he stood concealed in the darkness, his ears lifted for the sound of life. His blood thickened in his face, his thighs tensed and tightened beneath the clenched hands in his pockets which sweated a pool in his grip. The darkness was close; it touched him and pressed against him, fondling him, reaching along his stomach and arms, and pressing cold wet lips on his hot brow and touching his open mouth with cold-tipped teeth. . . . "Don't do it, Vince!" he cried

250

despairingly in the muffled darkness, losing sight of Vince in the night and filling the night with his own hot body, larger than it had ever been, and stumbling as though down a long stairs toward mornings. . . .

Joey was breathing deeply when he climbed into bed. He was aware of Vince's empty bed, in which only Rudolph lay, whimpering in the darkness; and as he lay against Joey's bony spine, he thought a long time about Vince and where he might be, and whether he was bad, and why he couldn't feel that he was bad although he tried. He thought of the burning moments on the dark hills, and again his body burst into flame, and in his dreams the Succubus came to lie with him.

14.

He took the back way to the parish house, following the alleys. He came that way because he had seen a company of six troopers going through town out to the hills. He came by alley because alley was less public, though he didn't know why he needed secrecy.

The alley was walled almost solidly on both sides by dark wind-beaten and weather-beaten cow-sheds, smelling sometimes sharply of dung, sometimes blandly. Where there were fences, he could see the dark yards beyond, with their neatly measured-out beds of vegetables. Blown-up paper bags swung restlessly from white strings; some beds still had plants under fruit jars, and paper bags had been capped over rows of celery to bleach them. A toy wooden windmill spun busily, although he could feel no wind. On the roofs of the sheds the ore dust still lay; a huge lightning-scarred cottonwood held up amputated limbs to the sky, and a long livid strip lay bare to the sun, reaching from the lowest branch to the ground.

He opened the parish gate with a heavy pressure on his heart. The yard was green: everywhere, by contrast, it was filled with flower bushes. He walked reluctantly through the yard, and before he knocked on the door stooped to look under the porch for the cats and kittens which he had never found the courage to drown. There was nothing there but webs. Nobody answered his knock: he had expected this, and so after another sharp knock, he immediately turned the knob and entered the kitchen. The geranium pot still sat on the window sill, but the flower was missing. He saw water under the icebox and brought out the pan beneath, which had overflowed, and emptied it into the sink. The kitchen smelled of food, but the air of sanctity was not completely obliterated: it was there underneath, the smell of incensed candles and leather books, of salt water and silk, of dusty robes, the odor of a burning wick.

He went through the ever-dark hallway, conscious of the gleaming Christ only abstractedly, and hesitated before he knocked on the inner door. The house was quiet. Perhaps, he thought, Father Dahr was upstairs? He knocked: and immediately there was a response: it was Father Dahr's voice; and he entered.

Father Dahr wasn't sitting at the window, as he had half-expected him to be. Instead, he was standing in his woolen underwear at the secretary, which stood dark and secretive against the wall near the corner, and was tearing up papers and letters.

"Father," Benedict began contritely; and then drew back, and ended in a flat voice: "I'm sorry I didn't come yesterday."

He was irritated because Father Dahr was in his winter underwear. He had taken his coat and shirt off, and didn't look like a priest at all: he looked like a butcher, with his uneven ragged hair and his cheeks, which were sagging now, filled with blue-and-red spots and dried patches where the little blood vessels were gathered like thin worms tangled together.

Father Dahr turned to him, holding a letter in his hands, and seemed to need a moment to remember him. Benedict felt that slight twinge of humiliation with which he had waited in the confessional for Father Dahr to identify him.

"Oh!" the old man suddenly cried, laughing at himself and his hair shaking windily, "Benedict! Come in, come in."

Benedict took a step farther into the room.

"I'm glad to see you're better," he said grudgingly.

252

"Oh," Father Dahr laughed, tearing the letter into halves and then fourths, "better, better! So improved I'm going traveling!"

Benedict wasn't sure, sometimes, that Father Dahr was always aware of what he was saying.

"You traveling?" he repeated skeptically but patiently.

Father Dahr turned around to face him, threw up his hands and clapped them together in an unexpected thunder clap: "Yes!"

Benedict looked about the room now, noticing, although nothing seemed to be moved, a slight touch of disorder.

"Where would *you* visit?" he said scornfully, and waited for Father Dahr to reveal the joke.

"But still I'm going," Father Dahr said grimly, and he turned back to the secretary and opened one of the drawers. He looked at the handwriting on a letter, then pulled the letter out and read a few lines; before he was through he quit reading and tore it into shreds.

"But, Father——" Benedict said helplessly, with a laugh. "Where *could* you go?"

Father Dahr didn't turn to answer him. "To the Poor House," he said quietly.

Benedict started. "What?" he said.

Father Dahr was tearing more letters with a kind of blind passion, without reading them.

"Father," Benedict said, "Father, what did you say?"

"I'm going to St. Thomas' Home for the Aged," Father Dahr said, opening one letter to scan it. "Will you come and see me?"

In this moment of silence he heard for the first time the sound of men's voices outside the front of the house. Somebody was cursing, oblivious to the fact that he was near a church. He tasted dust.

As though he understood that Benedict would not easily be convinced, Father Dahr now turned and said sharply: "Yes, yes." Benedict was standing tensely in the room, listening. Father Dahr stared at him and then slowly crossed the room on bare padded feet, and took him silently by the elbow to the window. He parted the curtains and let him look.

The curses were real. They came from a gang of men who were

standing at the front of the church looking up. And looking up with them, Benedict saw two men on the slanted roof. They held crow bars in their hands, and they were prying the slate off the roof. The loosened slate rode down the side and crashed in a million fragments on the street. Two trucks were standing at the curb, being filled with broken slate.

Benedict turned shocked eyes to Father Dahr, and Father Dahr shrugged and nodded.

"Fixing the roof?" Benedict pleaded.

Father Dahr didn't answer. He returned to the secretary, and opened another drawer.

"Father!" Benedict cried from the window, holding the curtain with his hand. "You've got to stop them!" He stared out at the working men, unable to tear his eyes away. "Father," he cried. "Father, do you know what they're doing?"

But Father Dahr seemed not to hear him. There was already a big pile of torn paper on the floor (the waste basket was filled), and he continued to add to it. Occasionally, he shook his head with a half-embarrassed, half-surprised smile as he read.

Benedict dropped the curtains and stared back at him. His face was pale, and he worked his fist before he cried: "Father, I didn't tell on you!"

Father Dahr turned to the window, with the letter half-torn.

"Father Brumbaugh *asked* me to go!" Benedict cried.

Father Dahr laughed. "What, what?" he said lightly. "What are you trying to say?"

Benedict lowered his voice. "He said the Bishop wanted to see me." He looked at the floor.

Father Dahr stared at him and then cried: "Of course! Of course!"

Benedict said, staring down at the carpet: "The church is sold, Father." He lifted his head and stared at it. "Isn't it?"

"Did you think it *wouldn't* be?" Father Dahr cried angrily. "The whole valley's sold!"

"No, not the houses! My father didn't sell!" Benedict cried hotly, proudly. His tongue stumbled. He wanted to add that he *knew*, he *knew*—because he had seen them all out in the woods!

254

"They will be sold," Father Dahr said with his lips tight.

Hot waves of shame broke over Benedict. He trembled, wet his lips.

"It was *my* fault, Father!" he croaked.

Father Dahr looked at him with astonishment and then laughed.

"Your fault!" he said, and turned back to the letters. As he tore one in half Benedict remembered how he had torn the letter from the Company—torn it in pieces and thrown it like a snow over the young priest.

There was a crash in the street, and Benedict turned wildly to the window again. They were lowering the stone crucifix with a rope and it had hit against the church wall, knocking one of the cross beams off, and this had crashed to the ground. The men had leaped away, and were looking with upturned heads, shaking their fists at the men on the roof as he parted the curtains. A police wagon went by at that moment, a policeman sitting with his leg blocking the exit. The wagon was full; he glimpsed their gray faces.

He turned to Father Dahr and in a voice filled with accusation cried: "The church *is* sold!"

Father Dahr was bending over to stare near-sightedly into the drawer of the desk. His unkempt hair fell over like a cockscomb. Benedict stared at him. From him he turned to stare again at the room, looking at it now with a certain bold confrontation, as though he had gained a certain authority to do so, to see it outside of his own implication in it: the arm chair, rubbed down by Father Dahr's head and arms and back, the straight-backed carved chairs, with lion's head feet, the African mementos, the crossed spears, the bracelet of teeth, on the window an African violet, the bowl of blue fish, the gilt-framed pictures that stared down on the room from behind a darkness as thick as of a time of only nights, one over the other. There were shelves for books, books that had not been disturbed for years, books of ecclesiastical history and law, bound in rubbed buckram; the secretary of dark teakwood, looking somewhat Oriental: all of it standing with a kind of dwindling dust on it, not perceptible, only felt. Already the room was stricken with decay and abandonment. It was vulnerable, it was a dying room.

All of it would be moved, the house would be torn down, the foundation would be locked forever under tons of rock. The garden outside would suddenly die, in full bloom; a flame would come from nowhere and kill, in a sudden blow, the violets and irises, the snowball bushes, the lilies and lilacs, the grapes hanging on the trellis; and if nobody succeeded in getting the cats out, the cats, too. The kittens he would drown. . . .

He felt an enormous silence lapping them up in a velvet wave and sinking them slowly into a depth so still, so deep that he could no longer imagine his own motion, or even the breath of his thoughts. But the silence would be hard and solid, not soft, not liquid: hard and solid, encasing them like iron that has been melted and cooled, and then cooled forever.

And then suddenly in the betrayed room he noticed an old man, a man whom he had never quite seen before: who was now with an odd unsure intensity looking over a batch of yellowing papers, tearing some, putting a few aside to be torn by others, stopping sometimes to scratch under his arm where the union suit itched. He knew that he shouldn't feel suddenly that he wanted to help this old man—to sweep up the torn papers for him, anyhow, and tell him it was getting late. (Late for whatever was next.) Then, he wanted to cry briefly but knew that if the old man turned to him with an astounded expression and asked him querulously *What are you crying for?* he could not tell him. For he would be crying for this old man! He would have to run out of the house, before he could talk, feeling that he had committed a great crime for which there was no way of making amends, no way of making up for pitying someone you had no right ever to pity! He felt sad, as though somehow he had come into possession before his time and unwillingly of a terrible secret, one he had no right to: a power that changed the priest standing on the other side of the room into an old man tearing up old letters and papers, shaking his head over some, knitting his brows over others, lingering over others still, and then tearing them, too, finally, as though he had given up trying to remember who had written them or what it was all about, and smiling to himself with tired astonishment that so much of life could have slipped so irrevocably away, and the key to it lost forever. Benedict felt pity for the old priest, and this was his secret. . . .

Father Dahr sighed. "Look!" he cried, pointing to the pile of papers. "Look at all that!"

Benedict shook himself. He parted the curtains slightly and looked out again. A truck was already filled with slate and was starting its motor. The crash of slate went on.

"Father," he said, "are you too old?"

"Look," Father Dahr repeated, kicking the pile of papers with his toe, "all that."

"But you could find another parish," Benedict said.

Father Dahr drew in his breath and lifted a letter to the light: ". . . and see you Tuesday," he read. He lifted his head. "What Tuesday?"

"But you *want* a parish, don't you?" Benedict demanded.

"What?" Father Dahr said, without lifting his eyes.

"A parish," Benedict murmured. "Don't you?"

Father Dahr's lips moved and he began to smile with slowly gathering surprise. He read on and laughed unbelievingly to himself, knuckled his eyes and squinted at the paper. "Eighteen eighty-two," he mumbled.

"I could go to the Bishop," Benedict said.

"What?" Father Dahr asked vaguely without looking up.

"I could go to the Bishop," Benedict repeated.

Father Dahr picked up the letter again. "Oh," he said.

"But Father!" Benedict cried. "What are we going to do?"

Father Dahr put the letter down at this note of despair, and beckoned Benedict to him. When Benedict was within reach, he put his arm around his shoulders and drew him closer. Benedict could smell the wool of the underwear, the odor of his arms.

"Benedict," he said, "what are you trying to say to me?"

Benedict turned his head away.

"There's nothing you can do," he said. "Nor I. Soon we'll have a new church. You'll attend it, and serve with Father Brumbaugh as well as you know how. That's all."

"But you, Father?"

"And I will do what old men do," he said impatiently.

There was a louder crash than ever outside.

"But why are they tearing——"

He took Benedict by the shoulder and led him to the chair, where he sat down with a heavy sigh.

"There's nothing left here," he said wearily, pinching his eyes. "That's why they're tearing it down." He closed his eyes and drew in his breath deeply and said in a low voice: "In this life, Benedict, the poor are doomed always to lose. The worker always to fall in defeat. . . ." He opened his dying eyes and said: "Don't blame us, Benedict. . . ."

There was only the sound of crashing; the far sound of men.

Benedict lifted his head, at last, and looked into the old man's eyes; and when the old priest brought his eyes to meet Benedict's, Benedict turned away and said tonelessly: "I went to see the Bishop with Father Brumbaugh."

"Oh, Benedict," Father Dahr cried, reaching over and punching him gently. "I *made* Father Brumbaugh take you! It was my promise to you, wasn't it, to help you enter a seminary?"

"The Bishop said——"

Father Dahr cut him short with a sharp wave of his hand. "The Bishop, the Bishop!" he cried. "I don't want to hear! All my life all I've heard was, 'The Bishop said this, the Bishop said that!' Thank God, that's over now! Whatever the Bishop said, keep it locked in your heart as your secret forever. Nothing would be new to me!"

He patted Benedict over the heart as though the secret lay there, and added reproachfully: "What a fine priest you'll make!"

Benedict smiled too sadly at this, and Father Dahr cried, with a touch of exasperation, "Why are you so gloomy?"

And Benedict turned a look so full of naked pity for him that he jerked his head back with surprise; then his face flooded with shame, then crimsoned with anger, and he cried: "What did you come to see me about?"

Benedict stammered: "See you?"

"Yes! Yes! What business have you with me?" Father Dahr cried, rubbing his head.

Benedict thought; he lifted his face to the old man and said slowly: "Suppose, Father," and he turned his piteous look to the old man. "Suppose I talk to Father Brumbaugh, and then——"

He had never seen Father Dahr's eyes so cold! They flashed fire, too, in spite of their age. The old man got up with a violent surge from his chair, leaving it rocking angrily back and forth. He strode to the secretary and viciously began tearing the papers at random. Benedict stared at his back in horror. He tried to form other words with his tight lips but could not. He turned suddenly to the window where a shattering crash came. He swung back to the old man, and again tried to say something. The shoulders were working furiously and his head was bent over, rigidly.

He was suddenly at the door. He wanted to step through it quickly and run down the hall before he had a chance to think again. But at the door he hesitated and looked back at the bent shoulders.

"Father, I'll pray for you!" he cried, and closed shut the door.

15.

Benedict couldn't leave the house immediately. He sat in the kitchen for a while and looked around the room as though he were memorizing it before leaving it forever. When the cat scratched against the screendoor, he opened it and picked it up and looked into its sleepy green eyes, and stroked its yielding gray fur. Then he went out into the garden and stared at it as though troubled by its ambiguous appearance: that it was the parish garden—and soon would not be. He went to the grape arbor that had been built over a well that no longer was used and pulled off a tiny bunch of hard green fox-grapes, so carefully cultivated by Father Dahr, no bigger than peas, and rolled them thoughtfully between his fingers. Those grapes seldom ripened, for the kids stole them when they were still green; but they were supposed to get almost white. He stared at their innocence: at their hanging from the trellis with the sun on them, slowly growing, as though this would be a year as long as last year and the year before. Everything was innnocent he thought, feeling the flight of innocence from himself —turning to look back at the house, the kittens, which had mysteriously appeared from under the porch and were now tumbling with each other, at the fence which Mrs. Rumyer had painted . . . but she could have skipped it this year! He stared at the little kittens, and shuddered a bit, and thought of drowning them. So innocent!

The crashing of slate and the yelling of the men was clearer out here in the open. He couldn't see them from the back of the house. He walked to the door opening into the sacristy, and observed—he felt, for the first time: this, the kitchen, the garden —that the copper door latch was twisted into a snake doubling on itself and forming a handle. Why had he never noticed that? He fingered it curiously before he put his whole hand on it—remembering that he had done this once before; then he pulled the heavy door open and stepped inside.

A frosted window let in a wintry light. But he was so familiar with this room that he could have found his way in it blindfolded! The floor was tile. Across from the door was the huge chest of drawers, surmounted by a crucifix, whose paint was peeling along Christ's slender legs. Beside the drawer on the right was a prie-dieu, to the left was the porcelain sink, and beside it the basin in which he had washed the chalice, oh, hundreds of times, turning the gleaming gold vessel in his hands and staring down at the balloon face distorted in its curved side. He had been struck dumb, he remembered, when he was told that the drain pipe led straight into the ground and not into the sewer: this had amazed him because he had felt a kind of guilt as he realized sharply that in his ignorance he had supposed that *this* water, which had washed the sacred chalice, the vessel in which wine was turned into Christ's sacred blood, had also gone down the common sewer to the river. This revelation had made him nervous about all his knowledge. How many sins was he committing unknown to himself?

He walked to the tall cupboard and opened it. The odor of old moth balls and yellow soap and the clean smell of neat clothes, rushed out. His surplice and cassock were hanging there on a clothes branch. He stared at them, suddenly surprised to see them, and slightly dazed. They had been hanging there through all the time (for it seemed so much time had passed), through all the infinite growth, through the murder of men, through hunger, through so much pain! They had hung there as though nothing had happened, exactly his old size, exactly fitting the Benedict he had been —a stillness in time and space, a balanced nothingness, oblivion in life. It was as though he had stumbled upon, in some frightening way, in some disturbing and upsetting way—if such a thing could be—a corpse of himself, a memory of himself that had no right to intrude into this new—and only now was he struck with this fact!—life, and new self. He closed the doors suddenly, and shut his eyes and shook his head gently back and forth. And then, as though trying once again to fly, "I'm in *church,*" he whispered desperately to himself.

He turned the key in the closet: a brass key that always remained in the lock; then moved on. He paused before the entrance to the sanctuary to dip his fingers in a holy water fount and slowly to wet his forehead: "In the name of the Father, and of the Son . . ." he whispered. If he rang the bell, the shadows would tremble inside the church; someone would hear him outside and run away, thinking there were ghosts. Slowly he crossed the sanctuary floor, genuflecting before the altar, and raising his head to stare at it for a long time. The altar was bare, the Tabernacle was open and empty; but there had been a morning Mass: the wicks of the dead candles gleamed still with oil. Christ looked down on him from His agonized height, His arms outstretched, and nailed, His feet placed one on the other, and nailed through with one spike— but not of gold!—His breast was bleeding; the crown of thorns sitting above beads of blood on His forehead. Hail, O, King! For years he had not dared to look at Him: the bloody wounds had turned him a little sick. Then after a while he never really saw Him anymore, only vaguely felt His presence, His intense agony weighing on the air. But now he felt that harsh sick feeling as though for the first time, and the wounds were alive. Christ, too, had suffered, he thought, thinking of his father in the Mill. It was suffering that had brought him close to Christ. Christ had once been alive, and had suffered human pain! It was through pain that he reached for Him when his vision of sainthood faltered. He wanted to ponder longer about it, feeling that he was on the verge of a great truth. But instead, he rose from his knees and turned to survey the church.

Kyrie, eleison! Christe, eleison!

How human the voices sounded! He heard them somehow in the dusty shadows of the choir loft, where the organ had not been played for years: for it had not been repaired. He heard his own voice, as though it were an echo, *Christe, eleison!*—and the elevation of his heart with the elevation of the Host. Incense clung to his nostrils; mixed with it, as he turned through the communion rail to the benches, he smelled the steeped odor of sawdust and kerosene; and a closeness as though from a thousand moths gathered together in the suffocating dust of their wings. There was a smell of human grease that hung in the church like a windless cloud: it saturated the walls and the benches and even the floor, and no wind would ever quite drive it out. Father Brumbaugh had detected it immediately: his nose had twitched; in the first days he had pumped gallons of rose-water into the church, hoping to kill it off. Through the walls, too, the gritty steel smoke from the Mill sifted as though the walls were porous, and stained the walls from the inside, and helped to give the church a faint taste of the rolling mill, which the noses of the workers accepted, as they fell to their knees, with a kind of relief.

Benedict turned to the side of the church, where in the dimpled walls, behind votive candles covered with dust, middle-sized representations of Christ's Gethsemane and climb to Golgotha stood in carved tableau. Seven panels on this wall, and seven on the opposite traced His martyrdom, and Benedict drew near to the first one and knelt before it, and lowered his head. How long they had saved, and how Father Dahr had begged and threatened and fought for the money from his parishioners, to erect these! How his heart had swollen with reverent pride when the last one was installed and blessed and he had been—was he the first one? In his pride!—one of those who had followed Christ in His agony —until his own knees were raw and bleeding! He whispered to himself, lifting his head in the middle of his thoughts to stare at the ceiling from which dust was falling. It fell in a slowly-descending haze, as though of tiny fruit: and then he heard the dulled thud on the roof, and remembered that men were above him tearing at the church. A sudden anger rose up in him, and his fists gripped, and he felt the pain of them. He wanted to run out of the church and scream something to the men—to the sky, the valley, the world!—something, *what, what?* He turned bitterly back to the First Station of the Cross, and stared at the roughly carved features of Christ, as He stood between two Roman guards, looking down on the jeering populace, already crowned with thorns, already condemned to die. How often had *he* stood just that way looking down on them with that infinite pity in his eyes! He felt the tug of that memory, and he shrugged, suddenly, and passed to the Second Station.

Here, Christ is on His knees with arms outstretched, while the great cross descends on His flimsy shoulders: and His jailers are there with the scourge, and the first fiery blows descend crackling on His back. How many times, he thought, had he felt that cross fall on his own shoulders; how many times had he himself started on the rocky climb to Calvary, while his back bled and his knees—for in the Third Station He falls under the weight of the cross and the blows—were cut to the bone. At the Fourth Station—O, my God (Benedict trembled)—Jesus met His mother. What a torture was that! How they wept for each other! How vainly she reached for His hands, for the back that was draining blood as though from a storm of blood! At the Fifth Station, the executioners believe that He will never reach the crucifixion and force Simon to carry the cross for Him. (Gladly, Benedict reaches for the cross and bears it on his shoulders.) And then in the Sixth, Veronica held forth a towel to Him, and He wiped the blood and sweat from His face. And the Seventh—Benedict stopped and stared at it as though he had never seen it before—Jesus lay sprawled under the heavy cross bearing Him down, for this was the Second Fall. A soldier has his heavy arm upraised with a lash. Benedict reached out into the carving to hold back the arm; and then, with a frown, withdrew his arm from his mind's eye, as he stared at the rigid images which had no life in them, none at all. . . .

He shook his shoulders with slight vexation and looked across the church to the other seven panels, which brought Christ to the cross, to His dying, and then to the sepulchre, from which, in three days, He rose again. The panels returned to the sanctuary, and he couldn't see the last ones. A sparrow, which had blundered into the church, and had been sitting quietly high up in the arch, suddenly left its perch and began madly flying around and around in the church, stirring dust and light like a wheel. Finally, it burst through a broken window pane and disappeared, leaving the church stiller than before.

Benedict stopped beside the curtained confessionals and fingered the yellowed curtain. He felt the darkness and the odd coldness inside, a coldness which arose through the floor from the dirt cellar below with a damp rot. He parted the curtains and entered: sank to his knees, finding the tiny bench there, and sketched a tiny cross over his head and shoulders, and waited for the clatter of the board between them and the wheeze of the old priest's lungs, and his monumental profile, and the sour sting of his breath. Benedict felt giddy, and leaned his head against the screen. "No, Father, I have no sins to confess." "No, Father, I have not sinned." "Father, my ambition is to be a saint—but no, Father, not ambition but consecration." "I wish to remain poor, I wish only to serve my people." He kept his head averted, overwhelmed by the old man's breath, praying deep in his mind that God would relieve them of this old man in some quiet, sinless way. . . .

"*Oh, God. . . !*" He stumbled out of the confessional, lurching against the back of the bench, and groped his way to the door. Slate crashed over his head onto the stone steps and he stared blindly out into the blazing sunlight, with one hand above his head with the five fingers rigidly outspread.

A truck growled, and as his eyes focused again, he saw two men staring at him.

"I thought the church was empty!" one of them said.

Benedict clattered down the steps, and turned away from them, and began to walk. His arm hurt terribly, as though the slate had hit it.

16.

It was five o'clock before Father Brumbaugh returned. Benedict saw him get out of a car, wave to somebody inside, and then with a roll of blueprints stuck under his arm, come briskly up the walk to the parish house.

He walked differently now — quickly and confidently, with authority in his look. Benedict's heart sank. Without exactly planning to, he found himself half-hiding behind a tree and hoping that Father Brumbaugh would pass him by without noticing. But Father Brumbaugh at this moment caught sight of him and hailed him cheerfully: "Benedict, hello, hello!"

His voice was fresh, and he looked both younger and older. His eyes sparkled, his usual pale face was flushed and—apparently he'd been out in the sun all day—almost tanned. Benedict had never seen him like this. There was a smudge across his chin, a shocking thing to see, and his knuckles were skinned. His smart black hat was perfectly shaped and in place, and there was a black smear across his white collar.

"What were you doing there?" he asked laughingly. "Waiting for me? Long?" he added with regret.

"I went to see Father Dahr," Benedict mumbled.

"How does he feel?" Father Brumbaugh asked cordially, putting his arm on Benedict's shoulder and pressing it affectionately. He waited with slightly raised eyebrows for Benedict to answer, but Benedict couldn't answer. "I suppose he told you about the new church?" he said.

Benedict's shoulders jumped, and Father Brumbaugh looked at him curiously.

"Did he?" he asked, looking into Benedict's eyes with a waiting smile.

"Well, good!" Father Brumbaugh said freshly. "Then you know! What news, what news," he almost carolled, lifting up the blue-prints before him. Benedict shrank into his skin. "Where were you yesterday?" the priest demanded reproachfully. "Did you know?"

Benedict shook his head tightly from side to side, with his lips set.

"*Didn't* you know?" Father Brumbaugh continued with some surprise. "The whole valley's going, the whole valley. . . ."

"They're tearing down the church, Father!" Benedict cried in a muffled tormented voice.

"What?" Father Brumbaugh exclaimed, startled by his tortured look.

Benedict stopped and drew away from Father Brumbaugh's arm and pointed. A pile of slate stood in front of the church.

"Yes?" Father Brumbaugh asked, puzzled. He looked from the pile to Benedict's bitter eyes and cried: "Benedict!"—with such profound regret that Benedict turned impulsively to him, his lips quivering. He brought Benedict back into the curve of his arm and crooned: "It doesn't mean much, Benedict. It had to go—it's an old church. We'd have had to get a new one anyhow. God needs at least," he smiled with his joke at Benedict, "at *least* a clean place, free of mice!" He patted Benedict on the head. "What are you so bitter for? There are so many things you don't know about the church. Benedict," he cried, tipping Benedict's head up, "look at me! We couldn't keep it here—the people are too poor. We *had* to move—even if this hadn't happened, if the Company hadn't needed the land, still we would have had to move. There are more people in the City. *These* people will be in the City——"

"But they haven't given up!" Benedict cried. "They're *not* moving——"

The priest stared down at him, his eyes patient, slightly narrowed. He said, finally: "What can they do?" He touched Benedict's elbow. "A church isn't a building—you know that. The building is merely the shell. Look at it—can't you see? The church is empty now: its soul has gone. Let us bury it." He turned Benedict's head toward the bruised building. Benedict stared at it again: the top beam of the roof was all exposed now; one side was torn loose as though by a mighty hand. Gray dust covered the side. He turned away.

"Father Dahr is leaving," he mumbled.

Father Brumbaugh pulled Benedict nearer to him, and once again put his arms around him, and forced him to walk with him. "Don't worry about Father Dahr," he said quietly. "Father Dahr's too old to serve. He understands."

"No, he doesn't understand!" Benedict answered.

Father Brumbaugh looked at him with a flush. "What did he tell you?" he asked.

"Nothing!" Benedict cried scornfully.

Father Brumbaugh searched his eyes again, and then said: "But he does understand." He tightened his grip on Benedict's shoulder and added: "I know you loved him, but don't let your feelings for him blind you. The old man," he hesitated, "was not —pure."

Benedict stiffened: the street disappeared; he swung loosely, blinded.

Father Brumbaugh hadn't noticed. His eyebrows were arched, and his lips had the tiny smile Benedict had seen before, and he expected the priest to raise his fingers and caress it. They came to the front yard gate, and Father Brumbaugh opened it with difficulty, keeping his arm around Benedict's shoulder as though not wanting to let him go. They mounted the three steps to the porch, and Father Brumbaugh brought him to the swing and sat down on it.

"Now," he said efficiently as though he had been waiting until they arrived here to produce his most convincing argument, "here's what the new church will be like." He unrolled one of the blueprints. "It's all lines and squares now, but it's a church anyhow. See how much larger? That's the nave." His voice became absorbed, his eyes fascinated, and in a minute he was running along eagerly not waiting any more to make certain that Benedict was following him. He recited figures and numbers, times and weights, and the sanctified elements of the church flowed from his lips in terms of feet and inches. His finger ran professionally along the white lines. His eyes glowed, his voice was lyrical.

Benedict stared off the porch to the church. A dog was sniffing along the steps. A pigeon curtsied in the sky and then sought for the cornice, certain that it was there, implicit with faith. Father Brumbaugh's silver voice ran on: numbers tumbled out; he was sucking one of his bleeding knuckles which had been scratched somewhere. His blond eyebrows were knitted and his blond eyelashes looked sunburned.

"If the church sells," Benedict said in a monotone, "then others will sell, and then the Company will win."

But Father Brumbaugh was unrolling the second blueprint, crackling and unfolding the paper.

"They'll think," Benedict said in the same toneless voice, "that if the church sells, then there's no use to keep on fighting. Father Dahr promised never to——"

"Oh," Father Brumbaugh exclaimed, looking up for a moment. "You mean the strike! But that'll soon be over."

Benedict looked at him and said as though throwing his words a long distance: "But the workers don't want it to be over."

"They'll come to their senses," the young priest replied confidently. He looked up, caught Benedict's expression and laughed: "Oh, they'll come to their senses, Benedict! Don't worry about it!" He patted Benedict on the side of the face. "Smile a little," he admonished.

"Father," Benedict said, "I feel so bad."

Father Brumbaugh laid the blueprints to one side. "I know, Benedict," he said sincerely, "it's hard to give up the old things, the things you've known all your life and—loved. But you'll get over it. Wait until you see the new church. You'll come and watch them building it. Every day more will be added—every day something new, something different; and one day, it'll be finished. We'll go inside—you and I. And then, *then*, Benedict—think of the day, of *that* day!" His face was lit with vision, and Benedict smiled wanly into his shining eyes. "Mass," he said. "You'll be there," he promised. "Benedict," he cried, "don't look so gloomy!"

Father Dahr had said that!

"That's better!" the priest said with relief. "You'll feel badly at first. But you'll see!" He looked thoughtfully, curiously, at Benedict. "Didn't it bother you," he asked with surprise, "didn't it bother you to know that the church was so old and infested with all kinds of things, and that the rain came through the roof?"

He stopped. "What's wrong, Benedict?" he cried.

Benedict tried to turn his face away, his raw eyes of horror. The young priest caught it and turned it into the light. "What's wrong?" he cried again, his voice catching. He dropped the blueprints on the porch and jumped up. "Lie down!" he commanded, and laid Benedict down on the swing. "I'll get you some water!"

He sprang whitefaced through the door, and Benedict could hear his feet running through the house to the kitchen. He lifted himself painfully to a sitting position on the lurching swing, and sat there with his eyes closed to stop the rocking motion in them. Then he pulled himself off the swing, and stood on the porch. The blueprints crackled under his feet. He stumbled down the steps, and looked back with his hand on the gate. The curtains of the window of the front room behind the swing were parted, and for a moment it seemed that someone was there, had been there all the while, watching him.

He left the gate open behind him.

PART THREE

1.

The day was hot and humid. There were flat meadows of heat waves stretching as far as the aching eye could see. The air smelled of heat. Thunder charged restlessly beyond the hills. Ducks and chickens sought the cool underside of the cow sheds, and out in the fields the cows formed a lolling circle around the single tree of the field.

There seemed to be more of them, but there were actually only about a hundred mounted and foot troopers and police, reinforced by a few local and Mill police. Their horses walked with heads already down, their forelocks brushing against the tall grass. The troopers themselves let the reins dangle, and opened the collars of their shirts. Sweat ran down their hard, tanned faces, and the intense heat produced universal scowls as they sat in their wet saddles.

They came over the flue dust dunes, over the flat plateau of packed slag, and rode into the scrubby outskirts of the woods. Here, the going was tougher but they still sat their horses. But soon the underbrush grew thicker, and the pits in the hills, covered by vines and bushes, were harder to detect and were more closely set together; they had to dismount then and lead their horses, picking their way by foot through the woods.

The heat was like a roof of flame over them. Even the leaves were heavy as they pushed them out of their way. The dry alkaline smell from the mine-water creeks made them feel thirstier, and they had to fight their horses from trying to drink the sour water. Then even the horses couldn't go farther. They tended to slip into the pits. They were left behind, under guard, and the men continued on foot, with rifles and revolvers on the ready.

Word had reached the men that the troopers were coming. There was a meeting around the picnic table, over which Dobrik presided. Benedict could see them from afar. He stood with Mother Burns, watching.

"What do you think's happening?" he asked.

"Can't tell," she replied.

"What are they so excited for?"

"Don't know," she answered.

Benedict examined the men. They were almost equally divided among white and Negro, and he turned to Mother Burns.

"The troopers are coming," he said with conviction. He looked up at her and said anxiously: "Don't you think you better go somewhere?"

She didn't change the direction of her eyes.

"Where?"

"Out of here," Benedict replied.

She looked down on him. "Where to?" she demanded. She looked away from him and added: "Every rabbit in his hole."

He stared at her frail bony face, with its tiny skull covered with white; he looked at her tiny hands and bones. "But find a place to hide," he insisted.

"Got no place," she said sharply.

He looked around the camp, and saw his father. His father was nailing cut wood together into chairs, rustic chairs, as if for summer picnics.

He turned to her and asked curiously: "Why did you come *here?*"

But she didn't answer.

Things had changed between them; or he had just noticed the change. He had been wanting to ask her what had happened to her studies, but something had held him back. Nor did she talk to him with as much respect as before; and suddenly she seemed to grow not only much older—that she was—but more secretive, wiser, as though she saw through him, and he felt uneasy. What had happened? It seemed to him that sometimes she was just bitter, and other times that it was something else: not bitterness, and not even personal, but something even harder than that. If she had sometimes been amused by him, and tolerated him, now she spoke to him as though he were a truce-bearer—a messenger from a hostile people bearing a white flag. She resented not him, he felt, not directly him: himself-when-grown up, he thought. And he wanted to say. . . .

"All whites are like cats," she said grimly, as he turned with surprise, "cats in the woods, killing all the singing birds."

Me? his wounded eyes asked her; but her face remained set.

"Dobrik?" he cried aloud, tilting his head toward the table where they sat.

She looked over to where they were, and said slowly, almost against her conviction: "Mr. Dobrik is like a colored man," she answered.

He felt as though she had defined him out of her sympathy. She turned to him and said: "It's time *you* go hide!"

"Me?" he said.

"Yes," she replied. "Time you run away. Leave us colored folk to fight this out!"

He stared at her.

"But we, too——"

She turned from him abruptly and went to her lean-to.She entered it as though nothing would force her out. He followed her and entered, too. She stood up and looked at him standing near the door.

"What you want, boy?" she asked.

"I——" Benedict began.

"Now, go away," she said sharply. "Let me be."

"I have to *help* you!" Benedict cried.

She turned a look of fiery scorn on him. "Help yourself, boy!" she said.

"But, Mother," he cried, "*I'm* not like that!" He lifted his anguished face toward her. "*I'm* not like that!" he repeated desperately, obscurely understanding what her hostility came from. He remembered her running that day to a house that was already empty, and soon would go up in flames. *He had sat there by the side and let her go!* He turned his face from her and said, in a lower voice, troubled and filled with pain: "I don't *want* to be like that!"

She looked at him and her face softened.

"You ain't *now*," she said.

His face flashed up at her. "You think when I——?"

She shrugged.

"But Mother," he said, "how *could* I?"

She gave a short, mirthless laugh. "You'll find the way."

He continued to look at her with his face stricken. "But why," he demanded, "why didn't Dobrik?"

She sucked her lip in; her eyes narrowed in thought. Then she said simply: "Dobrik, you see, he's a Communist; and they don't allow it."

Over their head the thunder rolled and a crack like a gigantic whip exploded across the heavens.

"Going to rain," she said at last, kindly.

Her remark focused his attention on the roof. "The rain'll come through that," he said.

"Stay, if you like," she said.

"But the troopers!"

"I'm not going to pay no mind to them," she replied.

She sat down on a little cot, and reached behind her for a pillow. He went over and found it for her.

"Thank you," she said. "You always had manners."

"I'll get you another one," he said.

"Ain't but one," she replied.

Another clap of thunder burst overhead, and he looked uncertainly up to the roof, which was made of thatched grass, cardboard, tin and wood.

"You oughtn't to stay here," he said helplessly.

"Can't outrun the devil," she said with a grim laugh, closing her eyes.

The rain began to fall. He stood in the little dirt-floor room and listened to the chatter of the raindrops, and stared at the old woman lying on a bed of sacks and many-colored quilts, which she had rescued from the fire, and thought about his father, and Father Dahr, and thought about his mother and about Vince.

The sack curtain over the door was moved aside and a Negro man entered. He stared at Benedict and then at Mother Burns, and his eyes filled with amusement.

"Still together," he said. It was Clifford King; Benedict flinched helplessly. The other smiled but said nothing.

"Out of here, Mother," he said directly. "Mother," he added when Mother Burns had not responded, "we want everybody out." He turned to Benedict. "What's the matter with the old woman?" he asked.

Benedict shrugged. "She's tired," he said.

Clifford went to the cot and touched her on the shoulder.

"I've got orders, old lady, to clear out the huts. You better come along with me."

Mother Burns opened her eyes. "Cliff," she said, "don't you know me?"

"Yes, Mam, I know you," he answered.

Mother Burns looked at him for a full moment, and then turned on her side. "I run *once*," she said.

"What's she mean?" Clifford asked Benedict.

"She's tired," Benedict said. "I'll stay with her. I'll try to get her to leave."

Clifford looked again at the slightly bent, obdurate body of the old woman, lying like a nail, and said: "We're going to have to carry her if she don't change her mind. You stay with her."

"What's happening?" Benedict cried.

Clifford looked at him solemnly. "Son, nothing to worry about. We got everything under control."

He left the hut, and Benedict stared out into the rain. He pushed the sack curtain apart and stared out across the slanting rain to the other huts. There was no sign of activity. The camp was already desolate, the rain was rising in fury. A fine gray spray covered his face, and he wiped it clear with his sleeve.

"I'll be back, Mother," he promised the silent body on the cot.

He leaned into the rain and crossed the clearing behind the huts. There a larger tent had been built, and here men and women were crowded. His father was among them. Dobrik stood on a table and was speaking:

"Up on the slag heap," he said, "and keep them off for an hour or as long as we can. You'll make the old Robbins mine by then, and our men will take you down. The troopers are stuck back in the woods, but they'll keep coming. . . ."

They stared intently at him, looking, from time to time, out into the driving rain, shivering at the thought of plunging into it and into the soaking woods for several miles yet before they could reach the worked-out Robbins mine, where twelve men lay buried deep in its unknown depths. There they would hide like animals from the troopers and the rain.

Men were furiously packing. Benedict touched his father.

"Papa," he said, "are you cold?"

His father stared at him.

"Don't you have a hat?" he asked Benedict.

"No," Benedict replied.

Benedict touched his father on the elbow and returned to the hut.

"Mother," he said. "The troopers are coming. You've got to go."

She was breathing quietly, and he tiptoed to her side. In the quiet he looked down upon her sleeping face, aware that probably for the first time since he knew her he was *looking* at her. Her face had relaxed, but still, sunk in it, and almost as though visible under a layer of water, the grim, stubborn expression still lingered. Not even sleep could quite soften it. Her face was cracked into patches like a dried-mud pond bottom; her nose caught the uncertain rain-dimmed light of the hut which followed the line of the flare of her nostrils, with their touch of fierceness. He held his breath as he watched, as though he were stealing this privileged glance; and as he looked at her strong set face, he suddenly flushed with reluctant admiration and, thinking of himself teaching her, with humility. She had just wanted company, he realized now: this old woman sitting most of the night long exiled in that patch down near the Ditch watching the tumbling fire roll down the hill and spit into the water. He had come conscientiously and importantly along every Sunday morning, holding his catechism next to his heart: and in his eagerness to ask her, *Who is God? Who made us?* he had forgotten to ask her who she was and who made her. He caught for one fleeting instant the enormous advantage that being white, even hunky white, had bestowed on him—so that this old lady had never been any more to him than just an old Negro woman whom he could lecture and patronize, in the name of God, as he would never have dared anyone else. For the first time since he knew her, he felt like a boy before her.

"Mrs. Burns," he said, sending a hand out to touch her, and drawing it back. Suddenly he felt shy.

The rain beat relentlessly on the roof, and water soaked through and fell to the ground. His own hair was soaked and lay flat on his head, and the rain seeped slowly through his clothes, and the raindrops on his face and eyelashes made him seem to be crying. He felt chained to her. He sat down by the bed and folded his hands in his lap, bracing himself for her first waking glance. Would she see *him?* he wondered. . . .

There were no sounds from the camp, only the rushing about of the wind and rain. He knew now that they had gone. An emptier silence than before spread over the camp. The rain had increased, and was tattooing the ground like tiny bombs, exploding as they hit. The roof was soaked through. He raised a blanket over the bed, and the water collected in the blanket and made a tiny bulge in the center. There was nothing else in the room but a chair, and a box.

He thought he heard gun shots through the rain, and stood at the door to listen. A dense roar of rain came from the muffled woods. The clearing glistened in the gray light. Again the troubled sound of guns. It was cold, and he returned to the center of the hut and looked for wood. There was a little wooden box, which he broke and stacked in the middle of the floor. He lit a match to paper under the wood and blew on it. Smoke stung his eyes, and real tears came. The smoke then rose twisting up to the roof and clung to the top. The wood caught, and he blew on it with all his might to make it burn better. His eyes stung and he went to the door to cool them. He stood there, staring out again in the never-relenting rain. It seemed to him that he saw something moving, and he called to it.

Two men came to the hut. One was Clifford King, who had tried to get Mother Burns to leave: and he was bleeding. A bullet had gone through both cheeks. The other man, a white worker, stood panting beside him, his face splashed with the wounded man's blood. He was cursing the rain. *What color will it be? Red, red, red!*

"Sit down," he told Clifford, whose eyes already had a thin covering of glaze like rime on a pond. As if seeing Benedict for the first time, he said, with his eyes clearing slightly, and a slight mocking expression in them: "We scared all hell out of them." He shrugged however and added: "Got some water?"

Benedict laughed nervously. The water was almost pouring through the roof!

"I'll get some," he said, and picked up a pail and ran through the door, and down the slippery path through the woods to the same spring where he had met Mother Burns. He filled the pail and slogged back. Mother Burns was getting up, and the other man was helping the wounded one on the bed, saying, "Just a scratch, just a scratch. . . ."

"Why didn't you take *two* buckets?" she scolded him.

2.

The man's groans were in his ears all night, and he didn't sleep well. He sat huddled in a corner on a piece of sack on the ground. It was cold. During the night several men came in to take a look at the wounded man. Once Dobrik entered. He said a few words but the wounded man was already out of his head. Dobrik didn't even see Benedict. Benedict wanted to pull his coat, like a little child, and make him look down. But he was too tired: he only dreamed of doing it. Mother Burns came to him with a cup of bitter tea, and he drank it and lay down and slept for a long while, he thought. He could hear Clifford's agony in his sleep, and once he screamed in his sleep, and felt a hand that smelled of alum touch his head.

The cold came up from the ground, as though the ground was still unthawed beneath. He saw Father Dahr groaning up the spiny hill, staggering under the heavy cross, and a Roman guard was lashing him. Three gigantic crosses stood on the hill. He hung from one of them. He felt the spikes in his hands, the warm blood that glued his fingers; he felt the spike parting the bones of his feet, cutting through the instep and flattening against the wood. It seemed that this pain was a pain within a greater pain that filled the world: air was pain. "You're one of the thieves," somebody announced. He was hanging from the cross and dared not look at Jesus. "No, I'm not a thief," he replied in a whisper. "I brought the wagon back, you know." "You're a hunky from N----r Ditch," the voice then said. He felt a great glee. "You're wrong," he thought to himself. "You don't know me. I'm not colored." He felt safe now. Soon, they would come and take him from the cross; somehow there would be tears and laughter and apologies. "You're not a Negro!" he heard them say indignantly. "Why are you up on the cross?" Was that Mr. Brill's face? "I know *you!*" Mr. Brill said. "But I'm not colored," his own voice replied proudly. Mr. Brill smiled. He was from Boston; he knew Father Brumbaugh there. "I know you," he repeated. "I only go there on Sundays to teach Mother Burns," he explained. He was talking to Father Brumbaugh—no, it wasn't Father Brumbaugh. He was talking with somebody who had taken Father Brumbaugh's face. It was Mr. Brill himself. Benedict laughed. He saw through the trick! He knew Father Brumbaugh was in the house getting a glass of water. He'd be back soon and Mr. Brill would have to explain.

"You have five minutes, Mr. Brill!" Mr. Brill was sweating: Benedict could wait with confidence. "Three minutes, Mr. Brill." "I don't know you," Father Brumbaugh would say, "you were never in Boston." But Mr. Brill was in a hurry: he kept pointing to people in the crowd: Benedict's father, his mother, Joey, Vince,

Dobrik—and the police came and picked them up and took them away. "You see," Mr. Brill said, "I can tell at a glance where you're from, and what you're thinking. You're all Communists." His voice had changed however. Benedict was irritated at these tricks. Why didn't he keep his own voice? Now he had taken Father Brumbaugh's voice, too—or rather the Bishop's. *Why* didn't Father Brumbaugh come out of the house? He didn't want the water anymore! He decided not to answer Mr. Brill. After all, nobody had even *told* him about Communism! Mr. Brill was a fool; he wanted to jail them all just because they came from Hunky Hollow! But Mr. Brill was pointing people out of the crowd again, and the police were busy picking them up. Now the spikes were hurting. "Better-class people don't hang there." Benedict was confused. The voice still sounded like Father Brumbaugh's but the face was now Mr. Brill's. "But I'm not colored!" Benedict cried. Again the change took place. Mr. Brill was flustered. But his face cleared. "All right," Father Brumbaugh's voice said. "Then we'll take *her*. *She's* colored!" They started to walk toward Mother Burns. Benedict strained against the spikes and screamed. . . .

"What's got into the boy?" Mother Burns said.

He stared at her and lifted his hand to touch her face. Outside dawn had come. But it was still raining. The wounded man was no longer moaning.

3.

He was running recklessly. The soaking woods shed fat drops on him, and the rain still came. The woods were heavy and bent over, like unmilked cows in a kind of pain; the huge glistening green arch hung over him as he slipped and fought his way through the spongy undergrowth.

"The Hollow's flooded!" The man, his eyes spread wide, had screamed: "They're caught in the flood!" A woman had shrieked, and men had burst out of the cabins and sunk into the woods. The words had stunned him and he had sat on the damp dirt floor, staring out into the gray skies unable to move. Then he had flung himself out of the hut, across the clearing and into the woods again. There was no trail to lead him to the Robbins mine where his father had gone with the others; but he felt it, as though his need was so imperious it forced through obstacles. Under his feet the overgrown donkey trail, which had faded into the earth completely except for some faint trace which was imperceptible to anything but his driving feet, led him through the drowning green. Whether it was morning or not, he no longer knew: and as he ran, slipping and pulling himself up by the slippery weeds, smelling the heavy soaked musk of snails and naked worms, mixed with rotting acorns and wet fungus, he felt as though the morning was still contained in the feeling of the night; and even as he ran he searched his memory, breathing hard, for his dream. Who screamed? The ache in his chest burned. . . .

They had forgotten the troopers. These men huddled under pup tents and blankets, cursing the foul weather, and smoking soaked cigarettes. The horses left behind under the dripping trees snuffled and twitched, snorted at the rain and nuzzled their heads against the rough bark of the trees, smelling the live dust. Men slipped like green shadows between the trees on their way back to the Hollow. The troopers sensed their passage through the woods, and sent men slogging after them; sometimes they would send a shot that died in the wetness. They complained and groused: murder was wet business.

Benedict sensed the mine opening, and stopped to lift his head, as though somehow to catch it on the fine skin of his face. It was wet, and his inflamed nose twitched, and the faint, unshaven lip mustache had its little berries of rain clinging to the delicate down. His hair was plastered down and made a star over his forehead. He decided, and swept through a tiny opening in the woods: and there was the shaft with its broken tipple lying on the ground and half-sunken into the woods. The shaft opening was hidden: a huge tree grew out of it; it grew from beneath the lip of the opening, from the side; and they had let it grow, hiding the entrance. A man was hidden in it, and Benedict yelled at him: "The Hollow's flooded! I want to see my father!"

A hand-wound cage lowered them down into the tangy darkness, down into the dripping chambers. The cage stopped and the wire gate opened with groans. The men and women were huddled around a coke fire in the middle of the first room. They had already erected supports to hold back the slate roof from which the cold fell like rain. Their faces turned to Benedict as he entered: holding back the fear in the flatness of their faces. His father was standing. He was doing something with his hands. Before he spoke, Benedict was seized with a kind of nostalgia to learn what his father was doing. He came to his side. "Papa," he said slowly, looking at his hands, "the Hollow's flooded. We better go back and get Mama and Joey and Rudolph."

His father raised his head, but not his eyes. He lifted his hand. He was fitting a splint to a bird's wing. The bright little eyes stared at Benedict.

"Papa," Benedict said.

"What does Dobrik say?" his father asked finally.

Benedict stared at him and then shrugged. He twisted guiltily. "But Mama——" he began.

"And what about these?" his father said, with a slight move of his shoulder. The bird lay in his hands now with eyes lidded. It was an ordinary sparrow. Benedict stared at the people, who had now turned away from him and were eating *kilbasai*. There were about fifty older men and women. The roof creaked. Small clouds of dust floated through the room whose old beams were icy. Dust shuddered from the ceiling. The coke fire lit occasionally a corner of the wall, and shards of coal gleamed for a moment.

Suddenly somebody shouted. Benedict shuddered as though, in spite of himself, the fear swollen in his brain had burst out of his mouth: "The Hollow's flooded!" There were sudden shrill cries, and the people surged toward the cage and filled it, and like caged prisoners ascended from the darkness into the yellow rain. The cage came down and again it rose; and again descended. And the people ran through the woods, slashing through the wet branches.

281

Benedict wanted to ask his father to let him carry the sparrow. They ran together, and now he was more frightened than ever before because he saw his father's face grow lean and white. His fingers gripped, and Benedict couldn't raise his voice above the suffocating rain. The little bird opened its eyes, and opened its orange beak, and closed both again.

His lungs ached as though dragging sand. His father's face was violently inflamed with fear; but his lips were white and soaked. Puddles originated before them and they sank to their ankles in them. Sudden brooks, bursting tumultuously through the grass, appeared magically beside them, racing with the same kind of violence as themselves in the same direction. Benedict felt outstripped by water.

As they passed someone, that person groaned as though he were beaten: a man fell on the ground and wouldn't move, looking up at the sky with his free cold eye. A woman stretched her hand at them as they passed, as though to help her go as fast as they. Benedict looked with horror at her. *Mrs. Tubelis*, he cried in his brain; but he couldn't stop his feet. His father was gasping and sweat grew under the rain on his face. His fists gripped. Benedict cried to him, but he couldn't make his father hear. He sobbed and threw his hand out to stop his father, dragging on him. His father leaned against a tree, with his eyes shut.

"Papa!" Benedict cried in horror, taking his father's gripped fingers and unloosening them. The bird's feathers moved, and the tiny head fell to the side with its white hooded eyes. His father stared at it and then lifted it and put it to his ear like a watch. He stared then at Benedict, and then at his hand. Finally he laid the bird down on the ground.

They didn't run any longer.

The ore dunes were a vast red sea. They sank above their ankles in the bloody soup. Rivulets cut deep veins in the ore-dust hills. The sour creek was swollen over its banks: it looked like a rushing lake. It roared down through the ore dunes, down over the lava-plateau, down into the Hollow where it discharged its tons of water into the Hollow. The culvert had long been stopped up. It was drowned under twenty feet of water. Where the Ditch had

282

once been now only an ocean of soapy water raged. The tiny entrance to the culvert had an uprooted stump wedged in it like a cork. The creek swarmed over. The near houses were under up to their roofs, but the water mounted the valley. Roofs were crowned with chickens and small animals. A row of white hens sat along a house ridge; a rooster crowed from a chimney.

Already men in row boats were going in and out among the upper windows of the drowned houses. Highland Avenue was gone completely. The water had climbed up Shady Avenue to Washington Avenue; it had reached to the west and flooded the church and gone as far as the incinerator dump. Garbage floated grandly along. The incinerator stack stuck up out of the sea, but there was no smoke coming out of it. The foot of Honey Bee Hill was lapped by the gray water, and it threatened to climb the wooden steps with its foamy feet.

From the hill Benedict searched first for their house. There it was—the water was up to the bedroom windows! On the roof a roost of chickens had perched. A cow swung down the streets, mooing dolefully. A dog barked. They couldn't go down. Honey Bee Hill was crowded with people. Bedding lay like daisies on the gray hill. Mothers stood with their children fastened around them. Men ran and slipped through the dirty grass, and got into row boats and rowed back. A huge fire was burning on the hill and the smoke billowed up to the sky, and then fell back. Far to the east, the sky was lit with fire; and those who noticed it in this darkness knew that a cast was being made in the Mill, and the fire was burning there, too.

They threaded through the crowd, searching. Day rose higher, and the hill accumulated more of the valley. People from the City came down to watch the agony. Through the gray afternoon, the troopers returned, bringing with them men they had caught in the woods. They rode around the hill looking down on the swirling city with bitter bloodshot eyes; their heads ached; they wanted to kill something. Dobrik sat among them, his hands cuffed, smiling through the blood on his face. They kicked their horses and rode off into the City, and then took the men to jail: and from jail, the men went back to work. Smoke rose from the Mill stacks.

"Mama!" Benedict screamed.

She sat stonily on the wet ground, holding Rudolph against her breast. She didn't answer him. He shook her and tried to pull her face to him.

"Mama!" he cried. And then rising shouted over the heads of the people: "Papa!"

Her shoulders slumped when his father arrived. He sat down beside her and put his arms around her, and then lowered her head into his lap. She lay as though crying, then raised her head, and Benedict saw that it had remained the same. Her yellow face was cold. She whispered something to his father, as though he shouldn't hear.

"Come on," his father said, turning from her abruptly.

They found a row boat and set off in the dark. They passed the church, and Benedict stared at it. The roof had already been ripped off. The water had climbed the steps and gone through the open door: it had entered, genuflected, run down the aisle, climbed the altar steps, beat its breast three times; it had swallowed the altar, the Christ, the candles; it had gone off into the sacristy and had burst into the garden. Then it had entered the back door of the parish house, catching the kittens and drowning them. Its other self entered the front: it had found no one there, not what it sought. Father Dahr hadn't finished his packing, so it had moved the trunk out of the upper window, and taken it down the street. A dead cat had caught at the chimney, and as though still clinging to it in death four kittens clung to it, also dead. Papers swung from the broken window as though the house were an inexhaustible store of them: papers and more papers, and they sailed along the gray water and separated, some going east, some going west. A wooden image bobbed against the unbroken pane of a window, staring out with its gilt eye, imprisoned behind the glass.

They swung into Highland Avenue, and worked their way among the floating chairs and tables, the crowing roosters and struggling goats. Clothes, billowing as though they held drowned and swollen bodies, floated around them. A tree sailed in surprise between the houses. A newspaper, its black headline speaking of two Italian martyrs, melted into the water.

284

They couldn't find their house at first. Only the upper windows were visible. They tried several. They knew it was the right one at last when they pushed through the broken window into the flooded room, for here they found him. He was floating with his face down in the dark water, knocking with his forehead gently against Benedict's home-made chapel.

"Joey!" Benedict screamed, as though he could hear.

4.

A day after the funeral, which was conducted in the Irish church, Father Brumbaugh, who had assisted, sought Benedict out, and said: "I didn't realize he was your brother, Benedict, until today."

They were walking uptown through the City. Benedict carried a bag of oranges, which he had bought out of money left over from the funeral, for which a subscription had been made. He said nothing.

"You have another brother, haven't you?" Father Brumbaugh asked.

Benedict nodded.

"What are you carrying?" the priest asked.

"Oranges," Benedict replied.

The priest looked at him but Benedict added nothing more. It was a clear day now. The sun shone peacefully, as though it had spent itself. The air was cool. Some green leaves flew through the mild air, and for a moment it seemed to be a day in October.

Father Brumbaugh slipped his hand through Benedict's arm. "Come along," he said. "I want to show you something."

He turned Benedict off the main street into a shaded side-street, along which they walked for several blocks, passing that same lawn, the same lilac bush, but Benedict hardly noticed. Then the houses jumped between lots. Children of a different class played here. Finally there was a big lot, and Father Brumbaugh hurried Benedict along. Benedict stared at him, studied him with calm eyes. The priest's eyes were excited and his feet quickened when the lot came into view. Surveyors were already working on it: they had been working for days: nothing had stopped them. They were knocking stakes into the earth. Father Brumbaugh pulled Benedict over to them, and said to the surveyor: "How are you?"

"Fine," the man replied, squinting through his instrument.

Father Brumbaugh said confidentially to Benedict: "They'll break ground in a week."

An ore slip loomed over the town. The Mill was working furiously again, and down near the river the sky was smudged. Benedict stared at the huge red cloud that floated slowly across the sky. He wanted to say: "Where is Father Dahr?" The words formed in his mind without force. He looked at Father Brumbaugh to see what would happen to the aristocratic face that was now leaning hungrily into the work of the surveyor. First, it would look blank; then a little hurt, perhaps, then it would assume an expression on which the words would comfortably rest: "Father Dahr has gone to the Institute, where he is quite happy."

Benedict didn't say them. Father Brumbaugh turned to him. "It'll be built in a year," he said. "In just a year!"

His eyes had in them such naked rapture that Benedict could say nothing. "Yes, Father," he murmured to this alien who looked at him from over his white collar.

"And then," Father Brumbaugh continued, lowering his face and speaking softly as though his words were too dear to emphasize, "and then you and I, Benedict—for the first Mass, you and I."

"Yes, Father," he answered.

He looked once again over the brown field where the men were stretching white lines back and forth. Above him the red cloud floated. He turned and began to walk back. He heard the young priest call after him, his voice tilted with surprise, with slight reproach.

"Benedict!"

But he made no motion to turn. He continued on through town

to Honey Bee Hill, and at the top of the steps that led down into the slimy floor of the Hollow, where the water still stood several feet deep, and where dead animals still floated in its dark waters, he stood looking as he looked once with Father Brumbaugh.

Across the Hollow a train of hot-metal cars had just arrived, and he waited for the first fiery boulder to come tumbling down the hill. The church looked as though some vicious wind had torn off its roof. Little men were even now back on it. The bell-tower was gone, and even from this point he felt that he could see into the soaked depths; the dark depth from which his prayers had fled like souls released: the endless prayers of his childhood that had bombarded the sky, had saturated the air with entreaty, and had fled leaving the church to water and foul air. Only its shell remained, Father Brumbaugh had explained to him. Who, he wondered, in this limbo between the old and new church had been appointed guardian of its soul?

The first fiery ball came tumbling down the hill and disappeared with a great hiss and a tail of smoke into the deep water. And hardly had this disappeared than the second one followed: it rolled and sent sparks sailing through the air and hitting the water with a dozen explosions before it, too, slid into the gray sea. The slag hill steamed.

"Here I am, Benny."

Benedict didn't turn. He had watched his brother—home from where?—weep hidden in the back of the church among the crowd, not daring to show himself to his father.

"Papa wants you to come home," he said.

Vince turned his yellow eyes from the drowned valley and spat. "Why?" he asked.

Benedict said: "He wants to see you."

"No," Vince replied.

Benedict turned to look at him. He was wearing a brown, torn sweater, which clung to his almost skinny body; he wore faded, oil-stained dungarees. He looked back at Benedict with defiant, haunted eyes.

"Come on home," Benedict said.

"Where do you live?"

"On Carnegie," Benedict replied. "We got two rooms there."

"Where would I sleep?"

Benedict paused. "With me," he said.

Bitter tears came into his yellow eyes.

"Joey slept with you," he said. "I'd always remind you."

He hitched his dungarees and spat again. "No," he said. "I'm not going home. I'm going back on the bum. I always did hate this town. Pap won't miss me." He looked out at the burning hill and spit. "To hell with it," he said, and turned off.

Benedict watched him go. Vince was not running this time.

Now, he, too, turned and continued downtown, reversing the route he and Father Dahr had once traveled. He stopped before the jail house to stare at it; then shook himself and walked through the polished brass doors, holding his bag of oranges.

He recognized the officer at the desk, and said: "My name is Benedict Bulmanis. Remember me?"

The officer looked at him. "Yes, I remember you. But your fine is paid. Didn't you know? That old priest paid it. Is that why you came?"

Benedict stared up at him and said in a low voice: "No, I want to see some one. I have some oranges here."

"Who do you want to see?"

"I want to see Dobrik."

The officer laughed. "You mean the Communist?"

Benedict stared beyond him into the corridor down which he had once been dragged.

"Yes," he said. "The Communist."

THE END

288